Reluctant Cuckold

Reluctant Cuckold

David McManus

fanny press
Seattle, WA

Published by Fanny Press
PO Box 70515
Seattle, WA 98127
For more information, visit www.fannypress.com

This is a work of fiction. The names, characters, and incidents are products of the author's imagination and are used fictitiously. Any resemblance to actual events or people, living or dead, is entirely coincidental.

Cover design by Sabrina Sun

Reluctant Cuckold
Copyright © 2012 by David McManus

ISBN: 978-1-60381-502-4 (Paper)
ISBN: 978-1-60381-503-1 (eBook)

Printed in the United States of America

CHAPTER ONE

"There's this rumor going around at work."

That's what my wife said.

That's how it all began.

It was the halting way she said it that jarred me to attention.

Until then, it had been just an ordinary Tuesday night, talking casually over cocktails, about nothing in particular. I swiveled my chair away from the Yankees' game on the bar TV and watched her sip her gin and tonic before saying, "So what's the rumor, Ashley?"

"It's nothing, really. But you know what a rumor mill it is where I work."

"I guess I didn't realize."

"Well yes, and the guys can be even worse."

I let her expound before asking, "So what is it this time? The rumor, I mean?"

"Well, you know the party we were at the other weekend?"

"The one at your friend's from work? In the Village?"

"Yeah."

"Sure, what about it?"

"Well there's a rumor that Jim Murta and I hooked up there."

"What?" I asked, miffed and incredulous.

"I know. It really pissed me off, and it is so high-school-ish. So, Craig didn't say anything to you?"

"Craig?" I replied. "No, I haven't talked to him, why?"

"Nothing. I just figured he'd probably said something to you."

"I haven't talked to him since I hung out with him that night. Who started the rumor? Was it Jim?"

"I don't know. I've been trying to figure it out. There's this one notorious gossipmonger Ellen who was there, and I could see her starting the whole stupid thing."

"So the rumor is that you and Jim Murta supposedly hooked up, meaning what? Hooked up, how?"

"You know, hooked up like we kissed or fooled around or something. I don't know. Ellen's the jealous, bitchy type. She probably has a thing for Jim, saw us talking for a minute, and goes off telling stories, y'know."

"Yeah sure, so you were talking to him? You were talking to Jim at the party?"

"Yeah I talked to him, but I talked to a lot of people that night."

"Of course; it's a party," I replied, "but I can discuss it with Craig if you want."

"What? Why?"

"I was thinking, maybe I can help get to the bottom of it. Perhaps he knows who started it."

"No that's OK, I don't want to make too much of it. It's more annoying than anything else. I just wanted to tell you."

"Are you sure?" I asked, "'cause it's not a problem to call him."

"No don't, I'm fine, it's no big deal. I can handle it, but I just wanted to let you know and appreciate you listening."

"Sure, Ashley, anytime, I'm glad you told me. And if this nonsense continues or any other, please let me know, OK?"

"I will, but no one takes it seriously. Some new rumor will replace it next week, I'm sure."

With that, she put her hand on my knee, asked what was going on in the Yankees' game, and suggested we get another drink.

I told her that the Yankees would move into first with a win and she asked me if the pitcher was about to be pulled, and at some point it struck me, that her sudden interest in a baseball game was unusual.

****

As Ashley fell asleep beside me, I started thinking about what she'd said.

I knew Jim Murta, but only in a "hey, what's up" kind of way.

I'd met him maybe a half dozen times at a few of Ashley's work parties and happy hours. He was just some junior salesman. I don't remember Ashley ever mentioning his name.

I wondered who the hell was spreading this rumor about my wife. And what exactly was meant by "hooked up." Had someone seen them talking a little too intimately? Or misread a hug as a kiss? Or was someone maliciously trying to smear my wife?

I had been with Ashley at that party.

Granted she'd been off talking to her friends, as I'd been with mine. We weren't keeping tabs on each other, but that's just how we are. Although the party had been ten days ago, it was still relatively fresh in my memory.

I began replaying that night in my head, starting from when we'd left our apartment.

I remembered the mild contention in our conversation during the cab ride down.

"But suppose there are Red Sox fans there tonight?" she was asking.

"So what if there are?" I replied. "Look, I know wearing a baseball cap can be frat boy college-y, and no, I'm not trying to look ten years younger. But the Yankees won big today and it'll be a conversation starter at the party. It's not like I'll know many people."

"You will too know people."

"They're your work friends," I said. "C'mon, I've met them, what, a handful of times."

"Well, Craig's your friend. He'll be there."

"Yeah, Ashley, I know that, and I'm psyched to see him."

"And, you know Tamara."

"Oh sure," I said, "Like she's going be chewing my ear off. C'mon, please."

"Please what?"

"You and I both know that Tamara could give two craps about anything I have to say. Which is fine. She doesn't have to like me."

"She likes you, Dave. You just need to engage her in things that interest her."

"Sure," I said, "I'll talk foreign films or pastel drawings. Or whatever boyfriend of the week she's dating."

"OK, fine," Ashley said, "don't bother getting to know her."

"Look, I'm just saying, she sees me as some corporate finance guy. In her mind, she's too cool for me. I told her once I liked some Coldplay song and she rolled her eyes like that made me a dork."

"I think you're just overly sensitive," Ashley said. "Tamara likes you and she doesn't think you're a dork, but wearing that Yankee cap tonight—"

"Fine," I said, taking it off, "put it in your purse. I won't wear it, okay?"

"Good."

"Happy, now?" I said, smiling. "I put on jeans, changed my shirt and now you've stripped me of beloved Yankee cap."

"So much better," Ashley said. "Now we just tousle your hair a little, and there, you're good to go. Trust me."

"OK," I said, "I trust your fashion sense. I just thought this party was ultra casual. Didn't you say there'd be a keg?"

"Yeah, the party's casual, but it's also Saturday night in Manhattan."

****

Two girls who lived there—work friends of Ashley's—gave us the tour when we arrived.

Walking into their sunken living room, I saw the circular staircase and realized it was a duplex.

Then I saw all the people already outside on the terrace.

"This place is huge," I whispered to Ashley as I put the beer I'd brought in the fridge. "Your two friends are only a couple years out of college, right?"

"Yeah, they lucked out" she said. "It sure beats the closet studio I had after I graduated."

"They can't be making much more than entry level salaries. How do they freaking afford this place?"

"Well, it is big, but it's kind of run-down. This kitchen is like out of the '70s, and these walls are crying out for some serious Benjamin Moore."

"I hear you, but the rent's got to be—"

"Well, they have a third roommate who's away, and they also have rich fathers."

"OK, got it," I said.

I didn't proceed further. Ashley could say that about me. I made good money, but if not for my father, we wouldn't have been able to afford our apartment.

****

Ashley got a big welcome when we walked outside.

We had just returned from a week-long vacation at my parents' condo, and her friends were complimenting her on her dark tan.

I knew about half of the people there—work friends of Ashley's I'd met before.

It was a young crowd. Not the kind of party the higher-ups would be invited to. Ashley had recently been promoted to marketing director, but these were Ashley's peeps—her peers, her friends.

I made the rounds, saying hello as she said, "You remember my husband, David."

Everyone was friendly enough.

After I gave one of her friends a hug, I stepped back and said, "I love the Yankee cap you're wearing. Nice hat, isn't it Ashley?"

"It looks good on her," she replied, giving me a playful punch in my side.

****

I remembered moving toward the railing and running into Tamara.

She was looking her usual gorgeous self, with her long blond layered hair and large breasts practically bursting out of her dress.

Ashley was finishing up another conversation, and Tamara asked me about our vacation.

"Yeah," I said, "it was great, very relaxing."

"So I hear you had a *Baywatch* moment."

"Oh yeah," I said. "Ashley told you. We were swimming in the ocean when we saw this fin surface about thirty feet away. Suddenly, the theme from *Jaws* was playing in my head."

Tamara smiled and asked, "Did you channel your inner David Hasselhoff?"

"I can't really say that. It was more like I channeled my get-us-both-to-shore-and-pronto instinct. Ashley thought it was a porpoise, but I wasn't taking any chances. But yeah, that's what it turned out to be."

"I'm surprised Ashley didn't want to go and play with it."

"Oh she did," I said, laughing. "She was bummed when it didn't return."

"You were on the Gulf side, right?"

"Yeah, we were in Naples. Ever been?"

"Naples, Italy, yes. Naples, Florida, no."

"Naples, Italy," I said. "We were there on our honeymoon."

"I know."

"So Ashley showed me some of your photography the other night, and I have to say I really liked—"

But now Ashley had finished her conversation and turned to Tamara. "What's up, Miss BFF, did you miss me this week?"

"You know it, girl. Lunch just wasn't the same without you."

****

I turned to look at the view of lower Manhattan and saw a few young salesmen who work with Ashley standing nearby.

Jim Murta had been one of them—the guy in Ashley's rumor.

I asked if any of them had seen the Yankees' game, and that got the conversation rolling. Then it turned to area restaurants. Having been to virtually every one they mentioned, I offered my opinion, making sure not to dominate the conversation.

Even though these guys were only probably five years younger, I felt like the seasoned adult, the guy who had been around the block a lot more.

I knew their type. We have them where I work. Guys who use swagger as a way of compensating for experience. I didn't begrudge them that. I was established in my career. These guys were still just trying to get noticed

A few of them began speculating if a hot summer intern was going to show with her friends. When I heard the girl was nineteen, I said, "I like pretty young interns as much as the next guy, but remember there's an alcohol issue."

When I heard the boos start, I smiled and said, "I'm just saying."

"So, Dave," one of them said, "you're like Mr. Hedge Fund Guy, right?"

"Yeah," I deadpanned, "I'm Mr. Hedge Fund Guy, Brian."

"I didn't mean anything by it," he said, "but I was watching a documentary on Bernie Madoff, and what exactly is a split strike conversion? It sounded cool."

"It's basically a collar," I replied, then realized I was quickly boring them with details.

"Anyway," I said, "it limits loss but also profits. The SEC should have known his returns were phantom. At the time, he gave honest, legitimate hedge funds a black eye."

They had asked for stock tips—a question I hated.

Suddenly Ashley came up and said, "Are you talking shop? Are you all sufficiently bored now?"

"I was just explaining," I said, "I'm no Nostradamus. Taking my advice would be like listening to some old timer on what horse is gonna win the Belmont."

"Yeah," Ashley said, "go with the old-timer on the ponies."

I appreciated the conversational rescue.

At the keg we met up with my friend Craig. He and I were friends from college. I'd referred him to Ashley when she told me they were looking for higher-level IT people.

He was a big Yankees' fan as well. And when we started in on the thrashing they had just given the Red Sox, Ashley said that was her cue.

I didn't mind. It was how we were at parties like this. We'd mingle together, and once in a conversational groove, we'd do our own thing, which I liked about our relationship.

A few of Craig's IT guys joined us, and soon we'd formed a

group by a corner railing, talking sports as the sun set behind us. They all reported to Craig, so he and I were doing more of the talking, like we were holding court. As the scene became more crowded, I saw Ashley go inside with Tamara. I was perfectly content with the little nook we had, and liked the ambience as the terrace lights turned on.

****

I remembered going in to piss.

Ashley was sitting on the kitchen counter talking to Tamara, while another girl pointed me to the bathroom. It struck me when I went in, that Ashley was right about the place. Yeah, it was large, but also older, a little ratty. The bathroom needed renovation as well.

When I returned to the terrace, Craig had introduced me to two British guys who had just arrived, friends of one of his IT boys. We debated American football versus soccer, but in a joking kind of way. One of the Brits was passing around a bottle of Yaegermeister, and I took a swig.

One of the girls who lived there came by and asked us if we were having a good time. She was not amused when I said, "I love your terrace. You should really think about getting a couple basketball hoops installed on both ends. If someone throws an air ball, oh well, it just falls eleven stories to the sidewalk below."

The indoor part of the party had moved to the second floor when I walked in to take another piss. After waiting a while, I wound up knocking on the bathroom door and shaking the lock. Tamara's voice from inside said, "Dave?"

"Tamara?"

"Dave, there's another bathroom upstairs. Use that one."

I was just psyched to learn of a free bathroom. I liked their spiral staircase. And the upstairs bathroom was considerably nicer.

I heard a lot of talk and laughter from the bedrooms down the hall when I came out. I figured Ashley had migrated up there because it sounded like a girls-from-her-job scene.

Lying in bed now, I wondered if the rumor had come from Ashley in one of those bedrooms.

****

Back down on the terrace, I hung out with Craig and his IT team. At some point a guy approached us, saying he was a neighbor from downstairs. "Who's up for bungee jumping?" he asked

"What do you mean, mate?" one of the Brits asked.

"I've got some cords in my apartment," the guy slurred back. "I've got a friend across the street. We're gonna throw a line to the roof there and secure it real good. Then you just make your way on out to the middle and I'll secure the cables. I do this all the time. It's such a rush jumping down over Avenue A, like you're about to hit a cab and shit, before the bungee pulls you back up."

The Brits told him he was crazy and there was no way they were doing that.

"Bring your cables," I said, calling his bluff, "I'll go first."

"I'm fucking serious dude," he said.

"So am I, *dude*," I said, "and maybe you can make one of them cords a little too long for the jump. I like a little risk and danger. We can play a little bungee roulette."

When he just stared at me, I said, "Maybe you could use another beer, my friend."

When Ashley eventually walked back out, I told her, "I've made some new friends tonight. This is Pete and this is Guy, just over from the UK. And this guy here has been nice enough to offer us free bungee jumping rides right over Avenue A if you want to stick around while he gets his equipment."

Ashley was gracious and polite before asking if I was about ready to leave. She didn't seem drunk or anything, and the terrace was starting to clear out as we said our usual goodbyes. I'm pretty sure we were asleep within minutes of arriving home.

CHAPTER TWO

The rumor continued to bother me in the shower the next morning.

Who in hell was talking trash about my wife? Had something happened that had been misconstrued? Was there an innocent explanation? Had Ashley been involved in some party game like *Truth or Dare*, and had Ashley been dared to give Jim Murta a quick peck? If so, then why wouldn't Ashley have explained that? And "hooking up," generally means more than just a peck.

Or was it like Ashley said. That is was just some jealous girl, talking shit.

I decided to call my friend Craig and didn't think much when he didn't return my call until late afternoon. When I mentioned the "rumor," he said, "I take it you've heard?"

I was peeved by his response. Like, why hadn't he picked up the phone and called me?

I told him I was going to be in his area and suggested we meet for a beer after work. "I'm buying," I added.

It took me saying, "C'mon, one quick beer. Come *on*, man," before he replied, "OK."

We met at an Irish pub, four blocks from where he and Ashley worked. It was by his subway stop, far enough away and sufficiently nondescript to avoid running into any of his and Ashley's co-workers.

I ordered a pint of Harp. When he finally arrived, I smiled and gave him a hug. After some brief small talk about work and sports, I told him how my wife had informed me about the rumor. "So you know what I'm referring to?"

"Yeah," he replied tersely, before asking, "what did she say?"

"That there was a rumor at work about her and Jim Murta at that party the other weekend. That they 'hooked up' or something."

"Yeah," he said, "that's what I heard."

"So what's the story?" I said.

Craig shifted uncomfortably. He was making me nervous

"Craig, c'mon, you're my boy, talk to me, what did you hear?"

"That he was with her at the party."

"*With* her?" I asked. "What does that mean? What are you telling me? They made out?" When he hesitated, I laughed and added, "What? Did they have sex or something?"

"Yes, that's what I heard."

I looked at Craig. His eyes weren't making contact with mine.

"They had sex?"

Craig hesitated before saying, "Yes."

I looked around the bar. The other men were older, no one I recognized, and no one looking our way.

I lowered my voice and said, "So you're telling me the rumor is that they had sex? What, that he fucked her?"

"That's what I heard, Dave."

"At the party?"

"Yes."

I was stunned.

It seemed crazy, incredible.

"Craig, you were with me at that party—"

"I know," he said.

"Did you see anything? Know of anything?"

"No, I didn't know anything until I heard about it at work that Monday."

"So Jim was telling people this?"

"I heard it from others. I don't know who started it. Everyone was talking about it."

"Did you hear where this supposedly took place?" I said. "One of the bedrooms upstairs?"

"In the bathroom."

"Which bathroom?"

"The bathroom," Craig replied, "I don't know, the bathroom inside when you come off the balcony."

"So the two of them just went into the bathroom and fucked? Is that what you heard?"

It seemed insanely ludicrous.

"Well, Tamara was in there with them."

I was startled. Hearing her name made my heart drop.

"Tamara?" I said.

"Yes."

"OK, continue, and—?"

Craig looked exasperated, almost squirming in his chair.

"What did you hear, Craig?" I said finally "Please, I need to hear this. What is the rumor, exactly? So Tamara was in there?"

"Dave, I work there and it's really none of my business."

"Craig, we've been buddies since college. Please, bro, if there's talk going around about my own wife… please, let me know the rumor."

"OK," he said, sighing, "I'll tell you, Dave."

I silently braced myself

"It was basically this," he said. "At some point, I don't know when, Ashley and Tamara went into the bathroom together."

"OK, and—?"

"Well, Tamara then invited Jim into the bathroom. I heard they put on a little lesbian show."

"Lesbian show? Meaning what?"

"It was supposedly just an act. It was like a mock pseudo kind of show type thing. They kissed and got topless in the tub."

"Mock pseudo?" I said. "Ashley and Tamara? Who was the show for? It was for Jim?"

"Yes."

"OK and then?"

"Well, then Tamara told him to take it out and stroke himself."

" What? Take it out? You mean, his dick?"

"Yes."

"He stroked his dick in front of them?"

"That's what I heard, yes."

"OK so my wife was topless in the bathtub and Jim Murta was stroking his dick, looking at her?"

"Tamara was also in the tub with her."

"OK, all right, and then?"

"And then Tamara asked him.... Tamara asked him which one of them he wanted."

"Wanted?"

"Supposedly Tamara said, 'Which one of us do you want to fuck?' "

Tamara's comment made my stomach sink.

I could picture her saying something like that. But I continued, "OK and—?"

"And he chose, uh—"

"He chose my wife? He chose Ashley?"

He didn't reply at first and then nodded, "Yes."

"And then he had sex with her?"

"Yes."

I tried to keep my emotions in check and focus. I wanted to get it straight, make sure I was hearing this all correctly.

"OK, so the rumor was that Ashley and Tamara went into the bathroom during the party—the one off the kitchen downstairs—and Tamara invited Jim Murta in. They did some lesbian show, and Tamara told him to take out his dick and stroke it for them."

Craig nodded, "Yes."

"And then Tamara asked Jim 'Which one of us do you want to fuck?' And Jim chose my wife. And then Jim had sex with Ashley right there at the party—I mean in the bathroom—as the party was going on?"

"Yes, that's what I heard."

"Did you hear *where* in the bathroom?"

"What?" Craig asked.

"Where in the bathroom?"

"Over the sink," Craig mumbled, looking away.

Then I looked away. I was stunned, unable to process the sheer idea of it.

"I'm sorry to be the one to tell you," Craig added.

"Oh hey, Craig, no, thank you. I appreciate you telling me."

We sat in silence for a minute.

"So this rumor," I asked, turning back to him, "do people think there's truth to it? Office gossip is pretty typical there, right?"

"Typical?"

"Like it's a big-time rumor mill over there?"

"I haven't noticed that. I mean maybe it is, and people just don't include me."

"So, rumors like this aren't typical?"

"I don't know. After last year's Christmas party, there was talk of a VP making out with his Assistant."

"Do people believe it?"

"Yeah, there were several witnesses. And the VP got a dressing down about it."

"I mean about this? About Jim and Ashley? Do people believe it?"

"Yeah, it seems that way."

"A lot of people were talking about it?"

"It wasn't like there was a crowd at the water cooler chatting about it. But sure, it definitely got around."

"But did they think maybe Jim concocted it? Or Tamara?"

Craig looked at me oddly, like that was a reach.

"Why not?" I asked.

"I don't know. Why would they?"

"So you believe it?"

Craig looked away and said, "I don't know."

"But people believe it's true, that's what you're saying, right?"

"Dave, I don't know. It seemed that way to me, but who am I to know for sure."

I began zoning out until Craig gave me a nudge to get my attention.

"Oh, sorry, can I get you another?" I asked.

"No thanks, I need to get going. I'm meeting my girl for dinner."

"Sure, I understand," I said. "Well, thanks a lot for coming out and telling me this. I mean it. I really appreciate it."

"I'm really sorry," he said. "You're not going to tell Ashley I told you this, right?"

"No."

"I work with her, so it wouldn't be cool, you understand?"

"Of course."

We shook hands, and he patted my back as we said goodbye.

I swiveled back, but as I began zoning out, Craig tapped me on the shoulder. "You going to be OK, Dave?"

"Yeah," I said, trying to brave-face it.

"You sure?" he said with an expression of pity, like he clearly believed the story to be true.

"Yeah, I'm fine, really, I'm good," I said, attempting a smile.

"OK," he said, patting me again. "Let's grab a beer soon."

****

I couldn't believe what I'd heard. It would be one thing if Ashley had just drunkenly kissed the guy. But I could never have imagined a rumor like this—that Jim Murta had fucked my wife in a bathroom, at a party where I was on the terrace outside.

It seemed so ludicrous and utterly implausible. Ashley wasn't like that. It would be insanely out of character. We'd been together for over five years, been married over eighteen months. She wasn't going to fuck her co-worker just because her friend gave him a choice.

The rumor should have been laughable. How could it have gained traction? No one should have believed it, not even for a minute.

And yet, according to Craig, people did believe it. His reluctance to tell me, and the way he said goodbye, suggested he believed it, too.

I walked out into the crowded, rush hour streets, heading home. I was having a mental back and forth. For a while, the "no possible way in hell" side won out. Then I started thinking about that night at the party, and had creeping recollections of what seemed like nothing at the time. I started thinking about going inside to piss. I could hear Tamara's voice saying "Dave, there's another bathroom upstairs. Use that one."

I hadn't seen Ashley for a while before that. Come to think of it, I hadn't seen her for perhaps an hour. My heart started racing and my pace quickened. The story Craig had told me seemed so outlandish and freakish, yet strangely peculiar—peculiarly *detailed*. It wasn't the run-of-the-mill office story—in fact, the contrary.

"Which one of us do you want to fuck?"

Jesus Christ. That sounded exactly like something Tamara might say.

Suddenly, it seemed potentially possible that Ashley, Tamara and Jim had all been in that bathroom when I had knocked.

Part of me wanted to rationalize it. Perhaps they were in the bathroom smoking a joint. But if so, why wouldn't Ashley simply tell me that, or at least try and account for the rumor? And how would a story like that come out of nowhere? Why was Craig so reluctant to tell me? Why had he seemed to believe it? Was there even more to the story?

I started thinking how Ashley never actually denied it. She referred to it as a rumor, sure, but by definition a rumor means it's not confirmed to be true. It doesn't mean it didn't happen.

One thought quickly led to the next. She seemed to have told me about the rumor only because she had assumed I'd hear it from Craig. Would she have even mentioned it otherwise? The rumor had been going on since the prior Monday, over a week before she told me. Did she not want to trouble me or dignify it? Or was she working potential damage control on the assumption I already knew? Why, I wondered, had she told me not to bother asking Craig about it?

If the incident hadn't happened, and people were spreading lies, Ashley would have stormed into HR that very Monday. Granted it's not some ultra-corporate firm, but that's how she is. Her dad's a lawyer, for Christ's-sake.

I thought back to her demeanor as we were leaving the party. She seemed happy but sober as she said goodnight to her friends, like she always does on any other typical night out.

But I couldn't get past the fact that Tamara was in that bathroom when I knocked. Or how I didn't remember seeing my wife at the time, or Jim for that matter. And Tamara's line, "Which one of us do you want to fuck?"

Heading up Central Park West, I began to wonder … suppose everything Craig had just told me really was true?

All I had to fall back on was, Ashley would never do something like that. She's absolutely not that kind of girl. Letting a co-worker fuck her in a bathroom at a party with her own husband nearby was off-the-charts-crazy.

Yet none of the tea leaves or strange road signs pointed to "this didn't happen." Instead, all the data points were lining up, like weird mental planets in alignment. Impossibility suddenly seemed possible, or maybe probable, or even highly likely.

Holy shit, I thought.

I said the words to myself in my head: Ashley fucked Jim Murta in that bathroom that night. Jim Murta fucked my wife.

****

I walked into my apartment feeling dizzy, dazed, stupefied.

My marriage, the future, everything I had planned on, seemed suddenly hurled into jeopardy. I felt tears in my eyes. I don't think I've cried since I was a kid. I was alone but grateful she wasn't there. Ashley had texted me earlier, about some birthday party she was going to.

I looked around at the new gray Italia Charles sofa we had recently bought, the bathroom we'd had renovated in the spring, the new floral comforter for the summer, the funky lamp we had bought last month in Soho.

I looked at the smiling photos of friends and relatives she had put up on our fridge and her cutely written Post-it note reminders.

I looked at photos of us—smiling, arms around each other, on vacation, family holidays, on our wedding day, on our honeymoon.

I began thinking of my wife in that bathroom that night. Wondered how it was possible. If I were to pick anyone to have been in the bathroom, it would have been Tamara. Unlike Ashley's more conservative and now-married friends from college, Tamara is bold, busty, single, flirty, vivacious, daring—and exudes sexuality.

Tamara was one of Ashley's bridesmaids, and barely smiled in the photos that day.

I wondered why Jim had chosen Ashley. Perhaps it was that she'd seemed more untouchable, less attainable, a greater challenge. The fact she was married and that I was right outside. That she was higher ranked at work. I wondered if he'd been thinking that, what else he'd been thinking, how it all went down.

My thoughts were all runaway train, and I had to stabilize them. So I went into our home office and started cleaning. Ashley had been on me about it for a while. I had allowed the office to become more of a storage room. I spent the next hour hauling boxes down to the basement.

****

I was lying on the living room sofa when I heard Ashley unlock the door. I pretended to have dozed off, saying, "Oh, hi Ash."

I was struck by how sweet and pretty she looked in just jeans and a Virginia Tech t-shirt.

"How was Lisa's b-day shindig?"

"Good," she said, leaning in to give me a kiss. "What's up with Mr. Sleepy head? It's not even eleven. Grueling day at work?"

"It was OK," I said. "I had some number crunching tonight. I just fell asleep for a few minutes. So you had a good time?"

"Yeah. It was kind of subdued, actually. A few peeps canceled at the last minute, which was kind of lame, but we still had fun."

"Cool."

"So, check this out," Ashley said, handing me a wrapped, brown roll of coins.

"What's this?"

"The cab was twelve-fifty. I gave him a twenty and asked for five back. But Mr. Cabbie had no cash on him. Literally none. Can you believe that? All I had was twenties. So he gave me this. I was like, what the hell is that? What am I to do with a five dollar roll of nickels?"

She was laughing, and I laughed with her. "Did you say anything to him about it?"

"I asked him if he was serious. But he seemed embarrassed, so I didn't give him a hard time. Besides, I was late."

Ashley noticed the folded up cardboard by the kitchen counter. "What's that?" she asked.

"Check it out," I said, pointing to our home office room.

It was reassuring when she exclaimed, "Wow!"

"Looks great," she said, coming back out. "Thank you so much for doing that, honey!"

"No thanks necessary," I said. "I know I've been blowing it off for a while now."

Ashley said she was going to get ready for bed, so I said I'd do the same.

****

I lay in bed, my mind racing.

Where was the logical explanation? And if this *rumor* was true, how could Ashley sleep so peacefully beside me? Had she been reassured by my not having heard the rumor? Did she assume I wouldn't follow up with Craig after telling me not to? That I would remain forever in the dark? Was this a symptom of something seriously wrong in our marriage?

And yet she had acted as if everything was fine and normal when she arrived home. As though our conversation of the prior night had already been paved over. It wasn't like she was proposing that we have a "serious talk."

But now there was a growing possibility that I was all too oblivious that night. That I had been clueless while a crazy incident unfolded, starring my wife.

I couldn't help but think that Ashley had been in that bathroom with Tamara when I knocked. Tamara addressed me by name. If Ashley had been in there, she definitely would have known that I was the one knocking outside.

And If Jim Murta were already inside, he would have known as well.

I began to assume all three of them had been in there when I knocked. That would explain why Tamara had been so quick to tell me to go upstairs.

I had a sickening, gut feeling that the rumor Craig had recounted had been unfolding at that very moment. Had I knocked before or after Tamara asked, "Which one of us do you want to fuck?" That one line kept echoing through my brain, sounding so authentically Tamara.

And then there was the sheer audaciousness of that comment. She could simply have asked, "Which of us do you want?" Or, even "Do you want to have sex with one of us?" But that was too subtle.

Instead Tamara had to go with "fuck." Saying it to a guy who had been stroking himself, looking at the both of them.

Why would Ashley go along with such a thing? Wasn't that the moment when she should have pulled the ripcord and left? Ashley wasn't easily peer pressured—not even by Tamara.

I thought back to my knock on the door. Was Ashley already fucking him, or had Ashley heard my voice, known I was outside, and still went on to fuck him?

Good God, I thought, it's 4 a.m.

CHAPTER THREE

I took a walk in Bryant Park the following day.

I couldn't get past my growing belief that the story Craig had told me was true. But I needed to mentally step back from wondering about the minutia of that night.

I wasn't the first husband in the world to learn his wife had cheated. Quite the contrary, it was an age-old story. Hell, I even had a friend who had experienced this.

Two years ago, my friend Greg learned his wife was having an affair with her boss. *What a kick in the balls that must have been at the time*, I thought.

He had told me he thought about divorcing her. Then they went to counseling. He didn't talk much about it after a while. But eventually they reconciled. As far as I could tell, things were very good with them now.

I remembered his friends questioning his decision to take her back. Hell, admittedly I was one of them. Some guys were pretty harsh about it, telling him to "dump that bitch."

But apparently he thought their marriage was worth saving. None of us were in his shoes.

I compared my situation to his. Mine was different. His wife was having a full-blown affair that she had hidden for six months, maybe even a year.

With Ashley, it was a one-night, completely out-of-nowhere event. And if Tamara hadn't propelled it forward, it would probably never have happened.

Still, the fact that it did, or *probably* did happen, meant something.

I could only mentally whitewash so much.

I thought of calling my older brother. But I knew what Sean would say. He'd be clearly on the "dump that bitch" side of the fence.

It's all black and white with him. I could imagine him saying, "She cheated, that's it, toss all her stuff onto the street and change the locks tonight."

I imagined my friends giving me a similar response.

And that would be after just hearing she'd cheated. If they knew it was at a party I was at, where I had even knocked on the door, I'd be hearing the "dump that bitch now" refrain in unison.

But I knew in my heart that not losing Ashley was my number-one priority. I loved her too much and had invested too much.

And none of my friends or family knew what had happened.

Yes, Craig did, but he wasn't part of my regular social circle. So long as I didn't talk about it, it would remain a secret.

Whatever issues this had exposed, Ashley and I could work through them in private. There was no way I going to just throw our marriage away now.

I was going to become more engaged. When she talked about work or friends or what was going on in her life, I wasn't going to be half-there, distracted or dismissive. She was going to have my full attention.

****

Ashley was still at the gym when I arrived home from stopping off at the supermarket.

I had uncorked a bottle of wine and was cooking a pasta dish.

I'm not much of a chef, but my mom taught me the basics growing up. I have about a dozen meals I'm confident about, and this was a particular favorite with Ashley.

She walked in saying, "mmm, something smells good —yum!"

When she came out of the shower, I had dinner on the table and we toasted each other.

We talked freely, as if everything was fine. I discussed work politics I was negotiating through, and my parents' recent trip to

Australia. She mentioned a Lennon documentary about John and Yoko's time living in the city.

We polished off the first bottle and broke into the second.

"There's something else," I told her, pulling out a Netflix envelope. "Your movie arrived a few days early."

Ashley widened her eyes, affecting a child's expression, and said "Yay!"

It was a children's Disney-type movie that had gotten four star reviews. She had wanted to take her eight-year-old cousin to it the last time she was in town. But something had happened. Either they had gotten the times wrong or she or her cousin didn't want the 3-D version.

She would normally watch something like that on her laptop using her ear buds. But I surprised her by offering to watch it on TV with her.

So she grabbed a small blanket and lay beside me. It wasn't even half over when Ashley fell asleep on my shoulder.

Stroking her hair, I lowered the TV sound and thought of the first time I'd met her, five summers ago, at a Columbia alumni party at an Upper West Side bar. Five blocks from where we now lived.

She wore a stylish, black, cocktail-type dress, and she captured my eye the moment I spotted her.

She was a classic, dark-haired beauty. I was struck by her excellent posture and the grace and ease of her movements.

Her smile was warm and girl-next-door American. Her slightly Asian looking eyes gave her an exotic quality. Her legs were thin and tanned. And her breasts, though revealing almost no cleavage, stood out magnificently in that dress—full, firm and natural.

I'd always been drawn to big breasts. And thin, tight, compact brunettes. In my early teens, I watched reruns of *Dallas* and lusted over Victoria Principal. Ashley reminded me of her.

At 5'4" and barely one hundred pounds, I found her unbelievably hot. I couldn't take my eyes off her.

I was determined to at least introduce myself. I asked my few friends there, but no one knew her. One said she looked like she was still a freshman.

Finally I walked over and asked the three girls in her group how they were doing. I didn't claim to have organized the event, but I tried to create the impression that I was important—a significant alumnus.

I asked their graduation class and surmised they were around twenty-five.

I mentioned that I worked at a hedge fund in midtown, propped up my position there, but that was a conversational bust.

So I went from boasting to humility.

"You know," I said, "I nearly dropped out after my first month." They all gave me a look that invited me to continue talking and explaining myself. "Well," I began, "I had broken my arm just before and arrived a week late. Cliques had already formed. My roommate was a football player who was never around. "But mostly," I continued, "my econ professor asked me after class why the school would admit a dunce like me. Told me I would be lucky to last past the semester. For the first time in my life, I started thinking I was dumb. You know, where you've been told you're smart throughout high school, and then there you are in New York City. It can be a cold and lonely place when you're a seventeen-year-old kid on his own for the first time."

"I know what you mean," Ashley said, stepping conversationally forward. "I had never experienced city life. It took a long time for Manhattan to grow on me. I didn't grow up on Zuckerman's farm or anything, but the pace and crowds and noise had me mega-homesick. And I'd studied piano since I was six. I planned to major in music. I thought I could go professional. But when you're not in that top one-half of one percent, all you get is rejection for anything serious."

"Zuckerman's Farm?" I asked.

"It's nothing, just a silly reference from *Charlotte's Web.*"

Soon we were talking one-on-one and I couldn't believe it when she said she was single and agreed to a first date.

It became coincidental that she would refer to that book. I later introduced her to a friend when we were first dating who told me,

"Ashley has such a soothing voice. I would love for her to read me *Charlotte's Web*, and just before drifting off to sleep, I'd blow a load in her face."

I wasn't offended, I laughed. I had no idea the relationship would continue. I told him he lived in a fantasy world but agreed that Ashley spoke in a uniquely calming way.

****

As for my first actual date with Ashley, I was mighty nervous, and impressing her was the priority.

It was an August evening, and I was in my work suit, taking a cab down to Tribeca Grill. Ashley was working in that neighborhood at the time. I had never been to the restaurant, but it had gotten high marks on Zagat's.

As I shut the cab door, I checked my pants, the breast pockets of my jacket and then my back pockets. I suddenly realized I had left my wallet in the backseat of the cab. I waved frantically, trying to get the cabbie's attention in his rearview as I watched the cab speed uptown.

I'd never lost my wallet before. I always check the seats when leaving a cab. But I had been distracted with a work call.

The timing couldn't have been worse. I had no money, not even a couple bucks for coffee. I was going to make a terrible first impression.

I called my parents. My driver's license still listed their address. My dad told me to start canceling credit cards. But I was already late.

I spotted Ashley waiting for me outside. She looked angelic and curvy in her fitted business suit.

I greeted her as normally as possible, giving her a hug. Then I said, "This is going to sound really strange, but my wallet is in the backseat of a cab, probably at Times Square by now."

She looked at me puzzled, and I added, "I just lost my wallet. I left it in the cab. My money, all my credit cards are in it."

At first she regarded me as if my excuse were of the "dog ate my homework" variety, but my expression of sincere angst soon convinced her otherwise.

"It's OK" she said, "I can get it."

It was a huge gesture and I was so grateful for the offer. But Tribeca Grill was five-dollar-signs expensive, and I suspected she wasn't making much money. Besides, I didn't want her paying.

"How about we just grab a drink somewhere, so I can figure out what to do?"

As we walked, I told her about a surfer-type friend of mine from California. How he would always talk about karma. I wasn't much a believer myself. "But" I said, "I found a wallet once before, in a cab actually, and I called the girl when I got into work. She came and picked it up. It had over 200 bucks, and that's how I gave it to her. Where's this thing called karma now, when I need it?"

Ashley bought me a beer and herself a glass of wine. I was trying hard to make small talk, despite being distracted.

When my cell rang, and I didn't recognize the number, I quickly picked up and heard, "Hi, is this David Martens?"

"You found my wallet?" I asked.

He had indeed! He'd called information and gotten my number from my parents.

"Thank you so much man, you don't know how much I appreciate this."

I asked where I could meet him. He told me he was going to a movie at the Angelica. I told him I'd meet him there. He asked where I was. I asked the bartender for the name and location of the place we were at.

"Tell you what," he said, "I'll just bike down on my way there."

"Are you sure?" I asked, "I can meet you anywhere."

"No, I'll just bike down there."

I couldn't believe it. Incredible relief rushed over me. The whole mood of the evening had suddenly changed.

I could talk to Ashley now, in high spirits, undistracted.

A half hour later, this guy walked in.

"Are you David?"

I got up and gave him a hug.

He handed me my wallet and I reached for a twenty, but he waved me off.

"Please," I said, "just for your time and effort. You biked all the way down here. C'mon, you did me such a freaking solid, please man, I'd really appreciate you taking this."

Finally he said, "OK, I'll donate it to charity."

I sat back down with Ashley and told her about the encounter.

"What an incredibly nice guy," I said. "I feel like writing a letter to the *Post*. New Yorkers get this reputation of being uncaring a-holes, and you get jaded about human nature at times, but there really are good people out there. And you know," I added, "I bet you that guy really is going to donate it to charity."

I was ecstatic. I could treat Ashley to a proper dinner. Our date had turned from disaster to magical and auspicious.

We stayed out past midnight on a work night. We shared a cab uptown. I gave her a quick kiss on her cheek as I dropped her off.

I was giddy and enthralled.

I had a skip in my step as I walked through the lobby.

I did a little jig back up in my apartment living room.

It was nice to think about that magical date as she slept on my shoulder.

I gave her a slight nudge and said, "Let's move to the bed, babe, it's late."

****

The next morning at 7 a.m., Ashley was already dressed in full business presentation mode. As I lay there in bed, I silently marveled at her beauty, watching her shuffle between our bedroom and bathroom. In her trim little, fitted suit and blazer, getting ready in front of the mirror, she was in A-game mode.

I pictured her standing in front of a roomful of sales people, mostly men, who had probably all heard the story of that night at the party. I imagined them strolling in with their coffee, checking my wife out. They would stare at her tits as she talked, check out her ass as she leaned over to straighten the projector. They would be mentally undressing her, thinking of her now in a different light— no longer the wholesome, proper, untouchable, faithful married girl in the office. Now she was the married girl who got fucked by a junior salesman in a sleazy little bathroom.

Maybe they'd be thinking they had a chance of fucking her, too. After all, she got fucked with her husband there. If a junior salesman can close the deal, what would that say to others?

I asked Ashley if she was nervous, and she replied, "Yeah, right now I am, but that's par for the course. I'll be fine once I start talking and I'm a few sentences in."

I was sure she was right. She's a very, polished and natural public speaker.

But I knew Ashley had to realize what the guys would be thinking. They would be objectifying her. Thinking of her having sex. She would have to block that out and maintain the focus of a field goal kicker. But I admired the way she was brave-facing it.

****

Friday afternoon had me on another walk, thinking about that night at the party.

I thought the story must have come from either Jim Murta or Tamara—at least originally.

Who else would be privy to such specific details?

I had mostly ruled out the possibility that it was pre-planned. If Ashley had intended to have sex with Jim Murta, she would have chosen a far more discrete place. She would have anticipated the potential danger, consequences, and drama of such a public location.

I also couldn't see Tamara setting this up beforehand. Tamara considered Ashley a BFF. She might not like me, but she wouldn't deliberately put Ashley in a situation she might regret.

Instead it seemed spur of the moment, with one thing quickly and unexpectedly leading to the next.

Craig had told me Ashley and Tamara went into the bathroom together before inviting Jim Murta in.

Why did the two of them go into that bathroom together, I wondered. I understand going to the women's room together—I've seen them do that. But this was an apartment bathroom with one toilet.

I knew Tamara smokes pot, and Ashley has joined her at times.

That was a possibility. Or perhaps Tamara had told Jim prior to coming in that she'd give him the signal to enter the bathroom under a pretense of them all getting high.

I thought about the "pseudo mock lesbian show." Craig said it involved kissing and some topless fondling in the bathtub. That sounded very Tamara-inspired, in a "let's be provocative and surprise him" kind of way.

But I could also picture a guy like Jim Murta pushing the envelope, to see how far they would go. If they were kissing, perhaps he suggested they take their tops off.

Either way, my wife's tits were on display for him.

Then, Good God, Tamara suggests he whip his cock out. I pictured him displaying a big hard-on as it came out of his pants. I thought of him standing, his hand stroking his cock, looking down at my topless wife.

Then Tamara had to go and drop that verbal nuclear bomb, "Which one of us do you want to fuck?"

Could she have been any less crass, bold, and blunt? Or realize my wife wasn't to be offered up like some A or B coin toss?

I started getting wobbly, just thinking about it.

I had the afternoon at work to get through, and focused on that, walking back to the office.

****

Ashley and I were meeting another couple that night for dinner. We sat at the bar, waiting for them to arrive.

After I came back from the men's room, the bartender was chatting up Ashley. I quickly took my seat next to her, and the guy went to serve another customer, but it made me uneasy.

I'd seen my wife hit on before, lots of times. It had never bothered me. My friends had made cracks about wanting a crack at Ashley, and I'd always laughed it off, as "in your dreams."

Two months after getting married, Ashley and I were having dinner at a restaurant in Florida. When I left for the men's room, some guy from another table went over to her and gave her his number. Ashley showed me the napkin when I returned in a "can you believe this guy" kind of way.

****

I was just glad when I spotted our friends coming through the door. We were having dinner with the Morrisons. Kim could be OK after a couple drinks, but her husband Jim was a bore who fancied himself an intellectual—the absolute last guy who should have the name Jim Morrison.

Dinner proved to be more painfully boring than I imagined. Ashley playfully kicked me in the leg twice during the most excruciating parts. She has a knack for catching me when I'm conversationally zoning.

During the cab ride home, Ashley said, "Well, that was a big fat dud, huh?"

"Um, that would be a yes."

"I don't know why Kim was so quiet tonight. I thought you were going to lose it when Jim went on and on about that movie."

"Well it was freaking ridiculous," I said, "I mean, I know he's Mr. Irish heritage boy, but he spent thirty literal minutes describing the plot of that movie. And he'd back-track, and re-explain stuff and give pointless details about the architecture. Like the architecture is a freaking Hollywood set. I wouldn't subject people to a ten-minute story. But if I did, it would be a real life experience story. Not retelling the plot of a movie that sounded freaking totally dumb and boring in the first place."

Ashley smiled and said, "You had this 'give-me-a-gun so I can blow my brains out now' expression at one point that was priceless."

"Hey," I said, "if anyone ever recommends that movie to me, I swear to God, I'm going to tell them to royally go fuck themselves."

Ashley burst out laughing and leaned into me.

It felt good having her beside me, and she fell asleep in the cab.

I rightly assumed sex was not in the cards that night.

And within minutes of arriving home, I was conking out myself.

CHAPTER FOUR

Saturday morning and we were off to visit my parents in Westchester.

We had made the earlier train, so we decided to surprise them by walking from the station and just showing up at their front door. The walk would take twenty minutes—tops. We started up a sleepy suburban street, the kind you imagine block parties and kids on bicycles. Just past the first house, it started to drizzle. We had no umbrellas, and started walking faster. Another minute later, the drizzle turned to rain. Ashley and I took cover under a tree on someone's front lawn. I called my parents but got voicemail.

I went on my iPhone and weather.com'd our location. It was showing green precipitation heading through the area for the next few hours. I looked behind at an old lady, peering out, wondering what we were doing standing in her front yard, under a tree.

Ashley said, "This tree is too small and it's dripping. What do you say we run to that big one, two houses up?"

"You can run in those shoes?" I asked.

"I can sure try; let's go for it."

Now we were standing by another family's front lawn. Only this time there was a dog by the glass front door. It wasn't barking, but was definitely eyeing us as if we were intruders on his land.

Then Ashley sprinted to another tree, calling to me, "Come here, this one's better." I hugged her close beside that tree, not caring how potentially ridiculous we looked. "We might be here for a while," she said, "and those people in their spiffy cars can't appreciate this."

"Appreciate what?" I asked.

"The rain. I'm not saying I like it, but we're bonding with caveman peeps. I'm sure this happened to them all the time. Granted we don't have saber tooth tigers hiding behind some rock, but it's kind of fun, isn't it?"

"I hear you," I said and gave her a kiss.

The rain let up briefly and we ran two houses farther. When that tree didn't work, we ran to the next house.

I was no longer thinking of calling my parents or trying to explain to a cab company, how we were under a tree in some family's front yard. We continued sprinting to different trees until we were in my parents' driveway.

"Wow," Ashley said, "I'm so going to need to use your parents' dryer."

"You got it," I said.

"But it was kind of cool, you know. It made me think of trees in a whole new way. When you're a kid, they're things to climb and when you're an adult, they're pretty things to look at. But them trees were gangster today. They had our backs. They were our friends— we gave them purpose. I'll always think of this walk to your parents now, based on the best trees to hide under."

"Something new for Google maps" I said, "you know, the 'in case you're in the pouring rain and hoofing it' feature."

****

"No worries, it was an adventure," Ashley said as my mom asked why we didn't call for a ride.

We sat with my parents in the kitchen, drinking coffee, as the rain began to really pour.

"You know," my mom said, "that house on Greenleaf has been lowered in price and would make a charming starter home."

Ashley gave me a look, like "you're gonna field this one champ, right?"

I just smiled at my mom and said, "We're enjoying city life for now."

We had talked to my parents about moving to suburbia before we were married. There had been an original two-year plan when we bought our Manhattan apartment. Or more appropriately, when my dad made the down payment. Starting a family was the plan. But we didn't feel rushed. Ashley had just turned thirty last spring, and I wouldn't be thirty-five until January.

Ashley had expressed concerns about moving to the suburbs too soon. She liked having her circle of friends nearby. As it was, we could both walk home from work. Plus, we had city conveniences as soon as we walked out the door.

My dad shuffled Ashley into the living room after coffee. "We just got the piano tuned," he said, gesturing her toward it.

"Mmm, sounds tempting, but I don't want to be anti-social."

"Oh please, go ahead," my mom said, "we would love to hear you."

"Well, if you insist."

Ashley started with some classical numbers. Beethoven was one I recognized. Her hands danced around the keys in a fury. Then she asked for requests. My parents had her playing "Moon River" and some Beatles songs. Her performance had me reminiscing about the first time Ashley came to the house. She had met my parents once in the city, but then she came out for Christmas Eve. I think that's when my parents fell in love with her. She had talked passionately about her job and career aspirations. And then moved on to literary figures, understanding all my dad's obscure references, from Plato to Gina Lollobrigida.

Ashley's grandmother was from Brazil, and her grandfather was from Hungary. An odd mix that gave her that slightly exotic look. She brought my mom some very pricey, aged wine from Hungary and my dad a Brazil soccer jersey for the World Cup that summer. My dad is a big fan of England, but he wore that Brazil jersey during the tournament—at least the two times we showed up.

On New Year's Eve, I told Ashley I loved her. I had never been the first in a relationship to say "I love you." That line had always come first from prior girls I dated, and I typically had a "good grief" kind of reaction.

But I wanted to be the first to say it to Ashley, because I meant it, and I wanted the declaration to be unprompted. She didn't tell me she loved me back. It took another month for that. But I didn't care. I had told her I loved her first. That was important to me.

****

After her piano playing, Ashley and my mom went shopping and my dad talked business, the economy, interest rates, stocks, etc.

It was because of my dad that I was in finance. He had opened doors for me and I always respected what he had to say.

Nonetheless, given all the crazy thoughts that continued traversing my brain, I struggled to pay full attention and engage.

The sun suddenly came out after my mom and Ashley returned. Ashley had brought her suit on that chance, and soon we were sitting next to the pool. Ashley was a little wary, looking over at my neighbors' house. Last year, she had seen their seventh grade son jerking off from the fence while watching her sunbathe. My parents had been out of town that weekend, and I was determined to confront him or tell his parents.

She pleaded with me, "Don't, we don't know it for sure and he's just a little kid."

So I didn't. But Ashley didn't spend any more time by the pool that weekend—at least not in a swimsuit.

****

On the train back, I was thinking of making love to Ashley, just having sweet sex with my wife. It had been five days. I had a hard-on the whole ride.

I had always believed we had a pretty good sex life. It wasn't crazy, in the thralls of passion sex like in the movies, but it was always loving, tender, and bonding.

We were hardly the most adventurous couple in bed, but I always felt we were in sync; we clicked and it worked.

When I came out of the bathroom, having just gotten ready for bed, Ashley was sleeping above the covers.

My dumb luck, I thought.

Opportunity lost.

Still, it had been a really special day.

****

Sunday was considerably stranger.

Ashley headed out to Connecticut to see a college friend. I comforted in the seeming normality of things. It was like the conversation about the rumor had never taken place.

Had I not talked with Craig and heard the details, I might well have mentally slid it under the rug as well.

I pulled out a photo album from last year. There was a picture of Ashley in a white bikini in Florida, her boobs on display, sipping a margarita by the pool. Ashley's smile looked so wholesome and innocent, her complexion so smooth and youthful that it still gets her routinely carded.

I was imagining what Jim Murta had been thinking as he looked at her in that bathroom. That's when I suddenly sprouted an erection—a major what-the-fuck-moment. And it didn't go away. I had never masturbated in front of Ashley, and here was Jim Murta jerking his cock in front of my wife. Had he been a few feet away or was she watching him stroke it up close? Suddenly I had my dick out and was stroking myself. How did he answer Tamara's "which one of us do you want to fuck question"? Had he said, "I want Ashley"—or had he signaled his choice by pointing his cock at my wife?

What was Ashley's reaction to being chosen? Had she thought, this is crazy, my husband's right outside? Had she hesitated? Or had her expression given him the green light?

I pictured Ashley standing up, getting out of the tub, and Jim Murta watching as she took off her miniskirt and thong. I imagined his moment of triumph when he first slid his cock inside her. He had his cock inside little Ashley Martens. What a coup it must've seemed. Within a half hour or so, he was going all the way with my wife. He was hitting pay dirt. The seemingly conservative and unattainable married girl—the hot, polished, director from work—

and with her own freaking husband right outside, no less.

What must Ashley have thought, having crossed such an insane threshold? She had another man's penis inside her, knowing I was right outside. Was she humping back on it? Was she moaning? Was she saying things back to him?

"Oh God, Ashley," I whispered, staring at her in that revealing bikini.

And suddenly I came, really hard. I wasn't prepared for that.

****

"Get a mother-fucking-grip," I said to myself, as I ran for a tissue. It's one thing to jerk off, but it's another thing to jerk off thinking about Ashley being fucked by another guy.

I pulled out some supplies from the kitchen, cranked music, and began cleaning the bathroom. I reminded myself of the fun, normal time we'd had yesterday, the way she had leaned into me in the cab the other night, the way nothing seemed to have changed.

But after I was done, with our bathroom now pristine, I sat on top of the sink.

The motherfucker fucked my wife in a ratty little bathroom, with people—including her own husband—right outside.

God, what a dumb-luck gift he'd been given.

A married co-worker sitting in a bathtub with her big tits displayed in front of him. Had Ashley made eye contact or had her eyes been fixated on his cock as he stroked it? Good God, she knew I was at the party—what had stopped her from putting her top back on and leaving?

Instead Jim tells her he wants to fuck her and she's OK with that? Are you serious Ashley—just like that—you're gonna take his cock inside you?

What a dirty, slutty little scene that must have been. I imagined Ashley's black miniskirt and thong tossed in the corner of that dirty bathroom floor, strewn like afterthoughts.

Suddenly I had my pants down and my bare ass on the porcelain sink. I imagined Ashley's bare ass on a similar sink, my wife's pussy exposed to Jim Murta's eyes. As soon as he had his condom around his hard cock, he knew he'd be fucking my wife.

The won-the-lottery satisfaction Jim must have felt as he slid his cock inside her.

They all would have known I had knocked on the door. I pictured Ashley crying "Oh God" and Jim French-kissing her, as his cock went all the way inside. And from that point on, Jim Murta was now fucking my wife. I thought of Ashley's tits bouncing with each pump and thrust from his cock.

I thought of Tamara looking on, encouragingly.

Ashley was getting full-throttle fucked with her clueless husband right outside. I thought of people talking about it afterwards.

Jim Murta balled Ashley Martens …

He dicked Dave's wife …

In a bathroom at the party …

He nailed her …

He banged her …

Jim boned Ashley …

With her own husband right outside …

Goddammit Jim Murta …

You fucked my wife …

You fucked my Ashley …

And then I came, splashing the tiled floor below. It was like coming out of a trance, sitting bare-assed on the bathroom sink.

****

Good God, I thought, if anyone knew I'd just masturbated thinking about this ….

But I reminded myself of the stress of the past week. Being alone had left me idle, restless, stir crazy, whatever. It had simply been a weird day with weird thoughts.

"I've been through a lot," I reminded myself. "Don't beat yourself up, just put it behind you."

I went out and picked up groceries and then watched some of the Yankee game.

But that rumor kept creeping back. I thought about how Craig had said he'd done Ashley over the sink.

Jim Murta had taken my wife doggy. *Fucking doggy?*

Ashley and I had tried that a few times, but on a bed. How would that even work standing up?

I went into the bathroom and leaned over the sink.

Jim Murta was a strapping 6'3" guy. I wondered if Ashley had to stand on something or on her tiptoes. What a slutty position to fuck in, something she'd never done with me. That must have been his idea He was asserting his dominance by fucking her that way. She might rank higher at work, but in the confines of this little bathroom, he seemed determined to give Mrs. Ashley Martens an authoritative fucking from behind. I imagined him slapping her toned ass, saying something like, "C'mon Ashley tilt up higher, I want to see that pussy pop out from behind."

He must have marveled at how easily it all happened as they got synced into rhythm. Less than an hour earlier, he'd been drinking beer with some work buddies, shaking their hands—with me, even.

And now he was having Ashley look at herself in the bathroom mirror, and he could watch Ashley's fuck-face expressions, as my wife took his cock.

I shook my head. Good God, another erection. But I figured, I'd already done it twice, what was one last time? Ashley wouldn't be home for a while. And I'd get a grip, return to normal tomorrow.

I grabbed another bikini photo from a vacation album, lay it on the living room sofa and pulled my dick out. I wondered what they'd been doing when I knocked on that bathroom door. Had they already been in the middle of fucking, only pausing while Tamara sent me upstairs?

Had they all known it was me—Ashley's husband at the door—before Jim had gone on to fuck my wife?

The power-rush he must have felt, getting my wife to submit to his doggy fuck as her husband bumbled away, oblivious, upstairs. Had Jim pointed that out? "You're getting fucked, Ashley" he might have said, "with your husband right outside."

"I know, it's crazy," she might have said back, as he pumped inside my soul-mate.

Repeat it back to me," Jim Murta would have said as he bent my wife over the sink like his personal fuck doll, "What are you doing Ashley, tell me?"

"I'm getting fucked, Jim."

"With your husband right outside."

"With my husband right outside."

"Look at yourself, watch yourself in the mirror as you get fucked, and tell me that again."

"I'm getting fucked … with my husband … right … outside."

"Again."

"I'm getting fucked … with my … Oh god… my husband … right … out … side."

I came hard again.

Then I came back down to earth, big-time.

What the fuck?

Some strange, foreign thoughts had barged through my mind's front door today. And now I wanted to lock box them all up and throw them off a bridge. But I didn't want to dwell on or rationalize what I was doing. It had been a crazed, stressful week.

It had happened, and it wouldn't again. Move on and forget it.

****

Ashley startled me an hour later as I came out of the shower. I hadn't expected her home so soon.

"I know the kitchen's a mess," I said, giving her a hug, "I was just about to clean up."

"It's OK, how was your day?"

"Pretty good," I replied. "I got some groceries, did some work stuff, watched the Yankee game. How's Leah, how was your day?"

"She's good, we had fun, we ended up back here. We had some time before meeting her mom for dinner, so we took a walk through the Park. We ended up by the zoo and were like, 'Let's check out the animals.' "

"Cool. How was the zoo?"

"Well right before that, we stumbled upon a fight between a clown and a magician."

"A fight?" I asked.

"It was like a turf war fight. I think the magician had set up shop right by the clown's usual spot. It was the place where two pathways intersect before you enter the zoo. That's prime real estate right?"

"Yeah," I said, just following along.

"Well, the clown was pissed. I mean fuming. 'Cause the magician had a crowd of kids around him and the clown had lost his audience to the magician. So the clown started swearing 'This is my fucking spot.' The magician hollered back, 'Stop scaring the children.' He'd go back to doing his magic, but with the clown yelling 'Fuck you,' the parents got their kids on out of there, so they were both SOL."

"Wow," I said.

"Yeah, it was interesting. So then we were like, we're right here, let's see the zoo."

"Sure."

"Well, the main zoo was OK. We've been there. Central Park ain't no Bronx Zoo."

"No, it's small—a twenty minute zoo."

"Yeah, so we checked out the Children's zoo. I don't know why we've never gone."

"How was it?"

"It was fun, actually. You just need to make sure to bring quarters."

"Why?"

"Leah had some on her, so we were OK. What makes it fun is feeding the farm animals. An animal gumball machine spits out these pellets. I guess sheep and goats just love them pellets, 'cause they run up to you and eat them right out of your hand."

"Sounds fun," I said, "and how was dinner?"

"One last thing," she said.

"Yeah sorry, what's that?"

"The last animal was this weird platypus-looking thing. The only animal by himself. He was shy and wouldn't come out with all the kids by the fence. But when the kids left, he came right up to me. And his tongue was sandpaper rough, an interesting texture. I fed him all the pellets I had. And then he looked me in the eyes with this forlorn expression that said, 'Please don't go.' "

"Please don't go?"

"Yeah, and I felt bad leaving, because his eyes would follow me. So I went back to pet him again, like to tell him he'd be OK. And he looked up at me like 'I know I'm ugly looking, and all the other animals make fun of me, but I've got a heart of gold and you're the only being besides my mother who really understands me. Please take me home with you.'

"I swear to God, Dave," Ashley continued, "I felt so bad having to say goodbye to his sad little face."

I just smiled.

"What do you say," she added, "late tonight—you and me—we'll sneak in there and rescue that little guy?"

"What, your Platypus friend? Steal him from the zoo?"

"He doesn't want to be there. "

"And then what, as we have this thing in our cab?"

"We take him here. He would love this place. That room would work for him. We clear it out, throw down some hay, and give him a little basket for sleeping."

Suddenly she looked at me inquisitively and asked, "Are you OK?"

"What? Yeah."

"You seem really quiet … distracted."

"Oh yeah, maybe I am—you know with work tomorrow—but I'm fine."

She stood up, leaned over me, and began rubbing my shoulders. "You seem really tense, honey."

"It's just thinking about work."

Then she came back to the sofa and started kissing me. Under normal circumstances, this would lead me to getting her clothes off and having sex. But I was nervous, self-conscious, awkward.

CHAPTER FIVE

Monday was a new day.

And while I dread the weekly managers' meeting that starts my workweek, I was anxious to get things started, thinking, bring it on.

I called Ashley right afterwards and suggested we go out to dinner, to a quiet little Italian place we discovered a few months back.

"I'll reserve that corner nook we like."

"Perfect."

By six o'clock, I was high-tailing it down the elevator. Fifteen minutes later, I was buying wine, flowers and picking out a card.

Ashley met me there. We relaxed amidst the dim lighting and chill, background music. I felt vaguely nostalgic. The last time we'd eaten there was before the rumor, when everything had seemed so blue-sky certain.

But listening to her talk so animatedly, like nothing had changed, was soothing.

When we arrived home, I surprised her with the flowers. "They're beautiful" she said, "I love them."

Then I gave her the card as I poured her some wine.

"Happy Anniversary?" she asked puzzled, reading the card.

"Nineteen months today," I said.

She looked at me oddly before reading my note aloud:

Nineteen months ago, you were walking down the aisle, the prettiest bride any man's ever laid eyes on. You make me so happy and I look forward to every month of our lifetime together.

"Awww," she said, "that's so sweet, thank you. I'm sorry I didn't get you anything. I feel like a heel."

"I'll get you back on our twentieth, OK?" she added, smiling, before giving me a kiss.

"I'm not setting some monthly precedent," I replied, "I just thought of it this morning, when I was getting ready for work. How it was nineteen months ago today. I figured since I chickened out on the late-night kidnapping of the platypus, this might be a small gesture to make it up to you."

"You're not going to help me steal him?" she said, "Actually, it's not stealing. It would be a rescue mission. If we left now, we could have him roaming around here in an hour."

****

After our first glass of wine, we began making out on the couch.

I was putting the weirdness of Sunday behind me. I was trying to be thoughtful and demonstrative. I had wanted to make love to my wife all day. I was determined to make that happen now.

We quickly moved to the bedroom. I had her breasts in my hands, cupping them both, my tongue going from one nipple to the other. I was kissing her neck, massaging her back, sliding my hands on her ass, under her thong. When I felt Ashley getting wet, I held her hand and went down on her with gusto. My tongue was going slowly but enthusiastically up and down, licking her exquisite pussy, and she began to really moan. When she said "I want to feel you inside me," I felt rock hard and more than ready.

Ashley's been on the pill since right before we got married. I don't even have condoms in my drawer anymore.

She put her hand on my dick and slid it inside her. "Yes," she said as I drove it all the way in. Then I pulled back and drove it right back in again. On my third stroke, she cried out, "Oh God."

Suddenly I thought of Jim Murta. Fucking her knowing I was outside. I felt as if I were in Jim Murta's shoes, inside Ashley's pussy.

And that's when Mayday warnings went off. I tried to pull out to get a grip, but there was no stopping it.

I suddenly came. Within a half-minute, before we had barely even started.

"Did you just—?"

"Yeah, I'm so sorry."

"Don't be sorry."

"I think it's 'cause you're looking so sexy, and it's been like a week, I couldn't control myself."

"It's OK, honey," she said, "it's fine."

"I love you, Ashley," I said.

"I love you, too."

In the bathroom, alone afterwards, I was unsteady. I was embarrassed by how quickly I'd cum. But I knew what thoughts had triggered it. They had crept back from yesterday and pulled that fire alarm.

I had just prematurely ejaculated inside Ashley. She hadn't even come close to orgasm. Here I'd set this up as a night of significance, and when the penultimate moment finally arrived, I was three quick pumps and done.

We didn't bring it up afterwards.

I just knew I couldn't let that happen again.

****

The next afternoon I was planning on making Ashley dinner—and initiating sex again—to stamp out last night's memory. But then she called me.

She was going out with Tamara for drinks.

I felt crushed. Especially hearing Tamara's name, but I did my best to sound normal. To sound not phased in the slightest. "OK, so I'll see you later tonight—have fun."

I paced my office, feeling slightly ill. Ashley and Tamara go out together a few times a month. This wasn't unusual. It had never bothered me before, but now I had reason to be bothered. This was the girl who had basically offered my wife up to Jim Murta.

It wasn't until I got home that I really had a chance to think about it. I pictured the two of them sitting at a table, ordering designer cocktails, and dishing about the last couple weeks.

Obviously they would be talking about the "rumor." How could they not? They both had starring roles in it. It's possible Tamara was embarrassed, but I doubted it. She was single and hadn't been the one getting fucked. Sure, she had been provocative, but that was her personality. While she probably tones it down at work, people would already have that perception of her.

I assumed she did feel bad for Ashley, and how the story had spread like wildfire around the office. But I could also see her taking satisfaction from it. Tamara had gotten Ashley to stray, from the husband she's never liked. She had gotten Ashley to spread her pussy and take another man's cock, with her husband right outside. She might have been nervous hearing my voice when I first knocked —afraid my knocking might derail whatever had started. But when she realized it hadn't, she must have relished sending me upstairs. Had she included my name, just to make sure Jim Murta knew exactly who was being relegated upstairs?

What nerve Tamara had inviting him in. And what gall to tell him to pull out his cock in front of my wife, utterly dismissing me, my feelings, our marriage, asking him, "Which one of us do you want to fuck?"

I pictured Ashley and Tamara sitting at the bar. Ashley would be telling her what she had said to me last week.

"So he hadn't heard?" Tamara would ask.

"No," Ashley would say. "When I realized he hadn't, I downplayed it like it was nothing."

How much did Ashley confide in Tamara? Girls talk. Had Ashley talked to her about our sex life before? Told her explicit things? Expressed dissatisfaction?

Tamara was probably more aware of how happy or unhappy my wife was in our marriage than I was. She was no doubt privy to things about Ashley that I was not. Could Ashley be telling her about our sex the prior night?

"How premature is 'premature'?" Tamara would ask.

"Um, I don't know" Ashley might tell her, "about thirty seconds."

Tamara would burst out laughing.

I took out the photo album and found a photo of Tamara from Halloween. She leaned into the camera, a flirtatious, mischievous smile on her face as it captured her cleavage.

What a fool that girl had made of me that night! Sending me, the husband, away, so my wife could get fucked. And now my wife was having drinks with this girl.

Tamara knew all about that night. She had been there, watching everything. She knew exactly what was happening when I knocked on that door. She knew if Ashley had sucked his cock.

Had she rooted Jim on as he fucked my wife?

Goddamn Tamara, were you cheerleading it?

I unbelted my pants and pulled out my dick. I shook my head, telling myself I shouldn't be doing this. But I also thought that if I jerked off now, it might ensure full stamina later tonight—when Ashley came home.

Fuck it, I thought, and began stroking.

Was his cock in Ashley's mouth when I'd knocked? They'd stay motionless for a moment, Jim's hand on Ashley's hair, his cock in her mouth. Perhaps Jim had shoved it in even farther and held it there at the sound of my voice. Then Tamara had shooed me upstairs, and he'd given her the green light to go back to sucking—sucking the cock that was about to fuck her.

I looked at Tamara in the photo, picturing what she was saying as she urged him on: "Go for it Ashley, don't worry, I sent clueless Dave upstairs. Oh yeah, ride that cock Ashley—you're getting good and fucked now, girl."

I looked at Tamara in the photo and then at Ashley beside her, and I came hard, looking at my wife.

I felt dumb and embarrassed in the moments afterwards, sitting there with my pants down. I cleaned up and put the photo book away. I thought, *what the fuck was that again*, but I didn't want to dwell on it.

There were more important things.

I began wondering if Ashley was still interested in Jim Murta. Had they been together since? What kind of impression had that night left on her? Could Jim Murta possibly be out with her tonight? Had Jim Murta been a better fuck than me? Was Ashley comparing me to him? I knew last night had been a disaster, but had she been comparing him to me before all this?

Did he have a bigger cock?

Suddenly, that last question had me reeling. I had never felt I was small. My dick did the job. It passed the pass-fail test.

A friend used to tell me he was a "standard six." The only bragging was in his honesty. He was confident enough to state it. It was reassuring to me as well. After all, I was average, or at least close—a solid five and a half, anyway.

But I began to wonder, was Jim Murta bigger? Could Ashley have even told him that? When he pulled it out and stroked it in front of her, did she remark on its size?

Like "Oh my God, wow!"

"Bigger than your husband's, Ashley?"

Good God, I told myself, stop driving yourself crazy.

And so I started making some dinner. I made extra in case Ashley was hungry when she came home.

I realized I needed to have a talk with her about this rumor. I'd have to position it delicately, in an understanding, non-accusatory way. But, I couldn't continue to sweep it under the rug. I needed to get a sense of where her head was.

Was she still interested in Jim Murta? Was she not happy in our marriage? I needed answers.

I'd call Craig in the morning. I could at least ask if any sort of relationship seemed to be happening between them. He couldn't begrudge me that.

****

Ashley was a little buzzed when she arrived home.

"So Tamara was pitching me on going to Burning Man for Labor Day," she said, as she sat down. "You know what that is, right?"

"Yeah" I said, "I've heard of it."

"She wants to rent an RV for a week and was gung-ho'ing me on it."

"Is she serious about actually going?"

"She talked like she was. She wanted to go last year."

"It's where—Nevada?"

"Yeah, exactly, three hours outside of Reno."

"Isn't it just a big rave-type event in the desert like some Nuevo-hippie group love-in?"

"No," Ashley said dismissively. "It's this whole community, built out of nothing. It's all about self-expression and self-reliance. Tamara's trying to marshal up a crew, and wants to build this artsy lounge for people to chill in."

"So like a girl's week away?"

"No, her friend Trevor would be the one really organizing it, and some of his friends. You've met Trevor, he threw that Cinco de Mayo party."

"The gay guy?"

"Yeah, he's gay" she replied, "He had that exhibit in Dumbo. He seems to be making a decent living at it."

"Are you really thinking about going?"

"Oh, I don't know. Not sure if I could really take all that time off. But it sounds like a once-in-a-lifetime experience. "

"Hanging outside in the desert for a week worshipping some pagan burning man?"

"Oh please," Ashley said, "don't be all fuddy-duddy on me. If you just went with it, you might find your own inner burning man."

"Am I even invited?"

"Of course you are. You could even wrap it around one of your San Francisco trips. It's a short flight to Reno."

"I don't think Tamara would want me there."

"Of course she would. Oh, she said to say hi tonight, by the way."

****

I served up Ashley a late dinner and was about to make love to her as we lay in bed.

I went down on her slowly, then quickly picked up the pace. I was determined to bring her to orgasm and felt such relief when she cried out, "Oh my God, I'm cumming."

Then, now self-conscious from the night before, I went inside her.

Don't think about Jim Murta, I said to myself as I slid in.

I made it past four strokes and was beginning to get into a rhythm. A few strokes later, it happened. I was suddenly cumming again.

"Jeez, I'm sorry" I said, "I don't know what my problem is. It's just that I have been looking forward to this tonight, maybe a little too much."

"It's OK," she said.

"You had an orgasm?" I asked.

"Oh yeah, couldn't you tell?"

"Just making sure."

CHAPTER SIX

Craig picked up when I called the next morning. He was either distracted or not happy to hear my voice, but then his tone tempered and he said, "Hey Dave, how ya doing?"

"Hey Craig," I said, "I'm sorry to bother you at work, and so early. I know you're probably wicked busy, but I just wanted to know if you could spare fifteen minutes after work to meet for a drink by your place. I swear it will be brief, and it would mean a lot to me."

I think my speed-talking threw him off guard. There was a pause before he said "Sure Dave, six o'clock, same bar."

When he arrived that evening, I hugged him, and he reiterated he had to be quick.

"Sure," I said as I ordered him a beer. I threw away any script of pretenses, like small talk about sports. "I was wondering if Jim might still be seeing Ashley," I said.

"Dave, you're asking the wrong person. I have no idea."

"But have you seen them talking at work? Like in the hallway? Or going out for lunch?"

"No."

"And you've heard nothing to suggest that?"

"To suggest what?"

"That they might be seeing each other now."

"No, I have not."

Craig turned his seat toward me. "Look, I have enough stuff going on at work, and I don't engage in gossip, but I don't see Ashley wanting to be even seen fucking talking to Jim Murta now."

"You mean, because of the rumor?"

"Yeah, of course because of the rumor. I can't see Ashley wanting anything to do with Jim. I think you have nothing to worry about."

"OK."

"Are you guys fighting about it? I'm sorry—don't answer that question—it's none of my business."

"We're not fighting, it's fine. You can ask me, Craig."

"This is awkward, Dave. You're my friend, but Ashley got me my job, and I report to her on many projects."

"Yeah, I know, and I'm not saying anything to her, relax."

"OK, so, how are you holding up, Dave?"

"I'm OK, I really am."

"OK that's good to hear."

"But I was just curious, about that rumor. When they were having sex, did you hear if it was interrupted or did he complete it?"

Craig looked at me inquisitively. "What do you mean?"

"I mean did he complete the act? Having sex with her? It wasn't stopped in the middle?"

"Um, yeah, no, I don't think it was stopped in the middle."

"One last thing," I said, trying to sound dispassionate. "He used a condom, right? I mean, did you hear if he used a condom?"

Craig hesitated before saying, "No."

"No, you didn't hear?"

"No, I heard he didn't."

"He didn't?"

"I heard he did not."

"He didn't use a condom. He finished inside her?"

Craig looked at me, treating it like a rhetorical question, saying nothing.

"So he did?"

"I'm sorry, Dave."

He was giving me that pitying look like the last time. I hated being looked at like that.

"Well, I don't want to keep you," I said as he finished his beer.

"Dave, are you OK?"

"I'm fine Craig, honestly. Ashley and I are working through this. Nothing that other couples haven't been through, right?"

"Right."

"Yeah, so I'm OK. We're not fighting, we're getting along, we just have to work through this."

"Sure, I understand."

"And also, I really appreciate you availing yourself at the last minute and being honest with me. I'm not saying anything to Ashley—so don't worry there. Also, I'm not telling my friends, so if you can keep quiet about it, I would appreciate it."

"Dude, I ain't saying shit to no one."

"Thanks, man," I said and asked for the check.

It was the second time in less than a week that I felt emotionally pummeled leaving that bar. I never wanted to go back there again.

I walked to the subway, disoriented and lost.

Jim Murta went bareback in my wife that night. He blew his sperm in Ashley's pussy. It was too much to process.

I must have had a beaten-up expression on my face as I headed downtown to the Village.

****

I was meeting Ashley there. I figured I wouldn't have time to get out of my suit, so I just took the subway from the bar. I was meeting her in a parking lot. The whole thing sounded ridiculous, but Ashley's friend was starring in something called *Shakespeare in the Parking Lot.*

It was very low-budget and a twist on *Shakespeare in the Park—* the professional production they do in Central Park during the summer. It was about as far Off-Broadway as you can get—a literal parking lot.

Ashley texted me that she was just heading down, and I talked with her friend Natalie for a few minutes. She was telling me how nervous she was, asking if I could tell. I said "no" and told her I was sure she'd be great. She wasn't going to be performing in front of much of an audience—about thirty friends of people in the play sitting on asphalt, some with six-packs of beer.

Natalie had graduated from Columbia the same year as Ashley. I liked her well enough. She was a good girl. She had a high-paying, overseas-traveling job for a while, but she had given that up to pursue acting. I thought it was the height of foolishness. Ashley questioned it, too. But Natalie had said, "I'd rather fail at acting than succeed at anything else." OK, whatever.

Ashley arrived just as the play was starting and I waved her over. I tried to block out what Craig had told me, and she gave me a kiss as she sat down.

They were performing *Macbeth*. There were no sets. It seemed ultra-amateur to me, everyone over-acting with fake British accents. I was utterly bored. I couldn't follow it and had no interest in trying. But I did my best to seem like I was paying attention and laughed when others did.

It was only an hour but seemed to go on for two and a half; then we had to go out with "all them acting folks." I had nothing in common with them and nothing to say. But I wanted to be a trooper for Ashley's sake.

I did my best to laugh and seem engaged, but inside, I was just waiting to leave. All of them seemed to think they were one small step away from breakout fame.

When I complimented one guy, he told me he would thank me in his Academy Award speech. I pretended to be appreciative.

By the time we arrived home, it was just after midnight.

****

Once Ashley fell asleep, I thought about what Craig had told me earlier.

Jim Murta hadn't used a condom. He'd fucked Ashley bare. He'd gone bareback inside my wife.

I wondered if talk of using a condom had ever even come up. Had Tamara explained she had none on her? Had Jim said he hadn't either? Had Ashley so much as hesitated?

Oh God, the sheer brazenness of it all. Jim Murta had blown his sperm up Ashley's pussy. He had pussy-jizzed my fucking wife. What a coup that must have been. Not just fucking my wife, but busting his nut right up inside her. How triumphant he must have felt as his head touched up against Ashley's pussy. and once inside her, he could relax, take his time, enjoy her pussy, and just savor the fuck.

At some point he must've thought, "I'm so going to do this. Ashley Martens is going to take my sperm."

Did Ashley tell him not to? Or had she whispered, "It's OK, I'm on the pill"? Did Jim even ask? Or did that not matter?

He probably didn't even ask for permission. He was just determined to do it. He was going to seed Ashley's pussy with a fat load of Jim Murta sperm.

I imagined him holding Ashley firmly on that final thrust, holding her down on his cock, thinking, "You're taking my fucking sperm, baby."

What satisfaction he must have felt as his cock spewed glob after glob of hot sperm inside her. Did he wonder if maybe he'd just impregnated my wife, knocked Ashley up, given her a baby—his baby?

What was Ashley thinking as she felt it shooting up inside her? Was there any disbelief? Or back to earth reality?

What a stud he must have felt like as he slowly pulled his cock out of my wife's freshly seeded pussy.

How easily he proceeded from walking inside that bathroom to giving my wife a hard, raw, bare, animalistic fuck. And then he added that humiliating punctuation mark. He had uncorked his sperm, his baby-seed, inside my wife.

Was it entertaining for Jim as he zipped up and put his cock back inside his pants? Watching my wife get hurriedly dressed, nervously fixing herself in the mirror, knowing she would have to go greet people outside, including her own husband. Trying hard to look like she hadn't just been fucked.

"Now go outside and say hello to your husband with my sperm inside your puss," I pictured him thinking.

I got out of bed and went to the bathroom down the hall. I sat on the sink.

Oh God, Ashley, I thought, you didn't just let him fuck you, you let him fuck you bare, you let him pump his sperm inside you, knowing I was right outside. You let him seed your pussy, oh God Jim, don't, please, pull out, you're not going to let him do it, Ashley, you're not going to let Jim seed you, oh my God you are, you're really going to let him cum inside you. Jim Murta blew his sperm-load inside my wife's pussy!

I had tears in my eyes.

Then I came ultra-hard.

Immediately I started to come down. I was sitting in a bathroom with cum in my hand, as my wife slept a few rooms away.

This is fucking crazy, I thought. I need to have a talk with Ashley. I needed to get a grip on our marriage and myself.

We were overdue for a heart-to-heart.

****

I waited until Saturday to have the talk, after chickening out the night before. We'd just finished dinner at a place nearby.

"Hey Ash," I said, "If I may change the subject ..."

That's how I started, as we sat at a high table in a quiet bar.

I took a deep breath. I was nervous, but I told myself, *Just do it.*

"There's something I've been thinking about," I said, "and if I don't bring it up, I'd wonder about it down the road."

"OK," she replied.

"It's nothing bad," I said, returning her gaze, "I swear, it's not."

"OK."

"I've just been thinking. I mean, I love you so much, and our marriage is far and away the most important and precious thing in my life. I know you know that, but I wanted to say it again, because it's so true."

Ashley replied, "Me, too."

"Well, I just wanted to say that you can be completely open with me. Nothing would change how I feel about you. The love I have for you has no boundaries. It's, it's unequivocal.

"And so," I continued, "I think the key for us is open communication. I think if we have that, everything else follows. I want you to feel like you can tell me anything, and I'll understand. And so," I stuttered, "I know how things can happen, I totally understand that. I want you to know I do or that I would, that I have no judgments."

"OK," she said.

"It's just that I've been wondering, I mean, just so we can put it behind us and move forward … that night … at your friend's party … it's OK if it did … I understand how things can just kind of happen, I really do … but, like that night, you mentioned Jim Murta and I was just wondering … because you can be totally honest with me, and I won't feel differently. But if there was something between the two of you that night, I mean—"

Ashley took my hand, cut me off, and said "Yes."

I looked back up at her and quietly asked, "Yes?"

"You're asking if something happened with Jim that night."

"Yeah," I said.

"Yes, we did hook up that night."

Ashley was still holding my hand, trying to make eye contact.

"'Hooked up' as in 'had sex'?"

"It's like you said, it just kind of happened."

"But you had sex?"

"Yes, we did."

It was as if Ashley had just punched me hard in the gut. Even though I was sure it had happened, just the reality of her admission had me emotionally reeling. Like I was trying to conversationally get back up off the floor.

"I kind of figured that you had," she said.

"You did? Why?"

"I had just gotten that impression. And I'm sorry. I should have been upfront about it when I told you. It's just I was scared about how you would take it. And I was embarrassed. That first week at work, I was mortified—knowing people were talking about me."

"I understand," I said, "but there's something else I've wondered about. Are you still interested in Jim?"

"Oh God, Dave. Not at all."

"You sure? I mean you could tell me—"

Ashley patted my arm. "Jim is an immature jerk. He's how the rumor got started. The last thing I need now is more gossip about me."

"So there's nothing between you and Jim now?"

"No, nada, zilcho. There's zero between us."

We were both quiet, but I found it hard to look her in the eye.

"You OK?"

"Yeah, of course," I said, "I'm just glad we got it out in the open so we can move on."

"Me, too," she said.

"I love you, Ashley?" I said, phrased more as a question. I was desperate for reciprocation.

"And I love you," she replied. "I appreciate you being so loving and understanding"

"Of course, Ash."

"I mean it," she said, "I really appreciate how cool and sweet you've been. That first week at work really had me freaking out. Being gossiped about. I thought I would have to start getting my résumé in order."

"But it's gotten better?"

"Yeah, as Tamara said the other night, 'Just let time do its thing.'"

"Ashley," I said, "can I ask one more question?"

"Of course."

"I'm not really sure how to say this. But was he, um, was uh, I mean Jim, was he bigger, I mean, bigger than me?"

Ashley looked at me like she wasn't sure of the question.

I looked down at the floor and said, "You know, his penis ... was it bigger than mine?"

She waited for my eyes to get back off the floor.

"He was ... wasn't he?" I asked.

Ashley looked pained, as though having to tell a kid the truth about Santa Claus. "Yeah" she said.

"How much bigger?"

The way I blurted out the question caused her to laugh slightly.

"Just bigger, OK," she replied.

"OK," I said, utterly floored, emotionally reeling, mentally stumbling. "Well," I added, "I understand how things can get out of control or how you can get caught up in the moment."

"Yeah, and I'm sorry, I should have told you before tonight."

"It's OK, Ash, no worries, I'm just glad we talked about it. I felt it was important."

"Me, too."

"So," I said, "anything new with your mom? I mean, it looks like she's coming out here in September?"

****

I didn't initiate sex that night. I was still reeling, and Ashley conked out on our bed pretty quickly. I spent another night lying there thinking. My wife had just admitted to me—her husband—that she'd indeed let another man fuck her at a party we were both at. And now she was sleeping serenely beside me.

Her apology seemed insanely marginal. She hadn't said, "I'm sorry I did that."

She hadn't said, "I'm sorry I let a guy fuck me at a party you were at," or "We all heard you knocking on the bathroom door, and I'm sorry, I was just too horny, I just had to fuck him."

The only "sorry" she'd offered was for not being upfront afterwards. What kind of apology was that? She might as well have said, "I'm sorry, I forgot to pay the cable bill." Was it possible she didn't recognize the magnitude of what she'd admitted? Where were the tears, the begging for forgiveness?

You just told me another man fucked you, Ashley! And you simply feel bad for not telling me earlier? That's the only thing you're sorry for? You're sorry for the rumors at work? Really? That's your main concern? Your reputation trumps our marriage? All I get is, "you OK?"

Could she really think this hadn't affected me? Or was that what she meant when she said she figured I knew? Why? Because I seemed more nervous around her, less self-assured? Because I cum within a minute of fucking her now?

Is that how you put two and two together, Ashley? You assumed I knew, and yet you didn't even bring the subject back up with me? You left it for me to do. You let some junior punk salesman fuck you in a ratty little apartment bathroom with your own husband outside, and it's the work rumors you're concerned with? Not how your own husband feels about it? You can't even offer a real 'sorry'? Instead I get a 'thanks' for being so cool and understanding?

Was she fucking serious?

"You let Jim Murta fuck you and cream inside your pussy while I stood outside knocking. And now that we've finally talked about it, you can sleep peacefully."

And Jim fucking Murta ....

"Oh God no, Dave, I have no interest in him now."

Why Ashley? Because the guy fucking blabbed to your fellow work colleagues how he fucked and spermed you? Is that the only reason you have no interest now? If he had kept his fucking trap shut, would you have fucked him again? Would you still be fucking him? And then, good God, you tell me Jim Murta's cock is bigger than mine.

Sure I asked the question and sure I suspected that answer, but couldn't she have at least lied or downplayed it? Said something like "not really"?

And that fucking brief laugh when I asked "how much bigger?" Could she be any more condescending?

"How much bigger Ashley?"

"Just bigger, OK?"

What was with the "OK"?

Like, "you don't pay it any more mind, don't trouble yourself with the details, just know that it was bigger." And conversely, the implication was, my dick is smaller.

How fucking big was it, Ashley? Obviously it wasn't just marginally bigger, or you would have told me that. Was it seven and one half, eight, eight and one-half? Was it porn-star big?

Had she really misunderstood my original question? Did I have to squirm and actually have to say, "Was his penis bigger than mine?"

Do you not see how humiliating and embarrassing that was?

Good God Ashley, how fucking big was he?

I got out of bed and went to the hallway bathroom.

I knew I shouldn't, but I had gotten hard just thinking about it and felt compelled. I was back on the sink again with my boxers down. My wife had just admitted to fucking Jim Murta that night and strongly implied that his cock was significantly bigger than mine.

Had Ashley stared, mesmerized by its size, as Jim Murta stroked it in front of her? Was it irresistible? Was she so intrigued and tempted by the prospect of feeling it inside her that she didn't care her own husband was outside? Had knocked on the goddamn fucking door?

He had stroked it, pointing his big cock right at her, as he looked down on her in the bathtub, staring at her tits. When Tamara asked, "Which one of us do you want to fuck?" was Ashley hoping Jim Murta would pick her? That she would have the honor and privilege of being fucked by Jim Murta and his big, fat, cock?

God fucking dammit, Ashley. You let him take you bare. You let him drain his big fat balls inside you. You let that horse-cock fucking seed your pussy.

And then I came hard.

This is so fucked up, I said to myself.

"What kind of a pussy are you," I whispered as I looked at myself in the mirror.

CHAPTER SEVEN

"I think I'm breaking my bike out" Ashley said the next morning, "it's a gorgeous day."

I offered to join her, telling her I could rent one from a place nearby.

An hour later, we were riding through Central Park. She was wearing snug white shorts, and I just looked at her small, firm ass as I followed behind. Soon, we were darting through city streets, making our way to a bike path on the East Side.

We stopped at a Dog Park, twenty or so dogs running around in a fenced-off area as their owners sat on benches.

"What a big old party," Ashley remarked. "Look at little Napoleon; he may be runty and small, but he ain't taking shit from no one." When Napoleon started humping another, much bigger dog, she burst out laughing.

We rode uptown, crossing over to Wards Island. Neither of us had been there. It was like a sanctuary—picturesque, full of trees, and free of people. In the distance we could see the Hell Gate Bridge.

"That's the bridge you and your dad used to picnic by, right?"

"Yeah," I said. "When I was five years old it was my favorite bridge. I mean it's kind of ridiculous, picnicking by a bridge, but my dad indulged me."

"Aww, that's all cute," she said.

We biked right up to it.

The Hell Gate Bridge is a steel railroad bridge that crosses the East River. I didn't think it was even still in use, until we watched an Amtrak train glide across.

The area was quiet, almost eerily. We were talking about the castle-like structure that supports both sides, when a park employee came up from behind and startled us. He seemed to have a certain fondness for the bridge himself. Ashley told him about my boyhood fascination with it.

"It was remarkably constructed" he said, "Made to last."

Then he told us that if humanity went extinct tomorrow, virtually all the bridges in the world would collapse within three hundred years from lack of maintenance.

"But that bridge," he said, "would be the very last to fall. It would take one thousand years."

Ashley looked at him funny.

"I'm not making it up," he said. "Look it up on Wikipedia."

He was an older man, maybe mid-fifties, but I could tell he was checking my wife out as he talked; he was obviously staring at her tits.

We got back on our bikes, and Ashley yelled back, "Hurry up, slow-poke."

Staring at her as ass, I followed quickly behind.

We arrived at some sort of facility. Then we saw a bunch of men looking at us from behind a chain fence.

"Oh my God," Ashley said, "I think there's a big psychiatric center here, like for the violently deranged."

She was right. I looked it up when we got home. That was exactly what it looked like. No one behind the fence appeared in any way normal.

"What do you say, Ash," I asked, "do any of them loonies have a face that says 'you're the only one who understands me, please take me home'?"

Ashley punched me playfully in the side. That felt good. Next we attempted the bike path on the Triborough Bridge. It's insanely steep, so we quickly switched to walking our bikes.

"This is a bridge for Sir Edmund Hillary," Ashley remarked.

Once we got to the flat part, where the bridge really begins, we had second thoughts.

"What do you say we just ride back down and start heading home?" she said.

"Sounds good to me."

And so I followed behind her as we glided back down. It was as long as a ski trail, reminded me of the Alpine Slide I'd taken as a kid. I watched her hair fly and her exhilaration as she looked back at me. *Remember this moment*, I said to myself. *Appreciate this. Savor it. A wonderful day with my wife.*

****

Sunday 4 a.m. and I couldn't get back to sleep. I'd ejaculated prematurely again with Ashley and was thinking back to the night of the party fuck.

How Ashley could have let this guy just walk in there and sperm her pussy, knowing I was outside.

I mean really, Ashley, I thought. Did Jim Murta spend every day of the last five years working on building a relationship with you? Did he spend 20K on a 2+ carat ring with a nice diamond cut? Did his parents pony up $30,000 to help cover the cost of your wedding? Did he take three days off from work last spring when you were sick? Did he take you on trips to Europe, Hawaii, Brazil and the Caribbean? Did he contribute $80,000 of his own money to help with the down payment on our apartment? Did he drive you down to Virginia when your grandmother was in the hospital? Does he take care of your bills and finances and do your taxes each year? Does he hug you when you need a hug?

No, of course not. He's done none of that. It's me. I've done all that.

I've invested everything for five years, and this guy just walks in, fucks you bare, sperms your pussy, knowing I'm right outside, and walks back out to the party.

Had he given a rat's ass that I was there? Of course not.

He didn't hesitate for a second. He probably got off on the fact I was there. An extra notch on his belt. Fucking a married colleague with her husband outside. It probably added to the thrill. Getting Ashley to be so slutty, while her own husband bumbled around oblivious, right outside.

Had he worried at all that I would find out? No, he blabbed away. And blabbed away the extra humiliating detail of busting his nut up inside her. Talk about not giving a fuck.

And what did it say about Ashley that she would let him fuck her? What a slut she must have seemed. His cock looked so appetizing, delicious, and significantly bigger than mine that she just had to have it.

I went to the bathroom and got on the sink.

He must have felt like the king of the world. What a chump I must have seemed like to him.

I pictured him calling me that to my wife, getting Ashley to say it back to him as she looked at herself being fucked in the mirror: "I'm getting fucked … with my chump husband … right outside."

"You're about to get your pussy seeded Ashley, now say it …"

"I'm about to have my pussy seeded, Jim, with my chump husband … right … out … side …"

And then I came hard.

This was not good. It was quite the contrary of good. It was pretty fucked-up. Off the map fucked-up, actually.

I started thinking I should see a therapist. Someone I could talk to about this.

Look into that tomorrow, I told myself.

****

The alarm clock might as well have been flipping me the bird as Monday morning arrived. It was going to be a three-coffee morning for sure.

I thought of being asked in the elevator heading up to my office, "How was your weekend, Dave?"

I imagined the cartoon absurdity of being completely honest: "Well, if you really want to know," I'd reply, "my wife came clean and admitted she really did fuck this co-worker at a party I was at. And she told me the guy had a bigger cock than mine. The reason I look tired is because I was up late last night jerking off in the bathroom thinking about it. But enough about me, how was your weekend?"

I was putting on my cufflinks, looking for my watch as I heard a song Ashley had playing in the shower. I remembered it from *The Wedding Singer* soundtrack—The B-52s.

The chorus kept repeating, "You're living in your own private Idaho," and I internalized it, like it was being sung directly to me.

****

At lunch, I closed my door and Google'd "therapists in Manhattan." I found marriage counselors and relationship specialists, but I wasn't looking for couples' therapy, I was looking for myself.

I found some personal therapists near my office, but then I suddenly wondered, how am I going to answer the question, "So David, why are you here?"

I could explain that my wife cheated, and that I was scared and worried by the implications. I could certainly admit to that; they probably heard stories about infidelity all the time. But that would only be part of the story.

The therapist idea would come to me during the comedown from masturbating. I was mystified by my strange reaction to Ashley's cheating. But how, I wondered, could I ever sit across a therapist's desk and explain that?

"OK," I pictured the therapist saying, "so you learned your wife cheated. I'm assuming you've confronted her?"

"Yes," I would reply, "we've talked."

"And how did that go? She apologized? She's broken it off?"

How do I begin to even respond?

"Well you see, it was at a party. She had sex in a bathroom with a man she works with. There was no real relationship to break off, and I don't think she's interested in him now because he blabbed the whole story to everyone they work with."

"But she apologized?" the therapist might interject.

"Well, she apologized for not admitting it sooner and I know she's sorry about the rumor being spread around her office."

"Did she specifically apologize to you for having sex with this other man?"

"No," I'd reply.

"So, how did you respond to that?"

"I basically thanked her for being honest with me."

What kind of 'what-the-fuck' look would the therapist give me then?

"Oh," I'd go on to explain, "it was particularly humiliating because you see, I was there at the party. I even knocked on the bathroom door. Her friend—who was in there with her watching her have sex—told me to find a different bathroom. I was unaware what was going on."

How could I look across at a female therapist and tell her even that much?

"But the real reason I'm here is, I now masturbate regularly thinking about my wife having sex with that man at the party. And the incident has made me less confident around my wife. Now I ejaculate prematurely when I have sex with her. So I guess I'm here, so I can learn to correct this and de-program myself from obsessing about it."

Forget a female therapist, how could I confess that to anyone?

Then I considered saying, "well, you see, I have this friend, and my friend was at this party, and I was just asking, you know, for the sake of my friend."

"David," I imagined the reply, "I think you're going to have to seek help for your—ahem—*friend* elsewhere."

Therapy would be worthless if I wasn't honest.

I can table this for now, I thought. It's still an option, but I don't have to figure it out today. Besides, this might be a temporary reaction. It might just recede on its own. I can give it a week and see how I feel.

****

Ashley called me that afternoon, saying she wanted to cancel our dinner plans with another couple. "I'm just not feeling it tonight," she said, "and I thought we could have dinner on the roof, just the two of us, and talk."

"Sure," I said, "it should be really nice up there tonight. I can pick things up on the way home. You going to the gym beforehand?"

"I was planning to. Is that OK?"

"Yeah, of course," I said, "you OK, Ash? How's your workday going?"

"Not great, I'm fine, we can talk when I see you."

"Sure," I said.

"Oh, and Dave?"

"Yeah?" I asked, hanging onto her next words.

"Can you get that wine from the place on Columbus?"

****

I was a little uneasy after hanging up the phone. Ashley's generally not all zippity-doo-dah on Mondays, so that wasn't unusual, but cancelling on her friend at the eleventh hour was. And she wouldn't say 'just the two of us' unless there was something she wanted to talk to me about.

Perhaps she'd felt blindsided Saturday night when I brought up Jim Murta, or had since had time to reflect. Perhaps she felt bad for not really apologizing or realized how flippant, 'just bigger OK' came across.

I decided to be gracious about any apology she might give.

But back at the apartment, fixing a dinner platter, another possibility began to scare me.

"Dave," I imagined her saying, "I didn't want to tell you the other night, but this isn't working for me. I'm going to move in with Tamara for a while. It's not an easy or snap decision," she'd continue, "but I think we made a mistake getting married, or at least I made a mistake. I've given this a lot of thought, and I kept it all in, but it manifested itself that night at the party. I'm beginning to think seriously of divorce."

And what would I say back to that?

"Let's not be rash Ashley, I'm open to counseling, anything to make this work ... I love you so much, I can't imagine you not in my life, I'll stop getting caught up in my job, I'll be a better listener, we'll get over this speed-bump, this relationship hiccup, just please don't leave me Ashley."

I braced myself for anything.

****

"To the workday being over," I said as we clicked our wine glasses and she reached for the cheese platter.

"Amen to that."

"Do you want to talk about it? What happened?"

"Just our CFO tearing into my boss in front of the higher-ups. And me running around like an ambassador to his finance underlings."

"What was he going off about this time?"

"The fall convention, nitpicking the budget, why clients who've done no business with us were invited."

"Well, he's got a board to report to," I replied. "Cutting costs is how he earns his bonus."

"Well how is Sales going to drum up new business if we shut the door on new business prospects? And he didn't have to chew out my boss in public like that."

I thought about Ashley's boss when she went down to the bathroom. My one memorable conversation with him had been when we were at his house in Connecticut for his sixtieth birthday. He'd been married for thirty-two years and as he was putting down the scotch, he told me that he loved his wife now more than ever.

"I treasure every moment I'm home with her," he said, before grabbing me by the hand. "My wife's my best friend. Is Ashley your best friend?"

I told him she was, and that he was an inspiration and ideal to aspire to. I remember him being moved when I said that.

He had to have heard the story about Ashley and Jim. Stuff like that gets communicated to bosses.

I imagined him saying, "This was a private party when she was off-work, correct?"

When whomever told him nodded, I imagined him replying,

"In my day, a gentleman never kissed and told. Let it be known, I do not expect to overhear anyone talking about this anymore."

****

"I'm sorry, enough boring work talk," Ashley said when she sat back down. "I want to stop thinking about it." She paused for a moment and looked up at the sky. "Do you see that?" she asked, pointing.

"What?" I said.

"The moon—look how big it is tonight."

"Well, those clouds have it pretty much surrounded" I replied. "They're like, 'put your hands up, moon, we've got you cornered.' "

"Yeah, but those clouds don't know who they're messing with," Ashley said. "The moon's gonna bright light itself past any interference they try and pull."

We watched the moon silently for a few minutes. Every time it looked like the moon would be hidden by clouds, it came rebounding, shining back through.

"It looks like a jack-o-lantern now," Ashley said, "Can you see it, the little eyes, the cheerful smile?"

"I do see it actually," I said.

"He's looking at our cheese and thinking, 'looks mighty yummy.' "

"Nah," I replied, "the moon's thinking, 'hey Dave and Ash, that cheese you're munching on looks OK and all, but I'm the friggin' moon. It ain't nearly as tasty as the grade-A green cheese I'm made of.' "

Ashley laughed and put her head on my shoulder. We sat there like that for a few minutes until she said was tired from the wine and a little cold, and how maybe we should head back down to our apartment.

When she sat on the couch and turned on the TV, and I was putting leftovers in the fridge, it suddenly really hit me. That was it? No serious talk and no self-reflection about two nights ago? Instead, we were talking about the moon?

Are you serious Ashley? That's our conversation? The motherfucking moon? And how big it was tonight? How much bigger was it tonight Ashley? Or was it just fucking bigger, OK?

But then again … Maybe she really had wanted to follow up, but her own nervousness had caused her to back down. Perhaps she felt as awkward talking about it as I did. After all, I had chickened out the first time. Maybe she got cold feet, or thought the timing was wrong, or didn't want to get into heavy talk on a beautiful summer night.

I held Ashley close to me. Maybe she was in a purgatory of her own, wondering if I would suddenly pull the marital rug out from under her.

"I love you," I said softly and she replied back saying, "I love you, too."

There was something to take from that. She hadn't dropped any conversational A-bomb. She hadn't said she wanted to leave me. There was an A-OK, normalness to the evening.

****

"Are you OK with this movie?" she asked.

"Yeah, sure."

Ashley laughed and said, "That didn't sound very convincing. I promise you'll pick the next movie added to the cue."

She was leaning on me as we sat on our living room couch. She wore one of my Giants jerseys that fit her like a mini dress. I was in my boxers and t-shirt.

When she put her hand on my thigh, I popped a boner. Her hand grazed across it when she began to pull away. She saw me angle my boner towards her, and finally, she pulled my dick out of the fly and gently caressed it. But her eyes stayed focused on the movie, as I stared down on her soft, beautiful, hand on my dick.

C'mon baby, I thought to myself, put that movie on pause and put your gorgeous, succulent lips around it. You haven't blown me since Florida, since before Jim Murta. Show me what you probably showed Jim Murta. Get on your knees and blow me, Ashley, like maybe what you were doing when Tamara sent me upstairs.

Then I thought, *holy shit*, as I realized I was about to cum.

"Wait," I exclaimed, pushing her hand away. But I knew there was no stopping it now.

I stood and pulled my boxers up, as my dick started spurting right into them. I muttered, "Be right back" as I hightailed it for the kitchen. I could feel it dripping down my thighs. My boxers were a sopping, sticky mess.

I scurried into the bathroom and grabbed a handful of tissues. I put the boxers into a plastic bag and buried them in my closet, pulling out a new pair from my dresser.

Now I had to go back out and face Ashley. I didn't know how to explain myself. I had just creamed my fucking boxers. And all from a lazy, half-attentive handjob.

"Are you OK?" she asked when I returned.

"Yeah, I'm fine. That was weird," I replied, "Not sure what happened exactly."

"You just came?"

"Um I guess, I mean, yeah, a little. Just a bit strange. I'm fine though. Sorry about that. Um, so how are you? What did I miss?"

****

Lying in bed I wondered what Ashley was thinking about this new sexual debacle. Perhaps she had wanted sex, but her attempt at mild foreplay had put a quick end to that.

I didn't know what was worse—going prematurely from a handjob or creaming my underwear.

The last time I had to throw a pair of underwear away was in junior high, when I first began masturbating. At first I would stop before the tension got too much. But then one day, staring at some big-titted tenth-grade cheerleader in my brother's yearbook, I felt this new sensation. In a panic, I tried to stop it. My first orgasm was a 'what-the-fuck-is-happening' moment, as my dick went crazy, shooting into my white briefs. The next day I secretly took those briefs in a plastic bag and stuffed them in the garbage in my parent's garage.

And now here I was, twenty years later, just as shamed, about to trash another pair of underwear.

Ashley's become familiar with Mr. four-pumps guy, but a fucking lazy handjob? What would she think of me now?

Would she think, Well, I did just admit to getting fucked in that ratty bathroom. And I told him Jim Murta had a bigger cock.

Are dots like that really so hard to connect?

CHAPTER EIGHT

In the shower the next morning I kept thinking about what had happened.

Jim Murta surely wouldn't have cum prematurely from an Ashley Martens handjob. Stroking his cock, looking at Ashley's tits, he was probably close enough to shoot his load all over her. But Jim Murta had stamina. He wasn't going to bust his nut and miss an Ashley Martens full-throttle fuck-opportunity.

Stroking had been just a warm-up act. With Ashley's husband now relegated upstairs, he would take his sweet time, savoring the fuck. Had Ashley compared the two of us last night? Jim's big-cock stud-fuck performance and me creaming inside my boxers from a simple handjob?

I noticed Ashley's skin cleanser in the shower caddie and squirted it into my left palm. It had the look and consistency of cum. I kept pumping until I had a puddle of white cream in my hand. I imagined it as Jim Murta's monster load. As it began slipping through my fingers, I felt its thickness and heaviness, picturing how it had dripped out of my wife's pussy as she returned to the party. Had it puddled up and soaked Ashley's thong as she walked back outside? Might someone have noticed a stray glob of Jim Murta semen errantly sliding down her tanned bare leg?

Had she even put her thong back on? In the heat of the moment had Jim ripped it off, rendering it un-wearable? Or had he pocketed my wife's thong as a Jim Murta-Ashley Martens fuck trophy?

I thought of her knowing Jim Murta's sperm was inside her pussy as we took a cab ride home together, and suddenly came.

****

I knew Ashley would be at the gym for a while, so my plan was to quickly jerk off at home. I figured that would give me better stamina than yesterday, when I hadn't masturbated at all.

I hadn't looked at much Internet porn, certainly not since getting married. But now I searched free porn sites, entering the keywords, "amateur bathroom fuck." I was looking for a girl who resembled Ashley—a young, petite brunette with big tits. I finally found one of a college girl getting fucked by her boyfriend that looked real and amateurish—like they had drunkenly invited a friend to film them.

At the time they probably saw it as a fun and kinky thing to do. They were capturing themselves in the natural act of fucking. But how could the girl not possibly regret it now? It's one thing to have nude photos posted online, quite another to have a photo with your boyfriend's dick in your mouth, and yet another to have an actual video of yourself sucking and fucking, for anyone who stumbles upon it to watch.

I imagined the crawl-under-a-rock embarrassment when another classmate would tell her, "Last night we watched Alex fucking you. Sound familiar?"

Ashley could probably relate in some small way after having to face everyone and the rumor that Monday.

Of course the girl on the video had it worse—that graphic intimate video for anyone to see on the Internet into perpetuity. The girl in the video was younger but resembled Ashley in a general way—not as pretty, but with big tits, long hair, and similar proportions.

The video began with her on her knees sucking the guy's cock. He was pretty big, maybe eight inches.

How could Ashley not have sucked Jim's cock beforehand? Maybe he did go straight for the fuck, but as in this video, cock-sucking was a fairly common preamble.

I thought of myself knocking and being sent upstairs.

And then I watched the video really begin. The guy was sitting on the toilet, his big cock pointed to the ceiling. She eased herself down, guiding his cock with her hand, like they'd fucked plenty of times before. The guy wasn't using a condom and I was glad for that. I watched as his cock went up inside her.

I wondered if Tamara's view had been the same.

Then the real cock pumping ensued. She had her head tilted back, her big tits bouncing, as she rode him right down to his base, his balls.

Soon he had her lying on the sink counter, and I watched him pumping quickly. I listened through headphones. The girl was moaning, "Oh yes," "Oh God," "Oh baby."

Then it happened. He had her bent over the sink and he was doing her from behind. I couldn't see his cock from that angle, but I watched his body thrust into her and her tits bounce in front of the mirror. The girl grinded back into him, like it was her mission to get his cock to explode. Suddenly the guy pulled out and shot several good bursts onto the girl's ass. I froze the picture as the cameraman zoomed in. It was a good amount of cum.

Jim didn't shoot on Ashley's ass. All that cum that was sitting on that girl's ass had gone up my wife's pussy instead. Jim would have made a statement by simply pulling out and leaving his sperm on Ashley's ass. But he wanted the full enchilada. That's how Jim Murta rolls. He wanted my wife's pussy seeded.

I rewound the video clip slightly, watched the doggy bathroom fuck, and came.

****

I quickly washed up.

It was a cool summer night, and I thought I'd mix it up a bit by serving our Caesar salad in the living room and setting up the table there.

Ashley came home looking all sweaty in a cute and hot way, and by the time she came out of the shower, I had everything ready and laid out.

"This looks great," she said as she sat down across from me.

"How was your day?" I asked.

"Well, better than yesterday. It seems like accounting has eased up a bit and is going to approve a slightly scaled back budget on the convention."

"That's cool," I replied, "you're OK with that?"

"Yeah, it's just the whole jumping through hoops nonsense," she said, "I mean …"

Suddenly a huge black bug came screaming through the window, landing on the hardwood floor nearby. We were all frozen for a moment—me, Ashley and this big fat water bug. The bug seemed as freaked out as we were, sitting motionless, like it had just survived a kamikaze mission.

Ashley shrieked, "Oh my freaking God, Dave, do something!"

The bug made a lightning fast beeline right for the sofa.

I hustled into the bedroom and came back with a shoe.

"It's under the couch," Ashley screamed. "What's that going to do?"

"I'll get the Raid," I said, and ran into the kitchen.

Ashley pulled back the couch as it headed under our bookcase. "Oh my God," she said, "Did you see that? That thing was *flying*. God, this is so freaking disgusting."

"I'll get it," I said, spraying under the bookcase.

"You're getting it on all the books!"

"I'm trying, Ash."

I saw what Ashley meant as the Raid drove the bug out. It could kind of fly. Not like a bee—more like a bloated dirigible attempting to get off the ground. It rose several inches before hitting the counter and flying a few inches more. When it stopped briefly on the counter's edge, Ashley slammed it with a magazine.

She recoiled, muttering, "That is so gross."

It had left a disgusting mess—white splattered goop and black bug body parts. I grabbed paper towels and used the disinfectant wipes Ashley handed me.

She was shutting the window when I returned from the living

room. "What happened to the screens you said you were getting?" she asked.

"Yeah," I said, "I'm going to get them now."

"Dave, it's already August."

"Yeah," I said, "but we're on the eleventh floor. It's not like we've had bugs before."

"What did Jimmy say about construction across the street—that residents are signing up for the exterminator?"

"Ashley, I know what the doorman said, but we're up high. This was an anomaly."

"Anomaly? So, you analyzed the percentages? Being on the eleventh floor trumped what he said? Based on your analytics, we don't need screens?"

"Hey baby," I said, "calm down. I'm sorry, I will get the screens taken care of. It freaked me out as well. But it's over now. Let's just sit back down and have some dinner."

"Go for it," she said, "I'm done, I lost my appetite."

"Can I get you something else instead?"

"No, really, I'm fine. I'm not hungry anymore."

She told me she'd be on her laptop in the bedroom.

That fucking bug, I thought as I sat alone on the sofa. Of all the windows in New York City to kamikaze through, this freaking bug had to chose mine—and just as we were starting dinner.

****

I wasn't looking forward to joining her later in the bedroom. I was bracing for an "If only you had put that screen in like you said you would" type comment.

Instead she said, "Sorry I was such a bitch tonight. That bug really freaked me out."

"I understand," I said. "I will have those screens in by this weekend."

"No rush now. It's supposed to turn hot again tomorrow. It doesn't look like open-the-window kind of weather for the next week. Sorry I made such a big deal. It's just my bug phobia."

She motioned for me to lie beside her, and I quickly joined her.

"Well," I said, putting my arm around her, "that was one nasty bug. I've never seen one like that before, even in Florida or Costa Rica."

"Well, that's why we needed my platypus friend. He would have gobbled it up like a super-sized Happy Meal."

"Well," I said, "remember that spider web you had me knock down last week? He might have nabbed him."

"Oh please, this bug was a monster. That mini-spider would have said, 'What, are you crazy? He's all yours, guys.'"

"You never know," I said. "He might have seen it as a challenge. A spider is cunning."

"That would have to be one helluva spider" Ashley said, "and I'm not talking Charlotte."

"Yeah," I said, "maybe a team of spiders could have gotten Mr. Jumbo bug."

"OK, I'm with you, like they join forces and go after the really big bugs."

"Well, why stop with bugs?" I said. "They could have even larger blue-sky aspirations, right?"

"Sure, they just need a spider leader who gets them spinning one collective massive web."

"Yeah, and the leader would say, 'We're going big time, guys. We're gunning for small dogs, bratty little kids. We're gonna bag the old crabby lady out in her garden.'"

Ashley broke out laughing, and it made me feel good.

"You know that stupid job interview question," she said, "I've never been asked it, but the one where they ask, 'If you were an animal, what kind of animal would you be?'"

"Yeah," I said, holding her close.

"I'd say a spider."

"Well a spider's not an animal."

"It's a stupid question," she said, "so I'd ask for some leeway."

"I got you," I said, "so, you were saying—"

"I might not tell him that I'd bag old ladies, but I'd say, 'I'd be a spider.' And he would look at me funny, but nod for me to go on, so

I'd continue, 'Because I'm a leader, a team builder, and a visionary. I'd persuade other spiders to join the cause. We'd build a web that was the spider version of the Great Wall of China, and we'd go for broke. No ambition is too high. We'd get our feet wet with raccoons and squirrels, just to get the kinks out, and then, you name it: coyotes, pit bulls, pot-bellied pigs, wild bores, we'd bag them all. What do you think?"

"Mrs. Martens," I said, "in all my years of asking that question, I've never heard such a thoughtful and outside-the-box answer. We need a young go-getter like you running our team. You're hired. When can you start?"

Ashley laughed and held me tight.

Yeah, I thought to myself, you'd say all that with your tits upfront, and your pearly white smile, and you'd land the job on the spot. Me, if I ever said that in a job interview, I'd be taken out by security and blacklisted.

CHAPTER NINE

"I think I'm going to grab a drink with Tamara tonight."

Ashley might as well have just kicked me in the balls, when she told me that as I sat in my office the next afternoon.

"That's cool," I said, "so will you still want dinner when you come home? Should I make something?"

"No, we'll get a bite to eat, I'm sure. I can call you later in case you want to meet up with us."

I wasn't sure if that was even a real invitation, but I couldn't imagine why she would think I'd "want" to meet up with Tamara.

"Well," I said, "I'll probably stay in. I have some work to do and it's Yankees-Mariners tonight."

Goddamnit, I thought, as I said, "Have fun" and hung up the phone. What the fuck would Ashley be telling Tamara tonight? I started pacing, first in my office and then later at home. I knew they talked at work and went to lunch together, but now I pictured them toasting over margaritas and having closer one-on-one time.

"Really?" Tamara would exclaim, smiling, "so you told Dave the truth about what happened at the party?"

"Yeah, I came clean, I was honest," Ashley might reply.

"How honest?" Tamara would come back. "You told him Jim fucked you?"

"Yeah, I told him we had sex."

"And what did Dave say?"

"It was weird," Ashley might say, "he was all nervous, stumbling and bumbling, but mostly he just thanked me for being honest."

"He didn't get mad or look like he was going to storm off?"

"Not at all."

"Ashley—you admitted to fucking Jim, and he didn't have anything more to say other than 'Thank you for being honest'?"

"Well, it seemed like he already knew, but he looked a little nervous and shaken. He wanted to know if I still loved him, and I said I did."

"That's great," I could hear Tamara replying. "You didn't even need to explain yourself? I guess he's wrapped around your little finger."

"He asked a question about Jim."

"Oh yeah?"

"Well, after I admitted it—"

"Yeah," Tamara would break in, "after you admitted to your husband that another man fucked you, yeah? He asked what?"

"He asked if he was bigger."

"That is too funny," Tamara would laugh. "Tell me, how did Dave say it?"

"He stammered and sweated and then asked if he had a bigger penis."

Tamara would have a belly laugh over that one.

"Were you honest with him? Did you tell him 'Oh fuck yeah he was bigger'?"

"Of course not. I couldn't tell Dave that. I just told him that he was."

"Did you tell him how much of a better fuck he was?"

"I didn't rub it in by going into specifics."

"I know, you're so nice," Tamara would say. "So, how did Dave react when he learned his cock in no way measured up?"

"He quickly changed the subject."

"So there were no consequences? Dave gave you no grief?"

"No, just stuff about how he understands getting caught up in the moment."

"Wow, he's more of a pussy-whipped doormat than I even imagined."

"There's something else," Ashley might say.

"Oh do tell, girl," Tamara would reply.

Then Ashley would tell her how I creamed my boxer shorts from a lazy handjob. "He was pretty red-faced embarrassed about it," she'd say, "so I didn't say much afterwards, but I was barely stroking it and he ejaculated right into his boxer shorts."

If ever there was an uproarious laugh from Tamara, I pictured it coming then. "What is Dave, like a pubescent boy?"

Fuck you, Tamara, I thought.

****

I got on my laptop and went to the porn search engine. Among the assortment of recent videos on the main page, I saw the heading "big cock stroking."

Looking at other guys' cocks hadn't ever been my thing. I never sneaked a peek in the locker room or gym showers. I just wanted to imagine what Ashley had that night with Jim Murta.

The guy in the video had the camera zoomed up close to his cock, pointed up at the ceiling, as he sat in a chair. He never let his face show. He had a cock any man would be proud of, which is why he was probably filming himself and uploading it for the world to see. He was at least eight inches, probably nine.

Trent Reznor began singing, "I want to fuck you like an animal" in the background and the guy started stroking.

I began stroking myself.

The slit on his head would tilt down to the camera, before jerking up with the rhythm of his hand.

That's the kind of cock that fucked my wife, I thought, the kind Ashley watched being stroked in front of her, that she wanted in her pussy, bare, despite knowing I was right outside. I'm looking at Jim Murta's cock.

When the scene switched to him stroking hard over a wooden table, I knew he was about to cum. He had the camera on the other side of the table. His cock pointed directly at it. He removed his hand for a moment, letting it dangle and pulsate. And then it exploded in trajectories like fireworks. One shot went past the camera, but the rest splattered the wooden table. Then, finally, a few last bits just seeped out of him.

I replayed the cumshot in slow motion thinking, That's what you gave Ashley, that big cock, and that fat fuck load of sperm. Fuck you, Jim Murta!

And then I came myself.

After I wiped myself off, I felt sick and disgusted. I could rationalize what I'd done. I was simply imagining that I was looking at the cock that fucked my wife. *But good God*, I thought, *if I were ever to be busted jerking off while looking at something like that, what a dubious and convoluted explanation that would be.*

If Tamara knew my reaction to the two of them being out tonight was to masturbate while watching another guy blow his load—imagining it was Jim Murta's cock—she would laugh so condescendingly hard that it would echo in my brain for weeks. She'd have the satisfaction of knowing she had accomplished much more that night than she ever could have imagined.

****

Ashley texted me that she was still out drinking with Tamara but would be back in an hour.

I went through Ashley's photo album, looking for photos from last summer on Cape May. We had rented a beach house for the week with friends. Tamara had joined us the first weekend.

That first day at the beach, Tamara had unveiled a new thong bikini. She had tried to talk Ashley into buying one with her, but Ashley had demurred. The suit showed off her spanking tight, toned ass and attracted major attention on the beach.

Teenage boys were ogling while she ordered drinks at a snack bar. Where was her modesty and sense of decency, I'd wondered at the time.

In the third album I found the photos from that week. There was one of Ashley and Tamara holding drinks and posing by the pool in their bikinis.

I pulled the photo from the plastic and took it into the bathroom. After checking to make sure the bathtub was dry, I sat down in it. I wanted to better imagine how they looked to Jim Murta that night.

I stared at the photo, going back and forth over their tits in their bikinis. Jim Murta would be standing, towering over them, staring down at two sets of nice big tits.

I wondered exactly how Tamara phrased her suggestion: "Why don't you whip it out? Why don't you show us what you're packing? Why don't you show Ashley your cock, Jim?"

"Ashley," I pictured her saying, "the look on your face when you first saw Jim's cock was priceless."

I imagined him pointing it close at her as she watched it throbbing towards her.

Who in hell did Tamara think she was, offering up Ashley's pussy to him?

Did Jim Murta even hesitate? Sure, Tamara was hot, but opportunities to fuck a married co-worker with her husband outside didn't come along every day.

I stood up and sat on the sink. I imagined the moment when he slowly slid inside her.

"Oh my God," Ashley my wife would say, "it's so friggin' big."

"Bigger than your husband's, Ashley?"

"Oh my God, Jim, there's no comparison."

"It's still got a few inches to go, Ashley, but it will all be in you soon."

"Oh my God."

"Oh yeah, Ashley, it's going all the way inside you."

Jim Murta was off to the races now. He was getting his Jim Murta fuck on.

"Oh hell, yeah," Tamara might egg them on, "ride that big fat cock."

"Shh," Ashley might whisper, "David's outside."

"Fuck David," Jim would reply as his cock pumped deep inside her.

"Oh my God, I'm about to cum."

"Say 'Fuck David,' Ashley."

"Fuck David."

"Say 'Fuck David, fuck my husband.'"

"Fuck … oh God. Fuck Dave … David … fuck my husband."

I stared at the photo of Ashley, dropping it onto the counter as I came.

****

Ashley came home an hour later, a little buzzed, saying "I'se gots to pee."

When she came out, I asked her about Burning Man and she said, "Now she's talking next summer" and told me Tamara said "hi." She checked her email before asking if I'd mind if she called her Chicago friend Camilla, who was coming into town Friday.

I went into the bathroom and my stomach sank.

On the sink, right next to the tissues, I had left the photo of Ashley and Tamara in bikinis.

My heart started racing as I wondered how I could have been so stupid as to leave it there. Perhaps Ashley in her buzzed hurry to pee hadn't noticed. But what if she had? Why would I have taken a photo from her album of them in bikinis into the bathroom? What explanation was there, other than that I'd jerked myself looking at it?

If she had noticed it, why hadn't she called me out, saying, "What's this doing here?"

I put the photo in my back pocket and prepared myself for questions. Lame as it was, the only excuse I could come up with was, "I was on the phone with my mom tonight, and she mentioned the reception hall we had for our wedding. Well I got out your photo album, and I was flipping through it in the bathroom—well, obviously, I got the wrong one—and then the picture of you and Tamara fell out. I was still talking to my mom, so I just left it on the sink to return it later. And then my brother called, and well, which album are our wedding photos in, anyway?"

When I came back out, Ashley was typing on her laptop. She told me her friend Camilla would be coming in Friday night. "Oh, and she wanted me to tell you that her boyfriend Mark may have

Yankee tickets for Saturday. He'll invite you if he does, but the emphasis is on *may*."

"Oh, right on," I replied, "that would be cool."

I made my way into the bedroom and snuck the photo back into her album.

CHAPTER TEN

The next morning, Ashley made no mention of finding the photo.

The following night she had a presentation to prepare. I left her in the living room, went into the office, shut the door, and turned on some music. I was done looking at porn and catching up on financial news when I noticed the "chat room" icon on the upper right.

It had been several years since I talked in Internet chat rooms. When I did, it was mostly to talk sports. I used to frequent a specialty room called "Yankees Baseball." Sometimes Red Sox fans would infiltrate the room, and I'd join in the conversational Red Sox bashing. But the novelty of communicating with random strangers in real-time grew old pretty quickly.

I certainly never saw it as a way of meeting girls.

I clicked on the chat icon and went scrolling through the options. After a while, I found myself looking at the names of the "special interest" rooms in the User-Created Section. These were the adult-themed rooms and the majority of the room titles had something to do with sex. They had provocative names like "Women who Love Swallowing" or "Love Older Men" or "Submissive Women." Others, like "Men Look at Daughter" or "Family Fun," were downright creepy.

There was one called "Wife Likes Others," which I presumed had to do with cheating. But then I saw another room simply entitled "My Wife." I decided to check it out. There were about twenty-five people in the room, but most seemed on the conversational sideline. In the public scroll, only a few people were typing, and what they wrote was fairly generic:

"Jeremy 33, Kansas, any wives free to chat?"

"Mitch 49, Philadelphia, any swingers local—my wife's 45, DD."

"30m Las Vegas here—wanna talk phone about my hot Spanish wife."

"Anyone wife swap in the Tucson area?"

"Who's got pictures to trade tonight?"

I was about to exit the room, when I received a private message. "Hi Dave," it read, "NYC here as well."

"How did you know I'm in NYC?" I replied.

"I just looked at your profile."

I had forgotten I even had a profile. I had created it a few years ago. It gave my name, age, location, and that I was in a relationship.

"Oh, I got you," I typed.

"You married?"

"Yes."

"I have a hot 43 year old Filipino wife, care to trade photos?"

"No," I replied, "sorry," and clicked off the message.

Another message popped up: "Brooklyn here, do you share your wife?"

"No," I replied, "sorry."

Another guy asked, "Your wife like black?"

This was getting pointless, so I figured I'd type something of my own in the public scroll.

I looked at what I'd written for a few minutes before sending it: "Anyone here learn your wife cheated and how did you deal?"

That prompted a flurry of private messages:

"Your wife cheated?"

"Have a pic of her?"

"What happened with your wife?"

But then someone messaged me: "Yeah, it happened to me, my wife cheated on me."

"Hi," I replied, "I'm Dave, I'd be curious how you handled it."

"I was pissed but I eventually forgave her."

"How long ago was that?" I asked.

"Two years."

"And you're still with her?"

"Yeah."

"I'd be interested in hearing what happened," I typed, "if you don't mind discussing it."

"Not at all," he replied, "it all started with a cruise."

"That's where she cheated?"

"Yup."

"Were you with her?"

"No, she had gone on a cruise of the Caribbean with a recently divorced girlfriend of hers."

"OK," I typed, "and?"

"Well I didn't like the idea of her going, whatsoever. I even joked with her before about it being their 'Girls Gone Wild' week, but she assured me it was nothing like that, and that she was just going to be comforting a friend in need. I knew her friend and knew she would be looking for a rebound hook-up. But what was I going to say to my wife, 'No'? All I could say was have fun, but not too much fun, you know."

"Yeah," I typed, "I know the influence a friend can have. So what happened?"

"Well, she sent me emails that week saying she was having fun, but pretend G-Rated stuff. How they took in a musical, how she won some money gambling, lay out by the pool. How her friend's spirits were good. How we should take a cruise, the two of us, as a next vacation."

"Well, anyway," he continued, "when she got back, she seemed a bit depressed to be home. I understand the post-vacation blues, but this time seemed different. She was on her computer a lot the week afterwards and one day I saw she had left it on and was still signed on. She had written about her cruise vacation to two of her friends."

"So you read the emails?"

"Yeah, her laptop was just sitting there on the kitchen table."

"What did you learn?"

"Well," he replied, "The very first night she boarded that ship, she met an entertainment director, a guy who works on the cruise. And the guy bedded my wife that first night. It seemed pretty torrid. She had sex with this guy the whole week she was there."

"Wow," I replied, "how did you feel when you read all this?"

"I was mad as hell."

"Did you confront her?"

"Hell, yeah."

"How did she respond?"

"I'm sorry, I'm sorry, I love you, I don't know what got into me. She blamed her friend, even blamed me in a backhanded way. I told her I wanted her to stop emailing the guy and she said, 'Never again, I'm done.' "

"She was emailing him afterwards?" I asked. "You mean, when she got back home?"

"Yeah, she wrote him long emails about how fantastic he was and how she still thought about him all the time. But it was one-sided."

"One-sided?" I asked.

"Yeah, his replies back to her were brief. Like he was really busy. Three-sentence emails. Not blowing her off completely. He said maybe he could see her when he was in Tampa in the summer. But it was clear to me that it was just a fun little vacation relationship for him. I'm sure he was off fucking a new wife on vacation the following week."

"How do you mean?"

"I talked to a guy in this room who used to work for a cruise line. He said married women without their husbands are easy prey. He said he was constantly banging the married wives there alone. It's like a contest with them."

"Wow," I typed, "so what happened after you learned?"

"Well, she swore up and down that nothing like that would ever happen again and I eventually forgave her. She swore he had used a condom, but I was like 'Yeah, right,' and had her get tested. Then a few months later, I started rereading those emails. I saved them all. And I got kind of fascinated by it. This happened two years ago. I must have reread those letters a hundred times now."

"Were they graphic?" I asked.

"Not blow by blow, but there was enough for me to get a mental picture. It started to turn me on, the image of her with another man. This guy was young, around thirty, and she talked about how buff and strong he was, how well hung, how skillful he was in bed. How she knew that first evening he'd be sleeping with her that night. She was obsessed with this guy, but I think she meant nothing to him."

"Meant nothing?" I asked. "How so?"

"Check this out," he wrote. "The last day, she was out drinking by the pool and this guy took her to some secluded place on the ship. He works on the ship, it's probably his usual spot. Anyway, they had sex there and she wrote how afterwards she couldn't find her bikini bottom. So the guy told her he'd come back with a towel. Do you think he ever came back with a towel?"

"I guess he didn't?"

"Nope, she waited an hour and a half for this guy to return and he never did. So eventually, she had to make her way back to her room in broad daylight, running for visual barriers with her hands trying to cover her ass and pussy. She told her friend it was twenty minutes of running from one thing to the next, with other passengers catching glimpses. She said she was mortified when two men walked passed her as she was trying to slide the key in her door. Can you imagine that? Guys checking out my wife's ass as she's frantically trying to open the door? Having just been fucked. What a slut she must have looked like. I swear, if I could have video of that afternoon of my bottomless wife running that gauntlet in public—"

"Wow," I typed, "so did she ever see the guy after that?"

"Yeah, as a matter of fact, she did. You would think she would tell this guy to fuck off, right?"

"I would think so," I typed.

"So would I. But instead she saw him later that night at the bar and said, 'You never returned.' And he said he was sorry but he got called to work on the other side of the ship and couldn't make it back. And she said, 'that's OK' and then joked about it. She ate up that lame excuse like it was apple sauce. Now, you know that guy left her stranded on purpose, right?"

"I don't know, do you think so?"

"I'm sure of it. He probably had no intention of returning. Maybe he even tossed her bikini bottoms during sex. He probably enjoyed making that statement. Like 'I'm going to fuck you, cum inside you'—I don't believe the 'he used a condom' talk from her. And then he leaves her to walk back embarrassed and exposed."

"Why do you think that?"

"Because no other explanation makes sense and I know guys like that. It was the last day and he was telling her what he really thought of her, how little he ultimately regarded her. So you know what happened that last night, even after he pulled that shit on her earlier in the afternoon?"

"What?"

"She still wanted to fuck him. Where was her dignity? Instead, she wanted a final fuck goodbye. Or a fuck-off goodbye as I think it was for him, when he obliged her. You think he had any respect for her then? No, he was probably already thinking of the new blood about to come in the next week."

"But it turned you on, you said?" I asked.

"Eventually it did. Like I said I became fascinated by it. I can't tell you how many times I've wanked thinking about her with that guy."

"Do you still? I mean that was two years ago?"

"Oh sure," he replied, "When I wank, that's what I think about. It doesn't matter how long ago it was."

"Does she know it turns you on thinking about it?" I asked.

"Not to that per se, but she knows I'm now open to her being with another man. Only I would want to know about it, and there would have to be certain ground rules."

"Ground rules?" I asked.

"Yeah," he wrote, "something I would participate in setting up. It started as pillow talk, and she'll indulge in the fantasy, but she doesn't want to do something that jeopardizes our marriage or gives her buyer's remorse."

"Do you think she will do it?"

"I think with time, and some gentle encouragement, there's a good chance. But we'll have to see. I don't want to jeopardize our marriage either. For now, it's just a hot fantasy."

"How's your marriage now?"

"It's good, it's strong. I think we have our trust back now. In a weird way, it actually brought us closer. It's definitely improved our sex life. That is, I find her more attractive, like she has this wild side."

"That's good, I'm glad," I typed. "So would you say now that you don't really regret it?"

"Regret is a tricky word," he wrote. "It changed my view of her somewhat, that she allowed this guy to basically use her. But maybe it broadened her dimensionally for me. Just thinking of her being that wild. I certainly was hurt by it. But I think over time, assuming things remain good, whatever regret that might linger, will go away."

"Interesting," I typed, "I'm glad to hear that."

"Is this something you're going through?"

"Yeah," I replied, "only mine was a lot more recent."

"Turn you on?"

"Yeah, kind of," I admitted.

"It happens. That's normal. It hurts, but is a turn-on. Go figure, right?"

"Yeah," I typed, "it's a bit of a cluster fuck. Good to know I'm not the only one going through something like this and reacting like I have."

"Mean reacting by being turned on and wanking?"

"Yeah."

"Oh hell, don't sweat it. It's very common. I've talked to a lot of guys in this room. There's tons who get off thinking about their wives with other men."

"OK," I typed.

"I'm going to put you on my contact list. I want to hear all about what happened, but I've got to go pick up my son."

"OK," I typed.

"I'll look for you next time I'm on, and you can tell me."

"Sure," I replied.

"I'm Jack from Florida, 48."

"I'm Dave, 34, NYC."

"Nice to meet you Dave, we'll chat soon."

"I look forward to it."

"Hang in there Dave. It's OK, it's normal, you're human."

"Thanks, Jack."

****

I practically sprang out of my chair, relaxed, lighter, as if a load had been lifted from my shoulders. I wasn't alone.

Hallelujah, I thought, someone else had gone through a similar experience and reacted in a similar way.

And his marriage had survived it. Hell, according to him, it was now stronger. Talking with Jack had given me hope, a little beam of light—like the moon breaking through the clouds the other night with Ashley.

I thought about Jack's story. He had endured his own personal cluster fuck. Not just a one-night stand, but a whole week-long affair. He had her words in emails swirling in his head. And he had children, or at least one son. If he had to pick him up somewhere, his son was probably in his teens. What a fucked up thing for any son to learn—that while he and his dad were at home, his mom had been running naked through a cruise ship after being fucked by the entertainment director.

94

Jack probably had few people, if anyone, he could talk to. But I was an anonymous stranger, sincerely asking, and his openness had forged a bond.

****

I checked in with Ashley to see if I could help with her presentation or listen to her deliver it.

"I'd love to give it a run-through," she said, "in an hour or so."

"Sure," I said, and she gave me a kiss.

I shut the door and listened to Ashley's soothing voice as she recited her speech in the other room.

I thought about the emails Jack had read. I imagined finding one of Ashley's. She wouldn't be so graphic to a friend. It would be more akin to a diary entry: "Jim Murta was such a fantastic fuck. I think about his cock all the time. He was so manly and forceful, nothing at all like I'm used to with my dud husband Dave. Jim's cock is the kind a girl dreams about. When he first pulled it out, I was hypnotized—in complete awe.

"When Tamara sent Dave upstairs, I was so hoping Jim would pick me. I was so horny. I was like 'Dave who?' I wanted to feel that big cock pumping inside my pussy.

"And oh my God, did Jim feel good, balls deep inside me. And I mean balls deep. He was slapping it up into me so thick and hard. The kind of fucking a girl like me deserves.

"I knew I'd have to go back to the party, but I didn't care. He was giving me a cloud-nine orgasm, and I was like, 'just cum the fuck inside me.'

"Just fucking do it Jim, to hell with my husband, I want to feel your sperm inside me. And my God, did that man cum."

And then I came myself.

****

"How's the presentation going?" I asked.

Ashley had changed into the Yankee pajamas I had given her as a stocking stuffer last Christmas.

"Well," she replied, "maybe it's time for the painting to be taken away from me. I think I've re-worked it enough."

"Ready to run it past me?" I asked.

"Yeah, here's the PowerPoint. I'll snap my fingers when it's time to turn the page."

"You got it," I said.

"Good morning everyone, I'm Ashley Martens, director of marketing. And with the monsoon-like rain outside today, it's fitting that we're talking about a product that is essentially an umbrella—in this case, a security umbrella."

Ashley broke from the script to tell me, "There's supposed to be a heavy downpour tomorrow."

"And if the weatherman's wrong?" I asked.

"There will be plenty of time for questions afterwards," she said. Rolling her eyes at me and smiling, she continued, "And while the weathermen were wrong about today—what else is new—that doesn't mean we don't need umbrellas."

She went on, without missing a beat, and I just listened. I made sure to pay attention so I could offer feedback, but it wasn't easy. I kept hearing the soothing cadence of her voice and staring at her big tits in that Yankees top—so upright, without a bra.

When she finished, I really had no suggestions. The intro was a bit cutesy/cheesy, but the substance had flow and structure; she kept it interesting. I wasn't going to offer criticism for the sake of having something to say.

I meant it when I said, "That was great, babe! You're going to hit it out of the park for sure."

Ashley could see that I meant it but still had to ask the requisite, "Really?"

"Really, Ash, I wouldn't change a thing. You were clear, got across the relevant points, and infused it with humor and personality."

She made her way over to the couch and onto my lap and said, "Thank you."

I initiated making out. I kissed her hard, feeling up her breasts through her top. I thought of suggesting going to the bedroom but let it flow naturally. When she lifted off her top, I knew I was in business. I had her pajamas bottoms off and soon I was going down on her, right there on the couch.

It was spontaneous, organic, natural, and Ashley was into it. I licked up and down, sliding my tongue inside her pussy. She started to moan and I focused hard on keeping it up. She took my hand and said, "That's it, Dave, yes! I'm going to cum."

She squirmed, cried out, "Yes, yes, oh my God" and held my hand tightly.

She helped me with my jeans and, lying there on the couch, I slid inside her.

Just hold out there, I told myself.

But it felt so incredible, amazing, and I couldn't prevent thoughts of Jim Murta from creeping in.

She was starting to rhythm with me, saying "Oh yeah."

But five or six pumps later, I couldn't stop myself from cumming.

God fucking damnit, I thought.

"My God, Ash," I said, "you got me so turned on just watching you deliver that speech. God, I love you."

Ashley held me tight as I lay on top of her, both of us naked on the couch, and patted me on the back.

I didn't know how to interpret the pat. It was probably nothing. I knew I was paranoid. But it felt a little like, "It's OK, Dave, I know you're having trouble lasting lately."

"You're going to do just great on your presentation tomorrow," I said as a way to divert attention.

"You really thought it was good?"

"I thought it was awesome."

"Well, thanks for being such a good captive audience."

CHAPTER ELEVEN

We had dinner plans with Ashley's friend Camilla, who was in from Chicago with her boyfriend, Mark.

Ashley was laughing and spirited, basking in the relief of her presentation being well received.

They were an entertaining couple and I was looking forward to a few drinks as we walked the East Village streets afterwards.

I liked the bar Camilla chose, having been there before. But once inside, I said, "Good grief, are you freaking kidding me?"

Mark looked at me and asked "What?"

"It seems Friday night is Karaoke night at this place," I said.

Before I could say, "I know some other good places right around the corner," Camilla was exclaiming, "Oh, fun!"

"You sing karaoke, Mark?" Ashley asked.

"Sure, I've been known to on occasion."

Fucking thanks a lot, Mark, I thought.

"What do you say, Dave," Ashley said, "something different. How about it?"

"Sure," I said, feeling checkmated.

A few minutes later we were sitting at a table in the front.

This sucks, I thought.

It wasn't just the cheesy campiness of Karaoke that I didn't care for. If I could just hang out with my drink and watch, I wouldn't have minded. But the only time I've sung karaoke was drunk with my buddies, doing "Roadhouse Blues" at some random Jersey shore bar.

When Mark began looking through the song list, I knew what I was in for—I could hear it. "It's your turn, Dave, get on up there."

The guy on the stage was the DJ, doing his best white-guy imitation of an old Usher song. Of course he performed it well; he's the karaoke guy.

Ashley, Camilla and Mark put their song requests in, and I said I'd have to think about it.

Oh great, I thought, as the first people who came up seemed like they could actually sing.

Then some really old guy took the stage. He was at least seventy years old and looked like Grandpa Munster from the old TV show. I was expecting him to do some snooze-fest song like "Mack the Knife."

When the music for Coldplay's "Viva La Vida" came on, and he stood there waiting for the vocal part to start, I felt bad for the guy. But as soon as he started with "I used to the rule the world" in a deep, yet soft, vulnerable voice, he had the audience's full attention.

Even though it was a rock song from a modern time, the way he sang it echoed the past. He was making it his own.

The crowd roared when he finished, and he was so obviously moved that I was moved.

I imagined him widowed, heading back to an empty apartment, talking to his dog perhaps, saying, "I did good tonight, Rex. Maria would have been proud."

****

About a half hour later, Ashley was on stage doing the Cranberries song, "Zombie."

She had her fake Irish accent down and acted completely comfortable on stage. I did my own zombie-ing out when she started singing the line, "What's in your head boy …"

She was commanding the audience's attention and received a reception similar to the old guy's.

A few songs later, it was Mark's turn. He did Neil Young's "Rocking in the Free World."

Whatever he lacked in vocals, he made up for in energy.

When it was Camilla's turn, she asked Ashley to join her. "Hollaback Girl" isn't really a duet, but after Camilla chanted out the verse, Ashley backed her up on the chorus. Camilla's a good-looking girl as well, and they were eye candy as they pranced around on stage.

"I'm not much of a singer," I explained, when the inevitable goading began.

"Who cares?" Camilla offered ungenerously. "Neither am I. It's about having fun. Pick something and just do it."

Why is it so hard for people to understand that I didn't want to get up on stage in front of a crowd when I can't freaking sing?

"I've had a cold all week," I explained. "I'd take away from all the good performers like you guys."

They didn't press it after that. Their thinking I was a big fat stick in the mud was better than my making a fool of myself.

Ashley then performed the Fiona Apple song, "Criminal." With a few drinks in her, she was more theatrical.

I'd heard her sing that before, but it still got to me when she came to the line, "I've been careless with a delicate man."

I could see guys checking her out, and she got huge applause when she finished. Right afterwards the Karaoke DJ guy asked her if she knew some rap duet. Of course she did. Of course she said sure, she would try it with him. When she sat back down after more applause, she was exhilarated. I couldn't blame her or be upset. She has a great voice, which is why people applauded her freaking karaoke performance.

When I settled up and signed the bill, I felt lame for not even trying.

But I can't sing. What's so wrong with realizing that limitation?

****

As soon as we got in the cab, I offered, "You were brilliant tonight, I mean it, your singing was sensational."

"Really?" she asked. "Thank you. And thanks for putting up with it. I know karaoke's not your thing."

"Well, thanks for not calling me out on my 'having a cold' excuse, but you know I can't sing."

"Yeah, I know, but it's not like anyone takes it seriously."

"I hear you," I said, "but you guys set a pretty high bar, and I loved seeing you perform."

"It was fun," she said. "I haven't been on stage in public for a while."

I paid the cabbie and followed Ashley into our lobby. She made a beeline for our doorman. "Hi, Jimmy, can we get management to install screens in our apartment?" she asked.

"Sure, Mrs. Martens," he said.

"Like in the next couple days?" she asked. "We had a monster bug visit us the other night."

"I will put in the request first thing in the morning."

"Thanks, Jimmy."

"Thanks, Jimmy," I repeated lamely.

Ashley's next beeline was in our apartment; she headed straight for the bathroom and then to bed.

I wasn't tired, and went into the office.

****

I didn't see Jack online. I went back to the "My Wife" room and asked if anyone's wife cheated and how they reacted.

"My wife has a regular boyfriend," a guy from Illinois, messaged me.

"You mean she's seeing a guy on the side?" I asked.

"Yeah, she's been seeing him for nine months now."

"Does she know that you know?"

"Yeah, she doesn't hide it. She'll tell me when she's going over to stay the night with him."

"What? Are you serious?"

"Completely serious."

How do you feel about that?" I asked.

"I'm OK with it. I've kind of accepted that it's my place or lot in life, and I like when she tells me the details."

"It turns you on?" I typed.

"Yeah, and this arrangement is the only reason we're still together."

"How did it get to this point?" I asked. "I mean, to the point where she could be open and honest about seeing this guy?"

"Well, a few friends said she was marrying me for money. I had an inheritance when I was twenty-five. So, my wife was attracted to how I looked on paper—a mid-twenties guy who owned a big house, had some nice cars."

"You knew that when you married her?"

"Not consciously. But, deep down I had some inkling that she was only attracted to the idea of me. Her dad left her when she was a kid, so she has father-abandonment issues. Her family was poor and I provided something she didn't have—money and security."

"Do you regret having married her?"

"Sometimes I wish I had a do-over but I was fucked up before I met her."

"Fucked up, how? Coming into money?"

"No, I mean with women."

"Oh OK, fucked up how?"

"Well, I never had much confidence with the opposite sex in general. But then, my senior year in college I fell head over heels for this girl and she loved me back. We were inseparable. The girl was the love of my life, you know?"

"Sure," I typed, "I know what you mean."

"I proposed to her Graduation Weekend and we were supposed to get married the following summer. That would have been eight years ago."

"What happened?" I asked.

"Well, she wanted to work in London for the summer and I had done a semester abroad there two years before, so I told her I'd go with her. That was the plan after graduation."

"OK," I typed, "so you went to London with her?"

"Yeah. I even found a flat where we could stay. I had a friend there, an assistant professor who I had become friends with when I studied abroad my junior year. He was like a big brother to me."

"OK, so you stayed with him?"

"Yeah, he had a one-bedroom, so we slept on a bed in his living room."

"OK, so how did that go?"

"At first it was great. My friend Aaron was a great tour guide, and my fiancée Tara had never traveled abroad and was thrilled and excited to explore the city."

"Sure," I typed, "I understand."

"And the three of us got along really well. We'd drink wine off the balcony and stay up late, all of us talking, laughing, that kind of thing."

"Sure," I replied, "sounds fun."

"It was. I was never happier in my life, being in London with the girl I was going to marry. But then one night, something happened that changed my life, changed who I was, really."

"OK," I typed, "I'd be interested in hearing if you don't mind sharing."

"Sure. This was my first girlfriend. I was shy around girls growing up. And Tara came from a pretty traditional family—she's Catholic. So neither of us had sex before."

"You were virgins?" I asked.

"Yes, we were. And we'd decided, or really she asked, that we wait until we were married. I said sure, I was OK with waiting."

"Were you OK with waiting?"

"Yeah, I really was. Because I was in love and I'd waited twenty-two years to have sex, what's another year?"

"Yeah, I get it," I typed.

"So anyway, it was the fourteenth of July, and Aaron took us to a party at a French guy's place, because it was Bastille Day, the French version of the fourth of July."

"Sure," I typed, "OK."

"We drank a good bit there and then the three of us came back to our flat. Aaron kept the wine flowing and it was just talking and laughing. Then Aaron said he wanted to get another bottle and Tara said she'd go with him. I didn't care, because they'd be back in ten minutes. Then I lay down on the couch. I wasn't that drunk, but the wine had made me tired. So I briefly fell asleep. When I woke up, I heard Aaron tell her I was sleeping and I heard Tara say, 'Let him sleep.'"

"OK," I typed.

"So for some reason I pretended I was asleep and listened to them talking and laughing and having more wine in the kitchen. Then it got kind of quiet. The lights were turned off. I was just lying there listening with my eyes wide open."

"What did you think was going on?"

"I didn't know. Maybe I thought she'd say something to him about me, something she wouldn't want me to hear, because she assumed I was sleeping."

"Did she?"

"No, once the lights were off, I could hear him say, 'Come over here, Tara, lie on the bed with me for a bit.' And I heard her say, 'I shouldn't' and 'That's not a good idea.' But he persisted with 'C'mon, I'm not going to bite. Just for a minute.' "

"OK," I replied, "did she lie down with him?"

"Yes, after a couple minutes I heard her say, 'Okay, but just for a minute.' And so now my heart was pounding and I was bug-eyed looking up at the ceiling, just listening. And then I heard whispering and muffled laughter. I could hear her say 'I don't know'. But then I heard kissing and sucking sounds, and I knew Aaron was making out with my fiancée. Still, I just lay there, listening. About ten minutes later, I heard him say, 'Don't worry' and she was saying 'I don't know.' But then there was a lot of heavy breathing, and my heart was in my throat. It was like a dream. And I lay there, motionless."

"OK," I typed.

"There was a lot of whispering that I couldn't make out. That lasted about five minutes; then I heard more kissing and sucking sounds. Five minutes later I heard her cry out, 'Oh God,' and the bed started to creak. I knew what was happening. Aaron was fucking my virgin fiancée."

"Jeez, how did you feel?"

"My heart was beating a mile a minute, I was freaking. I was in shock. I didn't know what to think."

"OK."

"The creaking grew louder and now the bed was really starting to bounce. I couldn't believe it. But I was also sprouting an erection."

"So it turned you on?"

"Yeah, but I was going mental. It felt otherworldly. And I just listened. Aaron wasn't even trying to be quiet. I mean, the bed was creaking loudly. And I listened to Tara moan and skin slapping against skin. I heard her cry out, 'Oh God, oh God' and she may have had her first orgasm then. He said 'Mmmm' like he was cumming, and the creaking slowed down to quiet and whispering."

"Yikes man, that's crazy," I typed. "Did you just lie there on the couch?"

"Yeah, and then about a half hour later, he went into his bedroom and Tara came over and asked if I wanted to move to the bed. So I said sure. And she didn't say anything. She just went to sleep. I spent the night awake in a daze, scared and crying."

"Did you confront her or him?"

"No, I never brought it up. I wanted to pretend like it didn't happen. I didn't know what it all meant. That week we all had dinner together like it was normal, but she seemed different, more distant. By the end of the week she told me she was breaking off the engagement, that she didn't want to marry me."

"Did she say why?"

"She said she had given it a lot of thought and she didn't love me anymore. She had lost what had attracted her to me. For a few days I begged her to reconsider, but she would just say it's over, and that she was going to move out, unless I wanted to leave London. 'Maybe you should just leave,' she said."

"Wow," I typed.

"Yeah, so a few days later, I was flying back to the U.S., leaving her behind. I was miserable. I don't think I ever fully got over it. A month later she wrote me a letter. I hoped she was going to say she had reconsidered, but it basically said how she realized we were different people, how she wanted to explore life, how just a few weeks in London had changed her perspective."

"I'm sorry," I typed. "So she never mentioned having sex and you didn't, either?"

"No, it never came up."

"You ever talk to the guy, your friend from London?"

"When I said I was leaving, he said that with Tara breaking up with me, leaving was a good idea. He hugged me goodbye at the airport and we never spoke again. I did learn from another friend that Tara was still living with him two months later, so I assume he continued having sex with her."

"Damn," I typed, "that's harsh."

"I know. I never even got to fuck her. Not even once. The girl I was head over heels in love with."

"That is tough," I typed, "do you still think about that night?"

"Oh sure, something like that never leaves you. I'll still take out pictures of the three of us from those first few weeks and I'll jack off thinking of that night. Pretty strange, right?"

"I can understand it," I replied, "I can relate to the masturbating."

"It was like that night happened in slow motion, with me listening in agony. I introduced Tara to a guy who was supposed to be my friend. And then he goes and pops her virgin cherry on the bed we slept in, with me on the couch a few feet away."

"It must have been a triumph," I typed, "taking her cherry with her fiancée nearby—no offense."

"For Aaron?"

"Yeah, your London friend."

"Yeah, I'm sure it was. And like I said, it never left me. I took it into my marriage."

"How do you mean?" I asked.

"It just sent me off with a cuckold mindset."

"Cuckold?" I said.

"Yeah, I'm a cuckold to my wife."

"Meaning what?"

"You know what a cuckold is, don't you?"

I knew the term from Shakespeare but wasn't sure what he meant by it.

"Not sure," I replied.

"I let my wife have lovers and I basically just sit home and accept my place in the relationship. Only I don't even get the benefits other cuckolds get."

"Meaning what, you can't have sex with other women?"

"No, I mean, I don't get to watch or listen."

"Watch or listen to what? Your wife having sex? You wish you could?"

"Yeah, sure, but all I get are the details when she throws me a bone."

"And hearing the details turns you on?"

"Yeah, I jack off thinking about them."

"What's your sex life with her?"

"The last time I had sex with her was six months ago, on my birthday. But she lets me jack off looking at her sometimes as she tells me details."

"Damn," I typed, "have you ever thought of leaving her?"

"No, I love her, and maybe someday with another boyfriend she'll let me listen."

"Another boyfriend?"

"Her current boyfriend doesn't know I know. But some guys are into letting the husband listen. So that's why I say 'someday.' "

"Do you think she would ever leave you to marry her boyfriend?"

"She has a very cushy lifestyle being married to me. She has her cake and eats it, too."

"Do you ever feel humiliated by it?"

"Sure, that's a natural feeling, especially for cuckolds. Ever check out the cuckold chat room?"

"No," I typed, "I've seen a room called 'cuckold husband' scrolling through rooms, but didn't know what it was."

"Well there's a lot of guys there who have a similar relationship dynamic. But a lot of guys get to watch. I wish I had that situation, you know?"

"I guess," I typed.

"So what's going on with you and your wife?" he asked.

"It's a long story," I replied, not wanting to get into it with him, "and I have to get to bed. Can we talk later?"

"Sure," he wrote.

"Take care, man," I replied.

****

That is so fucked up, I thought.

His supposed friend pops his fiancée's cherry in the bed they slept in, while he listened. And then a week later his fiancée's telling him to pack his bags, it's over, take the next flight home. No wedding, no ever having sex with this girl you loved—no nothing.

No wonder it profoundly affected him.

What a Jim Murta that British bloke had pulled on him. He must've relished putting his cock in that virgin pussy with her poor-sap fiancé on the couch nearby. Another man, his presumed friend, had popped his fiancée's cherry, and he listened, paralyzed, while it happened.

It got me thinking. I wondered what I would have done if I'd heard something in that upstairs bathroom that night when I went upstairs to take a piss.

I imagined hearing sounds from the vent, coming up from the bathroom below. I'd realize someone was having sex downstairs, and put my ear to that vent—thinking it must be Tamara. I might have relished that.

Oh yeah, I'd think, you dirty little slut, let's hear it, Tamara, let's hear you get good and hard fucked girl.

I'd hear the balls slapping and the moaning and think, Oh yeah, I've got a front row audio seat to your dirty little bathroom fuck, so let's hear it baby—your secret's safe with me.

But suddenly the moaning, the voice would sound all too familiar. I'd press my head closer, and hear "Oh God" again.

No, it can't be, I'd say to myself.

Then I pictured hearing Tamara's voice, saying "Oh yeah, Ashley, that's it, ride it girl!"

I imagined that "Holy fuck" realization moment. The love of my life, my wife, was being fucked as I listened through the bathroom vent upstairs.

Maybe then I would have barreled down the stairs, banged on the door and yelled, "Open the motherfucking door, Goddamnit!"

Or maybe I'd have been paralyzed, in shock. Or even popped a boner, crouched, listening in surreal disbelief.

Sitting in the bathroom now, masturbating, I would pay good money for an audio of what I would have heard that night.

"You're a little married cock whore Ashley," I imagined Tamara saying, "You're taking some serious cock, aren't you girlfriend?"

"Oh God, yes."

"Oh God yes what?"

"I'm taking some serious cock."

"And you're a little married cock whore."

"I'm a … married … cock … whore."

"And I'm about to seed your married pussy," Jim might chime in. "Where do you want my sperm, Ashley?"

"In my … married … pussy."

"Say 'fuck my chump husband, and seed my married pussy.' "

"Fuck my … chump … husband … and seed my … my married … pussy."

I thought of Jim blasting his sperm deep inside my wife and suddenly came.

CHAPTER TWELVE

Ashley was getting ready when I woke Saturday.

I lay in bed and watched as she dressed and packed a small bag.

"Where you meeting Camilla?"

"The East Fifties," she said, "the Jitney leaves at ten-fifteen, so I'll have to cab it, and drying my hair's out of the question."

"When's the bridal shower?" I asked, "I thought it wasn't until late afternoon."

"Yeah, it's not till four," she said, "but I told you, were you not listening? Camilla and I are going to get brunch and go shopping beforehand."

"Oh, that's right," I said, getting out of bed. "I remember now. Can I make you some breakfast?"

"No, I packed yogurt for the bus, thanks."

A quick kiss goodbye, and she was off.

****

I waited fifteen minutes to make sure she hadn't forgotten anything; then I went through her closet. I wasn't going to risk pulling any more photos from albums.

I quickly found her CDs of photos and began downloading them onto my laptop. They were chronological, beginning with photos of Ashley before I met her, and then during that magical fall when we first started dating.

I stared at us smiling at a Columbia-Yale football game. That day I bought her a hot chocolate and a Columbia blanket for us to wear in the stands. By the third quarter, Columbia was down three touchdowns, and we were freezing.

Ashley began asking me, "What are the first signs of frostbite?" I suggested we bail on the game, find a bar and warm up.

I remember her saying she wanted a "Hot Toddy."

"What's a Hot Toddy?"

"Some old Scottish drink, I think," she replied, "like something Bob Cratchit would drink."

"Bob Cratchit?"

"You know, Ebenezer Scrooge's boy in *A Christmas Carol*."

"Oh, sure," I said, "so what's in a Hot Toddy?"

"I'm not really sure, but it sounds mighty good right now, doesn't it?"

At the first place, the bartender looked at us blankly before asking us how it's made. But there was an Irish pub across the street, and Ashley got her Hot Toddy. I don't think we ever ordered one again, but I remember thinking—sitting next to her as feeling returned to my feet—that the warm whisky drink sure hit the spot.

****

The pictures awakened memories.

The first Christmas Ashley spent at my parents' place.

The two of us making Champagne toasts at our engagement party.

Ashley in cute shorts and a tight t-shirt on the day we walked across the Brooklyn Bridge.

The two of us on the slopes at Park City.

At a Napa Valley winery, the day before I proposed.

Framed by the California sunset, the night she said, "Yes, I'd love to marry you David."

Ashley's beautiful beaming smile on our wedding day.

My expression of relief and joy in the pre-reception photos on a hill overlooking the Hudson.

Tamara's unusually reserved smile in the wedding photo.

Ashley and me in Venice on our honeymoon.

****

I stared at photos of Ashley from the time she went skydiving with two college friends. She told me how scared and tentative she had been up in the plane, but you wouldn't know it from her smile in the minutes before she jumped. Afterwards Ashley raved about it and suggested we skydive together that summer in New Hampshire.

"I love you baby," I remember saying, "but I ain't jumping out of no plane."

With over four hundred photos downloaded, including Ashley in her bikini, I wondered why I hadn't done this before.

Then I recalled seeing Ashley's camera on her dresser. I went back in the bedroom. It was there—she had forgotten it. Her mom had given it to her last Christmas—after she'd lost her last one. She would email me occasional photos, but I hadn't been curious about what was on it.

Now, as I picked up her camera and looked for a USB cable, I was intensely curious. Had she brought the camera to the party? Were there pictures from that night? Were there any from that bathroom?

I watched as they began to download, 45, 95, 125 …

I felt uneasy about what I was doing. It wasn't like trying to get into her email, but she could view it as an invasion of privacy.

A few minutes later, I read the message, "215 photos successfully downloaded." I returned her camera to exactly where she'd left it and went back to my laptop.

The first photo was of Ashley and her older sister posing by a Christmas tree. Jennifer wasn't Ashley, but her sister was an attractive woman in her own right.

The next photo was of Ashley with her mom, also by the tree. Ashley's mom is in her mid-fifties, refined and elegant. Though taller, she is the source of Ashley's looks and large breasts.

They've had their share of mother-daughter issues. Ashley felt that nothing she ever did was good enough. But I think most of it stemmed from her mom divorcing her father when she was in high school.

In the next photos with her dad, Ashley looked more relaxed, more herself, like she was simply having fun.

Christmas last year had been tricky and stressful—dividing our time between her mom, her dad and my parents.

After the Christmas family photos, there was one of Ashley and me with another couple at a Manhattan steak house on New Year's.

Next up were photos of Central Park after a snowstorm. The pictures she took were Norman Rockwell-ish—kids sledding, some smiling kid making a snowman. I had taken one of Ashley doing a snow angel. In another she was armed with a snowball as if gunning for me—the photographer.

There were photos of the day we went skating at the outside rink at Rockefeller Center. I had dreaded putting on skates. Despite growing up in cold-wintered Westchester, I had only skated twice as a kid. Little kids sped by me, but I didn't fall, and I managed to look semi-competent.

The next photos were of a Mardi Gras party. I had been away in San Francisco on business. Ashley had gone with Tamara. I hadn't thought much about it at the time. In the first photo they were both showing cleavage, wearing beads, and smiling.

Would a forward click uncover a photo of them lifting up their tops, Mardi Gras style? It's wasn't as if they'd never gotten topless together, as I had recently discovered. Part of me wanted to see such a photo. If nothing else, I wanted to see Tamara flashing her tits, to see what Jim had also stroked to, and see what Jim passed over in going for my wife.

Maybe I just wanted to possess a photo of Tamara topless. It would be one small thing to have over her. I could think, "Yeah, you successfully encouraged my wife to take another man's cock, but I have a photo of your bare tits on my computer, bitch."

So I started clicking, thinking, C'mon give me one, show us your tits, Tamara.

But no luck.

It was just more photos of Tamara teasing the camera with cleavage.

The next set was of Ashley and Tamara at a St. Patrick's Day party. It was at a bar, downtown. I hadn't gone to that one, either; I had been at a Knicks game with a client.

I stared at one photo in particular: Ashley had face-painted the Irish flag on both her cheeks. I remembered her telling me that, but I'd never seen the photo. She looked super-cute and super-sweet.

In the next one, Ashley was posing with Tamara, wearing a green t-shirt with Charlie Brown's Snoopy on it, holding up a mug of beer and saying, "Cheers."

Tamara was dressed more extravagantly in an aqua-blue dress with a belted green coat. Her white thigh-highs had shamrocks on top. Her top hat and bowtie were iridescent greens and blues. It was an outfit that said, "Who's got what it takes to fuck me?"

I rolled my eyes. Tamara is Scandinavian or Northern European. She's certainly not remotely Irish.

When I came to our Florida vacation photos, I knew I was getting close. If any photos from that night existed, I'd see them soon.

I clicked slowly through the vacation photos. There were pictures of us on the beach and solo pictures I'd taken of Ashley in her new sky-blue bikini. I paused on one in particular. She was on the beach smiling, a full body shot I had taken of her on the last day before we flew home. Her pearly white teeth contrasted against her new dark tan, and her firm full breasts filled out her top, nipples protruding through the thin fabric.

This was the Ashley that Jim Murta would be fucking just two nights later. I bring her home all tanned from a relaxing, expensive vacation, and he takes her into a ratty bathroom and fucks her hard and bare, and uncorks his sperm inside her.

I slowed down over the last vacation photo, thinking, "Here goes."

And suddenly, I saw it. A photo from that night at the party. Ashley had indeed taken her camera.

She had posed with friends on the terrace, wearing that black miniskirt and pink top—her Jim Murta fuck-me outfit.

The next photo included Tamara. Then Ashley and Tamara together. I braced myself for what was to follow.

But that was it.

There was no pre-fuck photo of Ashley posing with Jim Murta. In the bathroom, her camera had gone unused. No post-fuck photos, either.

The next ones were of her with a college friend.

And the last photos were ones we'd taken by the Hell Gate Bridge.

"But this bridge would last a thousand years," the old man had said.

I went back to the three photos from the party, but I didn't see me or Jim Murta in the background.

Then I homed in on the photo of Ashley and Tamara. This was how they were dressed for him that night. I stared at Ashley's carefree smile. Could she have known, I wondered, that before long she'd have Jim Murta's big fat bare cock blasting his sperm inside her?

Staring at the photo was blinding.

"Jesus Christ," I muttered, "you were about to get fucked, Ashley. You didn't just kiss the guy. You were about to take office rumors to the stratosphere."

I pulled up the photo of Ashley in a bikini—two days before Jim fucked her. I lined it up on my laptop beside the one of Ashley and Tamara at the party, and enlarged to full screen.

I stared at her tits in her bikini. Jim Murta would soon have them for himself. The top would be off, he'd be groping and sucking, watching them bounce as he fucked her.

I had brought Ashley to the party. I had paid for the vacation, delivered her to Jim, with her sun-kissed skin, looking relaxed and even more fuckable than usual.

Jim saw my wife's bare tits and pussy—he saw the contrast of her tan against her ass and milky white tits.

Then I stared back at the photo of Ashley wearing the outfit he had fucked her in. And the post-fuck clothes she probably had to pick up off the bathroom floor and wear for the rest of the evening as Jim Murta's semen slowly seeped out of her.

I stared at Ashley posing beside Tamara at the party. For Jim, the choice must have been a no-brainer.

Tamara's super hot and all, I imagined him thinking, but I'm giving the newly married girl the royal Jim Murta treatment, while her husband waits oblivious outside as his wife's marital vows go overboard.

Suddenly, eyes darting from one photo to the other, I came hard.

This was becoming all too familiar.

I wondered if I had mentally waded farther from land. With all these photos so accessible, I was flirting with something new. I could enlarge and align them. They were powerful stimuli.

I then wondered if photos from that night had been posted on some friend-sharing photo website, the link emailed around Ashley's work. Were there any of me floating around? I remembered posing with Craig. One of the girls who lived there had taken it—had that been circulated? Were Ashley's co-workers or Jim Murta's sales buddies looking at it, saying "Look at that clueless dumbass doofus Dave, out on the roof, smiling, as his wife is inside being fucked"?

Suddenly I saw a 312 area code on my cell phone. It was Mark from last night. He was offering me a Yankees ticket to tonight's game.

"Hell, yeah," was my reaction.

He tried to describe where the seats were, but I said, "Just tell me where and when to meet you."

After I showered and put my Yankees hat and jersey on, I still had a few minutes before having to leave. So I quickly went back to my laptop.

I went to an adult photo-sharing website and downloaded a close-up photo of a big, fat, erect cock. I lined it up beside Ashley in her bikini, smiling.

"This is what you were about to take, Ashley," I said softly, "this is what you stared at. Those tits of yours are what he was looking at. You were about to bounce up and down on that fucking thing, without so much as a condom. You were gonna let that cock burst a full load of sperm up in you, and you didn't care that I had knocked. You wanted to get fucked by it as our own bridesmaid fucking cheered you on. You let Jim Murta's fat cock own your pussy. You let him humiliate me—giving you a big-cocked corporate fuck while clueless me was shooed the fuck away."

I stared at the cock and then back to Ashley and came hard looking at her tits.

****

I met up with Mark in the Bronx an hour before game time. He was with his younger brother and his brother's friend Franco—the guy who had scored the tickets.

They already had two pitchers of beer going. I hadn't drunk beer from pitchers like that since I was twenty-five—roughly their age.

I made sure to pull Franco aside and quickly pay for my ticket. The way he was chugging the beer, I didn't want him coming back, saying something like, "You know, I don't think your brother's friend paid me for the ticket."

I took it easy on the beer. The Yankees were playing the Blue Jays. They had lost to them the night before. I wasn't there to get drunk. I wanted to focus on the game.

Franco didn't seem like a Yankees fan or even a baseball fan. I learned he had gotten the tickets from his uncle.

At least *I* was going to appreciate the ticket, even if I did have to listen to Franco blabber on about his recent trip to Brazil and how hot the girls are there.

Um yeah, Franco, I thought to myself, my mother in law was freaking born in São Paulo, my wife's half-Brazilian.

I could tell Mark was bored by it all as well. But we were in a booth. There wasn't much opportunity for one-on-one conversation.

The subject of the Yankees or what the game meant never even came up.

Finally, when Franco suggested one more pitcher, I said, "No. It's twenty minutes till first pitch. I want to get to my seat."

"OK, we can settle up," Franco said, "but how about a pre-game shot of Jack all around?"

"I'm just into the game, man," I said, "I don't want to rush you guys. I'll meet you inside."

****

"Sorry Dave," Mark said, once we passed through security, "I've never been to the new stadium. I wanted to leave as much as you did."

"Don't sweat it," I replied, "it's just if I'm coming out to see baseball, I want to see baseball."

I knew the seats were good, but we were both like "hell yeah" when we were escorted to a box in the twelfth row by first base.

Mark's brother and Franco stumbled into our row at the start of the third. The Yankees were already up 3-0.

They had an "oh, there's a game going on" attitude as they showed up with their beers. I was grateful that Franco was sitting as far away as possible.

By the end of the seventh, the Yankees were up 7-1. That's when Mark nudged me, and said, "Franco has the hiccups."

"OK," I said, "do you know who's up batting for the Blue Jays?"

"I mean," Mark said, "he has the hiccups and can't get rid of them."

I looked over at Franco and saw him hiccup.

"OK, so?" I said.

"He wants to leave."

"So?"

"So, he's pushing my brother to take off as well."

"And?"

"Well, the game seems kind of done," Mark said. "I'm in an awkward spot with my brother. I thought you and I could just grab a beer somewhere back in Manhattan and talk."

"So when does Hiccup boy want to leave?"

"They want to go right now."

"Freaking sacrilege," I said.

"I know, I'm sorry."

"They want to leave right now?"

"Yeah."

"All right, fine, let's go."

Franco was still hiccupping as we left him and Mark's brother at the 125th street Harlem station.

****

"Between you and me," Mark said as we sipped gin martinis at an Upper West side bar, "I was kind of looking to get some perspective—relationship advice, I guess."

"How do you mean?" I asked.

Mark had gone to our wedding, but I didn't know him well.

"There's some turbulence going on right now between Camilla and me," he said, "and I see how solid you and Ashley are. I was looking for your thoughts."

That piqued my curiosity. I wondered what he was going to say. Had he learned Camilla was fucking another guy behind his back? Had he walked in on her having sex and witnessed another man's cock going, balls deep, inside his girl—precious little Camilla?

"Sure," I said, "what's the turbulence?"

"Well, you know people wonder about us."

"I didn't, Mark. What do they wonder about?"

"Well, we've been dating for four years, and people think, 'What's wrong with Mark? Why hasn't he slipped a ring on Camilla yet?'"

"Well it's not their business. I mean, who cares what people think, right?"

I could tell he found that response unhelpful.

"I'm sorry," I added, "are you just not ready for marriage? I mean is that the turbulence? She wants to and you don't?"

"No, I want to, I've wanted to propose for six months, but she's not sure."

Had Mark learned sweet but horny Camilla was getting another man's cock on the side? Was that it?

"Why is she not sure?" I asked.

"Because she wants to stay in Chicago and doesn't want kids—at least right now—and she knows I want to move back to Jersey and start a family."

"Oh," I said, "Why not compromise? Why not try for a baby but stay in Chicago?"

I was being too flip; the martini had gotten to me.

"David, my company's corporate headquarters are in Jersey. I've already turned down one job offer because of Camilla. They're going to offer me another one there soon. I know that. If I turn that down, I can kiss any future promotion goodbye. I'll be the dead-ender regional office guy."

"What does Camilla do again? An event planner, yes?"

"Yeah."

"And you make more money?"

"Yeah, a lot more."

"OK, so decision made. You have to take that job offer when it comes. Lay off the pressure on kids for now. She can do event planning in Jersey just as easily."

"But she has built all her contacts there."

"To hell with her contacts. She can make new ones."

"Yeah, but she loves Chicago and the idea of suburban Jersey living nauseates her."

"So you promise her you'll do weekends in the city. She went to school here, it's not like she doesn't have friends."

"All I'm saying, Mark," I continued, "is you need to explain to her that if you don't take this, all that you've worked for is shot to shreds. She will understand that. And if she still doesn't care, then leave her knowing that you and she weren't ultimately meant to be."

"Yeah," he said, "that's what I admire about you and Ashley."

I choked slightly on my martini.

"What do you mean?" I asked.

"I mean you both seem so on the same page."

"Yeah?" I said, "I wasn't feeling that last night at karaoke."

"Well at dinner, it seemed like you both have common purpose, and I envy that."

"Oh man, Mark, no one's relationship is perfect. I thought we'd be out in the suburbs now and starting to have kids ourselves. But Ashley wants to wait and enjoy our time now in the city. I had to compromise on that. It's your career; she's gotta compromise as well."

Mark pulled out his cell phone, saying, "Hold on."

The bartender asked if I wanted another. "Sure," I said, "and one for my friend."

"Just a Bud Light for me," Mark said.

"They just got back," he said to me. "They're taking a cab over to meet us."

"Huh?" I said as the bartender handed me my third martini.

"Camilla and Ashley."

"It's not even eleven."

"They caught an earlier bus."

****

Ten minutes later, they strolled on through in their shorts and tight tops.

"So how are you guys doing?" Ashley asked.

"Just bonding with my boy Mark," I said.

"I can see that. How was the game?"

"A blowout," Mark replied, "we left early."

"We left," I said, "because of Franco Hiccup-pottomus. Do you know why Franco Hiccup-pottumus made us all leave?"

"Franco's the guy who had the tickets," Mark explained.

"Because the Hiccup-pottomus had the hiccups," I said, "and when Franco Hiccup-pottoumus has the hiccups, what do you think happens? Everyone has to leave."

"Well, someone is mighty drunky drunky," Ashley said. "How many of those have you had? Never mind, it doesn't matter."

I kept quiet after that and just listened to them tell their stories of their day.

I remember saying, "I'm sorry" and "I love you" on the short cab ride home.

CHAPTER THIRTEEN

"I just had the strangest dream," Ashley told me the following morning.

"How so?"

"I was on the beach and a lot of our friends were there. And I started wondering if there was any truth to the whole flapping-your-arms thing."

"Flapping your arms?"

"Yeah," she said, laughing and standing up, "you know, like to fly."

"So I just started doing this," she said, stretching her arms out and flapping them.

Looking at Ashley like that—in her bra and thong—gave me a boner.

"And suddenly," she continued, "I was airborne, like a few feet at first, but then like twenty feet, thirty feet. I was like, 'This flapping your arms stuff really works. Why didn't I think to ever try this before?' And everyone was pointing up, saying, 'Look at Ashley—she's flying.'"

"Sounds fun," I said.

"Oh, it was a blast, I was bummed to wake up. But now it just doesn't seem to work so well, does it? What do you say, Dave, are my feet off the ground yet?"

"No," I replied, "but keep trying, you'll get the hang of it."

****

I'm sure to Ashley her dream meant nothing, and who knows what dreams really mean anyway.

But when she was at the gym, I Googled, "Flying dreams" and "meaning." Many dreamers describe the ability to fly in their dreams as an exhilarating, joyful, and liberating experience. If you are flying with ease and are enjoying the scene and landscape below, then it suggests you are on top of a situation. You have risen above something. It may also mean that you have gained new perspective. Flying dreams and the ability to control your flight represent your own personal sense of power.

What the fuck, I thought.

Had fucking Jim Murta in that bathroom been exhilarating? Did she feel liberated, knowing I accepted it? Did she feel more powerful in our relationship? Did she understand the incredible power she had given that prick that night? Had it been exhilarating to be the center of attention in her dream, flying above everyone in her bikini—or maybe even naked—her tits bouncing for everyone to see?

Where was I in her dream?

****

Ashley called me an hour later, on her way home from the gym, asking, "Aren't your parents away this weekend?"

"Yeah," I replied, "are you thinking a pool day?"

"Well, it's hot already and I just heard it's going up to 95."

"I'd be game," I said, "but my mom told me she'd given a few pool passes to a couple neighbors before she left. So if you don't mind a few potential freeloaders—"

"I don't mind. We can make some bloodies at your house."

"Sure, you got it, Ash."

No one was there when we arrived. Ashley skimmed the few insects and leaves from the pool while I did the vacuuming.

"Looks better than a pool at a posh hotel," she said when we finished.

"Yeah, and hotel pools don't have diving boards—or even deep ends these days."

"Or a lush floral, rock garden behind it, right?"

I gave her a long kiss before she went back in to make the

bloodies. But Ashley had forgotten to bring celery salt.

What seemed like a simple thing turned into me going to three different supermarkets.

Ashley was already outside on a recliner when I returned. She was wearing that sky-blue bikini from the photo in Florida—the one I had just masturbated to yesterday. The next-door neighbor kid from last summer would be all over the view I had of her from the kitchen.

****

The neighbors showed as Ashley was pouring us a second Bloody Mary. They were two older couples in their mid-fifties I'd met before.

"Hi David, I'm sorry, your mom said—" one of the wives began.

"Not at all, Mrs. Seever, I'm the one pool-hopping," I replied. "My wife and I heard the forecast, and we just had to flee the city."

I introduced the Seevers and Marshmans to Ashley. They had met her before and said so; the Seevers had attended our wedding. But I'm sure she looked a bit different now, in nothing but her blue bikini.

"We've got a pitcher of bloodies," Ashley said, "what do you say, Jane?"

"It sounds like we came to the right place," she said.

When the Marshmans said they'd have one, Ashley turned to Mr. Seevers, asking, "Bill, is it 'yeas' all around or what?"

"Don't need to twist my arm," he said, "sounds good."

Ashley went to work, running around in her bikini, asking all of them how it tasted … "more mix, more vodka, more spicy?"

"It's great Ashley," Jane said. "C'mon, have a seat."

Ashley began chatting up the wives, so I moved my chair in and talked up their husbands. Neither of them followed baseball, so we talked business, the economy, interest rates … the over-priced home at the end of the street on the market for over a year.

Perhaps Ashley's conversation had gotten boring as well, because she was encouraging the two ladies into the pool. Once that was accomplished, Ashley began pitching us men.

"The pool thermometer says eighty-one," she said, "and your wives are waiting for you."

"Well maybe now you really will have to twist my arm," Mr. Seevers replied.

"OK, Greg," Ashley said, walking up to him pretending to reach for his arm.

"I'm going, I'm going," he said and took off his shirt.

Mr. Marshman hesitated. He was a heavy guy and seemed self-conscious. But I could relate to his checkmate feeling. In a short time, he was in the pool.

Ashley brought out plastic cups and served everyone from the edge of the pool. She was on such display. I watched Mr. Marshman look over at his wife, deep in conversation, before copping another view of Ashley as she set up the iPod deck. She joined us in the pool as Bono sang, "It's a beautiful day."

****

About an hour and another bloody later, another neighbor arrived.

Mrs. Seever had told me Jay might show, but also how "with his schedule, you never know." I had hoped he'd be a no-show. The half-dozen times I'd met Jay in as many years, I'd never cared for him. My parents liked him, or my mom anyway. He built a sunroom on the house a few years ago.

Jay was a blue-collar type living in a white-collar town. Despite owning his own construction business, he had the requisite chip on his shoulder—or at least that's how it seemed to me—when he walked through the gate with his "I take no bullshit" expression.

But Jay smiled broadly when the neighbors greeted him, saying, "I didn't know I was coming over to a party."

"You just made the party official, Jay," Mrs. Marshman said.

Ashley got out of the pool and introduced herself.

"Hi, Ashley," I watched him say, "we met at a cook-out last summer. July-Fourth weekend, if I'm not mistaken."

"Good memory," Ashley replied, "I thought you looked familiar."

"Yeah, you had recently gotten married," he added, "to Dave—how you doing Dave?"

"I'm good. How're you, Jay?" I said from the pool.

"What are you drinking?" Ashley asked as the water dripped off her. "We've got Bloody Marys or there's beer or soda or—"

"A beer sounds good," Jay said, "what kind do you have?"

"Hmm, that's a really good question," Ashley said, before turning to me, like I was going to rattle off the beer list.

When I didn't immediately answer, she replied "Just come inside with me, and decide what you like."

And I just watched as this older construction guy followed my bikini-clad wife into my parents' kitchen.

Can you stop being a hostess for one friggin' second, Ashley? I thought. Can you not see how a guy like that might misinterpret your Ashley Martens' welcome wagon?

I thought of the whole golly-gee way she got out of the pool and greeted him.

"Hi, I'm Ashley, and these are my big tits. You can see my nipples in my bikini. Can I get you something? Some alcohol to drink? And going inside, I can give you a close-up view of my petite, toned ass."

Being on a beach with Ashley never bothered me. Sure, I noticed guys checking her out. I had a "can't blame them" attitude—but they'd get nothing more than a look. But then I thought of Ashley's friends. Sure, Tamara pushed the envelope, but many of them wore one-pieces or bottoms with miniskirts. How is a bikini much different than bra and panties? It's just two small pieces of cloth away from being naked. Didn't Ashley know she was giving this construction guy a hard-on or an image he might jerk off to later?

****

When they came back out, Ashley was chatting him up about a house he'd built last year, and he was making her laugh by describing the owner's idiosyncrasies. "The guy was a real clown," Jay said, "a fool with money." Then he took off his t-shirt and stood by the side of the pool drinking his Budweiser.

"Wow," Ashley said, "You are really ripped."

"Thanks, not bad for a guy about to turn fifty."

"Fifty?" Ashley said. "Not bad at all."

"Well I'll be fifty August twenty-second. You guys should come to the party they're throwing for me."

"We'd love to," Ashley said, turning to me, like, "right?"

I wasn't sure if she was serious or yes-manning him.

"Yeah, sure," I said.

Ashley encouraged Jay to join her in getting into the pool and the three of us sipped our drinks in the shallow end.

"I like your tat," Ashley told him, looking to me for comment.

It was a tattoo of an angry bald eagle with the inscription, 'Live to ride, ride to live.' "

"Yeah, it's nice," I said, thinking what-the-fuck-ever.

"Harley Davidson," Jay said, "You ride, Dave?"

"Motorcycles? No, I never have," I replied.

"Never?" he said. "You should try it sometime. There's nothing like it. Have you, Ashley?"

"Oh sure," Ashley said, "I love ripping it up with a good pasta rocket."

"Oh yeah, you like the Italian bikes, do you? I have a black Ducati in my garage."

"I'm just kidding," Ashley replied. "It was just a fun thing to say. I've been a passenger a few times but I was too scared to try it myself."

"So you've ridden, but just as a passenger?"

"Yeah."

"Cool. I'm sure you made a cute little fender bunny."

Jay shot me a look—to note my reaction—then turned back to Ashley. I was still processing his comment.

"Thanks," Ashley said, smiling, "but I was glad when it was time to take the helmet off."

****

I was a bit self-conscious when we got out of the pool.

Ashley was sitting in her bikini, her big tits on parade, and Jay was shirtless in a nearby chair, looking tan and muscled.

The rest of the men put their shirts back on quickly, and their wives wore towels.

I'm typically not shy about going shirtless—I'm a thin guy—but at that moment, I felt pale and under-muscled. So I lay on the recliner, closed my eyes, and let the sun dry me off.

What the fuck, I thought, who is this character?

He's inviting my wife to his fiftieth birthday party and telling her she'd make a "cute little fender bunny"? And she's admiring how ripped he is? What's next? Is she going to ask him to rub suntan lotion on her back?

If he knew about what Ashley had done with Jim Murta—how easily he'd taken Ashley—Jay would consider my wife a fuck-prospect. Maybe he already did.

Maybe he was getting a vibe. Perhaps he could sense that Ashley was capable of bold, risky cheating; after all, she'd done it once before.

Could she be attracted to this guy? This one-track Mr. blue-collar construction worker asshole? He was old enough to be her father. She might have complimented him just to be social and friendly. She might find the idea of a fifty-year-old guy scamming on her revolting. Or then again, she might be intrigued by his looks, confidence, and experience. I couldn't get a read.

I put my sunglasses on and lay there thinking.

****

I pictured Ashley saying she was going inside to use the bathroom. A few minutes later Jay would casually make his way inside himself.

I pictured him waiting for Ashley by the bathroom door. She would know he wasn't simply waiting to take a piss. His eyes would say exactly why he was there.

Ashley would give him a look, like, "Are you suggesting what I think you are?"

And that's when Jay would strike, leading her back into the bathroom, passionately kissing my wife against the wall.

I suddenly popped a boner.

I told everyone I had to make a work phone call, and that I had to go inside for a few minutes.

I was in the upstairs bathroom, watching through the trees as Ashley and Jay talked by the pool below. If he thought there was an opening, Jay would no doubt take it. He wouldn't care about this being his neighbors' house or that he was hitting on his neighbors' son's wife.

He probably thinks I'm some elitist, privileged wimp who doesn't deserve my wife.

I yanked off my swim trunks and sat on the sink. I began to imagine Jay and Ashley upstairs in the bathroom I was in now. I would be outside, vaguely wondering what was taking Ashley so long as I tried to entertain the guests by the pool below.

They would be making out against the bathroom wall.

"Do you feel what's rubbing against you, Ashley?

"Yeah."

"What's rubbing up against you, Ashley?"

"Your cock is, Jay."

"That's right Ashley. It's my cock. How does my cock feel up against you?"

"It feels big and hard."

"What feels big and hard, Ashley?"

"Your cock, Jay."

"You've been thinking about my cock, haven't you, Ashley, since the moment I walked through the backyard gate today?"

"I have?" Ashley might say, ambivalently.

"Yes, you have, Ashley, we both know it. I've seen you staring at my crotch. I've seen you sneaking peeks when your husband wasn't looking. You've been staring at my cock, Ashley, hoping it might poke out."

"I have?"

"Yes, even your husband noticed your wandering eyes, but you didn't care. Instead you flirted with me in front of him, jiggling your nice, big tits, trying to get my cock hard, like the cock tease that you are. Well you've teased my cock, Ashley, and now you've got it big and hard."

"I know. I can feel it."

"And now you're curious about my cock. Admit to me you're curious, Ashley."

"I'm curious, Jay," she'd say as he licked her neck.

"What are you curious about, Ashley?"

"But it's my in-laws' bathroom. My husband's right outside."

"We both know that's not going to stop you, right, Ashley?"

"I don't know, Jay."

"Tell me what you're curious about, Ashley."

"I guess I'm wondering how big your cock is."

"You want to know just how much bigger I am than your husband right?"

"Well, yeah."

"And what it would feel like inside that tight, young pussy of yours. I bet you haven't been properly fucked in a long time, isn't that right, Ashley?"

"Kind of."

"I can tell—your husband's cock doesn't satisfy you, right?"

"Um, I guess not so much."

"Not so much what?"

"My husband doesn't satisfy me, Jay."

"I know, how could a wimp like him satisfy you? Your pussy's craving a real man's cock, the one that's rubbing up against you, isn't it, Ashley?"

"I guess, kind of."

"No guess kind of's, Ashley. I want you to say 'Yes, I've been craving a real man's cock.' "

"Yes Jay, I've been craving a real man's cock."

"I'm old enough to be your father. I want you to say 'Yes, daddy, I'm craving daddy's cock.' "

"This is so crazy, Jay—"

"Ashley, I'm feeling how wet that bikini bottom of yours is. You're all horny for this. Now say what you want to see, baby."

"Please show me your cock, daddy."

"Oh yeah, that's a good girl, now daddy wants you on your knees."

"I can't believe I'm doing this. OK, is this good? I'm on knees for you, daddy."

"You have a body that was made to be on its knees. I love looking down at your cleavage and you looking so innocently back up at me. You ready to see a nice big cock, girl?"

"Yes."

"Yes, what?"

"I'm ready to see your big cock, daddy."

"Get your face up there real close as you pull my swimsuit down."

"OK, I'm like an inch away now."

"Yank them down, Ashley."

"Oh my God, Jay."

"Yeah, Ashley, my cock just slapped your face."

"It's so freaking big."

"You like big cocks, Ashley?"

"Yes."

"Yes, what?"

"I like big cocks, Jay, I mean daddy."

"Well you've got a big fat hard one, right in front of you as you kneel for me in your in-laws' upstairs bathroom. Stare at it. You want to be fucked by it, don't you?"

"I can't say the thought hasn't crossed my mind."

"Say it, Ashley."

"What?"

"Look at my cock and say what you want from it."

"This is so crazy, but I guess, Jay, I want to be fucked by it."

"You will, baby, but I think you know what you're gonna do first."

"Suck it?"

"You ever suck a cock this big, Ashley?"

"No."

"Well, let's start off easy, stick out your tongue and give it a friendly kiss. See? It likes you," I imagined him saying.

"I like it as well."

"Then show me how much you like it. Open that pretty mouth of yours wide. Oh yeah, that's it, lick my shaft. Now suck my balls, mmm yeah. Now start really taking it into your mouth."

I imagined Jay looking out the window I had just looked out of, watching me.

"Now, no hands, Ashley, I want them wrapped around my ass. Oh yeah, that's it, you can take more. Slobber on it, yes, feast on it, oh fuck yeah, you've got most of my cock in your mouth now girl. I bet if your husband knew I was up here getting a blowjob from his wife right now, he'd be too meek and timid to come up and stop it, even knowing I was about to fuck you. He'd do nothing. You know that's about to happen, don't you?"

"Mmm hmm," she'd mumble as Jay's cock pumped her mouth.

"Take my cock out of your mouth and tell me, Ashley. What do you want to happen now?"

"I want you to fuck me, Jay."

"Let me help you up. That's it, now off with that bikini bottom, before I rip it off."

"Yes, Jay," she'd say as she untied the straps and they fell to the floor.

"Beautifully trimmed pussy, baby. Now the top. Oh yeah, as big, firm and lush as I imagined. Beautiful nipples. Now turn around and open the window, Ashley."

"Yes Jay."

"Yeah lift that window all the way up, that's good, now stick your head out—that's it—do you see your husband?"

"Yeah."

"What's he doing?"

"Talking to the Seevers."

Suddenly Ashley would feel Jay's hand smacking her ass, going back and forth against each cheek.

"Oh God," she would moan.

"Now hold onto these, Ashley, I want you holding them out the window. Your bikini bottom in your left hand and your top in your right—that's it—now tell me you want to feel daddy's cock—"

"I want to feel daddy's cock, Jay—"

"Say, 'Fuck me, daddy' as you look out at your husband."

"Fuck me, daddy."

"It's going inside, Ashley. You're about to take a real man's cock."

"Oh my God, Jay."

"Oh yeah Ashley, it's tight, but I'm easing into it, trust daddy, you're gonna take this whole fucking thing."

"Oh my God."

"Another inch, in it goes."

"Oh my fucking God."

"C'mon keep going girl, you can take it."

"Holy fuck, Jay."

"Oh fuck, yeah, it's fucking in you now Ashley, you're taking daddy's big cock, I am full on fucking you now. That's it, pump back on it, oh yeah, nice Ashley, grind back on it."

"Oh my God, it's so freaking big, Jay."

"Trust me Ashley, this is the kind of real man's cock that pussy of yours needs. You're gonna crave it after this. It feels good, doesn't it, Ashley?"

"It feels fucking great, Jay, I think I'm about to cum, oh my God, I am going to cum."

"Keep looking at your husband. I want you looking at him as you cum."

"Oh my God, oh fuck, Jay I'm cumming."

"That's it, you just came on my fucking cock. How did it feel, baby?"

"Wow, Jay, it felt freaking amazing!"

"Well, we're not done yet. You're gonna cum again, Ashley. Now you're really going to get fucked."

"Oh my God."

"Arch your legs, tilt that ass up, oh yeah, how do you like it now, Ashley?"

"Oh my fucking God Jay."

"Just keep staring at your husband. Imagine if he looked up and saw you now, his newlywed wife getting fucked bare by his parent's blue collar neighbor in the house he grew up in—"

"Oh my God."

"Do you love your husband, Ashley?"

"Yes."

"Look at him and tell me you love him."

"I love my … husband … I love … David."

"I want to hear that again as I fuck you hard, Ashley."

"I love my—oh God, Jay—my husband."

"How about your in-laws? Do you love them, the Martens—"

"Yeah … I love them … oh God."

"Say 'I love my husband and my in-laws' as you take my fat fucking cock."

"I love my husband and … my in-laws."

"Again."

"Oh fuck, Jay, your cock … I'm going to cum again."

"Say it, Ashley."

"I love my … husband … and my … in-laws."

"Keep staring at Dave and hold onto your bikini, girl. Don't let it slip from your hands. It would be tough to explain to hubby why your bikini's sitting in the grass below."

"I'm … holding it … oh God … firmly."

"You're getting fucked in your in-laws' home, in their upstairs bathroom, looking at their friends and son—and your own fucking husband. Now say it again … tell me you love them."

"I … oh God … I love … I love … oh God."

"Say it, Ashley."

"I'm going to … cum again, Jay."

"Let me hear you say it."

"I love … my in-laws … and I … I love my husband."

"You're a slutty daughter-in-law, fucking another man in their house."

"I'm a slutty … daughter-in-law … Oh God, I'm gonna cum."

"They invited their blue collar neighbor over to use their pool, and an hour later, I'm using their son's wife. I'm going to blow right up in your Ivy League pussy ... and then we're going to walk back out together with my cum filling up in your bikini."

"I'm cumming, Jay, oh my fucking God, oh God."

"Here comes my sperm baby, I want you looking right at your husband as I blast inside you ... hold on to that bikini ... oh fuck, yeah, oh yeah, right up in you, you Ivy League slut!"

Suddenly I came incredibly hard.

****

I was in a daze.

"What the fuck," I whispered to myself.

Then I felt wobbly and weak in the knees. I had tears in my eyes and a pit in my stomach.

I could rationalize that masturbating was the only way to lose the hard-on, but there was no way to rationalize thinking about blue-collar Jay pulling his own Jim Murta on my ass.

I looked back out the window. He was still talking up Ashley.

I had just masturbated thinking of this blue-collar a-hole brazenly taking my wife in my parent's house—fucking her in the bathroom I'd just jerked off in—while he flirted with my wife, in her bikini, outside, unattended.

He was making moves on her in my parents' backyard as I sat bare-assed on the sink with my boner in my hand.

Was Ashley interested in him? Had I just give him an opportunity to make his move? Would Jay read something in my face when I returned, have some sixth sense of what I had just been thinking? Would my attempts at expressions of confidence betray me?

Would he think I was a sucker for leaving him alone with my wife—and read some new weakness in me?

After I walked back down I saw a bottle of vodka on the kitchen counter and took a slug from it. And I put my sunglasses on. "Just be cool," I said to myself, "I don't have the word 'pussy' scrawled on my forehead."

****

Ashley and Jay were still sitting in chairs by the pool, talking, as the others sat around the table. I pulled up my chair, like I suspected nothing untoward.

"But I'm thirty years old," Ashley said.

"You look like you're still in college," he said. "I'm telling you, you should consider it."

"Consider what?" I asked.

"Jay was just saying," Ashley explained, "that I could get a gig at this motorcycle show at the Javitz center."

"Huh?" I replied.

"Displaying motorcycles at a booth," she replied, "like posing on them, how girls make a lot of *dinero* for just showing new bikes off for a weekend."

"Don't you think she'd be a natural?" Jay asked me.

"Modeling bikes at a biker show?" I asked, incredulous.

"Yeah," Jay said, "there's an annual convention this October. I think Ashley would be perfect. She's certainly got the body for it."

"Well, I'm really flattered," Ashley replied. "Let me think about that one."

"Sure," Jay said. "Well, you have my card now, my cell's on the back. And you guys are around in three weeks, right?"

"What?" I said.

"That's when Jay's having his big fiftieth shindig," Ashley said.

"Oh," I replied

"We just need to make sure we're in town," Ashley replied.

"Yeah, we still have to figure it out," I said, "anyway, that was my boss who called. I need to get him some reports tonight, so we're gonna have to clean up and train on back to the city."

"You sure?" Jay asked. "It's only four-thirty, the party's just started."

"I wish we could stay, but I need to get back to my boss ASAP."

When the Marshmans began packing up, I asked them in private for a ride to the station. Ashley and I changed back into our clothes and threw our swimsuits and towels into the wash.

Just as we all were leaving, Jay offered to take us instead, but I had already put our bags in the Marshmans' car.

"We're good," I said, and Mrs. Marshman added that it was on their way home.

"Well, it was great meeting you again," Ashley said as she gave Jay a hug goodbye.

"Nice seeing you," I said, shaking his hand.

"You too, Dave," he said patting me on my back, "don't miss the party, you both will enjoy it."

"Yeah," I said, "if we're in town, sure, sounds cool."

****

On the train home, Ashley said, "Well, that was fun. We got a little party vibe going there, right?"

"Yeah," I said, "they seemed into it."

"And Jay seems like a definite character for that town."

"Yeah," I replied, "he is."

"It was interesting to hear about his take on architects. I didn't realize the contention between the architect and the guy who actually builds it. Though it sounds like he's got a good partner now."

"Yeah," I said before casually asking, "Did I hear he gave you his number?"

"Yeah, when you were inside, he gave me his business card."

"He wants you to call him," I asked, "for what? For his fiftieth birthday party?"

"I don't know, or to tell him I've reconsidered trying out for a motorcycle modeling gig. Why, do you not want to go the party?"

"Not really. My parents have told me some things about that guy."

"Like what?"

"That he's kind of unstable. You know he's divorced?"

"Yeah, he mentioned that. Not long ago. Last summer?"

"Yeah, I heard he was abusive. My mom didn't go into details, but there was like a stalking or menacing thing going on."

"Really?"

"That's what I heard. It was covered up, I think, but pretty ugly. Sounded like bad news."

"Hmm," Ashley replied, "good to know."

"Well," I said, "and trekking out to the suburbs for a fiftieth birthday, I don't know how much of a good time that would be anyway."

"I hear you," she replied.

Then she put her head on my shoulder and within a few minutes fell asleep. The sun and the drinks had tired me out as well. But I cradled her chin so it wouldn't slip, and kept my shoulder steady so as not to wake her.

What I had said about Jay was a total lie. I didn't know why he got divorced or if the guy was stable or not. But I knew I didn't like the guy and didn't like that he had given Ashley his card.

Ashley seemed to believe me, but I wondered why she replied, "Good to know."

Why was it "good to know?" Had it given her pause, like I intended it? Why hadn't she thrown his card in the garbage before we even got on the train?

If Jay had overheard the libel I was saying about him, he'd want to kick my ass for sure. But what business did he have giving my wife his number while I was away? He was a guest at my parents' home, hitting on my wife right the fuck in front of me.

CHAPTER FOURTEEN

Ashley had another presentation to prepare for when she came home Monday night. This one was for a bigger client and carried more weight, and she was giving herself two nights to prepare.

I went into our office and back into the chat rooms. This time the "My Wife" room was full, so I scrolled up to "Cuckold Husbands" to simply check it out.

I didn't write anything in the public scroll, but soon had private messages saying, "Hello David—NYC here too" and "Are you a cuck?"

Then I received a message from a guy, asking, "Fellow cuckold?"

"No," I replied, "I was just seeing what the room is about. I talked to a guy a few nights ago who suggested I check out the room, just a curiosity thing."

"What did you talk to him about?" he asked. "Why did he suggest you check out this room?"

"Well, my wife recently cheated," I replied, "and it's done a number on my head. I don't know why he recommended it."

"So, your wife had sex with another man?"

"Yes," I replied, "a one-time thing at a party."

"Well, technically, you are a cuckold, because you're a husband whose wife was unfaithful. But most cuckolds here are into the lifestyle and have a clear and established cuckold relationship. So, you don't have an open cuckold relationship with your wife?"

"Meaning what, exactly?"

"That you've accepted your wife having sex with other guys, while you stay home or listen or watch."

"No, nothing like that whatsoever," I replied, "like I said, my wife cheated recently. One time. It was a bit of a head-fuck. I was simply curious about what this room was about."

"What are you curious about?"

"I don't know," I replied, "the guy said how his fiancée cheating had led him to being a cuckold, and I guess I was wondering what leads someone down this path."

"Oh," he answered, "the nature/nurture question. Like how big is the universe or how was it created. That's a bit above my pay grade. As for me I felt I was born with a submissive side, but then again, it was sculpted by experiences."

"How so?" I replied.

"It's a bit to go into."

"I'd like to hear, if you have time. I'm David, 34, NYC."

"OK, David from NYC, I'll give you my perspective if you like. I'm Mitch, 37, from Ohio."

"Nice to meet you Mitch," I typed, "I'd certainly appreciate hearing what happened."

"Well as I said," he wrote, "I think I was born this way, but experience does shape a person, doesn't it?"

"Sure, of course," I replied.

"Well, did you ever hear your parents having sex?"

"Uh no, not really man."

"Never at all?"

"I guess a couple times. But any memory of that would be vague. Before I fully knew what sex was. Just unusual noises from their bedroom, and I knew to shut my door and turn the TV on, or something."

"So you didn't listen?"

"Not at all," I replied.

"Well, my parents divorced when I was in kindergarten. Or my dad left my mom, to be more precise. Anyway, in what might be called my formative years, she would bring men home."

"OK," I typed, "and?"

"Well, I was curious. I would listen."

"And your reaction?"

"I don't remember my reaction. I just remember listening outside the door. When she brought a man home, her bedroom was off limits. It wasn't every night. She wasn't a whore. But when she did, I knew the drill, I'd go to my bedroom and then sneak out and listen outside her door."

"That must've had some impact, especially as a kid."

"I'm sure it did. But exactly what it did, like I said, it's above my pay grade."

"I hear you," I replied, "but that's what you think led you to this?"

"You tell me," he wrote, "When you were in high school, did you have a prom? Did you ever take a girl to the prom?"

"Yeah," I replied, "the girl I was dating my senior year."

"Did you get laid that night? Or were you already having regular sex with her?"

"No," I said, "we made out, some foreplay, but I didn't have sex until I got to college."

"Yeah, I didn't have sex till I went to college, either, but I had been going with this girl, and there was a lot of anticipation leading up to the prom. That was going to be the night I was going to have sex. We hadn't been together too long, but she'd had sex before, and I had felt her up, and what's the expression? I had gotten to 'third base' with her."

"OK," I replied, "what's third base again? You had fingered her? Or she had blown you?"

"Fingered her, not a blowjob. I had never cum with her. And I didn't know what I was doing when I fingered her. She didn't orgasm. I was just happy to get there."

"Sure," I typed.

"Well, we went to this house party afterwards. They had a keg. The parents were out of town."

"Sure, I've been to those kind of parties."

"Well, I hadn't," he wrote, "that is, I never drank much. Nor did she. We didn't get crazy drunk or anything, but a few beers back then had an effect."

"Sure," I said.

"Well, this football jock showed an interest in my date. He'd just broken up with his girlfriend. He was this studly guy and they were doing beer bongs—you know what that is?"

"I think so," I replied, "we called them funnels. Where you chug a beer through a tube?"

"Yes, that's it. Well, he wanted me to do one. I had the bad luck of being in the kitchen watching these guys do them. Now the spotlight was on me."

"Sure, I know what that's like."

"Ever do a beer bong?"

"In college, sure, freshman year, a few times."

"Did you fuck it up or did it go smoothly?"

"It's a beer bong," I replied, "just open your mouth and drain the thing, right?"

"Well I didn't," he said, "I spat it out and the whole thing spilled all over the floor. And the guy whose house it was got pissed and yelled at me. The other jocks laughed as I was handed a cloth to clean up the floor. I look back at it now, thinking give me a break. How was I to know? But at the time, it was as if I had made a total fool of myself."

"Sure," I said, "I can see that."

"Well, about ten minutes later, I was still the 'who invited this guy' guy, and this jock pointed to my girl to do it, the beer bong, I mean. Well, I don't think she ever had done one either, because she was very reluctant. But peer pressure got to her, and she did it easily, no problem. The jocks high-fived her."

"OK," I typed.

"I'll never forget my date in her prom dress, sucking from this tube like it was nothing."

"OK, and?"

"And pretty soon this jock was laying the rap on my girl. He was a popular stud type. He could have lots of girls and did. But that night, prom night, he was interested in mine. The girl I had rented a tuxedo for. The girl I had gotten a limo for. Or my step-dad had. My step-dad—that made it worse, actually."

"What made it worse? Did you not like your step-dad?"

"He was OK, I guess. I mean we didn't relate, but he probably meant well. He was a gym teacher and former army officer. The kind of dad who wakes you up on weekends by blaring big band music and yelling stuff into your bedroom, like 'Hit the deck!' "

"You an only child?" I asked.

"No, I have two sisters, but several years older. My mom married him when I started high school, so they were already out of the house. Anyway, that's not really my point."

"Sure, I understand, what's the more primary point?".

"Well, this jock was putting the moves on my date, and I felt awkward and lame. And he would look over at me, knowing what he was doing. I just watched as he took my date upstairs. It was like I wasn't even there. He took her up to one of the bedrooms."

"What did you do? Go upstairs?"

"No, what was I to do? I wasn't cool in high school. I was always the 'what's he doing here' guy. And it was obvious when he came back downstairs with my date, that he had fucked her. And then I called for the limo and dropped her back home. After that we broke up."

"You mentioned your step-dad and how that made it worse," I said. "What made it worse?"

"Well," he replied, "he loaned me three hundred dollars for that prom. So I spent the summer mowing the lawn to pay off that debt. My step-dad was big on stuff like that—a man pays his debts. So I spent the whole summer mowing the lawn to work off what? To work off going to a prom where someone else fucked my date."

"I got you," I said, "so that was the pivotal moment that led you to this?"

"It was one of them, probably, right?"

"There was another?" I asked.

"Yeah," he replied, "the next time was probably the moment that clinched things. Where your life becomes a foregone conclusion."

"OK," I typed, "I'd certainly be interested in hearing."

"OK," he wrote, "so when I was twenty, I was dating a girl in town. I went to community college and we started dating. She lived one town over."

"OK," I said.

"Well, it was summer. We went to this party, and I got pretty shit-faced. It wasn't like I was an amateur to drinking by then, but I was pretty drunk."

"Sure," I said.

"Well, I wound up crashing for a couple hours."

"OK," I typed.

"I woke up on a couch and I heard the sounds of sex. So I got up and stumbled over. And by stumbled, I mean really stumbled. It was like a dream. But there were these two guys who were in the marines. These guys hung out at the restaurant I waitered at during summers, so I knew them."

"OK," I typed.

"Well, suddenly I realized they were tag-teaming this drunk girl on another couch. She was getting fucked from behind with the other guy's cock in her mouth. That's when reality dawned on me. The girl was Erin. They were tag-teaming my girlfriend."

"Jesus," I said, "what did you do?"

"I was in a daze. Besides, what could I really do at that point? I was still drunk and these were hardcore marines."

"Sure," I said, "so did you watch?"

"Yeah, but like I said, I was in a real fog. I sat on a chair nearby and watched them use my girlfriend."

"What was your reaction?"

"I didn't have much of one. I just watched, stunned, and they looked over at me and said things like, 'You see what we're doing to your girlfriend?' and I just nodded, watching. Like I was totally stoned or something."

"Damn," I typed, "that's crazy."

"Well, you want to hear crazy," he wrote. "So I'm sitting there, watching them fuck her, right?"

"Yeah," I said.

"So the marine doing her from behind pulls out and walks over to me, and with his big hard cock pointed at me, he shoots his cum right on my face."

"Jesus," I said, "that is freaking super crazy. What did you do?"

"What was I to do? I just sat there and took it. A minute later, the other marine, the one my girlfriend was sucking off, pulls out, walks over and blasts his load on me as well, on my already semen-covered face."

"What the fuck?" I typed, "They were gay?"

"Not at all," he replied. "They were just asserting their dominance."

"What did you do?"

"I just took it. A few minutes later, they got dressed and left. My girlfriend's on the couch naked and I've got their cum dripping down my face."

"Oh my God," I typed. "Did you ever see them again or have to face them?"

"Yeah, they came by the restaurant afterwards. I talked to them."

"Did they say anything about it?"

"Not that I know of. Not to the people I waitered with, anyway. It was like this inside joke kind of thing. My girlfriend broke up with me shortly afterwards and they'd make cracks, like 'You dating anyone? You are? Bring her by, we want to meet her.' "

"And?"

"And nothing. It was a joke. I just laughed."

"Were you pissed?"

"Not really. These guys were hardcore alpha males and I had respect for them. I knew I wasn't or never could be like them. It was like they had the right to do that to me."

"Did they ever do that again, I mean, cum on your face?"

"No, like I said, they weren't gay and neither am I. It was about showing me my place. And they weren't assholes about it after. It was like this memory we all had."

"Wow."

"Yeah. I certainly will never forget that night," he wrote. "Ever suck another man off?"

"No" I replied, "I'm not gay curious in the slightest."

"It's not about being gay. It's about being submissive to a dominant man. My wife's lover makes me blow him in front of my wife."

I was starting to get creeped out and told him I had to go.

So fucked up.

What those two marines had done to him was a royal fuck you. Talk about rubbing it in. Not only had they sent him a message tag-teaming his girlfriend in front of him, they wanted to rub it in his face, literally.

And they reduced him in front of his girlfriend. She must have been equally shocked when they pulled out and coated her boyfriend's face.

Damn, how could the guy even look his girlfriend in the eyes after that? No surprise that she broke up with him. How could she have any respect for him? How could he look back at her with the cum of two marines who had just DP'd her, dripping down his face?

No wonder he's fucked up now.

Still, as he said, part of him was born that way. Despite what he said, there had to be some gay tendencies going on, especially since he's sucking cock in front of his wife.

Jesus, I thought. There are men out there who are way more fucked up than me.

CHAPTER FIFTEEN

Ashley was still working on her presentation the following night. I left her alone and went back into the chat rooms. Only this time, I waited until the "My Wife" room was free. I typed into the public scroll, "Anyone learn their wife cheated and how did you react?"

I got a few of the same "Have a pic of your wife?" replies before I got a message from a guy who introduced himself as Phil from New York.

"I take it something happened with the wife?" he asked.

"Yeah," I replied, "has it happened to you?"

"I'm not married, but my girlfriend fucked another guy," he said, "and it was the first time I'd ever been cheated on."

"How did you react?" I asked.

"I kept trying to think of questions to ask and wanted to know every detail, to the point that she was getting very annoyed. Well, I've got a very liberal view on sex."

"So you were OK with it?"

"We had just started dating and I was taken aback. But she told me right away and I appreciated that. And to be honest, it turns me on thinking of her fucking another guy. So what's your situation?"

"Well" I typed back, "my wife f'd a guy in a bathroom several weeks ago, with me outside clueless. She told me about it, but portrayed it as a rumor. She only told me because she thought I'd already heard."

"Tell me more," he replied, and I told him the details of what I had learned about that night—how I had knocked on the door, how Tamara sent me upstairs, and what Craig had told me.

"Who was the guy? A friend of hers or yours?"

"A guy she works with."

"Her boss?" he asked.

"No, a junior salesman from a different department, but word got around at her work and I felt like the last to know."

"Hmm, that sucks," he wrote, "but let me ask you an honest question. What bugs you more? The fact that she cheated or that you were the last to know? I know it's tough to answer because they both probably bothered you, but it's an important distinction."

"It's all wrapped together. It's just a colossal head fuck."

"OK, let's try to figure out the root issues, though," he said, and then asked basic bio questions—how long married, how long dated, our ages, where in NYC, was it the first marriage for both.

"OK," he wrote, "so back to my question—although I know it's all wrapped up together—the most important thing to figure out is if you feel mad at the thought of her fucking someone else, or mad that you were excluded and humiliated. Because if you think she's worth staying with, it's important to try and make that distinction. Clearly there's something she needs or wants for her to cheat—especially like that—the question is whether you truly want to figure out what that is and work on it with her."

"I don't know if mad is the word," I said. "I felt gutted when I heard what happened. And I cried, which I've haven't done in years. I know I should have confronted her or him, but I was scared of losing her. And I know my friends or brother would tell me to kick her to the curb if they knew."

"Yes, it's a lonely feeling, I understand," he said, "and the best thing to do is NOT get your family involved because then there is even less chance for recovery. And for the record, NEVER worry about crying about something like this—it's human to have that emotion and you should feel no embarrassment."

I told him more details—about my talk with her, how she'd replied, "Just bigger, OK?"

"You need to have open dialogue with her," he wrote. "That's the only way to real recovery—and you may not like the answers that come out in that discussion, so be prepared. So why do you think she cheated? Be honest, I know it's a tough question."

"I don't know. I thought our sex life was good but obviously it left something to be desired. Maybe she was just curious or maybe her friend influenced her."

"Is your wife a pretty wild gal in general?"

"No, this came out of left field."

"Has she ever talked about fucking other guys?"

"No, I know about a few past boyfriends, but we never got into sex talks about them."

"So you beat off thinking about your wife at the party?"

"Yeah, which is embarrassing to admit and way fucked up. I feel like a pussy about it."

"No need to feel like a pussy," he replied, "I understand your self-deprecation, but you have to take it easy on yourself and not hold the blame. Too bad you're not in Brooklyn, because I was going to suggest we get a beer."

"Thanks, but I couldn't get away anyway tonight."

"I cheated on my ex-wife," he wrote, "so I understand that side of it, and have been cheated on, so it gives me both perspectives. I think you need to talk openly with her about what she needs sexually. You might have to accept that she might be sluttier than you realized—I don't mean that harshly, just something to prepare for. Taking into consideration the other stuff you told me, she might have—well, probably has—cheated before."

"I know I should talk with her more about it," I replied.

"You've been fucking her since all this started?"

"Yeah," I said.

"As often as you did before?"

"No, less often."

"Do you fuck her dirty or nicely?"

"I guess the answer is nicely because that's how I thought she likes it."

"Ever call her a slut while fucking her?"

"No, I'm not sure how that would go over."

"You should just fuck her hard tonight, USE her," he wrote. "It's taken me a long time to realize that I am most attracted to slutty women. I think you might have one here, my friend. Those are the best women—a lady in the parlor and a whore in the bedroom. I should moderate a convo between you and your wife over beers. By the way, you got a picture of your wife for me to check out?"

"No, I'm sorry," I said, "I actually have to get going."

"OK, I've added to you my buddy list."

"OK," I typed, "good night and thanks for talking with me."

I couldn't believe how much I had just confessed to a total stranger. But, I felt a sense of liberation. He didn't think I was crazy. He seemed to understand and relate. I wasn't alone in some Ziggy-Stardust, Major-Tom space capsule. He was like the first guy I had chatted with the week before, telling me to keep my chin up, that I wasn't abnormal, that he could relate to what I was going through and how I was reacting.

And other guys were so much further out there.

Phil from NY sounded normal, a regular guy just as curious about the details of his girlfriend cheating as I was. He told me to "take it easy" and that I wasn't "a pussy" Basically he was telling me, "you're simply human and you can live with that, can't you?"

A load had just been taken off.

And then, before leaving the room, I quietly masturbated, looking at Ashley in her blue bikini.

****

Later that night in the bedroom, Ashley began returning my kisses. I wasn't sure if she was going to say, "I have to get up early," so I proceeded slowly, licking her neck, then rubbing my hand against her breasts.

Then back to kissing. Back to her breasts, pulling her bra down and looking at her beautiful erect nipples. I lowered myself and began licking each one.

A few minutes later, feeling the wetness on her panties, I slid my finger inside. This was my green light, my off-to-the races signal, and I slid farther down and began licking her precious pussy, immersing my face in it, French-kissing it.

About ten later minutes, I heard her cry out, "Oh God" and listened joyously as she reached orgasm.

I got on top of her quickly afterwards, thinking confident thoughts, praying to the patron saint of stamina.

As soon as I slid inside her, my dick was again in over-excited mode. I took it slow, trying to distract myself, like I wasn't there. I started thinking of Yankee scores from the prior week … Yanks 7, Orioles 2, Orioles 3, Yanks 1. I had been watching the clock on Ashley's nightstand from when I went inside her. 10:42 had become 10:44. 10:45 had become 10:46. I thought of an auctioneer with his megaphone … "10:46! Do I hear 10:47?"

But Ashley's pussy just felt so good, and when I heard her moan "Oh yeah," there were only so many mental acrobats I could do. I pulled out suddenly to try and hold it, but it was too late. I went back inside her and came within seconds. I thought of Jim Murta cumming up inside her and gave it an extra umph at the end.

"That was good," Ashley said, holding me as I lay on top of her, both of us naked.

It was good, I thought, as I told her "I love you so much."

We pulled up the covers and she rested her head on my chest and within minutes I could tell she was sleeping.

It was a huge improvement … I had gone a solid three to four minutes. I wasn't back to my pre-rumor self, but hell, I was on my way.

I felt relaxed and euphoric. She was my wife, we had just made love, and she was naked, sleeping ever so peacefully beside me.

CHAPTER SIXTEEN

"How did the presentation go?" I asked Ashley when she called that afternoon.

"Really great, I got lots of compliments—a relief *that's* over."

"Do you want to get drinks and celebrate tonight?"

"I would love to," she said, "but I'm already committed to see a movie with Jen."

"Oh, that's right."

"But I'm not leaving for Candlewood Lake until Saturday now. You're around Friday night, right?"

"Yeah," I said, "what are you thinking?"

"They're having a happy hour this Friday. Would you be up for going?"

"What? A work happy hour of yours?"

"Yeah, it's casual, very informal, but it's at Old Bridge and I know you like that outside area they have."

"Oh, yeah," I said, "I think I can swing that, this Friday, yeah, sure, sounds good."

****

Was she fucking kidding me?

Ashley had just invited me to face people who all knew the rumor. To them, I was the clueless husband bumbling outside while one of their colleagues fucked his wife. And now Ashley wanted me to show up and socialize with them.

Hell, there was a good chance Jim Murta would be there. I might have to say hello, make pleasantries, even shake hands with that self-satisfied, cocky prick—in front of everyone, no less.

How could she possibly think I'd be "up for going?"

I had thought she was asking if I were free on Friday, because she wanted the two of us to do something. Instead she gets me to say I'm free, only to drop the happy hour A-bomb.

She was throwing me to the lions. Could she not see how incredibly embarrassing and humiliating this would be? I'd be the sap, chump husband on display for everyone's amusement.

They all knew what happened that Monday, a week and a half before me. And they probably knew a lot more details. Craig had probably only given me the condensed version and hadn't the heart to offer up everything he heard.

Wouldn't Jim have blabbed about what was going on when Tamara relegated me to the upstairs bathroom? Wouldn't that be part of the full rumor? Had Ashley let on to Mr. "Just Bigger OK" Jim Murta that she was particularly impressed with the size of his cock? Might she have added it was a lot bigger than she was used to? If she had, wouldn't Jim have included that juicy detail when he blabbed? I'd show up as Ashley's smaller-dicked chump husband— the guy who bumbled around outside while his own wife's pussy was being seeded by another man's larger cock in a ratty little bathroom.

Could Ashley not realize how incredibly mortifying that would be? Did she want to humiliate me? Did she not know how much she humiliated me that night? Did she want to add insult to injury? Or was she just incredibly clueless to how I was feeling?

Where was the, "I understand if it's awkward and you don't want to go?".

Well, I had no intention of going. Not freaking happening.

I said "Yes" because I had been put on the spot.

A last-minute excuse was going to sound more believable. And I quickly agreed, like it was no big thing, to make my eleventh hour rain-check sound that much more believable.

I was going to have to have unanticipated extra work Friday night.

****

When I got back home that night, I went online, into the "My Wife" chat room.

I decided to be more specific in the scroll. I typed, "My wife cheated and it's royally messed with my head."

Soon, others were publically writing back, "What happened Dave?"

I hesitated about opening up further, but after a few more comments asking for an explanation, I typed, "My wife had sex with a co-worker at a party I was at."

"Tell us about it Dave," I read in the scroll. It struck me then that being on the public stage—even if the twenty-five people reading it were anonymous strangers—was a little reckless.

Then the instant messages started: "NYC here" or "Can I see a pic of her?"

I read one that said, "It does mess with one's head, doesn't it? Tony, 45M, Baltimore."

I figured he might have something to offer, some insight or perspective, so I replied, "Yeah, has been a colossal mind-f*ck to say the least."

He asked me to tell him the story and kept replying "Wow" as I relayed the details of the last month.

"And then today," I said, "my wife invited me to a work happy hour of hers."

"Is the guy who fucked your wife going to be there?"

"Yeah, I think so."

"How do you feel about going, knowing everyone there knows what happened?"

"Well that's the thing," I said, "I can't handle that. It would be just too humiliating. I think about having to shake hands with the guy or having to look him in the eye. I told my wife I would go, but I'm going to back out at the last minute. Tell her I suddenly have to work late."

"Wait a second," he replied, "so you told your wife today you were going, but you're planning to be a no-show?"

"Yes, it would be just too much humble pie to eat."

"So you're just going to let your wife eat all that humble pie instead?"

"Huh?" I replied, "What do you mean?"

"How is your wife going to feel showing up without her husband?"

"She's gone to plenty of happy hours without me."

"But this is the first since the party right? Since this rumor started?"

"Yeah," I said.

"And she invited you for a reason. She wants you there. She's probably told people you're going. She wants you by her side, to show everyone that you still love and support her. And when you don't show up, she's going to be embarrassed. And others will gossip about how you stood your wife up. You want to do that to her?"

"I don't think she will feel stood up or embarrassed," I said. "I just don't think she realized how embarrassing it would be for me."

"Don't be a fool," he replied, "You don't think the rumor was embarrassing for her? Being gossiped about like that. She has to go into work every day and put on a smile and say hello to these people who all know what she did. And you can't suck it up, and face the embarrassment she's faced, for a measly few hours."

"It's just too humiliating," I typed.

"So be humiliated for an evening. Don't you see? It's a test of your love and devotion. You have to go and provide solidarity, to show all the talkers that you're 100% percent behind your wife, that you support her. And yes, even go up and shake hands and be polite to the guy who fucked her."

"I just picture the smug self-satisfaction he would have, shaking hands with me," I replied.

"No, the smug satisfaction should be all yours, because she's your wife and she goes home to you."

"I'll give it some thought," I said.

"No more thought. She invited you, and you said you would go. So swallow your pride, put your tail behind your legs, and show up at the party with your wife. And make sure to stand beside her and hold her hand a lot, especially when meeting the guy who fucked her. You should be a walking billboard for your love and devotion to her."

"I would just feel so awkward and foolish, like they'd be laughing behind my back."

"You want them laughing behind your wife's back when you don't show? And what do you think they'll think of you, being too scared to show? Too intimidated to be in the same room with the guy who fucked your wife."

"I understand," I typed.

"If you understand then say it."

"Say what?" I typed.

"I want you to tell me that you're gonna go, and that there'll be no excuses from you. Tell me that no matter how humiliating it may be, you're going to be a good little hubby and hold hands with your wife, and be polite and cordial to the guy who fucked your wife."

"OK," I typed.

"OK, what? Tell me you're going to the happy hour and you're going to be polite and cordial to the guy who fucked your wife."

"Fine," I replied, humoring him, typing back, "I'm going to the happy hour and I'll be polite and cordial to the guy who fucked my wife."

"See, that wasn't so hard now, was it? Between now and the party, I want you to repeat that to yourself and let the words really sink in. Now repeat it back to me."

"I'm going to be polite and cordial to the guy who fucked my wife."

"That a boy. And I've put you in my contacts and I'm going to message you after the party and you're going to give me all the details of how the happy hour went, right?"

"OK," I typed.

"Now let's see a photo of this wife of yours. And send me one of the two of you together as well."

"I don't have any on this computer, sorry."

"Don't lie to me, show her to me."

"It's my work laptop; I really don't."

"But you have some on your home computer, right?"

"Sure."

"OK," he typed back, "and next time, you are going to send me some photos, and you're going to give me all the details about that happy hour, OK?"

"OK," I replied, just to assuage him, "I have to go now."

"First, repeat what I told you back to me."

"I'm going to be polite to the guy who fucked my wife."

"And cordial."

"And cordial," I typed, "I really have to go."

✷✷✷✷

I thought about what the guy had just said about Ashley being left holding the bag if I didn't show. It was true that Ashley had suffered a huge indignity as well. Jim Murta blabbing had been a major "fuck you" to her as well. I had the luxury of not having to see them. But she had to work with these people and put on a brave face every single day—in meetings, presentations, going up the elevator, walking down the hallways.

Perhaps Ashley was feeling just as out on the moon. And maybe it was important to her that I go. Perhaps she wanted me showing her friends that I did support her and that our marriage was as strong as ever.

But good God, how I could possibly show my face at that event?

I decided to start dropping hints tomorrow about a big project to try and get a better read from her. I'd see which way she leaned by how she responded, either something like "No problem, I understand if you can't," or "It's really important to me that you come."

Then I thought of what the guy had messaged me at the end. His attitude had changed as our conversation progressed from helpful to almost badgering, like he was rubbing it in a little.

Perhaps his efforts to show me Ashley's perspective were sincere, but by insisting that I tell him the details afterwards, he appeared to be taking some enjoyment from my predicament.

And his demand to see photos felt like some kind of weird power assertion.

Then I thought, The guy was trying to fuck with me.

He probably got off on getting me to repeat twice back to him, "I'm going to be polite and cordial to the guy who fucked my wife."

I thought of him ordering me to repeat those words before I went to the happy hour. What a crazy thing that would be. I'd feel reduced before even showing up.

Jesus, that guy was trying to fuck with my head.

In his own small way, he was trying to do what Jim Murta had done, what the marines had done to that other guy. If he couldn't fuck my wife, he could at least try and fuck with my head.

I thought of Ashley's co-workers' eyes fixed on me as I said hello to Jim fucking Murta.

I thought of what the guy had asked me to say and started whispering it back to myself.

I had popped a boner and started masturbating in the chair. I felt reduced, the guy had wanted me to feel reduced, and there I was jerking off, repeating what he'd had me say to him.

"I'm going to be polite and cordial to the guy who fucked my wife ... I'm going to be polite and cordial ..." Before I had whispered it ten times, I came.

Two minutes later, I thought, *No way am I fucking going.*

****

I called Craig the following morning.

"Yeah, I'll be there," he said. "Ashley told me you're going."

"Yeah," I replied.

I wasn't about to let on that I was going to pull a last-minute bail.

"Are there going to be a lot of people?" I asked.

"Well, the usual happy hour group. But I heard a sales director will be throwing down his card, which helps turn-out. I think most of my team is going."

"Sure, I hear you," I said. "You think Jim Murta will be there?"

That question caused an awkward pause, and I didn't know how to follow it up.

"Probably," he finally replied. "I mean, if he's around, happy hours are kind of his thing, especially if it's being expensed. But who knows, turnout's depressed in the summer with people going out of town for the weekend."

"I got ya."

"Were you—I mean, are you thinking of saying something to him?"

"To Jim? Oh no, not at all. Everything's good with Ashley and me. I was just wondering about the scene was all."

"OK, glad things are good with the two of you."

I heard some office commotion in the background.

"I won't keep you, Craig, so I guess I'll just see you then."

"Sounds good, Dave."

****

I imagined Craig's IT right-hand guy being nearby.

"Did I hear that correctly?" he might ask, "Dave Martens is gonna show Friday?"

"Yeah, that's what he said."

"Does he know his wife's been the talk of the office?"

"Yeah, I told him the basics."

"He knows Jim Murta fucked her?"

"Yeah."

"Does he know what a horned up, horn-dog Murta said she was or how—"

"I spared him the blow-by-blow detail."

"Does he want to confront Jim about it?" the guy might ask.

"No, I suspect he's doing it for Ashley. He has to deal with events like this sometime, right?"

"Damn, I guess that's commendable. But I sure wouldn't want to be him there."

****

Then I thought of the more junior guys on his IT team hearing that I was going—guys I was talking to out on the balcony as Jim Murta was fucking my wife. They had listened to me ramble about the Yankees and give the British guys bluster about American football. They had acted interested and amused at the time. Or perhaps they were merely showing deference to their boss' friend. Maybe they thought of me as the buzzed, boorish, finance guy—cluelessly bloviating as Murta was going inside my wife.

Had they enjoyed a good laugh when they heard the rumors that Monday? Had these geeks jerked off thinking about my wife—the marketing director at their company—getting fucked by Jim Murta while her buzzed husband droned on to them? There were probably a number of guys at that company who jerked off thinking about taking Ashley like that.

So humiliating to think about.

And suddenly I was hard, just sitting there in my office.

****

I went to the library at lunch and headed for the men's room upstairs. No one was there, and I went into a corner stall and sat on the toilet. I pulled my dick out of the fly of my suit.

I knew how crazy it was, but I figured if I didn't, I'd be thinking about it for the rest of the afternoon.

I imagined hanging again with Craig's IT team, were I to show. I assumed they'd be friendly again, maybe more so, given the strange "That's the guy—Ashley's husband" celebrity status I would have with her co-workers. But I imagined one of them regarding me as that boorish, buzzed guy, yapping away.

I imagined his unspoken thoughts.

How's that high-horse you were on the night of the party working out for you now, Dave? I hope you've developed a taste for humble pie, because that'll be on your menu when you show up Friday. I hope you're put in the awkward situation of having to buy a drink for the guy who fucked your wife.

Boy, did Jim Murta do a number on you that night. He humiliated you real good. He not only had you sent upstairs so he could give your wife a proper fucking, but then he topped it off by putting that special cherry on top, busting his nut right inside your wife's pussy.

And that's how he finished fucking your wife, Dave, he topped it off with a cherry, by blasting his sperm seed up Ashley's little puss.

He topped it off with a cherry, Dave, he put that fucking cherry on top.

When I came, it got on my suit. I panicked, reaching for the toilet paper—which left little white flecks on the spot—before trying to wash it off at the sink.

What the fuck is wrong with me, I thought as I splashed water on my face. I had a 2:30 meeting I had to prepare for.

****

I thought about what I had imagined the IT guy saying again when I got home that evening.

The "fuck you" was Jim fucking my wife, knowing I was right outside. Putting the cherry on top was when he blasted his sperm inside her.

I started imagining watching in the bathroom as Jim Murta fucked my wife.

"Please don't top it off, just not inside Ashley, please pull out, cum on her ass, just not in her pussy, just not the cherry, don't top it off with that humiliating cherry."

"Oh, but I am so going to top it off Dave," I imagined Jim replying, "There's no way now that I'm not cumming inside the woman you love. I'm topping it off, Dave, with a special fuck-you Dave cherry, and your wife's gonna take it real good. I'm topping it off, oh yeah Dave, here it comes, now take that fucking cherry!"

I came hard.

I'm fucking losing my mind.

Then I thought Jim Murta had thrown another cherry on top when he told everyone about fucking my wife that night.

And now he'd probably relish topping it off again by trying to man-me down at the happy hour.

I thought of the imaginary IT guy saying, "He fucks your wife, and you find yourself in the awkward position of buying him a drink. How's that for topping it off with another cherry, bitch?"

****

Waiting for Ashley to return, I brought my laptop out and scattered work papers on our living room couch.

I went down to the bodega and bought two large coffees—dumping them out and leaving the empties beside me. I pretended to have dozed off with the computer in my lap when she came home.

"What's going on?" she asked.

"My boss called. We've got a last-minute pitch for next week. I have to get Jeff all the analytics before the weekend."

"Is that realistic?"

"It's going to have to be," I said, "I'll probably be up for a while tonight."

"I'm sorry," she said. "Are you stressing about it?"

"Yeah, a little. How was the movie?"

"So-so, kind of cliché and predictable," she said, "how does tomorrow night look for you now?"

"What?" I said.

"The happy hour."

"Oh right," I said, "well I definitely want to be there, but I kind of need to play it by ear. Is it OK if I have to show up later?"

"Yeah, of course, it will be probably go on for a while."

****

I fell asleep on the couch after Ashley went to bed.

At 4 a.m. I made my way to our bedroom. I was deliberately clumsy getting into bed. I wanted her to wake up briefly.

"What time is it?" she asked.

"Sshh," I said, whispering, "Just past four. Go back to sleep."

"Oh my God, Dave, have you been up working all this time?"

"Yeah, it's OK. Go back to sleep, Ash."

****

"How's the project going?" Ashley asked, when she called after lunch.

"It's going," I replied, "but my team's still pulling data. I think we'll get there; it's just a race to the finish."

"Are you exhausted?"

"I'm hanging in there, been chugging coffee, a little wired on adrenaline."

"What time do you think you'll finish?"

"Tough to say, I'm hoping to get out of here by six or seven. How late will the happy hour go?"

"People will probably be there until at least nine."

"OK," I said, "I'm just going to have to play it by ear. I'll call you around six and let you know my status. I'm really sorry about this. Is that OK?"

"Yeah, of course," she said, "no worries. Do what you have to do, baby."

****

By six, the office had cleared out. No one works late on a summer Friday, unless they absolutely have to.

Ashley called to tell me she'd just arrived, and what a beautiful night it was on the bar terrace.

I told her I had just gotten the last data runs back and was going to crank as quickly as possible. "Hopefully, I can be there by eight," I said. "I'll call you in an hour."

"OK," she said, "good luck, and hang in there. I know the office is the last place you want to be on a beautiful Friday night."

I had nothing in particular to do, but I decided I'd at least be productive. I did my expense report and started an employee review that wasn't due for two months.

When I called Ashley just after seven, she sounded a little buzzed. It was noisy, with lots of talking and laughter in the background.

"I'm going to try for nine, Ash," I said. "I just finished going through all the data, and I'm mad-rushing the second half of the report."

"I'm so sorry, honey. I miss you. I'll have a margarita on the rocks, no salt, waiting for you, if you can make it, but I understand if you can't."

I was bored, but determined to stay in my office for the duration. On every call to Ashley, I wanted my work number to show up.

This sucks, I thought, but it was better than being at that happy hour. I had to give credit to the online guy two nights ago. He'd at least made me consider Ashley's potential perspective on a last-minute bail. Because of him, I had laid down the groundwork the night before. And now I knew for sure she wasn't embarrassed going alone.

To anyone asking why I hadn't shown, well, a major project had come up. Her husband has an important job. "I feel bad," she could say, "he was up until four a.m. last night doing a major pitch."

No one could say, "Can't say I was surprised he'd chicken out. That's how a pussy like Dave Martens rolls."

I called her at eight and apologized, saying that I still had another couple hours. I told her to say hello to everyone for me, to tell Craig that I was sorry to have missed him.

She said that was too bad, but she would make sure to have a stiff drink waiting for me when I got home.

And she did just that. When I walked in at eleven, she gave me a big kiss and showed genuine sympathy for the extra long day I'd just endured.

I had escaped a very awkward social situation.

I acted disappointed to have missed it and asked who was there. She threw out the usual names like Tamara and Craig and others. Jim Murta's name never came up.

I felt calm and more relaxed than I had for ages. The guy online the other night was right. My wife was home with me. I had a drink in my hand, my wife beside me, and I had avoided the happy hour. Spending five additional hours where I didn't want to be—at work—had been worth it.

As I lay in bed, I remembered a *Flintstones* episode I'd seen as a kid. Fred and Barney were in a pickle. A hidden camera show had caught them carousing with dancing girls at the Buffalo Lodge. It was going to air that Saturday night. When they realized their wives were going to see the show, they spent all Friday night lassoing TV antennas off every house in Bedrock. Exhausted as they were at 5 a.m.—having yanked every last antenna—they felt satisfied and relieved.

That's how I felt. My efforts paid off.

CHAPTER SEVENTEEN

"What time are you heading to Candlewood Lake?" I asked as we lay in bed.

"Noon. I should probably leave by eleven-fifteen just to be safe."

"I feel like I've barely seen you all week—"

"I know, me too!" she said curling up into my arms.

"And now you're heading away," I said, affecting a kid's whine.

"I'm sorry, we've planned it for weeks, and I haven't seen Jessica since last Christmas."

We started kissing; then our tongues intertwined. Once I had her t-shirt off, I knew it was on.

I sucked on her beautiful breasts, cupping them, caressing her. I went down on her until she reached orgasm. Then I went inside her. I sensed I wasn't going to last. I tried to slow up, but I was too hard and turned-on.

Within a minute, it was happening. I was fucking cumming.

"God, I'm sorry," I said, "I think it's just that we haven't been doing this for a few days."

"It's OK," she replied, "I should probably get ready if I'm going to make the train."

God, I thought, after she left, what a pathetic send-off that was.

****

I called Craig.

I was surprised when he picked up.

"Hi Dave, how are you?"

"I'm good," I replied. "Sorry I couldn't see you last night—last minute work bullshit."

"Them long hours on a Friday night. That sucks."

"Yeah, I know, but I wanted to call because I said I'd be there."

"Don't sweat it. I understand."

"How was it?" I asked. "Good time?"

"Yeah, it was cool. We basically took over the outdoor deck."

"I wish I could have been there," I said. "Ashley said it was fun. I guess you'd concur?"

Then Craig paused. I thought I heard him sigh.

"But it was cool?" I said nervously.

"Dave, I'd like to apologize," he said, "for how I've been since the party. I mean, how I've been with you."

"No need to apologize, Craig."

"No I do need to. I know what happened to you had to be difficult. I was uncomfortable being the one to tell you. And it was just awkward. Because I don't like office politics, gossip, and bullshit. I like to keep above all that stuff and I do. It's how I am. And what happened had me in professional self-preservation mode."

"I understand Craig, no worries."

"Yeah, well, you're my friend, and I feel I should have been there for you more."

"I appreciate that Craig, but I really appreciate you telling me what you did. And as I said, we are working through it. We've talked. Ashley and I are in a good place."

"I'm glad to hear that bro," he said, "I really am. And I mean it about checking a Yankees game this summer. We should really do that."

"You bet," I said, "I'd like that."

"Me, too."

"But Craig, given what happened, I hope you don't blame me for asking this, but was the party uneventful? I mean, there aren't any new rumors that came out of last night?"

"No, Dave, it was a good time but uneventful."

"Was Jim there?"

"Yeah, but there were no rumors."

"Can I ask, did you see them talking to each other?"

"I don't think they talked at all, other than as part of a group. There were no one-on-ones or talking in a corner, if that's what you're asking."

"That's kind of what I'm asking, yes."

"Yeah, none of that. Ashley was at a table with the other girls. And she spoke with her boss by the bar for a while. And Tonya, the female sales manager—I saw her talking to Ashley. Murta mostly stood by the bar with his sales guys."

"Did the rumor about Ashley come up?"

"No, not at all. No one was going to be so classless as to bring that shit up."

"How about Tamara?"

"She was just bopping around, you know, being Tamara."

"OK, so there was nothing I should wonder about? I mean, it was just a regular happy hour? And Jim and Ashley weren't talking to each other?"

"Right, I swear, there was nothing you need to wonder about."

"Anyone ask about me? Like if I was showing or why I hadn't showed?"

"No, other than me asking Ashley. She told me it was fifty-fifty, and then when it got late, I figured you couldn't make it."

"OK, cool, but otherwise my name didn't come up?"

"No, not at all."

"That's what I assumed but just wanted to check with you. I appreciate you telling me."

"You OK, Dave?"

"Yeah, I'm good. Like I said, I really wanted to be there for Ashley, and couldn't, and then I guess given what happened, imagination gets the best of you sometimes."

"Of course," Craig replied, "I understand."

"Well, I don't want to keep you, man."

"OK sure, but seriously, let's do that Yankees game before the summer's over."

****

I got back from doing errands around six.

There was a certain what-the-fuck-to-do-with myself feeling as I broke out the shaker and fixed myself a martini.

Pretty soon I found myself on my laptop, checking the "My Wife" chat room. After a few big sips, I typed in the public scrawl, "My wife recently cheated & looking for perspective, advice on how others handled."

The now familiar flurry of private messages ensued.

One message seemed interesting enough. "I've been there, my friend, Tom 56, Charlotte, NC."

"What happened?" I asked.

"My wife cheated for eight years. My teenage kids were on to it before me. I was stupid or in denial or both. LOL."

"How do you find out? How did you react?"

"I was hurt, distraught, couldn't sleep, all those emotions of betrayal and rejection, but I didn't want to split up for the kids' sake and once I accepted it, I found it a real turn-on. I still do. Tell me about what happened with you, Dave."

I told him about the night at the party, the rumor, how I couldn't sleep, either, the fear I still have, how it felt like such a fuck-you, my humiliation, how I couldn't face the happy hour.

"I can understand she hurt you and I can relate," he replied, "but you have to admit what's happened is pretty hot. I mean, you know it's hot, right?"

"I guess, when I step out of myself or my ego, or think of it objectively, sure. I think about the details. I'd pay to hear them if I could do it anonymously."

"But just the details you have are a turn on, right? I mean you said you've been jerking off, right? You're imagining that night, right?"

"Yeah, but I know it's fucked up."

"She must have really wanted this guy to do it with him, even knowing you were outside."

"Yeah, I figure she got caught up in the moment."

"What's your wife's name?"

"Ashley"

"And you said she's thirty?"

"Yes."

"Mmm," he replied, "a great young age. Your wife must be very pretty for this guy to have chosen her."

"Yeah, she is," I typed, "She gets hit on a lot, which I used to not care about."

"I bet the guys at work hit on her a lot more now, right? Knowing she took a co-workers big cock bare at a party with her husband right outside."

"I've suspected so," I replied, "but I think she's learned her lesson there."

"The fact that she told you—her own husband—that he had a much bigger cock, right to your face … Wow, that is so hot to think about. She's got a real naughty side for sure."

"Yeah, I know," I said, "kind of stunned me speechless when she told me."

"I'll bet, but that got you even harder, right? You said you jerked off thinking about his size, right?"

"I've thought of his size but I know that's fucked up."

"Dave," he said, "you don't need to be uptight. It's OK that it gets you hard. I get hard thinking about my wife. And I'm really hard thinking about what your wife did and your situation. Can you do me a favor?"

"What's that?'

"Show Ashley to me. I got to see this girl. With my wife here, I'll delete after looking, but please send me a photo of your wife."

"BRB," I typed.

I went into the kitchen, poured my second martini and thought about it. I'd been asked for photos several dozen times now. I had hundreds now on my laptop. What harm would there be to send one to some old man in North Carolina?

I scrolled through the photo files and found one of her posing in Central Park in a summer floral dress, smiling.

"Just sent," I typed.

"Mmm, she's absolutely adorable. So naturally pretty. So innocent looking—and those tits on her!"

"Thanks," I said.

"Show me Ashley's tits, Dave."

"I don't have any nudes."

"How about a swimsuit, so I can really admire them?"

"One second," I replied.

I probably had thirty of her in a bikini, but I sent the one in the sky blue bikini, from Florida, two days before that night.

"Oh my fucking God," he replied, "what a fucking rack. Your wife's tits are amazing and luscious."

"Thanks."

"They are perfect for titty-fucking."

"Yeah," I said.

"No wonder that guy picked your wife when she displayed her big titties to him. I'm surprised he didn't just blast a load all over them, right then."

"Well her friend has big tits as well, if not slightly bigger."

"Oh God yeah, Dave, show me her friend. You have one of Ashley with the girl who watched in the bathroom? What's her friend's name?"

"Tamara," I said, "and yeah I do. Hold on, let me find one."

I sent him the one from the Mardi Gras party.

"Wow, yes, Tamara is a hottie as well, and great fuckable tits for sure. But I can see why the guy chose Ashley. I would, too. That guy really did hit the jackpot that night."

"Yeah, don't I know it."

"Do you mind if I pull my cock out and whack off looking at your wife, Dave?"

"No that's OK," I said before telling him I had to go.

****

On the elevator ride down and as I walked across the street, I thought about the photos I had just emailed.

I'm sure plenty of guys have jerked off thinking of my wife, especially guys at her work who know the rumor. Ashley's in plenty of photos floating around on Facebook. So some random old guy in North Carolina has a few pictures of my wife. It wasn't like they were compromising.

I switched to Gin and Tonics when I returned.

The "My Wife" room was full, so I entered the "Cuckold Husbands" room. *Fuck it*, I thought, and just wrote in the public scroll. "I'm not a cuckold but my wife cheated rather publicly at a party I was at & has screwed with my head,".

The "got pics" and "where in NY" followed, but then I saw one that was more of a greeting. "Hello, I have some experience with this. This is a strange thing to deal with."

After I told him the details, he replied, "Oh my, this is quite a situation. I'm Chris, what's your name?"

"David."

"Want me to be honest with you, David? I don't want to upset you—you seem like a good guy—but I think this is why you came into this room."

"I only came in here because the 'My Wife' room was full."

"Maybe so, but l I think the room name does describe you."

"Maybe technically, because my wife did cheat on me."

"It's more than that. It's the fact you've only been married a year and a half. Do you think this has never happened before or won't ever happen again?"

"I don't know. I never dreamed I would have reacted this way," I replied.

"There's no right or wrong way to react. Nobody should judge you for that. It's about what you want. There's nothing wrong with staying with her. Many husbands enjoy what some people call cuckold relationships. I just don't think you should fool yourself."

"This is a hard question" he continued, "but honestly, do you think your sex with her has been good enough? Do you mind if I ask how big you are?"

"Five and a half," I replied, "or six with a generous spot. I thought our sex life was good, but since I heard what happened, it's made me more self-conscious."

"You may need to think about more than just being self-conscious. Judging from what she did, it seems pretty clear that she's not satisfied with you sexually. That doesn't make it right for her to do it. But at least some of her dissatisfaction probably has to do with your size."

"I've wondered about that lately, of course."

"She didn't just have sex with him, Dave. She performed for him, to turn him on. And then let him choose her. And she let her friend watch what she did. What's your wife's name?"

"Ashley."

"I want you to think about Ashley. She's fooling around in this bathroom with her girlfriend, and this girl pulls him in to join this game—there was probably a reason for that. And maybe Ashley started out just playing or maybe she knew all along. But he took himself out, and then he chose her. So she must have shown that she was impressed or excited."

"I don't think it was planned," I replied. "She wouldn't be so recklessly public about it"

"There's something sexy about public. It's very naughty. She must have really wanted it. He must have really excited her. This may sound harsh, but can you imagine yourself—can you imagine YOU—making her so horny that she'd let you fuck her right there at a party with her friend watching? Maybe you don't put on the kind of show she would show to her friend."

"No," I said.

"This is the point," he continued, "this guy comes into the bathroom, he takes out his large penis, and both of those women want it enough to compete for him. She probably felt sexy when he picked her. And she let him have her, right there in the bathroom, even though she knew it would humiliate you, and he knew he was humiliating you when he was doing it."

"And the larger point," he went on, "is that you're masturbating to this, and you like it, or at least you like it sexually. Something must have been there already for you to have these thoughts."

"No," I replied, "I never thought like this before."

"Most men would have been furious and left her, or at least made her apologize to never do it again. But you didn't do any of those things. Instead, you analyzed it from a zillion different angles before even reacting. And now you're consumed with it."

"I'm saying there was nothing in me before. I was very content with my marriage and sex life."

"But Ashley wasn't. And I bet thinking about this has made you more turned on than you have been in a while. It's a very powerful experience."

"It just seemed so outlandish and out of character. I wonder about the details that others probably know."

"Yes, there are a lot of things to wonder," he replied, "but it all comes from the same place. And you're thinking the same answers to all those questions when you are touching yourself.

"Of course he had her," he continued, "but it's the reason why. She's not in love with this guy—she is probably in love with you—so why did she fuck him?"

"I have theories but no solid answers," I said.

"She did it because Ashley likes sex and he was a good fuck."

"If it was only that," I replied, "she could have met him for a drink in private, with discretion."

"That's why those questions bother you—because she wanted it too badly to care about any of that. Women are so careful with condoms, but she didn't even ask. She wanted him to fuck her so bad, she didn't care if he came in her. And he knew she needed it, so he didn't ask. Even though you knocked, and she might have felt a little bad, she had his big cock in her hand and she couldn't resist."

"Probably true," I replied.

"Look, strength is just an accident of another man's weakness. Is it really your fault if someone else has a bigger cock and can fuck your wife better?"

"What are you saying," I typed, "is that it's like when I was never good enough to make varsity in high school—it wasn't my fault."

"Yes, exactly. In my experience, guys who get in your place

already know the truth deep down and sense their limitations."

"Well, I didn't, I thought we had good sex life."

"I know, but where are you now? You've admitted you have trouble lasting and don't have a particularly large cock. It's just the way things are. Men are easy to please, easy to satisfy sexually most of the time. Women are much harder. Every time you have sex with her, you cum, but for her, it ends in frustration."

"I understand what you're saying."

"You need to look at the future. This is a time when you can redesign your life and expectations. But you have to be open and honest—not emotional—both of you. There may be serious consequences if you don't keep discussing this with her. If she has the propensity to play with others behind your back, you are going to have some serious emotional/mental problems."

"I'm going to have another talk with her."

"This may be the first of many. You need to make sure you're ready to handle it."

"OK," I said, "but have to go for run for now, sorry."

*****

I paced around, started drinking a beer, but was back at my computer screen before long.

"Hey Dave, Rob 43m from Brooklyn, how are you this Friday night?"

Suddenly I was telling this guy from Brooklyn the whole story.

"Wow, what an experience," he replied, "as you said, I guess she just got caught up in the moment. And oh man, the embarrassment and being the last to know is the hard part. It's pretty hot though. Can I see a picture of your lovely wife?"

I sent him one the one from Central Park.

"Man, she is beautiful. She has that innocent, fresh, young-Jennifer-Love-Hewitt look. You can see her fun personality. Can you send me some more, Dave? Like one that shows off her hot young body?"

I sent Rob the Florida bikini picture—then another of her on our honeymoon ... then another from the Jersey shore.

"Damn, you are one lucky guy. She is fucking hot—amazing tits on that girl. She looks like a real fun fuck. If I was that guy watching her ass ride my cock while I sat on the toilet reaching around squeezing those tits, I would have dumped a nice fat load in her too. I'm 8 inches and thick, send me another pic to get me nice and hard."

There was a moment of "What the fuck am I doing?" But I had a good buzz and forwarded a couple more from Florida.

"Oh my God, she is incredible. My cock is ready to bust out of my pants. I just got to take it out … ahh, that feels good, your wife has me rock hard right now. Describe Ashley's pussy for me. Is she shaved?"

"Not shaved, but trim."

"Nice pussy lips?"

"Yeah, picture perfect."

"Dude, your wife is picture perfect," he said. "This is good … letting another guy stroke himself while talking about your wife. What a little slut she must have been for that guy. A dirty whore. Dirty whores like getting bent over the sink and fucked.

"So," he continued, "do you want to see her get fucked hard again, but this time in front of you?"

"No, it's not like that," I replied, "I'm just trying to figure out where her head is at."

"You know where her head's at, don't kid yourself. This is not about her, it's about you. She's the one who did you wrong. You need to ask her if she wants another good fucking."

"I'm not asking her that."

"Why not?"

"For starters, what would she think of me? She'd never respect me."

"She went about this in the most disrespectful way. She doesn't have respect for you fucking a guy at a party and now all her friends know."

"I know it was disrespectful."

"If you're going to stay with her, you have to gain that respect back and get control … maybe confront her … If you let her get fucked in front of you, that will show you have control."

"I don't see getting respect back from that. I can't imagine how she'd react to such a crazy suggestion."

"Again it's not about her, it's about you. Tell her you need to get past this by actually seeing her with another guy—one of your choosing. That's how you take charge and gain control."

"I'll think about it," I said, "but I have to get going."

"Dave, I'm serious, I'm good-looking, clean cut, eight inches thick and will fuck her for you real hard—I'll punish her real good for you."

Good God, I thought. Who in hell am I talking to?

"I'll give it some real thought man."

"Dave, does she have a screen name on here?"

"What?" I said.

"I can talk to her for you and let you know what she says."

"No," I said, "she's not online here."

"How about an email? What's Ashley's email address?"

"I have to go."

"I'll give you my phone number, let's talk for a few minutes …"

****

I looked out our living room window, at the cabs and cars and people on 75th Street below. Then I looked down Columbus Avenue at the lights toward midtown.

I thought about the first time Ashley and I saw this apartment. When the realtor gave us a few minutes to explore, Ashley was playfully nudging me, singing an old Talking Heads' song, "This Must Be the Place."

We moved in on a Friday and spent that Saturday with the couch moved up to the window, watching the snow fall, like we were watching a movie.

****

There was a guy I used to work with who'd say, "I partied with myself last night." I'm not one to get drunk alone, but talking online had provided a social component.

I went back to my laptop and typed in the public scroll.

"Recently learned my wife cheated, rather blatantly, what a head f*ck that is."

When I told the story to a guy whose screenname was Superman666, he replied, "That's fucked up bro. Recently married, she's already fucked someone else. Man, she's playing you. Once a slut, always a slut. It's obvious, buddy. Sorry, I know that's not what you want to hear."

"I do believe she loves me," I said. "It just did a number on my self-esteem, which maybe she's picked up on."

"You said it perfectly," he replied, "she's picked up on it, and now she's got your number and knows you're not going anywhere, which you're not."

I tried to explain myself, how this was not me before.

"Look," he said, "sometimes we say we wouldn't let this or that happen cause it's the macho in us, but reality can be a different story."

"I know, but truth is, I don't know if any guy I know or am friends with would have reacted like I have."

"Don't be so sure. They're acting like you were before you found out—when the world according to you was perfect."

"They haven't been in my shoes, you mean."

"Yes, they haven't. Have you told her it's turned you on?"

"No," I replied. "How could I? How could she respect me?"

"She didn't think about that the night she was fucking him. She wanted his cock that night and she didn't care if you were outside or not—that's not respect."

"I know. It's made me feel reduced."

"You shouldn't feel reduced—SHE should. So her friend watched as he fucked your wife?"

"Yes."

"And she was the one who told you to go to the other bathroom?"

"Yeah, when I knocked."

"Sorry, but your wife was sucking his cock."

"I've imagined that as well," I said, "but I just don't know."

"I do agree with you that she should have took him someplace else, but her girlfriend had a lot to do with it."

"I'm sure she did," I replied.

"I bet the higher-ups where she works have all talked about it. Hell, some are probably hitting on her, thinking she's an easy piece of ass."

"She wouldn't do it again. She doesn't want the rumors."

"She may regret the rumors, but her pussy's wet when she thinks about that night. But I don't mean to rub it in. I know you're going through a lot. Can I give you a piece of advice?"

"Sure," I said.

"You said you were supposed to see him at a happy hour last night but didn't go?"

"Yeah."

"When you do see him again, I would just smile at him and say, 'I fuck her all the time, and you will never get to again.' "

He asked for photos so I sent him the one from Central Park.

"She is very pretty," he replied. I can see why he wanted to fuck her. If it had been me, I wouldn't have said shit about it, and I'd still be fucking her. Damn! I bet she looks really hot nude."

"Yeah, I don't have any."

"Well, given what you've told me, her head must be on other cocks or she wouldn't have fucked him like that. So you better get your shit straight or you're going to lose her."

****

"Hey, Dave, how are you?"

It was my brother Sean calling.

"OK, just hanging out."

"Are you ready for Vegas next weekend?"

"What?"

"Patrick's bachelor party. You ready for Vegas?"

"Oh sure, you bet, are you kidding?" I said, "I've been practicing blackjack on the computer every night. I've got a book on card counting and I think I've got it down."

"Yeah, I'm sure," he replied.

"I'm serious, Rain Man won't have nothing on me. They're going to nickname me Benny Binion Jr. before the weekend's through."

"So, what time are you arriving Friday?"

"Friday afternoon."

"I know, but what time?"

"Not sure, I'd have to check."

"Well, can you check now? I get in at 1:30 and we could take a cab if you're arriving around then."

"I booked it at work. Can I get back to you?"

"Were you out?"

"No, why?"

"You sound fucking drunk, little bro."

"Oh yeah. Earlier I was, and been a long week."

"Just get back to me with your flight info tomorrow, K?"

CHAPTER EIGHTEEN

I woke up on the couch in the office, confused, and then in a panic. After I realized it was Sunday and Ashley was in Connecticut, I calmed down—slightly.

There was a half-empty bottle of gin beside me.

I checked the call history on my cell and was relieved to have only spoken with my brother. I had vague recollections of what happened after that. I remembered going into the "Cuckolds" room when the "My Wife" room was full. I had a real sinking feeling.

I made my way over to the computer, which was on screen saver mode. My chat dialogues were still open. The last one was some guy asking if I was still there. That was at 5 a.m.

I looked at my "sent" emails folder.

I had sent photos of Ashley and me—on our wedding day and our honeymoon.

I felt like throwing up.

Then I noticed I had two new emails. The subject line of the first read, "Show this to Ashley"; the guy's cock was in the attachment. The second was a returned photo of Ashley at our wedding. The sender had blown his load on the photo—right on her face.

I put my head in my hands. I could still taste the fucking gin in my throat.

Then I read some of the still open chats and cringed. I had given out our names, ages, and how we lived on the Upper West Side.

I began furiously skimming through the different chats I'd had the late night before …

I would make Ashley say 'thank you.' Could you handle that, Dave? The last wife I fucked couldn't stop thanking me in me front of her husband.

So you cried when you found out. Haha … pussy!

He got you real good. I'm sure her friend was talking shit about you in the bathroom!

I would love to turn your wife out! You'll lose all confidence when I'm there!

I bet her friend laughed as she sent you upstairs like you didn't matter —because you fucking didn't.

They wouldn't let in you the bathroom as your own wife was being fucked.

I can see how that would be humiliating, very humiliating.

All these people know your wife slutted for another man.

Her friend must think you're a wimp, probably sensed what kind of man you are,

I'm going to fuck Ashley and humiliate and degrade you in front of her.

I'm going to take Ashley right the fuck in front of you.

You're gonna sit in a fucking school-boy chair and take it.

You're wife's going to see you jerk off as I fuck her.

Ashley's going to look in your eyes as she blows me.

I love breaking another man down—stripping away his manhood in front of his wife.

The look of defeat on his face as I fuck the woman he loves and cherishes.

I love virgin cuckolds …

Your wife's pussy will become my property.

You're done fucking her, '2-pumps and done' boy.

You're gonna be serving us breakfast in your bed with an apron on, bitch!

She's going to be my fuck toy.

Your cock whore wife is going to dress nice and bimbo slutty for me.

You're going to watch as I use her, and you're going to clean her up for my use.

Ever eat a creampie, boy?

I'm going to humiliate you completely. Is this understood Davey?

I'm going to bitch you out first. Make you my whore, and have you show up at my apartment wearing Ashley's lingerie.

"Jesus fucking Christ!" I said as I went to the living room. These guys had pulled their own online Jim Murta on me.

I opened the email again from the guy who sent me a photo of his cock and lined the image up against Ashley in her bikini. His cock was in a different league than mine. And he had gotten off on belittling me, personalizing it, talking about fucking Ashley in my apartment, right in front of me.

I thought of the guy who jerked off and came over my wife's face in the photo on our wedding day.

All these guys verbally taunted and humiliated me …

They wanted Ashley …

They'd fuck her in a heartbeat …

They'd fuck her right in front of me …

After I came, I just sat there catching my breath, thinking, what have I been reduced to? This is all your fault, Jim Murta. Did you have any idea what your actions would do to me? You've got me talking to strangers, masturbating looking at other cocks, imagining that they're yours.

****

"I just had a stare-down with a cow," Ashley said when I picked up my cell a half hour later.

"You what?" I replied.

"We took a drive this morning—Julie and Bob dubbed me their 'fresh air fund kid' for the weekend—so they saw this cow by the side of the road and they're like, 'Look Ashley it's a cow.' "

"Yeah, and—?"

"Well, they pulled over, and I walked right up to him by this fence, and I was like, 'Hi cow, I'm Ashley.' "

"And he was like, 'Hi Ashley, I'm a cow?' " I replied, still dazed.

"Mmm, not so much. He looked more puzzled, like, 'Who is this girl, and why is she so excited to see me?' "

"So did you form a special bond with your cow friend?"

"No, I motioned to pet him and he gave me a look like 'Don't even think about it.' "

"Oh well, did he at least give you a 'moo' "?

"Nope, I felt kind of gypped ... but we're heading out to her uncle's farm now. Maybe I can try milking one and bring a big jug back."

"Sounds good," I said. "We're pretty low on milk, but I'll scratch that off my grocery list, since you've got that covered."

"So what are you up to today?" she asked.

"Kind of a mellow morning," I replied, "just doing some work, about to go to the park."

"OK," Ashley, said. "Well, I'll probably have dinner up here, so I won't be back till late."

****

I still had a hangover, and so decided to fix myself a small drink, in a hair of the dog kind of way.

Then I saw a new message.

I realized I was still logged in.

"Hi Dave, I'm Mike, 32, so what brings you to the room?"

I thought about not replying, but then figured I could always just click him off. "I just learned the term 'cuckold' and was checking the room out of curiosity."

"What are you curious about?"

"Well," I typed, "someone had suggested I check out this room, but I just don't get the mentality of the guys here."

"LOL," he wrote, "yeah, it kind of runs the gamut. Who suggested you check out the room?"

"Some guy I met online last week in the 'My Wife' room. But I'm not a cuckold or anything. I was just perusing."

"Of course," he replied, "why did this man refer you here, do you think?"

"I had mentioned my wife had recently cheated."

"I see," he wrote. "How have you been handling it?"

"It's been the most fucked up thing that's ever happened to me."

"I'm sorry to hear you're upset. May I ask what happened?"

He kept asking questions, but he was different from the night before. He wasn't insulting, but rather, understanding. A half hour later, I had pretty much told him the full story.

"I can see why that would have you out of sorts," he wrote. "How are things now?"

"Ostensibly good," I replied, "but we've both kind of swept it under the rug."

"Do you think that's wise?"

"Probably not," I said, "but I've felt a bit paralyzed."

"That's very understandable, and emotions are raw, but communication is essential. Do you feel you can trust her?"

"I can't trust her like I did before."

"So is it fear that has you paralyzed?"

"That's certainly part of it."

"And what specifically scares you?"

"Her telling me she wants to leave me, or doesn't love me, or wants a divorce."

"Has she hinted at that?"

"No, she told me that she appreciated how understanding I've been and that she loves me."

"OK, that's encouraging and reassuring right?"

"Yeah."

"Good," he replied, "but it sounds like you still have more questions. What's your wife's name?"

"Ashley."

"OK, so it sounds like you have unanswered questions for Ashley?"

"Yeah."

"So why haven't you asked them? Out of fear?"

"I guess so, yeah."

"Fear of upsetting her or fear of what she might say?"

"I just don't want to drive her away."

"Makes sense, I get it. So what would you ask Ashley if there were no repercussions?"

"I want to know the rumor or story in full, the details her work people know."

"So you would like her to give you the full story of that night?"

"Yes, but I don't know how I could handle it coming from her."

"But hearing additional details would be erotic for you, right? I mean, it has turned you on thinking about that night?"

"Yeah, and I know how fucked up that sounds."

"It doesn't sound fucked up. You learned of another side of Ashley's sexuality and after the hurt and the shock, it began to excite you. That's a very common male reaction."

"Not in the men I know," I typed. "No guy or friend of mine would react that way."

"Don't be so sure, Dave. You would be surprised, believe me."

"Well, I've talked to guys online who've had similar reactions, but it's a skewed sample for sure."

"Trust me, Dave, it's a lot more common, and you'd be surprised what goes on behind closed doors. So, you masturbate thinking about your wife in the bathroom?"

"Yes."

"Very common," Mike replied, "and I want to get back to that … but it seems to me you're looking for reassurance. What would you like to hear from Ashley?"

"That it was an aberration. That she truly does love me, is happy with me, has no thoughts of leaving me."

"Why don't you ask her?"

"I did. She said she loves me, but I'm insecure."

"OK, did you ask her why she did it?"

"Not directly. I asked if she got caught up in the moment and she cribbed that back to me, saying, 'Yes, that's what happened.' "

"How did the conversation end?"

"I couldn't deal and I changed the subject."

"Do you think she would have elaborated or wanted to explain more, had you not changed the subject?"

"I don't know."

"Have you told her that while it hurt, part of it was a turn-on for you?"

"No, I could never tell her that."

"Why not?"

"I think she'd lose all respect for me. Or whatever respect she still has."

"She might have more respect for you for being honest and open about your feelings and emotions. Did you ever think of that?"

"I don't buy that."

"Why not?"

"Because she would think it was off the charts weird. She humiliated me that night, fucking this guy with me right outside, and I react by masturbating. I can't tell her that."

"You don't have to tell her that. You can tell her that part of you was turned on by her sexuality."

"No," I typed, "I just couldn't. There's too much to lose."

"I understand, and I realize you're scared and overwhelmed. But can I give you an outsider's perspective?"

"Sure," I typed.

"You have every right to be upset with her over what she did. And her mimicking back your rationale—that she got caught up in the moment—is kind of weak. But, even if she wasn't honest that first night, she did admit to it when you asked. I know you didn't like hearing the guy had a bigger cock than you, but you pressed the question, and she was just being honest. And maybe she had more to say, but you changed the subject."

"I was flustered," I typed.

"I understand that, Dave, but maybe realize you both have played a role in sweeping this under the rug. Ashley did eventually come clean, but you haven't come clean with her."

"How do you mean?"

"Ashley doesn't know that part of it turned you on, or how much you're consumed with it now, because you've shared none of that with her. You've become a lot more closed about it than she has. Honesty and openness is a two-way street, and right now they seem to be coming only from her."

"I can't tell her that."

"That elephant in the room is only going to get bigger. Every day you don't talk to her, you're simply feeding that elephant."

"Are you married?" I asked.

"No," he replied, "but I have friends who have gone through very similar stuff."

"How did it work out for them?"

"The ones who are together and whose marriages are stronger," he replied, "were open with their wives."

"I want to be honest with her," I typed, "but it's a very embarrassing thing to admit."

"What's embarrassing?"

"That I was turned on."

"Well, the rumor was embarrassing for her, yet she still told you."

"I think the only reason she told me was that she assumed I'd already heard."

"Maybe so, but she didn't run from it."

"Eventually, no."

"Where are you guys from?"

"Manhattan UWS."

"OK, I'm from Brooklyn myself. So telling Ashley it turned you on is not something you feel comfortable doing?"

"No."

"OK, so you want to find out if it truly was an aberrant 'caught up in the moment' event, or if she's still seeing or wants to see other guys. Is that it?"

"Yes," I said, "that's a lot of it."

"And the other part is you want to know the details, but that's really not the critical part, that would simply satisfy your curiosity?"

"Yeah," I typed, "I guess I want to know why she did it."

"OK, so, the questions are why did she do it and does she have inclinations to do something like it again."

"Yes, exactly."

"I get it," he replied, "so maybe you take what motivated her to do it first. That may well indicate if she's inclined to do it again."

"I don't know what motivated her."

"Dave, I'm just saying, in your next talk with her, you ask her questions that allow her to hint about her motivations. You don't have to tackle the world the first time out. But you do need to start talking to her about this."

"Yeah," I said, "well, I think her friend had a lot to do with it. When she told the guy to whip it out, I'm suspecting Ashley was intrigued by his size."

"Yeah, that may be, or maybe she was just being adventurous. Are you particularly small?"

"I'm like six."

"OK, so you don't have a big cock, but you're in the normal range."

"Yeah, but I told you about her 'Just bigger OK' comment."

"Which got you hard, right?"

"Yeah, but it made me feel inadequate, too, and probably added to my premature issues."

"Look, I do think the guy's cock size probably had something to do it with it. If you truly want answers, you're going to have to be prepared for that."

"How do you mean?"

"Well," he wrote, "he was stroking it right in front of her, so she saw he had a bigger cock than yours. And she was probably flattered and excited when she was picked—you said her friend is quite attractive, right?"

"Yeah."

"Well, when her friend asked which one he wanted to fuck your wife could have left, but instead she waited for his answer. And Ashley was probably excited to have been chosen. She was curious to know what his cock felt like. And she didn't put conditions on it. She didn't insist on condoms. She probably wanted to feel it in all its naturalness."

"I know," I said.

"I'm not trying to bring you down, but if her motivations are what you want, you're going to have to be prepared for those answers."

"Yeah, I know."

"But you're going to need those answers. Because if Ashley's curious about experimenting with another big cock, you don't want her running around behind your back, right?"

"No, I don't."

"OK," he said, "so prepare yourself for what you might hear and then have a talk with her. Sound like a plan?"

"Yeah, it does, actually, thank you. I appreciate you talking to me."

"No thanks necessary, bro. You seem like a cool guy in a tough situation."

"Yeah, kind of. I don't have anyone in regular life to talk to about this."

"What about the guys you've talked to online? Have you gotten helpful perspective?"

"Yeah, I talked to a few in a similar boat but got verbally bitch-slapped last night."

"Bitch-slapped?"

"Just guys trying to rub it in, telling me how they would fuck my wife and stuff."

"Did that turn you on?"

"I was drunk. I think I listened because it was how I imagined the guy who fucked my wife would talk to me. This morning I wanted to puke and felt like a fool."

"Why did you feel like a fool?"

"I sent out some wedding and honeymoon photos of her and us, and some of these guys were local."

"You didn't give them your phone number, did you?"

"No. I got asked for that and my wife's screen name and email, but thankfully, I wasn't drunk enough to do that."

"Well it's a very good thing you didn't," he replied, "sounds like you were talking to a bunch of vultures—chat rooms like this are full of them. They are about exploiting any vulnerability. If you had given out your wife's email, don't think for a second that they wouldn't be doing everything possible to try and seduce your wife."

"Oh I inferred that for sure."

"The photos of Ashley—was she nude?"

"No."

"Good. Were there any you would be embarrassed about?"

"No but one guy jerked off on a photo of us posing at our wedding and sent back to me with his cum on her face. Which was a fuck-you to me."

"Hmm, yeah, those type of guys can be like that."

"I was drunk and wasn't thinking."

"Let me get a sense of how what you sent."

"It was nothing she wouldn't have on Facebook."

"Well, I understand if you don't want to send them. I'm just looking to help."

"OK," I typed, "I'll forward them. One sec."

"Well you do have a beautiful wife there," he wrote. "I can see why you wouldn't want to lose her. You're an attractive couple."

"Thanks," I replied. "It's also that she has a great, down-to-earth personality."

"Yeah, she expresses that," he replied. "Who's the other blond girl in that beach photo?"

"The girl she was with at the party. That photo is from Florida."

"I just sent you a picture of me," Mike said, "just so you know who you're talking to. And my full name is Mike Janson. You can easily find me on Facebook—there's only one Mike Janson from Brooklyn, on Facebook at least."

I opened up the photo and looked at the guy, a young-looking, clean-cut guy with a friendly smile.

"I just wanted you to put a face on who you're talking to as well," he said. "I don't hide behind my computer like some other guys.

"Look," he continued, "the most pressing goal here seems to be figuring out whether it was a fluke thing or whether she's inclined to do something like this again, right?"

"Exactly."

"OK, and secondly, if she does open up, you want to make sure you're prepared. You don't want to be flustered and suddenly changing the subject."

"Yeah, I hear you."

"So when you are ready to talk to her again," he said, "don't start at the front door, go through the back door."

"Back door?"

"Well, she told you how embarrassed she was about people at work knowing, and how she might have to look for another job, right?"

"Yeah."

"So ask her if it's gotten any better there—has the rumor become yesterday's news—so then you're not talking about how it affected you, but you're asking how it's affecting her."

"That's a good point," I replied.

"And you can baby-step this and just listen to what she has to say. You may be able to discern a bit of how that night came to happen from what she says, and even if you don't, you've started a dialogue and can proceed further the next time."

"I hear you, man."

"You want to make this about her," he went on, "it's not about begrudging her for what she did, it's about making her feel comfortable to talk about it. Your opening is, 'Have things gotten better at work?' "

"That's great advice, Mike, thank you."

"You bet bro. You seem like an honest and thoughtful guy in a temporary sand trap. It happens. Think of me as a friend, because that's how I think of you."

"Thanks Mike, I really do appreciate it."

"Anytime … Oh, and Dave?"

"Yeah?"

"I have to run for now, but no more talking to guys who want to exploit you when you're down. They don't care about you or your marriage. They're looking for any window to sabotage it."

"Yeah, I know it was stupid."

"Don't sweat it, bro. We all get stupid sometimes, just something to learn from."

CHAPTER NINETEEN

shley and I met my parents for dinner Monday night. They had just come from a cocktail reception at MOMA, and Ashley was connecting with my mom on some impressionist paintings she'd seen.

"So," my dad asked me, "when are you meeting your brother out in Las Vegas?"

"Friday," I said. "I have to be in San Francisco for business on Wednesday and I'm flying to Vegas from there."

"You don't sound very enthusiastic," my mom observed.

"Well, it will be good to see Sean, but I really only got the bachelor party invite because I'm Sean's brother and he's the best man. It's not like Patrick and I are really friends."

"Oh, come on," my mom said. "You all grew up together. He invited you because he wants you there."

"Mom," I said, patting her, "that would work when I'm fifteen, but he's Sean's friend. At least he doesn't give me wedgies anymore, I'll grant you that."

"Yeah but it's still Vegas, right?" Ashley interjected. "I mean let's bright-side things."

"Honestly," I said, "if I wasn't already going to be on the West Coast, I'd be thinking of ways to bail."

"I'm sure it will be fun," my mom said.

"Well, knowing Sean and Patrick," my dad said, "they'll see to that, which is what worries me."

Ashley laughed and said, "What worries you?"

"You really want to know Ashley?" my dad said. "I'm not saying Sean's not responsible, but in a few years he'll be forty and he still sometimes thinks he's twenty-one."

"Did you ever feel that way about Dave?" Ashley asked.

My dad looked over at me.

"Hey, stop right now," I said with a smile. "We were simply talking about my Vegas trip."

"Even as a teenager, Ashley," my dad said, "David was more grounded."

"Can we please change the subject," I said.

"Oh, I almost forgot, Ashley," my mom said, "I heard from the Seevers that you were the consummate host the other weekend at the pool, and they loved your Bloody Marys."

"Oh my God," Ashley said. "I can't tell you what a godsend your pool was that day. It was such a great escape from the city. And your neighbors were a lot of fun."

"Oh, and I gave Jay your address," my mom said.

"What?" I said.

"He said he invited you to his birthday party."

"Yeah?" I said.

"He told me yesterday he wanted to send you an invitation."

"You gave him our home address?" I asked.

Ashley looked at me funny.

"Yes, he's turning fifty. He said he told you about it?"

"Yeah," I said, and then Ashley followed with "Yeah."

"Well, we'll be away on Block Island, but if you want to go, you can stay at the house, of course."

"Well, we're not sure what we're doing that weekend. We'll play it by ear," I said.

Conversation swiveled back to some book my mom was reading and Ashley was hitting her up with questions. My dad had read the book, too, and was chiming in.

I just sat there, pretending to care.

****

"Was your mom holding back?" Ashley asked, as we lay in bed.

"About what?"

"She didn't say anything about Jay being unstable or domestic abuse or stalker stuff."

"My mom's not going to gossip like that."

"I know," she replied, "but she'd say something, right, like don't go to his party?"

"Oh, she would, if she actually thought we would go," I said. "I wasn't making up that stuff about Jay."

"I know. I wasn't saying you were."

But after Ashley fell asleep, I thought about what my mom had done. She's not stupid, especially when it comes to a person's character. Why would Jay make an additional effort by asking my mom for our address? How could my mom not see his motivations? Could she think he would have ever invited me solo? No, he was only inviting me because he wanted to get with my wife. I'd be just some pesky, slightly inconvenient, obstacle for his friends to distract.

Mom, do you realize what Jay was actually asking?

"Can I get your son's address? I want to fuck your daughter-in-law, your son's wife. I want your son to bring her to me."

The fucking chutzpah of some guys.

Hey Jay! You think I'm going to RSVP "yes" and bring my wife out to you like some kind of birthday fuck present? That I'm going to dither obliviously while you take her up to your bedroom?

You are fucking out of your mind. You're fifty years old, you dirty old man. Yeah, I'm sure you could kick my ass, or try and make a fool of me with your blue-collar biker-type losers, or have them pull interference on me, but guess what? We're not fucking showing.

****

By Tuesday night there was a card in our mailbox.

There was a pretty generic "please join us" card inside, but on the back, Jay had left a personalized note:

> Ashley and Dave, I had a great time the other weekend
> and I would love to have you out to the house for the
> party. Ashley, if you can get out here early, I'd love to

take you for a ride on my pasta rocket—I'm sure you'll have a blast!

Jesus Christ, I thought, *was this guy fucking serious?* Ride on his fucking pasta rocket? How was he not implying he wanted Ashley riding on his big fat Italian cock? Jay had to know I would see the invite. Perhaps he didn't give a fuck. Just like he hadn't that day by the pool.

"I know you're not man enough to stand up to me," I pictured him saying.

****

I was leaving for the San Francisco office in the morning before going to Vegas on Friday.

I wasn't happy about being away from Ashley for four nights and started thinking of what to do with the invite. I left it under some papers on my desk.

"I forgot about it," I could always say later, "we weren't really planning on going out there anyway, right?"

Ashley had a work dinner, so I went back online and saw Mike. I had put the other guys who had messaged me on *Ignore*.

"I thought about what you said," I told him. "I'm heading out of town for business and a bachelor party, but I plan on having another talk with her when I get back."

"Good for you man," he replied, "and don't over-think it. Focus on the things you NEED to know, and save what you WANT to know for later."

"Right," I typed, "well, I liked your idea of cloaking it as asking about her job."

"Yeah, be gentle and understanding, but ask open-ended questions, nothing she can say yes or no to. You want her to simply start talking, communicating about this. You want to starve that elephant in the room, and send him running for the hills."

"Yeah, I hear you."

"How long are you away for?"

"Four nights. Leaving tomorrow night and back on Sunday."

"Does that worry you? Will you be wondering what she's up to?"

"Well, I'm going to miss her primarily, but yeah, I'm sure I will be wondering. There's some older guy where my parents live, who flirted with her the weekend before last, and he just sent us an invite to a party."

"Who's the guy?"

"Some construction guy who was ogling over Ashley when we were at my parents' pool."

"Who is he?"

"A neighbor with his own construction business. He's turning fifty. He gave Ashley his number and openly flirted with her."

"What was Ashley's reaction to him flirting?"

"It's hard to tell because she's friendly with everyone, but she was running in to get him beers and jiggling her tits in her bikini. And they talked a lot."

"How did you feel about that?"

"Awkward," I replied, "and a little intimidated, to be honest."

"But Ashley hasn't called him, has she?"

"I doubt it, no. Like I said, I think she was just trying to be the friendly hostess."

"What was the party invitation you mentioned?"

"He's throwing himself a happy-birthday-to-me party. Well, he invited us and we said we'd think about it. He asked my mom for our address and I got the invite tonight."

"Are you gonna go?" Mike asked.

"No, and what he wrote has me peeved."

"What did he write?"

"Well, as I mentioned, he was openly flirtatious with her, and he had talked about motorcycles and Ashley joked how she likes to ride 'pasta rockets', which I've since learned is slang for Italian bikes."

"Never heard the term myself."

"Yeah, and he wrote in the note for Ashley to come early, so he could give her a ride on his pasta rocket."

"OK, bro, you need to watch out with this guy. He wants to fuck her; that's quite obvious."

"Yeah, that's what I surmised."

"Do you think Ashley has any interest in him?"

"I don't think so, and he's twenty years older."

"You said you're going to a bachelor party?" Mike asked.

"Yeah, in Vegas on Friday—a friend of my brother's."

"Are you worried about Ashley meeting up with this construction guy while you're away?"

"It's crossed my mind, but I really don't think so. And it's not in my control."

"Well, this may sound crazy, Dave, but do you want me to try and keep an eye on her when you're away? I have to work, of course, but maybe if she said she was at some bar and you wanted it confirmed, if I had time, I could maybe reassure you that she was there."

"No, but thanks," I typed. "I don't want to spy on her."

"I hear you. It doesn't bode well if you're reduced to that. That can be a problem in itself."

"Yeah," I typed, "but I am committed to having a talk with her as soon as I get back."

"Well, start thinking of what you want to say while you're away," Mike said. "Hell, even on the plane ride tomorrow, start sketching it out in your mind. Don't kick the can too far down the road. You certainly won't have time when you're in Vegas."

"Yeah," I typed, "you're right. I'll jot some themes down on the flight."

"Yeah, and keep your notes loose. Just prepare yourself for different things she might say … and potential answers."

"Yeah," I typed, "all good points. Well she's going to be home soon. I should get going."

"OK, but Dave?"

"Yeah."

"Be careful when you're in Vegas bro. Don't be talking to your friends about what happened with Ashley at the party."

"Oh, I won't," I replied, "I can't and haven't talked to anyone I know about this."

"I know you haven't. I'm just throwing out a friendly caution. I know how I get talking after a lot of drinks. You might feel better getting it off your chest, but this is not a 'what happens in Vegas, stays in Vegas' kind of thing. It doesn't matter how close you are as friends. I've seen your wife, and if you got real with them, I guarantee they would see the open sign and be scheming to fuck her when you get back."

"There's no way I would tell them," I said, "but yeah, I am definitely going to back-pocket your reminder."

CHAPTER TWENTY

As she was leaving for work, Ashley pointed at me and said, "Now, no funny business in Vegas, mister."

"Oh all right" I said, like she'd just rained on my parade.

"And don't come back with any missing teeth."

"Yeah, Ash," I said, "I'm really going to miss you."

"I miss you already," she replied, before heading out the door.

****

My meetings in San Francisco went well. And on both nights Ashley and I talked for a while. I was glad to be boarding the quick flight. In two days I'd be back with my wife.

The Vegas heat hit me as soon I stepped onto the boarding ramp. "One hundred six degrees," one of the airline support guys said when he saw my expression.

My brother Sean was waiting for me in the airport bar. "Starting a little early," I said, as he stood up and gave me a hug. "Is that a shot?"

"It's tequila. You got to love Vegas. You order a beer, they offer a shot for three dollars more. I don't turn down good deals. I've been waiting so long for your sorry ass that this is my fifth."

"Jesus," I said.

"I'm kidding, my flight was late, too—this is only my second— but get ready, little bro, this is only the second of many."

****

"It's probably too early for check-in," he said, as we got in the taxi. "You don't mind making a pit stop?"

"A strip bar?" I asked, rolling my eyes.

"No, a spray tan."

"Are you freaking serious?" I said, "that's a little gay, now, isn't it, Sean?"

"Sure it is, but I read reviews about this place. You can't tell it's fake."

"Oh c'mon Sean."

"Hey, I plan on getting laid while I'm here, and with the rain in D.C. this summer ... anyway, you look whiter than me. You could use one yourself."

"Like hell, I'm not going back to work on Monday looking orange."

"You won't, bro, trust me, it will look good. C'mon, we're in Vegas, just roll with it."

****

Twenty minutes later, I was listening to an automated woman's voice telling me to strip naked and stand on metal footprints. I closed my eyes as this cold chemical sprayed both sides of my body.

"Pretty painless, right?" Sean said when I met him outside a few minutes later.

"No it won't look fake," I said. "Like who has a tanned ass? What are you going to tell the girl—how you spent the summer in Ibiza?"

"That's good," Sean said, "just one more pit stop, little bro."

"What now? A stripclub?"

"No, the supermarket. There's a fridge in the suite, and there's a Von's on Flamingo."

The supermarket was far enough from the Strip that we were shopping with Vegas locals, or locals from a certain depressed neighborhood. Everything about the shoppers said "down and out"—their vacant eyes, their missing teeth, the way they screamed at their kids. I was thinking, *crystal-meth addicts*.

It didn't seem to bother Sean as he filled the cart up with mixers and frozen food. I just wanted out of there. While I was waiting outside for the cab we'd called, a panhandler came up to me.

I didn't reply to his question, at first trying to ignore him.

"Are you foreign?" he asked. "Do you not speak English?"

"No habla," I said.

"Spanish, you speak Spanish?"

"Si," I replied. Then he rattled off something in Spanish. I'd forgotten all that I learned from high school.

"I'm just waiting, sorry," I said.

"So you do speak English?"

"What?"

"Well, fuck you, man."

This haggard old raggedy man with no teeth was suddenly pointing a finger in my chest. "You're a coward and a liar. Go fuck yourself. Did you hear what I said?"

"Yeah, I heard, I'm sorry," I replied.

"Go fuck yourself, man. I don't want your fucking money, it's shit people like fucking you—"

I saw the cab pull up and ran to flag it down.

****

We checked into our suite and hauled everything up.

I lifted my t-shirt as I looked in the mirror. That spray tan shit really worked.

Sean went down to scope out the pool as I put my clothes away and checked in with Ashley.

I thought the knock on the door was Sean having forgotten his key, but it was Patrick. "You fucking made it," he said, as he gave me a hug.

"Congratulations," I said, hugging him back. "Why would you even question that I would make it?"

Patrick responded by pretending to mimic my voice when I was twelve, "I'm sorry Sean, I mean, I meant to go to your football game, but you see, I set the alarm clock for p.m. instead of a.m., and it was raining, and dad took my umbrella, and I mean the high school is like at least a mile walk—"

"Jeez, Patrick" I broke in, "that story is over twenty years old. Isn't there a statute of limitations on shit like that?"

"It was our championship game!" he said and slapped my stomach. "I'm just kidding Dave, I'm really glad you came. So, where's big bro?"

****

Beers by the pool led to a steak dinner and then a strip club.

Of the ten guys there, the only other guy I knew was Badger. He and Sean were off talking up a stripper, and I felt like the rest of the guys were thinking, "Who invited this stick in the mud?"

One of the guys rode me for refusing a lap dance. I thought about what Mike had said about getting drunk and blabbing about what happened. Two of the guys were single and lived in New York—the kind who would pull a Jim Murta on my ass if they saw any opportunity.

Around midnight, I discreetly pulled Sean aside and told him I was heading back. He gave me the obligatory, drunken big brother hard time, but he was also distracted by girls. I put $150 down on the table where a few guys remained and hightailed my way on out of there.

I called Ashley and left a message.

Back in our suite, I sat on the balcony, waiting for Ashley's return call, watching planes land at McCarren's airport.

Three hours later, I was in bed, still waiting. Ashley still hadn't responded. No phone call, no text, no nothing.

Then I heard a commotion. It was Sean, who was soon in our bedroom. "Hey little bro, Badger and I brought a girl back."

"OK," I said.

"I mean, so I'm going to shut the door, OK?"

"What?"

"Bro, we're gonna try and pull off the tag-team. She's never tried it, but she's drunk and curious."

"Who's the girl?"

"A hot twenty-five-year-old UCLA grad student we met at the Bellagio."

"Oh," I said.

"She's here for her bachelorette party," Sean continued. "She's getting married in six weeks."

"You mean the girl you brought back is about to get married?" I said.

"Yeah, look I know you're trying to sleep and I know this is an imposition, but I'm gonna shut the door, but you understand?"

"Yeah, sure."

Suddenly hip-hop music started cranking and I could hear loud drunken talk and laughter. I went up to the door to listen, but the music drowned things out.

****

I woke up to the sound of Sean and Badger's voices in the other room. It was 11 a.m. in New York, and still no reply from Ashley.

I knocked on the door to make sure I wasn't interrupting. Sean was lying on one couch and Badger on the other.

"What happened to the girl?" I asked.

"She had to get back to her friends," Badger replied. "She left a few hours ago."

"So she was having her bachelorette party?" I said. "That's how you met her?"

"She was at a bar with her friends," Badger replied, "her actual party is tonight."

"Badge had his A-Game going last night," Sean said.

"How so?" I asked.

"He had this girl in his sights, laid down his rap, got Patrick and Casey to distract her friends, and that's when I came in."

"Yeah and—?" I said.

"Major props to you, bro," Sean said over to Badger.

"We were getting it done old school, bro," Badger replied, smiling.

"OK," I said, "so Sean said you were gonna tag team her last night—any luck?"

"Oh yeah," Badger replied.

"Both ends," Sean added.

"Meaning?" I said.

"Pussy and mouth," Sean said.

"Jesus," I said.

"That's what Vegas is about," Sean offered.

"I guess," I said. "So the girl was into it?"

"Oh hell, yeah," Badger replied, "she was all horned out, going to town like it was a full cock nine-ninety-nine, all you can eat buffet."

"Yeah," Sean followed, "we were high-fiving and shit, but Badger had to go an' piss her off."

"How so?" I said.

"OK," Sean said, "so I'm fucking this girl on the couch and she's blowing the Badge, and after a while I blew my load."

"Were you wearing a condom?"

"Yeah, of course."

"OK."

"So then Badger starts fucking her and she tells him she just came, so he pulls out, whips off his condom and tells her to blow him again."

"And?"

"So she went back to blowing him, but she kept saying, 'Don't cum in my mouth, cum on my tits.' "

"So what does this motherfucker do?" Sean asked me.

Badger started laughing.

"Came in her mouth?" I asked, looking over at Badger.

"No," Sean replied, "all over this girl's face."

"The girl was fucking stunned and just took it … but boy, was she pissed."

"What did she say?" I asked.

"Jesus Christ, you bastard," Badger said, trying to imitate a girl's voice, "I can't believe you just came on my face. Then she looked at herself in the mirror and she really freaked—"

"Dude, her face was coated in cum," Sean added. "It was like a freaking porno."

"Yeah," Badger added, "but then she saw I had gotten her hair."

"Yeah," Sean said, "she was freaking how she'd just gotten her hair done, and she had a big splash atop her head."

"Jesus," I said.

"So Badger's acting like what's the big deal, it's not like you've never taken a facial before."

"And?" I asked.

"She was like, 'Fuck you,' " Badger said, " 'I've never taken no fucking facial before, you asshole, I can't believe you just did that to me. I said to cum on my tits.' "

"Wow."

"So Badger says, 'Oh come on, I'm sure your fiancé's blasted on your face before,' and she's like, 'No, he never has. I can't believe this, look at me.' "

"I told her she looked hot all glazed," Badger said, laughing.

"Then she saw text messages on her phone," Sean added. "Her friends were looking for her. Badger offered to give her cab money back to the Bellagio, but she told him to fuck himself."

"So she left?"

"No, she kept bitching me out," Badger said, "and she kept looking at herself in the mirror, saying, 'I can't believe you just did this to me, I'm a fucking mess.' "

"Yeah," Sean said, "so Badger got tired of her ranting and handed back her clothes and told her the door was that-a-way."

"Oh my God."

"Crocodile tears," Badger said. "She enjoyed slobbering over my cock."

"Sure," Sean said, "and you respected what she said—'Don't cum in my mouth'—and you didn't. You tried for her tits, but hey, your aim was off."

"Here, check her out," Badger said, showing me a picture on his cell phone. "Her name's Jessica. She's getting married in Redondo Beach, Columbus Day weekend."

I was thinking he might have something explicit to show me, but here was just a pretty, young, blond girl smiling with Badger at the bar. She had a sweet girl-next-door look.

Not someone I'd expect to get tag-teamed by two older guys she met in a Vegas club.

****

After breakfast they all went to play Craps. I said I had to get back to my boss and went up to the room. I kept looking at my cell, making sure my battery was charged. It was now early afternoon in New York.

I lay in the bed thinking about what Sean and Badger had told me. Her poor fiancé was probably sitting home in L.A., waiting for Jessica to return from her bachelorette weekend. When she saw him, she'd be saying, "Oh, we just lay by the pool during the day, drank at the bars and gambled—goofy little bachelorette stuff."

She certainly wouldn't be telling him how she fucked two thirty-seven-year old guys back in their hotel room, taking one cock in her pussy and another in her mouth. And she certainly wouldn't be telling him how pissed off she was when one of them blasted his sperm right in her face, how she had to take the hotel elevator down with the guy's load dripping off her.

Good Lord, I thought, Badger had really done a number on this girl … the long trek back to her hotel, her clothes disheveled and his sperm dripping off her face.

Badger and Sean were Jim Murta types—strapping alpha males who saw in "taken" girls, opportunities. And Badger had no qualms about adding his own special cherry on top.

I thought of what I knew of the girl … Jessica, UCLA grad student, twenty-five, getting married in Redondo Beach, Columbus Day weekend. With some Google cross-referencing, I could probably find the girl's wedding announcement or wedding site. I was a total stranger who knew far more about what this girl did last night than her soon-to-be-husband ever would.

I started thinking of just how slutty bride-to-be Jessica had been. As Badger said, she had chosen to come back with them. She knew she'd be taking two cocks last night, and she had wanted that. She just wasn't expecting a face full of sperm.

Her fiancé back home wouldn't be able to even process that.

That's right chump, I thought … My thirty-seven-year-old brother and his buddy were tag-teaming your wife's UCLA-grad-student pussy this weekend in a Vegas hotel as she celebrated marrying you … While you were sitting at home watching TV, your bride to be was chugging cocks … That's right, plural … She was probably on her knees slobbering from one to the other before taking it both ways—her mouth and puss. She'll be thinking about it on her way home to see you … And Badger topped it off, laid down the cherry on you, boy … He blew a fat load in your fiancée's face— I hear it was dripping off her—and then, as she's trying to put her bra and panties back on, your fiancée's practically being pushed out into the hallway, and she's walking the streets of Vegas, her face smeared in cum …

Suddenly I thought back to Ashley. Badger would have no qualms about pulling the double-cock stunt on my wife if he sensed she was game. I doubted it would matter that I was Sean's brother. He'd seize the opportunity to slut any wife out, including mine.

Had Ashley ever thought of the more-than-one guy thing? Was she trying it this weekend—seizing the "My husband is thousands of miles away" opportunity?

Could she have pulled out Jay's card and called the prick? Was she riding up and down on Jay's fucking pasta rocket? Could Jay have invited one of his biker friends over to join him in seducing her … just like Sean and Badger had done with Jessica? Could Ashley have been chugging cock, while Jay was pumping his big cock into her pussy?

Holy fuck, Ashley, I thought, why haven't you fucking called me?

I pictured Jay and his biker friend switching positions as Ashley's pussy and mouth were filled with cock. Jay's the type of guy who would cum on a girl's face, who'd top it off with that kind of cherry.

"Oh my God, Jay, please, not my fucking wife … oh God, he's doing it, he's fucking my wife, he's doing the double Jim Murta on me, laughing at clueless me. Please Jay, no …"

"Too bad, chump. I'm so going to do it, Dave. I'm going to cum right in your wife's fucking face. Ashley's about to take a hot messy facial. How do you like them fucking apples, boy?"

Suddenly I came royally hard.

And then I felt royally empty and alone … thousands of miles from home.

****

I didn't hear from Ashley until I'd joined the group by the pool.

"Sorry about being MIA," she said. "I just got my phone back after leaving it in a cab last night."

"Where are you now?"

"On a train back to the city. I had to ride up to Katonah to get it back from the guy who found it. He works in Manhattan, but I didn't want to wait until Monday. I had to take a cab to his golf club—such a hassle."

I heard the Metro-North station announcement in the background.

"So what are you up to?" she asked.

"Just hanging by the pool"

"Wow, rub it in, why don't you."

"It's not that at all," I said. "I'd rather be hanging by my parents' pool with you right now."

"Aww, that's sweet. Me, too."

"Well, I'm looking forward to seeing you tomorrow. I've really missed you, Ash."

"I'm looking forward to it, too."

I felt relieved. I jumped into the pool and floated on my back, thinking that by this time tomorrow, I'd be on my way home.

CHAPTER TWENTY-ONE

I felt like kissing the ground as I got off the plane.
There was a text from Ashley, telling me to join her at a bar. She was with Tamara and two other girlfriends I didn't know. Tamara was the last person I wanted to see, but I really wanted to see my wife, and I was going to have to deal with Tamara sometime.

Ashley gave me a big hug and kiss when I showed up with my luggage in tow and summoned the waitress to get me a drink. Tamara stood up and gave me a hug. As I sat down I said "hi" to the other two friends.

"So how was Vegas?" Tamara asked.

"It was fun," I replied. "It's Vegas, right? How can you not have a good time? I lost a hundred bucks at blackjack, but who cares, right? It's the price of having fun."

"It was a bachelor party, right?" Tamara asked.

"Yeah," I said, "for a friend of my brother's."

"Well," she said, "did you behave yourself?"

"Oh, yeah. C'mon, of course."

"I was just kidding," Tamara replied. "I'm sure you did, Dave."

There was an awkward silence.

"You know," I said, "when a buddy is getting married, you do the obligatory strip club scene, which is so played and boring, but I'll tell you this much, I didn't lose a tooth or wake up with a tiger in the bathroom."

Tamara smiled as I said, "You see, Ash? All my teeth, all still here."

"Did you get some sleep on the plane?" Ashley asked.

"No, but I flew Virgin, so I had a TV. A CNBC documentary on the housing meltdown kept me distracted from Indiana to when I landed."

"And that didn't put you to sleep?" Tamara asked.

"Well, I also checked out HGTV," I replied. "I got tips on how to remodel a kitchen, which I can back-pocket for when Ash and I buy a house."

Finally, gratefully, one of the other girls talked about some old, batty woman she works with. The woman sent an email and clicked the "send to all" button. And where this old woman worked, that meant three hundred employees' email in-boxes.

"She was warning us all," the girl said, "about not drinking some soda out of a can and how the media wasn't reporting it. But she wrote how rats had recently infested a plant, and how five people from various states in the last two weeks had died from rat feces' poisoning. She bought into this obvious Internet hoax. She actually wrote the word 'feces' in a company-wide email."

"Can I asked a practical question?" I said. "Why hasn't this woman been shit-canned yet?"

Tamara laughed and gave me an unusually supportive glance.

This was my chance to leave on a good note. I didn't want to alter the all-girl dynamic for long.

"Hey Dave," Tamara said, "we're having a work happy hour this Friday night. I know you had to work late that last time, but you should come out if you can. It'll be fun."

"Oh yeah, sure," I said.

Ashley said she'd meet me back home in a bit and hugged me goodbye.

My stamina in bed with Ashley was only slightly improved that night.

****

After I came home from work the next day, I had laundry to do.

I take my shirts in, but we had a washer and dryer recently installed. On the second load, I went into Ashley's hamper, just to fill the washer up and help her out. As I was throwing her clothes in, I found a t-shirt that startled me. It was plain white, with the word

"Submissive" in black lettering on the front. Above it was some sort of calligraphy, vaguely Arabic, maybe the word 'Submissive' translated into another language.

I had never seen the shirt before and had a sinking feeling. Why and where would she be wearing a shirt proclaiming such a thing? How could the connotation be anything but sexual?

I left the t-shirt, washed and folded, sitting atop her clothes on a chair.

"So I see you were going through my hamper," Ashley said when she arrived back from the gym.

"I had a light load," I explained, "so I thought I'd help you out."

"So are you asking for me to explain it?" she said.

"What?"

"The t-shirt—you didn't just randomly leave it on the top of my clothes."

"I hadn't seen it before," I replied, "so I was curious. What's it from? I didn't see any tour dates on the back, so I figure it's not some new rock band."

"It's nothing, Dave, we got it as a goof."

"We? How do you mean?"

"Me and Tamara—for a party last weekend. The theme was to be provocative. Well, that was our last minute, lame effort."

"How do you mean?"

"We bought matching t-shirts, only I picked out hers and she picked out mine. The dare was to wear whatever the other selected."

"Oh, so Tamara wore one as well?"

"Yeah."

"You both wore matching shirts?"

"No, I chose 'slut' for her and she chose 'submissive' for me—it was all a goof."

"Oh, OK," I said. "I didn't mean anything by it. How did it go over? I mean, at the party?"

"We didn't win any prizes," she replied, "but at least we had something."

"OK," I said.

"Are you upset?"

"No, I was simply asking, Ashley. You explained it, no big deal. Let's forget it, babe."

But after she went to bed, I couldn't forget it.

****

I went online. Mike messaged when he saw me.

"Hey bro, how was Vegas?"

"Not great. It was my brother and his friends pushing the debauchery."

"Did you join them in the debauchery?" Mike wrote.

"No, I felt like the odd man out. I sat on the sidelines."

"And you didn't open up to them about what's going on with Ashley, right?"

"I didn't say shit, man."

"Good job."

"But here's the thing, Mike," I typed. "Tonight I found a t-shirt in Ashley's hamper that said 'submissive' on it. She explained that Tamara picked it out for her, and she picked one for Tamara, to wear as a goof, as a dare."

"Dare for what?"

"They wore it to some party where the theme was to dress provocatively."

"Does Ashley have submissive tendencies?"

"No, not that I know of, anyway."

"What did Ashley pick out for Tamara?"

"A t-shirt that said, 'slut'."

"Well, that fits Tamara, doesn't it? Why do you think Tamara would give Ashley the 'submissive' label?"

"I don't know, man."

"Do you think maybe that's how she was with the guy at the party? Submissive?"

"Can't say I haven't wondered that."

"I'm thinking there was a reason behind it, Dave. I mean, she could have given her a shirt like 'married but available' or 'easy,' but she chose 'submissive' for Ashley."

"Yeah, it's more disturbing the more I think about it."

"Did Ashley tell you about the party?"

"No, I didn't ask. I know it was this weekend. I called, but she didn't return my call until the following afternoon."

"That doesn't sound good, bro."

"Well she had a logical-sounding excuse, and Ashley doesn't make things up."

"OK, but she still went out to some party wearing a t-shirt that said 'submissive' on it, right?"

"Yes" I typed.

"While her husband was out of town."

"Yeah, I know."

"I don't know about this Tamara girl."

"I know. Me, too," I said. "I had to see her at a bar when I got back."

"How did that go?"

"She asked if I behaved myself in Vegas and when I said that I had, she said rather condescendingly, 'Of course you did,' like, 'I'm sure you were a good little boy.'"

"OK, Dave, so Tamara sounds like a conniving enabler, but what about the talk you were going to have with Ashley?"

"Tomorrow night."

"You feel confident about what you're going to say, my man? You've thought it out?"

"Yeah," I replied, "I'll be taking your advice about bringing it up when she talks about work."

"Just wait for an opening, my friend," he wrote. "Don't rush it, find the natural opening."

"Right."

"But Dave?"

"Yeah."

"Don't blow it off tomorrow. It's important—there's an urgency. You need to figure out where Ashley's head is at—like right now. You know what I'm saying?"

"Mike I totally do."

"Good man."

****

It was raining hard the next morning.

I couldn't find any of the five-dollar junk umbrellas I'd bought off the street. I had an important meeting and was wearing a thousand dollar suit. I looked for one of Ashley's large umbrellas in her bedroom closet.

"What are you doing, snooping?" Ashley asked, suddenly coming out of the bathroom.

"What?" I asked.

"What are you doing in my closet?"

"It's pouring outside. I just need an umbrella."

"Upper shelf to the left."

****

I was frantic with work meetings but on my walk home, I refocused on the conversation I would be having.

I had focused objectives.

I'd open communication by simply talking about it again. I wanted to get a better sense of where her head was at. Was it a fluke thing or did the experience still resonate? I still wanted to know more about that night, like what was going on when I knocked, but I'd feel awkward asking for details and they wouldn't be useful going forward, anyway. But sitting in the bathroom at home, I thought about her potential answer to that question.

"Yes of course I knew it was you knocking, Dave—we all knew it was you, when you said 'hello.' What was I doing when you knocked? Do you really want to know?"

"Yes, Ashley, I was just curious."

"I was sucking on Jim's big fat cock, Dave."

I imagined coughing, maybe spilling my drink a little.

"Pardon?"

"I was on my knees, my tits out in front of him, and I had his cock in my mouth when you knocked. After Tamara sent you upstairs, I went to town on Jim's big, fat, beautiful cock. Does that upset you?"

"No Ashley, I was just wondering."

"Then I took his balls in my mouth and swirled my tongue around as his cock throbbed against my face. I wanted to make that cock utterly rock hard, do you know why, Dave?"

"Why, Ashley?"

"Because I wanted it good and ultra hard for when he fucked me."

Suddenly I came.

****

Ashley and I had dinner at a neighborhood sushi restaurant.

The waiter knows us—knows what sake we like and to bring me the child version of chopsticks, because I've never bothered to master the regular kind. I was slightly distracted as Ashley talked about the upcoming weekend.

We'd be going to the Jersey shore. Mark and Camilla would be back in from Chicago, and one of Mark's friends had rented a house for the week.

At the bar after dinner, Ashley ordered a martini, so I told the bartender, "Make that two."

Ashley talked about Camilla's relationship. "Obviously I'd love for her to be out here, but I think the compromise for Mark is moving to the city," she said. "I just don't know how Camilla could handle suburban nowhere."

"Well Jersey gets a bad rap," I said. "A lot of the state is farms and picturesque grasslands."

"Oh, I know," Ashley replied, "but Mark's talking suburbia, and Camilla loves Chicago city life."

"Sure, I understand," I said, "so how are things going with that conference? You haven't mentioned it lately. Any updates?"

"Not really. The CFO's backed off somewhat on his hard-line stance, but we won't really know until we get it officially budgeted."

"OK, so it's not stressing you out as much as it was?"

"No, it's not in the positioning phase anymore, so it's kind of out of our hands."

"Have things gotten better there in general, lately?"

"How do you mean?" she asked curiously.

"Like that rumor that was going around? Has that become a thing of the past?"

"Yeah, I think to the people who matter, anyway."

"How do you mean?"

"Well, I don't think upper management holds it against me, and I don't think my boss does. It wasn't a company event. People realize you have private lives."

"So no one says anything to you?"

"Well no, of course not. I mean no one really did when it happened. It was Tamara who told me."

"Tamara told you?"

"Yeah, that there was a rumor going around about us that Monday. And yeah, I started thinking I should get my résumé in order."

"It must have been horrible," I said.

"Oh, it was. I'm not the kind of girl who cries at work, but I was in meltdown mode. I went into the ladies room and cried like crazy that Monday."

I reached out and patted her shoulder. "I'm sure it must have been incredibly difficult."

"Well that first week was really hard. It's embarrassing being gossiped about. And having to stand up and give a presentation to sales, knowing that they all had heard."

"I'm sure," I said, "I don't know how you handled that."

"Well, my boss has my back, and after the first week I realized something about myself."

"What's that?" I asked, "what did you realize?"

"That I wasn't going to let something like that break me or bring me down. And my friends are still my friends. And upper management judges me on my performance and ability."

"Sure."

"I mean I'm not naïve," she said.

"Not naive about what?"

"I'm not so naive to think people have forgotten what happened, and some people probably still do talk about me, but I'm not going to let it bother me. I'm like, 'To hell with them.' I'm not going to continue to be embarrassed. I've moved on."

"That's great," I said. "Do you feel like people treat you differently?"

"Some of the sales guys do, sure. Like they'll flirt now, where they wouldn't before. And I have a sixty-year-old client who I'm sure knows, because he's a lot more flirtatious since."

"How do you feel about that?"

"I let it roll off me. It's become a big-whatever."

"How about Jim?"

"What about him?"

"Do you have to interact with him? Is it weird?"

"It was, and I was mega-pissed at him, obviously. But last week, he asked if we could take a walk and he groveled and apologized profusely."

"What did he say?"

"Just how terribly sorry he was, how he never intended for any rumors to start."

"So he admitted he started it?"

"Yeah, but how that wasn't his intention."

"What did he say?"

"He said that when he was back out at the party, he told Chris and Greg—two sales guys who were there—what had happened in confidence."

"So later that night—like, afterwards—he told them? While at the party?"

"Yeah, he said he wasn't thinking and was buzzed and told them not to say anything. But then one of them told someone else and someone else told someone else. He was as surprised, upset and embarrassed to hear about it as I was. He said he was a monumental idiot and basically begged me to forgive him."

"What did you say back?"

"Well, I could hold a grudge and avoid him forever, or I could just write it off as him being buzzed and in a moment of immaturity. And I don't think he would have intentionally spread that story about me. So I forgave him."

"And things have been OK with him since?"

"Yeah, we got past it. Things are cool with us now."

"That's good," I replied, not knowing what else to say. We ordered up two more martinis and I stared off at some random soccer game.

"Well it's been a bit weird and embarrassing for me as well," I said.

"How so?"

"Well like when I got back from Vegas and hung out with your friends and Tamara—that was weird for me. I mean, I know how Tamara feels about me."

"What was weird?"

"I just felt like a third wheel, like I got a 'What's he doing here' vibe."

"Oh, not at all," Ashley replied. "She even asked where you were. When I told her your flight was coming in, she said, 'Tell Dave to swing by, it'd be good to see him.' "

"Well, I get a sense she doesn't like me much."

"She likes you, Dave. She even told me the other day that she was impressed with how maturely you've handled this."

"Well, it's been awkward," I said, "and it's part of the reason I didn't show up at that happy hour."

"The one where you had to work late?"

"Yeah."

"So you didn't really have to work late?"

"No, I did," I said, "but that just kind of added to it."

"So are you not coming to the happy hour on Friday?"

"No, I'm not saying that."

"What are you saying? That you're going to avoid any of my work social functions?"

"God no, Ashley, I wasn't saying that at all. I was just saying that if I didn't have to work late the last time, it would have been a little awkward seeing everyone is all."

"Well, you don't have to go on Friday if you don't want to."

"I want to go, Ashley, and I'll be there for sure."

"I don't want you to feel awkward."

"I'm OK with it, Ash" I said, as I took a big gulp of my martini. "Can I ask you one question, though?"

"Sure, of course."

"I mean about that night, at the party—"

"Yeah?"

"It's nothing, really, no big deal, but I was just wondering, and I want to be able to talk openly about anything and everything and communication is key—"

"OK?"

"I was wondering, I mean if you don't mind telling me, but at the party, I mean with him, did you have an orgasm that night?"

Ashley look startled at first. Then she took my hand and said, "Wow, really, do you really want to know?"

I nodded affirmative.

"Yes, I did."

I looked away, then back at her, before asking, "Was it intense?"

"Well, given that I had two, you could say that."

I nodded, straight-faced, like she had just told me what topping she likes on her pizza.

"I'm sorry," she said. "I shouldn't have said that."

"No, it's OK," I replied.

"No it's not, I think this second martini combined with the sake is starting to hit me. I'm really sorry, I apologize."

"It's OK," I said. "You were being truthful, and that's important."

"Are you OK?" she asked.

"Yeah, I'm good. I mean, it was good to talk through this."

"I appreciate you being understanding, I really do, Dave."

"Hey, I love you, Ash, nothing's ever going to change that."

"I love you, too."

"So there's not going to be any karaoke bars this weekend in Jersey?" I said. "I know how Mark and Camilla fancy themselves American Idol wannabes."

"Tell you what," Ashley replied, "I will feign laryngitis at the mere hint of that suggestion."

"OK, I like that," I said. "So, who all else is going to be down there this weekend?"

****

After we returned home, Ashley crashed out quickly. I went into the living room and saw that Mike was online.

"Hey bro," he wrote, "did you have the talk?"

"Yeah, I did. We just got back a little while ago."

"How did it go?"

"Not exactly great. And now I got myself roped into going to a work happy hour of hers on Friday. I don't know how I can show my face there."

"Tell me what happened, Dave."

"I did what we talked about. After getting her to talk about her job, I asked if the rumor had become yesterday's news."

"And?"

"She said she was mortified at first, but then I got this whatever-doesn't-kill-you-makes-you-stronger vibe from her."

"Well, that's good, right?"

"Yeah, but she said things are fine between Jim Murta and her now. He apologized and there's no hard feelings. She's forgiven him and moved on."

"So you think with her forgiving him, she might be interested in hooking up with him again?"

"Well no, I wasn't thinking that exactly—but sure, it's more possible now. Then I said I was embarrassed by the whole thing, and that was part of why I didn't show up to her last happy hour."

"OK and?"

"Well, that set off conversational fireworks," I typed. "She asked if I really didn't have to work late, and I was all flustered, trying to explain myself."

"OK," Mike replied, "I have some thoughts on that, but continue, Dave."

"Well I found myself in conversational retreat, with her asking,

'So, you're not going to go to any work functions with me?' I said of course I would, and then agreed to go on Friday. You don't know how embarrassing that is going to be."

"I take it this Jim Murta guy is going to be there?"

"I don't know for sure, but I'm assuming, and Tamara will be there and everyone there will know the rumor."

"OK, was there anything else?"

"Yeah, I knew I had only one chance to get at the 'Does it still resonate' question, so I asked her if she had an orgasm."

"And?"

"She said she had, and when I asked her if it was intense, she said, considering that she had a couple orgasms, you could say that."

"Hmm, OK."

"She apologized for telling me that, but yeah, she still said it."

"What did you say to that?"

"I dropped it. I changed the subject. I didn't know what else to say, and I didn't want to put my foot in my mouth even more."

"OK, so now you have this happy hour to contend with?"

"Yes, and I felt so checkmated. I don't see any way of getting out of it, without Ashley reading bullshit now. I'm so fucked, man. I have no choice but to go."

"I understand your anxiety, but you're not fucked, Dave. You're going to be fine, believe me."

"Everyone's going to look at me like, 'That's him, that's Ashley's chump husband.' "

"I doubt they will, Dave, and any lowlife gawker who thinks that way isn't worth sweating over. Just put your game face on, go on charm offensive, make a showing and that's it."

"It's just so humble pie humiliating."

"It's only a couple of hours of your life, and don't treat it like humble pie. Treat it like 'fuck you.' "

"Fuck you?"

"Yes, fuck you," Mike replied. "That's right, you gossiping fucks, I'm not intimidated, I'm here. I could give a fuck what any of you think. I've got a killer job making kick-ass money and that hot girl over there is my wife. She comes home to me, and I don't give a rat's ass about what you petty people think."

"Yeah," I said, "but it's more having to see the guy and shake his hand."

"Shake his hand if you have to, but dismiss him like the fucking peasant he is. He's a junior salesman, right?"

"Yeah."

"So remember that—the emphasis on junior. He had one random Haley's Comet night getting lucky with your wife, and he was so immature as to blab. He'll never have a chance again at what you have every night. Think 'bravado,' my friend."

"OK, I hear what you're saying."

"Dave, you're above their little petty peanut gallery. Fuck them! Don't give two craps for two seconds about what they think. Just act like the strong, confident husband. Two hours later, you'll be out of there. You can handle that, can't you?"

"When you put it that way, Mike, yeah, maybe I can."

"Sure you can. Hey, what are you doing tomorrow after work?"

"I don't know, why?"

"I have a meeting on the west side that'll be over by six-thirty. What do you say we meet up in your hood and get a drink and talk about this? I feel like we're friends now, and it would be cool to actually meet you and have a drink in person, and talk more about this happy hour crap you have to deal with."

"Yeah, I guess I could meet for a beer."

"How does seven work? Yankees-Orioles are playing. You have a local place that's cool?"

"Yeah, sure," I typed. "There's a place on Amsterdam."

"What's your cell, Dave? I'll text you tomorrow when I'm out of my meeting."

I gave him my number and sent him a link to the bar.

CHAPTER TWENTY-TWO

I was nervous waiting for Mike, drinking a beer.
He'd become a confidant, a counselor, the one person I could really talk to. Yet we'd never even talked on the phone. But we recognized each other instantly when he walked in, and he smiled broadly and gave me a hug.

"It's good to finally meet you bro," he said, as he sat down beside me

Mike was a tall guy, with a somewhat unkempt look, with his tie loosened, a Yankee cap on.

"This is a chill place," he said. "I like the TVs. Has the game started?"

"No score," I replied, "bottom of the first."

"To a new friend," he said, as he clicked my beer.

We small-talked for a good half-hour about the Yankees before Mike suggested we do a shot, and what did I want a shot of? "I'm buying," he added.

"So, you feeling any better about this happy hour?"

"I'm just going to do what you said," I replied, "cop a fuck-you attitude and just deal."

"Hold on bro. I don't mean to be all fuck-you to people," Mike said, "just to anyone who might snicker—and I doubt anyone will. Just act like you're above any junior high school chatter. Exude Dave Martens confidence. Be gracious, magnanimous, like you're there for your wife, and you're above it all."

"Yeah, I didn't mean I'd be flipping the bird to people."
Mike laughed.

"I just meant," I continued, "like if I have to see that Jim Murta guy, I'm going to say hello and move on."

"OK, hold on," Mike said.

"What?"

"This little prick ratted out what happened and embarrassed your wife, right?"

"Yeah, basically."

"And you feel weird or awkward about meeting him?"

"Yeah, I do."

"Dave, I am telling you, you have nothing to feel awkward about. He does."

"How do you mean?"

"This little punk told his friends—like he was a fucking twelve-year-old. And he knows his kiss-and-tell gossip damaged the reputation of a director he works with. He knows you have every right to want to kick his motherfucker punk ass."

"I'm not going to fight the guy, Mike."

"Yeah, I know, but he doesn't know that. You think he's going to be comfortable seeing you? You don't think it's going to be awkward for him? Make it awkward for him."

"How do you mean?"

"Be confident when you arrive, exude motherfucking confidence, and take your time before meeting him. When you do, walk over to him deliberately. You're just going to shake his hand, but for all he knows you're going to clock him one right in the face."

"OK," I said.

"Be cool and calm, but walk over deliberately, and make him think you might just punch him out."

"There's no way I'm going to punch him."

"You're not getting what I'm saying. Make him think anything is possible. You might punch him or you might just shake his hand. But give him no satisfaction—zero. The guy means nothing to you."

"OK, I get it," I replied.

"You're David fucking Martens," Mike said. "Remember that! You have a kick-ass powerful job and a hot wife, and you're miles above the petty bullshit. This Jim Murta dickhead ain't going to be with your wife ever again. She sleeps in your bed every night. Shake his hand and smile, and when you do, be thinking, 'Go fuck yourself loser.' "

"That's fucking good, Mike."

"Well if that's not enough. I'll show up there if you want."

"What?" I said.

"I will kick this little prick's ass for you."

"Are you serious?"

"What, you don't think I could?"

"I'm just not looking for that."

"I understand Dave. I just don't like the position you've been put in, and I'd wingman you or anything else you wanted Friday night, because like I said, I consider you a friend."

"I appreciate that, Mike."

"You're going to be fine, bro," he said. "Don't fucking sweat it. You're not walking in and meeting the guy who fucked your wife, you're walking in and meeting the guy who dissed your wife with his adolescent blabbing."

"You're right," I replied.

"Dave, right now it's about the happy hour and not giving anyone, including Jim Murta, satisfaction. But afterwards we should talk about the situation in general."

"How so?"

"Just focus on Friday night, my man," Mike said. "That's the main thing right now."

****

I texted Craig the next morning, telling him I was going to tomorrow's happy hour.

"Yeah, I'll be there. Look forward to seeing you, Dave."

I wanted to pick up the phone and ask him if Jim Murta would be showing, but I didn't want him feeling awkward or have him thinking I was obsessed. Besides, he might not know and would only be speculating. And I wanted to approach the night as if seeing Jim Murta was no big deal. Plus, there was a chance he wouldn't even be there. People go away for the weekend, particularly at the end of summer. There was a chance I could skate through this with minimal awkwardness.

****

Still, when I got home, I changed out of my suit and went into my office, where I pulled up the sky-blue bikini photo of Ashley.

I imagined Jim Murta talking to me.

"So you're really not going to puss out this time, Dave? It sure will be fun to see you squirm as I look you straight in the eye and shake your hand. And others will get a kick out of that as well— seeing Ashley's chump husband trying to stumble through small talk with me. I'll be thinking of how hot your wife looked with her blowjob lips around my cock when you knocked.

"So I hear you know that Ashley's forgiven me, that all's now good between us. I sweet-talked your wife, and we kissed and made up—oh not literally, yet—but she was so horny for my big cock that night. It's only a matter of time, bro, before she's grinding her married pussy on it again.

"Maybe we'll literally kiss and fully make up tomorrow. After a few drinks, maybe I'll be making out with your wife in front of you, in front of everyone, as you just look away uncomfortably. Maybe I'll be French-kissing her, just like I was doing at the party when I blew my sperm up in her, when I topped it off with that special cherry for you.

"I heard about the talks you've had with Ashley. Tamara told me everything, how you asked if I was 'bigger.' Maybe someday you'll see my cock, Dave, as it goes inside your wife; then you'll really see how much bigger, and you'll get to see how a real man fucks Ashley. You'll get to watch as your wife cums with my Jim Murta cock inside her. And this time, I'll be giving her more than two, I'll be giving her multiples. I'll hold off seeding your wife until she's fully satisfied. Not like your 'Mr. Three Pumps and Done'— Tamara told me about that—too funny. You'll get to see the kind of fuck from a real man's cock she craves and needs.

"I might just be fucking your wife tomorrow, Dave, in the bar's men's room, and there'll be nothing you can do about it. You won't cock-block me any more than you did the last time, when your knocking on the bathroom door didn't stop me. This time, the door will be open, and I'll let you watch. I'll tell you to stand back as I fuck your wife. I'll give you the finger right to your face as I spew a big fat load of my seed inside your precious wife's pussy. That's how I'll top it off, bitch, that's the cherry on top I've got for you, telling you to go fuck yourself as I sperm up Ashley's pussy, as you stand there, scared and fucking speechless."

And then I came hard again.

I shook my head as I washed myself off. In twenty-four hours, I might be seeing this prick, Jim Murta, face-to-face.

Stop thinking this and man-the-fuck-up.

****

A few minutes later, Mike called. "How you feeling bro? You ready for tomorrow?"

"Yeah," I said, "I confirmed my IT friend will be there, at least."

"Cool, you'll have a wing man."

"Yeah, and I'm just going to avoid potential awkward moments."

"Like what?"

"I'm going to keep tabs on where Jim Murta is, so I'm never alone and cornered."

"No, remember what I said last night. Say hello to people and make a point to go up to him—this is important, Dave—one, it will put him off-balance and two, you'll get it over with. You'll be able to relax the rest of the night."

"No, you're right," I said, "I am going to do that. I just meant like I'm going to avoid shit like running into him in the bathroom. I'm just making an appearance, staying for an hour or so, and then I told Ashley I have an old friend I'm meeting. She was cool with that."

"Are you actually meeting an old friend?"

"No, but she doesn't know that."

"Tell you what, Dave. I'm around tomorrow. After you're done, call me and I'll meet you at the bar from last night. You can relax and chill out. I'm going to be in Manhattan anyway."

"Yeah?" I said.

"Yeah, I want to be there for you, man. I'll be the old friend you're meeting. You won't even be lying. I'd hate to think of you stewing back at your apartment."

"OK, Mike, I appreciate that. I'll text you when I'm leaving, probably around seven-thirty or eight."

"Cool, I'll make my way uptown by then, and Dave?"

"Yeah?"

"Make sure to make the first move. You approach Jim Murta, not the other way around. I know it's not easy, but trust me, it's important. I'm not saying to be overly obvious, but you don't want to seem like you're avoiding him. You say hello to whoever he's with and you say hello to him like he's no different, and then you quickly move on to everyone else. Hang with your IT friend. Whatever power this Jim Murta guy has will be drained."

"OK, Mike, I got it."

"Confidence, Dave, remember, you're David fucking Martens and who the fuck are you, bitches."

****

I was getting more uneasy as Friday afternoon progressed.

I would be thinking "three hours from now" as I hopped on a conference call.

The bar was ten blocks from my office. It was a sunny, mild evening, and I decided to walk. Mike texted me saying "Good luck, you can do this, bro."

I stopped in a bar along the way. "A shot of tequila, please," I said to the young woman bartender.

"Would you like anything with that?"

"No, just the shot. Actually, wait … can you make it a double?"

"Was it that kind of day?" she asked as she brought it over.

"No," I replied, "but it's about to be that kind of night."

****

"Oh, hey, Jim, good to see you," I muttered to myself, one block before the bar, "nice night out. I can't believe it's about to be September. At least football will be starting soon. You a Giants fan?"

I paused at the top of the stairs to look out at the deck. I spotted Tamara first, getting up from a table. Then I saw Jim Murta talking with a few of his sales buddies by the bar.

They have business casual Friday's where Ashley works. Jim was wearing a polo shirt tucked into his jeans. Tamara was wearing a skirt and halter top.

In my suit, I was going to stand out even more.

I went downstairs and found the bathroom, and washed my face and told myself to be confident. I ordered a beer, so I'd have something to drink when I showed upstairs.

"Let's do this bro," I said to myself.

I focused on Tamara standing near the bar and beelined for her.

"Hey Tamara," I said, "great to see you."

"Hey, Dave," she said smiling, "I'm so glad you made it. How are you?"

"I'm doing great, Tamara, and what a beautiful night."

"And it's Friday," she added.

"Hi," I said, turning to her friend and offering my hand, "I'm Dave Martens, Ashley's—"

"Hi Dave, I met you a few months ago, nice to see you again."

A few minutes of social pleasantries later, I turned around and faced the Jim Murta music that I knew was behind me.

Just rip the band aid off and say hello to these punks.

"Hey, Will, good to see you," I said, shaking his hand.

Then, "Hey Ralph, how you doing?"

Then "Hey, Jim," as I shook Murta's hand, smiling and managing to make eye contact.

Then, "Hi, I'm Dave Martens," I said to a guy I hadn't met before. "What an awesome night to be on an outdoor terrace." Now I was addressing all four of them. "But I have to say, I'm jealous. You guys are dressed all casual, and I'm wearing this monkey suit. But hey, I've got a beer in my hand, so I can't complain."

They laughed politely.

"Well," I said to Jim and his sales buddies, "I guess I arrived a bit late. Everybody's already settled in. Ashley's here, right?"

"At that corner table," Jim said, pointing.

Of course he'd be the one to answer that question.

"Oh yeah, I see her, cool. Well, talk to you guys in a bit."

A splash of relief. I walked up to Ashley, who stood up and gave me a kiss. I looked around the table, making eye contact and nodding hello.

"Do you want to sit down?"

"In a bit," I said. "I just want to say hi to everyone."

And that's when I headed for Craig and his IT team.

"Glad you made it," Craig said.

"Yeah, good to see all you guys," I said to the group. "What a great bar to chill out at on a night like this."

Craig and his IT team were bantering back and forth and I was just glad to be cocooned in the conversation. When the Yankees came up, I chimed in, but made sure to do more listening.

A few more sales guys showed up and joined Jim by the bar, but I had my spot, my place, and was grateful for the way IT and Sales were siloed.

When the waitress walked over, I bought Craig and his team a round. I could stay put where I was.

After a while, I saw Ashley talking to Tamara up at the bar. Five minutes later, Jim and his buddies were talking up T & A. I had never thought of that abbreviation for Ashley and Tamara before. I wondered if that was how the sales guys referred to them.

I watched them continuing to talk. Jim leaned into Ashley to say something and I saw her laugh.

Jesus Christ, I thought to myself, apparently all has indeed been forgiven.

I knew I had to man-up. I could hear Mike telling me to go over and join them and exude cool confidence. So I took a big chug of my beer and walked over.

"Hey Dave," Tamara said, "having a good time?"

"Oh sure," I said, "but when those IT guys start going off on Citrix servers and dot-xml-asci codes, I knew that was my time to leave. How are you all doing?"

Everyone responded with versions of good or great.

"Do you need another drink?" Ashley asked.

"Probably not," I said, "I have to meet my friend."

"Oh, have another drink," Tamara said.

"Well, twist my arm, why don't you Tamara. Oh, OK."

Ashley was telling some story about a flakey client and I just laughed along, acting as comfortable and interested as I could. I glanced over at Jim a few feet away in our circle, but looked away and back to Ashley when I saw him staring at me.

His stare said "I fucked your wife." In that moment, there was no way to really look back at him. He'd shot his sperm inside her. Both he knew it and I knew it. I'm sure he continued staring, but my eyes were focused on anyone besides Jim fucking Murta.

Then Tamara broke out her camera and said, "Let's get a picture."

I knew immediately what she was up to. I wasn't paranoid. She wanted a photo of me with the guy who fucked my wife.

"I'm going to pass on photos," I said, "I look ridiculous enough wearing this monkey suit on a summer Friday night.."

"Oh come on, Dave, you look sharp," Tamara replied.

"Well, I appreciate the compliment," I said, "but I'll rain check for the next happy hour."

"I'll rain check as well," Ashley said, "I'm getting called back to the table as it is."

"Oh come on. It's one little photo. Humor me, it's the last happy hour of the summer."

When Ashley hesitated, Tamara put her arm out for her to move in. Now Ashley was standing beside Jim Murta.

"Now come on Dave, pose next to Ashley."

I felt fucked and didn't know what to say. Tamara reached her arm out to me saying "C'mon, get in there, you look great."

Suddenly I'm standing beside Ashley waiting for Tamara to snap the photo.

"One more time. Ashley was blinking."

And so I grinned and endured it again. I put my arm around her and then Jim put his arm around her as well.

"This looks great," Tamara said as she showed it to us.

I took a quick glance at the five of us posing and passed the camera back to Tamara. I acted like it was no big deal. It was just a photo. But Tamara had a self-satisfied grin. I suspected she had been waiting for that opportunity to pose Ashley between me and Jim fucking Murta.

Ashley asked if I wanted to join her back at the table and I told her I had to go, that my friend would be waiting.

Then I turned back to Tamara and said the same thing, giving her a good night hug. Then I said goodnight to the sales guys, shaking everyone's hand—including Jim Murta's—like I was late and in a hurry. I went back to Craig's group and did the same.

Out on the street, I called Mike.

****

"That's awesome," Mike said as I told him about the evening at the bar. "Sounds like you handled things perfectly."

"Yeah, Mike," I said, "but—"

"But what, Dave?"

"Something happened at the end."

"What?"

"OK," I said taking a hearty sip from my drink, "when I was about to leave, I saw Jim Murta talking to Ashley."

"Sure and?"

"Well I figured I should go over there."

"Good for you, Dave, that was the right call."

"Well yeah, it was" I said, "but then Tamara pulls out her camera and wants our group to pose. I didn't want to. Even Ashley didn't want to."

"And?"

"I wound up posing for the fucking photo."

"Yes, so?"

"Tamara photographed Jim and me posing beside Ashley, like we were bookends."

"It was just the three of you?"

"No, there were five of us, but if you cropped them out, Tamara had me posing with my wife and the guy who fucked her."

"OK, I get it. Was Tamara taking photos there in general, or do you think she pulled out her cam just for that?"

"She was taking pictures before, but c'mon, I'm not naïve, I know what's she's up to—that was a way for her to rub it in."

"OK, but it's just a picture right?"

"Mike, you know what's going to happen Monday? Tamara will send a link to some photo site to everyone who was there, so they can check out pictures from tonight. Everyone knows the rumor. How the fuck is that going to look? People will laugh their asses off. 'There's Dave Martens posing with the guy who fucked his wife.' But how was I was going to turn down Tamara telling me to pose beside my wife?"

"OK, so you sucked it up and posed for the photo. You were gracious about it."

"But don't you see what people will say?"

"Fuck those people," Mike said as he ordered us another drink. "Where's Ashley now?"

"Still at the party."

"Are you comfortable with that?"

"I kind of have to be, don't I?"

"Do you want me to go there now and keep an eye on what's going on? I know what Ashley and Tamara look like. They don't know me."

"Well my friend Craig said he was hanging out there for a while. I planned on calling him in the morning."

"And you trust him to tell you if he saw something?"

"Yeah, on this, I do. And even though Ashley's forgiven Jim, I don't think she would risk her reputation by being seen walking off with him or anything like that."

"OK, I hear you," Mike said. "Here's what I think: Forget the photo, Dave, that's a distraction. So people see it, and people who snickered before, snicker again, no big deal in the grand scheme."

"I guess, but it confirms what a scheming little bitch Tamara is."

"Oh yes, it does," Mike said. "She's going to continue to be that. And you can't prevent them from hanging out when she works with her."

"I know, and Ashley would be pissed if I even suggested that."

"No, that would exacerbate things."

"I know."

"What makes me wonder is, why is Ashley even talking to the guy, especially when she knows you can see her? Fuck everyone else; that alone is a red flag."

"I know," I said.

"That's what you need to focus on. Look, I'm sure nothing will happen tonight, but I think if it did resonate with her like you said, something very well may happen, if not next week, then maybe next month, and who knows what she was doing at the party where she wore that t-shirt."

"Mike, believe me, I know."

"I think it may be time for Plan B."

"Plan B?" I said.

"You said you guys are leaving tomorrow for the Jersey shore, right?"

"Yeah, in the morning."

"When are you getting back?"

"Sunday evening."

"And you're both going to be in town next week?"

"Yeah."

"OK, are you free Monday night to meet up for a drink?"

"Yeah."

"OK, so let's you and me meet up on Monday and figure out a plan for the three of us having a drink next week."

"You, me and Ashley?"

"Yes."

"I don't know."

"Dave, it sounds like Tamara's on sabotage patrol. There's a real urgency now. I can read women extremely well. I'm good at detecting body language. Women betray what they're trying to hide. But maybe I'll see that she's not hiding anything, and that it was a one-time fluke thing. And if so, I would want to give you that peace of my mind."

"So what, like you would observe us out together?"

"Yeah, exactly, we'd all have a drink or two together."

"Meaning you would talk with us?"

"Yeah, exactly."

"How would that happen? You'd just come up to us and start talking?"

"No, trust me, I did this once before for a buddy. He learned he had nothing to worry about. That was four years ago and they're still together, happier than ever."

"Not sure I'm getting this, Mike."

"We'll figure out the details on Monday," he said as another round arrived. "I'll be some old friend of yours—you said you're on Facebook, right?"

"Yeah, but hardly ever on."

"Me, either," Mike said, "but confirm my friend request tonight. I'm going to be an old friend who reconnected with you."

"OK," I said, "and then what?"

"Then we figure it out from there," Mike said.

"But you're talking about meeting up with Ashley and me?"

"Yes, to help you get a better sense of where her head is at. Your talk didn't really get you there. You're too close to this. I can provide some higher-level perspective. I think this will really help."

"I don't know, Mike."

"Well, forget it for now, bro. Let's focus on tonight. You went into a stressful situation and passed the test with flying colors. You went man-to-man with that a-hole and came out on top, the bigger, more established man."

"Yeah, other than the photo, it went better than I thought," I said.

"Of course it did. I told you it would. Fuck that guy, he's the chump, you showed him how little he is to you tonight."

"Yeah," I said, "but Mike, I have to be honest, I'm not exactly comfortable with this Plan B."

"Fuck Plan B right now," Mike said, as he cheered me over a shot. "To manning up to Jim Murta tonight. Jim Murta is a little fucking bitch. To Dave fucking Martens."

CHAPTER TWENTY-THREE

I woke up at six and couldn't get back to sleep. I looked over at Ashley, her face so serenely angelic.

I was hard. I wished I could wake her, but I didn't want the "What the hell time is it" rejection. I thought of jerking off under the cover, or getting up and masturbating as I sat on a chair, looking at her. Both were too obvious risks, and so I made my way to the bathroom.

I thought about that photo Tamara had now—Ashley smiling between me and Mr. Fucked My Wife, Jim Fucking Murta.

What conniving satisfaction Tamara must have felt.

I imagined the comments that would inevitably ensue when Tamara posted them.

"Oh my God, did you see that?"

"I know, isn't that hilarious."

"You could see how awkward he looked posing with the guy who fucked his wife."

"Oh, he looks like such a chump. If he knows what happened, what a pussy he is. And if he doesn't, what an idiot."

"He looks like he knows, given his uncomfortable expression. I bet he's just a pussy."

I imagined guys at her work looking at the photo from their home computers. I imagined them jerking off looking at Ashley, thinking, "Go fuck yourself, Dave Martens."

I thought of what they might be thinking …

"You got punked, bitch—what kind of man poses with the guy who fucked his wife? And look at Ashley, with her big tits bubbling out underneath that dress, allowing Jim to put his arms around her."

"Oh yeah, Dave, I'm looking right at you, you fucking pussy, and I'm not the only one, other guys at work are thinking the same thing. Oh yeah, he fucking nailed your wife and now you're fucking posing with him. Gobble gobble that humble pie, Dave. We're all fucking laughing at you now!"

"Yeah, Ashley, that's it, show your husband how much you don't give a fuck. You rode Jim's cock and now you got your husband to pose with him."

"Do you feel like a chump now? This is another cherry on top—posing with the guy who balled and creamed your precious Ashley, bitch!"

I came hard, and hung my head.

****

Mark and Camilla picked us up at our apartment just after nine.

Mark had his dad's BMW convertible and suggested I ride shotgun, so Ashley and Camilla could talk in the back. He had jam-type music playing and we didn't talk much over the wind. I kind of zoned out, enjoying the ride.

We met two couples—friends of Mark's—and they gave us the tour.

It was a three-bedroom beach house that Mark's friend, Chip, had rented for the week.

The six of them had split the cost. Ashley and I were last minute invites, simply free-loading for the night.

"There's couches for you guys to crash on," Chip explained, "one in the living room and another downstairs."

"That works," Ashley said.

"Yeah, and there's a Jacuzzi out here on the deck. Take that path and you're on the beach in less than a minute."

"This place rocks," Ashley said. "Love the ocean view. Thanks so much for having us."

"You bet," Chip said. "What do you all say about bringing the cooler down and hitting the beach?"

****

After staking out a more secluded section, Chip handed out beers in plastic cups and I watched as the girls stripped off their t-shirts and shorts.

I'm sure the other guys were checking out Ashley through their sunglasses. Ashley was wearing a white bikini with blue polka dots, which accentuated her breasts. Camilla was wearing a bikini as well, and was thin and tan with more modest-sized breasts. The other two girls were wearing one-pieces and were OK looking, but not in any noteworthy way.

When Ashley and Camilla suggested we go swimming, Mark and I joined them. The ocean waves were crashing hard, the kind of waves that can take a girl's top off. But we made it out to where it was above standing and Mark and I tossed a nerf football.

Then I joined up with Ashley and gave her a kiss, my arms around her wet hair. When I started to cop a feel of her breasts she said, "What are you doing?" in a 'this-is-a-family-beach' kind of way.

"I'm just kidding," I said as a pseudo apology.

Drying off, Mark mentioned there was a lighthouse at the end of the island.

Back at the house, everyone was lazing around, watching some old Will Ferrell movie.

"Do you want my car keys?" Mark asked.

"What?" I said.

"You can take Ashley up and check out the lighthouse. It's only ten miles north and a scenic ride."

"You don't want to go?"

"I think I may take a nap. Camilla and I got in late, plus the time difference."

"Time difference?" I said, "Central time is one freaking hour. What, does Daylight Savings Time knock you out as well?"

"Fuck you, man," he said ribbing me in the chest.

"Hey, if you're cool with it," I said, "I'd love to check out the lighthouse."

"Of course I'm cool with it. There's some champagne in the fridge if you want to take a bottle. Just don't get drunk and crash my dad's car."

"No worries there. That's very cool of you, Mark."

Ten minutes later, Ashley and I were off in Mark's dad's BMW.

"Is this 'Stand by Me'?" Ashley said as the breeze had our hair flying.

"Yeah, it's John Lennon, doing acoustic."

"It's really beautiful," she replied.

I pulled over onto a side street.

"What are you doing?"

I hit replay on Pandora, and we made out as the song started up again.

****

The group was out on the deck drinking when we returned. Ashley put her bikini on and joined the other girls in the Jacuzzi.

I helped Mark squeeze watermelon for watermelon margaritas. Then Chip's old college buddy friend came up the stairs. He was the last guest to arrive.

"I'm Miguel," he said, as he shook my hand.

"I'm Dave, is that a turkey you have in that tray?"

"It is," he said. "Ever have deep-fried turkey?"

"Uh, that would be a no."

"Well then, you're in for a treat, my friend."

I turned around and saw Ashley walking over to introduce herself. Why was she the only girl who felt compelled to get out of the Jacuzzi to greet him, I wondered. Soon she was inquiring about what flavoring the turkey was covered in, what he injected it with, and how you actually went about deep-frying turkey. He rattled off the details as Ashley stood there listening intently in her wet, polka dotted bikini.

****

The turkey was a hit, and for someone who doesn't enjoy Thanksgiving dinners, it was probably the best tasting turkey I'd ever had.

Mark's margaritas were also a hit—so much so, that a half hour later, he was asking me if I'd join him in getting another watermelon and another bottle of tequila in town.

Ashley and Camilla were talking to Miguel in their swimsuits about cook-out/tailgate meals, and I felt a little uneasy leaving. But Mark had lent me his convertible, and had invited me to a Yankees game, so I couldn't say, "No I want to stay here."

We'd already had a few drinks, so he called for a cab to take us. Only the cab driver refused to wait once we got there—he had another fare he was late for. He handed us the card for Surf City Taxi and pulled away.

****

"Unfucking believable," Mark said as he got off the phone, "twenty to thirty minutes—do you want to just hoof it?"

"Mark, it's got to be at least a mile, and we have a freaking watermelon to lug."

So we waited. Fifteen minutes later, the cab company was now telling us thirty minutes more.

"I can't stand waiting. Fuck the watermelon. Let's just bring the tequila and walk back."

"Are you sure you know the way?" I asked.

"Yeah, I've got it on my iPhone—1.3 miles."

"OK," I said.

Mark asked a few people walking into the store if they wanted a watermelon—"and could you drive us to North Fifteenth?" Finally he just gave it to a couple with kids and we set off on foot.

****

On the walk home, Mark opened the Cuervo and asked if I'd join him in a "social." We took two swigs each and walked down Long Beach Boulevard.

"I'm sorry about this," Mark said, "I fucked up. I thought this would be quick."

243

"Don't sweat it man, it was an adventure," I said. It was something Ashley would say.

"Well more like a misadventure, but I'm glad for the company."

"You bet."

"So I think Camilla's getting slightly more open to moving."

"Oh yeah?" I replied.

"At least she's saying things like, 'Well, if we move' and towns she'd be open to that are a quick train ride to the city."

"Well yeah, that sounds like progress, right?"

"Yeah, it is," Mark replied, "and I'm hoping that having fun relaxing this week will get her thinking Jersey's not so bad."

I reluctantly agreed to join him in one more social chug as we approached the house.

****

The two couples were sitting around on the deck talking when we returned.

"Where's Camilla?" Mark asked.

"Or Ashley?" I said.

"They walked down to the beach with Miguel."

"To swim?"

"Not sure," Chip replied, "maybe just to check out the beach."

"How long ago?" I asked.

"Maybe twenty minutes."

I turned to Mark and said, "I could see Ashley wanting to swim."

"Yeah," he replied, "and Camilla was in her swimsuit. Let's put our suits on and go down there."

"Yup," I replied, "I'm right with you."

Ashley and I had swum in the ocean at night plenty of times before. Sometimes after drinking. The next day, I always knew that was stupid. The Jersey shore can have rip tides. I hurried into my suit and met Mark back on the deck.

We started down the sandy path when we saw Camilla walking back up to us in her bikini.

"I was just coming out looking for you" Mark said, "Did you go swimming?"

"No, we just brought our drinks down and admired the ocean. The moon's illuminating it."

"Where's Ashley?" I asked.

"She and Miguel went to check out some ten million dollar house about ten houses down, but I'm barefoot."

"Well, we couldn't get a cab back to save our life," Mark replied, as he turned around and the three of us began walking back to the house, up the stairs, onto the deck.

I didn't know what to do. I wanted to go find Ashley but I felt weird asking Camilla to point me in the direction of this ten million dollar house that Ashley and Miguel had ventured off to.

"Did Ashley bring her cell?" I asked.

"No, isn't that hers on the top of her purse?"

"Oh yeah, that's hers."

Motherfucker, I thought, taking a piss.

Ashley was taking a stroll on a moonlit beach in her bikini with another man. Could others not see how that was just a little weird? Miguel was single, had complained about there being no single girls at the house, and now he was taking my wife on some quarter mile walk. And couldn't Ashley think I'd have to wonder? She'd admitted to fucking Jim Murta at the same party I was at. She'd told me less than a week ago that Jim had given her a couple orgasms.

Suddenly I felt weak in the knees.

Miguel is going to try to get with my buzzed, bikini-clad wife on a moonlit beach. Would he try and kiss her?

And if Ashley kissed him back, he'd move on to more ambitious goals, like getting her top off, feeling her tits, sucking on her nipples, getting her bikini off, having her feel his hard-on, putting her hand on his hard cock.

At this very moment, I thought, Ashley could be on the beach with Miguel's cock in her mouth. Or he could have her in a secluded area behind the brush, fucking her, Ashley's bikini in the sand.

How long had it taken Jim Murta to go from zero to sixty? Twenty minutes?

Maybe they had never made it to the ten million dollar house.

Maybe once Camilla left, there was no more third wheel.

He had my buzzed, bikini-clad wife all to himself. Perhaps right now, he was only a hundred yards from the house, fucking my wife hard in the sand as Ashley moaned over the sound of the ocean.

I could sneak out and go look for her, or say I was going to check out the view of the moon myself. I could yell out for her: "Ashley?"

It reminded me of this fat kid who moved next door when I was a boy. I was too caught up in trying to be somewhat cool in junior high to be remotely friendly to the kid. It seemed like his only real friend was his dog, Alfie. I remember lying in bed and hearing him walking down the street yelling out for his dog: "Alfie … Alfie!" It made me sad.

Would she even answer my "Ashley" call? Not if she was naked under the bushes with Miguel's cock inside her.

They'd probably freeze and get quiet as I walked only a few feet away from them and continued down the beach. As my cries grew more distant, she'd put his hands around his bare ass, gripping it, as he'd begin pumping away again on that sandy beach.

Oh my God.

Could Ashley be taking Miguel's bare cock right now? Why, he could be blowing his load at this very moment inside her. I imagined the moment after they both came.

"Oh my God what happened to my bikini, Miguel?"

"It's a few yards back down the beach."

"Miguel, it isn't, where in hell is it?"

"I don't know, Ashley, I don't see it."

"Oh my God, what the fuck."

"Relax, Ashley."

"Relax? I'm fucking naked!"

"I'll sneak you back."

"How?"

"There's an entrance downstairs."

I imagined Ashley walking back down that path, naked, with Miguel's cum inside her.

"What's wrong?" she would say.

"I don't know; it seems locked."

"What?"

"Hold on, I think the door's just jammed."

"Miguel!"

Then, hearing the commotion, Chip would turn on the spotlight. And Ashley would look up at all of us on the deck, including me. She'd awkwardly wrap one hand around her tits, the other around her pussy. When she turned around, her butt cheeks would be covered in wet sand. Mark might look back at me to see my frozen reaction. Everyone would know then. Miguel had just come back from fucking my wife.

Suddenly I came.

****

"Holy Shit" I said to myself, as I realized my body was shaking.

This wasn't like Jay flirting with Ashley by the pool. This Miguel guy was having real alone time with my wife. And here I was, a guest in the house, jerking off in the bathroom, my wife MIA.

The Jim Murta night had shown me anything was possible.

I splashed water on my face and rejoined the group.

Mark handed me a margarita but I was zoning. I had to suck it up and take it—the possibility my wife was getting fucked as I sat there.

About twenty seeming-like-eternity minutes later, there was talk coming up the stairs and I heard Ashley's voice. She was in her bikini and Miguel was in his swimsuit, without a shirt, looking fit and muscled.

"How did your watermelon margarita run go?" she asked as she gave me a quick kiss.

"Long story, cab problems," I replied. "Did you go swimming?"

"No, we just checked out this massive beach home down the shore."

"They were having a cookout," Miguel said to me, "but it was a little too intimate to try and crash it."

"I need a drink," Ashley replied. "So, no watermelon margaritas?"

"No" I said, "but there's margarita mix, I'm just drinking a regular one."

"Regular one it is then," Ashley said.

"I can make you one," Miguel said, and I watched the guy head into the kitchen to fix my wife a drink.

****

I made sure to keep Ashley nearby the rest of the night. I joined her in the Jacuzzi when she went in. I hung out in the kitchen when she was making more appetizers with Camilla.

Mark offered to sleep on the living room couch and give Ashley the bedroom with Camilla.

"Thanks," Ashley replied, "but you paid for that room, I'm just lucky to have a free couch. I'm sure it'll be ultra-comfy. I nap on our couch at home all the time."

I half expected Miguel to say, "I have a good sized bed in my room, Ashley."

So I kept close.

I hung out in the living room as Chip brought out blankets, and Ashley changed into a t-shirt and sweats. Then Chip showed me the couch downstairs. I had a nightcap with Mark in the kitchen as Ashley went to sleep.

Miguel and Chip came in from the deck and said they were going to crash. I waited for their bedroom doors to close before telling Mark I was going to bed as well.

But I couldn't sleep. I started wondering if Miguel would come out from his bedroom and ask Ashley to join him, with me, now presumably, asleep downstairs. If he had even simply kissed her on that beach earlier, it would be worth a shot for him.

Would Ashley say, "I'd love to Miguel, but Dave might come up and wonder where I am."

Or would she think she could finesse even that? "That couch was really uncomfortable Dave, so I just crashed out on Miguel's bed."

Maybe he was talking to her in the living room right now. Maybe they were making out on the couch. Perhaps he had Ashley's clothes off. Maybe they were getting off on the risk, hooking up in a public room, with chump husband Dave a staircase below. Maybe at this moment, Miguel was straddling my wife, sliding his cock between her tits, telling her to lean forward and lick it.

"A little more, Ashley, that's it, give my cock a good kiss, oh yeah, show me that tongue, nice, good girl."

I thought of slowly walking up those creaky stairs, trying not to make them creak. I imagined what I might see. Perhaps I'd peer out and see Miguel's ass, Ashley's legs wrapped around his back. Or maybe he'd have her turned around. So when I walked up, Miguel would see me quietly pop my head out to sneak a peek. Maybe he'd smile and mutter, "Hell, yeah!" as we made eye contact. And he'd pick up the pace, thrusting fast and hard as he stared me down, pounding Ashley extra loudly as she screamed out in orgasm.

"Watch this chump," his expression would say, "look at me as I cum deep inside your fucking wife."

Suddenly I came.

I just lay there, my heart racing. I couldn't hear anything over the din of the air conditioner. For all I knew, everyone was asleep in the house. And it was all in my crazy head.

****

I woke up, unsure of where I was.

Then I looked at my watch and couldn't believe how late I'd slept. The curtains had kept all the light out. I thought about Miguel having possibly done something with Ashley last night. It wasn't impossible that he'd fucked her on the beach and then fucked her again in his bedroom after I had gone down to sleep.

Then I thought of Ashley in that circular Jacuzzi. I imagined going upstairs and finding everyone already in there—Miguel and Camilla sitting between Ashley, and me squeezing in on the other side. The jets would be on lightly as we all sipped our drinks.

I imagined seeing Miguel put his hands under the water, like he was sliding off his swimsuit.

I imagined Camilla trying to control her "Oh my God" expression as she saw Miguel's cock point upwards under water.

I imagined seeing Ashley's arm go down, trying to discreetly give this guy a hand job, ten feet away from me—her husband.

I imagined Ashley's polka-dotted bottom being untied and held under water in her hand.

I pictured her suddenly on Miguel's lap. Everyone would keep talking as if everything was normal. Then Ashley would cry out, "Oh God."

People would look back at her.

"I mean, oh God, these jets are pretty hot."

But she'd continue to softly moan, looking up at the sky, back down at the water. Miguel's arms would be under water as he clutched her. Suddenly Miguel's swimsuit would rise to the surface, followed shortly by Ashley's bottoms.

I would sit there paralyzed looking at them. And then Miguel would untie my wife's top, leaving Ashley's tits exposed and bouncing in front of everyone. No one would not know what was going on. Miguel was fucking my wife in the Jacuzzi right the fuck in front of me.

Oh my God stop, I thought to myself, don't do it, Miguel, please pull out, please don't cum, not in Ashley's pussy.

I sat there on the basement couch with cum in my hand and no tissue.

****

"What's Hat Night?"

That's what Ashley was asking Miguel when I walked into the kitchen.

"About time, sleepy head," she said to me, "it's almost eleven."

"I know," I said, "it was dark downstairs and it took a while to fall asleep."

"Well," Miguel continued, "we all dress up in the most outrageous hats we can find, and bar-hop as a group. It's become a tradition."

"Sounds fun," Ashley replied, "I'll talk to Camilla about it."

"I'm telling you, it's a blast. You would love it," Miguel said.

"Think you could take Friday off?" Ashley asked me.

"What?" I said, as I looked for the coffee.

"We could come down Thursday night," Ashley said, "chill on the beach, and go out with everyone for Hat Night Friday."

"Oh I don't know," I said.

"I'm telling you, it's so much fun," Miguel said, "and the forecast for Friday is Sunny and 85."

"And it's Labor Day weekend," Ashley added. "It'll be half-day Friday anyway."

****

We had a 2 p.m. bus to catch.

I went downstairs and packed. Ashley was outside on the deck when I came out, drinking a bloody with Miguel. I suddenly wondered if she'd given him a goodbye blowjob while I was showering.

"I hope you can come down later this week," Miguel said as he hugged Ashley goodbye.

"Would love to have you down again," he said as he shook my hand.

"Hey Ash," I said on the bus ride home. "Did Tamara email you the happy hour photos from the other night?"

"No, she's out in the Hamptons."

"Well," I said, "you remember that photo she took of us with the sales guys?"

"Yeah."

"Well, Jim was in the photo, and it occurred to me that she might group-email the photos tomorrow at work."

"OK, maybe."

"Could you talk to her and ask her not to include that one? I mean, that might get people talking again about the rumor, me posing with Jim. It might be a good idea not to circulate that photo."

"I'm with you," she said. "Sure, I'll text her now."

****

"I've got issues, Mike," I said, when he called that night. "I could be paranoid, but whenever Ashley is friendly with a good-looking guy now, I start imagining stuff."

"What happened?"

"I went on a liquor run, and when I returned, Ashley was taking a moonlight beach walk in her bikini with this guy we'd just met. I started thinking he had fucked her on that beach."

"Do you think he did?"

"Probably not, but given what happened with Jim Murta, anything is possible. And then I think it could all be in my head."

"Would you rather it all be in your head?"

"What?" I said.

"Does part of you wish she had fucked this guy?"

"No, I'd like to think it's my imagination, but whose wife goes on a moonlight walk with another guy in her bikini when her husband is out?"

"I hear you," he said. "It could be innocent or it could be something."

"And then there's the whole 'submissive' t-shirt and just happening to lose her phone while I was away. And that guy this weekend invited us down for some 'Hat Night' event this weekend."

"What's 'Hat Night'?"

"Oh just some stupid tradition thing the house does each year. But for me, 'Hat Night' might as well be a euphemism for 'Fuck my Wife Night.'"

"Yes, my friend, I understand why you are wondering. And that talk you had with Ashley seems to have given you more questions than answers."

"I know," I said, "I'm no closer to figuring out where her head is at."

"Maybe even slightly farther away," he replied. "Have you thought about what we discussed?"

"You mean your Plan B suggestion?"

"The plan to help you figure this all out, yes."

"Yeah, I have."

"And?"

"I guess I'm willing to give it a try."

"OK, I'll see you tomorrow. As you said, given what happened at the party, you might indeed be thinking the worst. I want to get you an objective read."

"OK," I said, "I feel I need to do or try something."

"Cool, just be vague to Ashley about who you're meeting tomorrow. I'm just an old friend you reconnected with on Facebook. By the way, I invited you after we hung out Friday, but I didn't get a friend confirmation."

"Oh, I haven't been on. I'll connect with you now."

CHAPTER TWENTY-FOUR

When I met Mike the next night, he gave me a hug, asked if I ever had a "Sidecar" and said he was running a tab.

"We should probably discuss logistics," he said, after some small talk about sports.

"Logistics?"

"Yeah," he replied, "to get you a better read on Ashley."

"Sure."

"I'm thinking when you go home tonight, you should see if she's free Wednesday for the three of us to meet."

"Wednesday?" I said, "That's two days away."

"Yeah, there's some urgency here, bro, especially with 'Hat Night' on Friday."

"Well, there's no way we're going to that."

"Still, the sooner, the better, given the circumstances."

"OK," I said, "I'll ask her tonight."

"We should figure out a place to meet—does Ashley have a favorite local place?"

"Yeah, but I'm thinking probably not there. I'll think of something."

"Why not there?"

"It's the place where she first told me about the rumor."

"It's just a place," Mike said. "It's not like it's haunted. If she likes the place, I say let's go there."

"I'll ask her."

"OK," Mike said, "and we should also get our story down about how we know each other."

"I thought we were childhood friends who reconnected on

Facebook," I said, "I mean that's how I described it to Ashley today."

"OK, you did tell her that. Did she ask any questions?"

"No, we were both at work. It was a quick call."

"Sure, but she'll probably ask you more questions about us when you're home—or when you invite us all to meet, right?"

"Yeah."

"Well, I don't know about saying we met at school 'cause old yearbooks can be dug up."

"I don't have any yearbooks from grade school."

"Still," he said, "the school friends thing could trip us up."

"How do you mean?"

"I'm thinking," he replied, "did you and your family summer anywhere, like have a summer house?"

"No, I spent my summers at camp mostly."

"A sleep-away camp?"

"Yeah."

"Like where you were away for weeks doing typical summer camp activities?"

"Exactly."

"Where was the camp?"

"Upstate New York."

"What was its name?"

"Camp Marvins."

"How many summers did you go? How old were you?"

"Oh Jeez, from like when I was nine until fourteen."

"That's perfect, Dave. We're old buds from Camp Marvins. We spent our summers there together. And if she picks up that I'm a couple years younger, well, you were like a big brother to me."

"Yeah, I guess, OK."

"What activities or sports did you like—or what did you excel at?"

"Go-carts were the most fun," I said. "But I was a good swimmer, canoeist, and a pretty good second baseman."

"Great, and I played first base," he said. "We won lots of games together, didn't we? And you can bust on me for dropping some of your throws to first."

I looked at Mike with an expression of "Huh?"

"This is important Dave. Because if we're going to get a sense of where her head is at, Ashley needs to feel comfortable. I'm not some friend of yours from work she has to watch her words with. I'm your old buddy Mike. We go way back to the days at summer camp. If she asks how I'm doing now, say, 'He's doing well. He's successful, but we didn't really get into that.' Mostly that we reminisced about good times as kids at good ol' Camp ... what was the name again?"

"Marvins."

"Right, good ol' Camp Marvins. Have you talked to her much about your summer camp days?"

"No, the only story I really told her," I said, "was about this letter I nearly mailed home the first night I got there."

"What was the letter about?"

"Well, I was nervous on the five hour ride up there. And my dad said, 'If you don't like it, write a letter home and we'll be right back up to pick you up'."

"OK," Mike said, as he motioned to the bartender for another round.

"Well, my dad said, 'And just in case they're reading your mail, if you don't like it, simply say it's 'dandy.' "

"'Dandy,'" Mike repeated. "When did you go to camp—in the roaring twenties?"

"It was like a code word," I said. "I know it's corny, but my dad was like that. It was his way of giving me a parachute."

"I get it."

"Well, when I got there," I said, "I was in the second session, so a lot of kids already knew each other. And kids give the new kid a hard time, so I thought no one liked me. So that night I wrote a letter home. I wrote 'Dear Dad, camp is dandy. The kids are dandy, the food is dandy, the counselors are dandy. I'm having a real dandy time here.' "

"That's funny," Mike said, "so what happened?"

"Well I knew my dad wouldn't be happy driving back up there so soon, so I decided to wait a bit before mailing the letter. I kept it like a Linus security blanket for a few days. Pretty soon I'd made friends, was fitting in and having a great time. So when my dad came to pick me up, I handed him that sealed letter, and he opened it up and read it. My mom still has that letter somewhere at home."

"That's a really sweet story, bro," Mike said.

"Yeah, I guess so."

"Well it has me thinking that maybe I'll have a similar story."

"How do you mean?" I asked.

"Well, I felt like an outsider at Camp Marvins the day I started. And maybe you saw in me that same scared boy you were, when you first started."

"OK."

"Or maybe you befriended me because you're just like that, but either way, you rescued me. And we became good buds that summer. Then my family moved, I didn't go back and we lost touch. Only we reunited when I found you online, and here we are, having drinks together tonight."

"OK," I said. "Sure, that works, I guess."

The Yankees game was on TV, and Mike asked how I'd become a fan. Then he asked me if Ashley shared my enthusiasm.

"No, she's not much of a baseball fan. She likes going to games, but more for the fun of the event, not actually paying close attention to the game."

"And not much for football either?" Mike asked.

"Not pro football. She likes college football. Or Virginia Tech football anyway."

"Is that where she went to college?"

"No, she went to Columbia, like me. But her dad and sister went there, and her dad took her to a lot of games growing up."

"Is that how you guys met—at college?"

"No, afterwards, at an alumni event in the city."

"Gotcha. She like any other sports?"

"She's a huge tennis fan. That was her sport in college."

"She played on the college team?"

"Yeah, she was a co-captain."

"Wow," Mike said. "Do you play?"

"Not really, was never any good at it."

"Me, either," Mike said. "I bet she could whup the both of us, huh, if we played doubles against her?"

"Yeah," I said, laughing, "and if her older sister was with her, it'd be the 6-0, 6-0 thing."

"Does she like watching tennis, like pro tennis?"

"Oh yeah, she's been to Wimbledon and the French Open with her parents. She jokes that before we have kids, I have to take her to Australia for the Open there."

"That would be very cool."

"Well, Australia would be cool, other than the flight, but I'm not much of a tennis fan."

"You guys going to the Open?"

"We've gone in the past. Maybe if I can score some tickets at work."

"Yeah, I hear you. You know, you've got me thinking. I should probably know some basic interests of hers, so that we can include her in the conversation. So it's not just me and you talking summer camp stories."

"OK," I said.

"So tell me about her hobbies."

"Well, she was a big piano player growing up—she's classically trained—took lessons for like ten years."

"Who are her favorite composers?"

"Oh jeez, um, Chopin, Mozart, Liszt maybe, definitely Beethoven."

"Classical not your thing?"

"Not really."

"Mine either—how about new music?"

"We don't share the same taste there. She's into new alternative rock bands, hiphop and poppy stuff like Lady Gaga. She even used to like that F-U-C-K song."

"That Cee Lo song?"

"Well, she likes that as well, but I meant the Britney Spears song, 'If you seek Amy,' that sounds like F-U-C-K Amy."

"Oh, OK."

"Don't get me wrong," I said, "she likes good music too, like U2 and The Beatles and Pink Floyd, but I would think, for someone who almost majored in music, that she wouldn't like some of the bumble-gum crap she does."

"I hear you. So what was her major?"

"What?" I asked, a bit drunk now.

"You said she was going to major in music. What did she choose instead?"

"English."

"English?"

"You know, like the study of fiction, themes, interpreting novels, from *Beowulf* and Shakespeare to twentieth century."

"Yeah, I know what you meant. So who are Ashley's favorite authors?"

"Oh jeez, where do I begin. She likes women authors like Emily Brontë, Jane Austen, Emily Dickinson. Really likes Flannery O'Connor. And F. Scott Fitzgerald. Thinks Hemingway is way over-rated. Also thinks Vonnegut is an ass.

"But it's interesting," I continued, "when it comes to books, she never reads junk. Like she'll read the first page of a book, and if the writing's not strong—up to her standards—she'll dismiss it out of hand. Yet with music, she also likes the poppy throw-away."

"How about her movie tastes?" Mike asked.

"She's not into big-budget, Hollywood stuff. Like she wouldn't see a movie if she learned Tom Cruise was in it. And the romantic comedies bore her. She likes indie movies, which is good. I mean we have similar tastes there."

The conversation then turned to where she's traveled. How she went to Europe a lot with her parents. How we honeymooned in

Italy. Told him about a trip she took to Southeast Asia with her friend. How we went to Hawaii last fall.

"Does she speak any languages?" Mike asked.

"She's pretty good with French and can get by with Spanish. She picked up some Italian before our honeymoon."

"How about you?"

"I took Spanish, but don't remember much. I'm not good with languages."

"Me, either," Mike said. "I was in Belize once and I thought I was telling the cab driver I wanted a bar with girls and nightlife and he dropped me off at a whorehouse."

****

We talked some more, but I soon realized I needed to go—the sidecars were kicking my ass.

"I hear you," Mike replied, "I'm buzzing hard myself. I was just thinking, though. Why not text Ashley about meeting Wednesday?"

"What?"

"I said, 'Why not text Ashley about meeting Wednesday' now."

"Saying what?"

"Well she knows you're out with an old friend, right? And when you get home you can explain we were buds at Camp Marvins, right?"

"Yeah," I said.

"So text her that you're having a good time reuniting with your old childhood bud, that you'll be back soon, and ask if she's free Wednesday for the three of us to meet up. Like we want to lock it in if we can."

I looked up at the Yankee game, then back at Mike and said, "OK, I guess, why not?"

I typed, "Hey A, good time reuniting w/old friend, u around wed nite to meet up with us?"

Ten minutes later, Ashley texted back, "Sure, sounds fun."

"That's perfect," Mike said. "So Wednesday night it is."

"Yeah, I mean, I don't know how much of a read you'll get on her, but I'll talk to her about a place."

"Yeah, somewhere here in your neighborhood that's relaxed and comfortable, where the three of us can talk. Maybe that place you mentioned. Or whatever Ashley wants."

"OK, I'll talk to her and let you know where."

"OK, bro," Mike said once we were outside. "Remember, we met at Camp Marvins. There's nothing more to remember than that."

"Right," I said, and then he gave me a hug.

Mike headed to the subway, and I walked home.

One of my doormen gave me a look when he opened the door, and I mumbled how a client of mine is a big drinker and won't take no for an answer.

After a few minutes with Ashley, she said, "I think you need to get yourself to bed there, mister."

****

The next night Ashley and I checked out a movie at a local theater. It had gotten four-star reviews, but I kept looking at my watch, wondering when the thing would end.

Ashley's comment—"What in hell was that?"—gave me validation.

On the escalator to the exit, I heard the guy behind me tell his girl, "I want those two hours of my life back."

When I walked past the ticket booth guy, I gave him a two thumbs down sign, and Ashley laughed.

"Oh my God, I need a drink after that," Ashley said and suggested Gabriel's.

"So how about we meet your friend here—what time did you say, eight-thirty?"

"Yeah."

"Well, it's not crowded then, the music's not loud, and we can probably get seats at the bar. It's good for talking, right?"

"Yeah," I said.

"Or is this not the kind of scene you were looking for?"

"No, it is," I replied.

"Plus, the bartenders know us."

"Yeah, OK, I'll tell him to meet us here."

"Oh," Ashley said, "so what about going down for 'Hat Night'?"

"What?" I said.

"Taking Friday off and heading down to LBI Thursday night. We can come back with Mark and Camilla on Saturday."

"I don't know," I said, "I don't know if I can get Friday off."

"It's the Friday of Labor day, a half-day. Is it really critical that you be there?"

"Let me see what I can do."

CHAPTER TWENTY-FIVE

I called Mike in the morning to let him know the bar where we would meet. "It's pretty chill, we go there often," I said.

"Sounds like there's a 'but' in there, Dave."

"No, not really. It's just the place where Ashley came clean and said the 'Just bigger, OK' comment."

"Well, it sounds like a place we can talk and be comfortable," Mike said. "We'll keep things ultra-casual. I'm a good reader of women. We'll figure out where Ashley's head is at and get you some much-needed reassurance."

"OK. I have a meeting to run to, but 8:30 at Gabriel's."

"See you then, bro."

****

A crazed day at work had me scrambling to get ready. Mike called me at seven to make sure we were still on. I said, "Yeah," but probably hesitated, because Mike seemed to sense I was nervous. I explained I felt a little weird about the whole Camp Marvins story.

"Oh, Dave, it's the whitest of white lies. It's just a way for Ashley to be comfortable and for me to gain insight. Is she there now?"

"No, she's still at the gym."

"Relax, Dave, this is going to help. There'll be no more Tamara pulling interference on you. You're taking charge now, bro."

"OK," I said, "I appreciate that."

"Hey, Dave? One last thing."

"What's that?"

"I was thinking about what you said the other night. About how it might be difficult to get a read on her."

"Yeah?"

"Well, I thought about this last night. You mentioned you have a San Fran office. You were out there a few weeks ago, right?"

"Yeah."

"They call your cell after work sometimes, probably, right?"

"Yeah, why?"

"I was just thinking that for me to really get a read on Ashley, maybe you should go outside for a few minutes, saying you've got to take their call. That wouldn't be too unusual, right?"

"It wouldn't be that unusual, but the point being what?"

"It would give me a few minutes of alone time where maybe she'd be more open. Get a little more insight."

"I don't know, man. I'm already lying as it is."

"Trust me, Dave, I've thought this out. I will definitely get more insight from some brief alone-time with her."

"So, what are you saying? You want me to excuse myself?"

"Yeah, like, step out of the bar for a bit, so she can feel a little more comfortable talking."

"I'm running late but fine, I can step out for a few minutes."

"Cool. So, after we acquaint a bit, I'll give you a wink when she's not looking."

"OK."

"And Dave?"

"Yeah."

"Give me a little time, y'know, like say twenty minutes."

"Twenty minutes?"

"To try and get something of significance."

"Yeah, but—"

"Trust me Dave, OK? It will help you figure this all out."

It was late. There wasn't time to debate the merits of twenty minutes versus five minutes. "OK," I said.

"Cool, I'll be very discreet and signal you when to go. Then look at your phone or BlackBerry and tell us you have to take the call, OK?"

"OK," I said. "I have to get going. She's going to be home any minute."

****

Ashley had changed into a black dress and Gabriel's was close enough that she was OK walking there in heels.

"So your friend's name is Mike, right?"

"Yeah," I said "Mike Janson."

"So do you guys have some camp sing-along you're going to bust out in unison with?"

"No," I said, nervously.

Mike was already sitting at the bar when we walked in, chatting up the bartender as we came through the door. He smiled broadly when he saw me, stood up, and gave me a hug, saying, "Dave, my man." Then he said, "And you must be Ashley," and gave her a hug as well. "Please, have a seat. What can I get you both?"

We knew the bartender in a casual way, and he greeted us as we both ordered vodka-seltzers.

"Wow, Ashley," Mike said, "Dave told me you were beautiful and showed me a few photos, but you're far more beautiful in person. You must hear that a lot. My boy's a lucky guy," he added, as he rubbed my shoulders.

Mike wasn't wearing sweat pants this time, nor was he sporting the casual unkempt look I was accustomed to. He was wearing stylish, expensive jeans, trendy leather shoes and a black button down. He was clean-shaven and very polished. This GQ mode kind of threw me.

"Are you on Facebook, Ashley?"

"I'm on FB, but not actively."

"Just not into it?"

"Maybe I don't have time, or I'm in touch with my real friends. Those status updates can be so mundane."

"Yeah, I feel the same," Mike said, "but I'll give it props where props are due. It's how I reconnected with Dave."

"Yeah," Ashley said, "that's what I was thinking when Dave told me you guys connected. It would be fun to reunite with some childhood friends. It must have been strange to see each other after all these years."

"It was, in a very cool, strange way," Mike replied. "It gets you reflecting on your life and people who were really important to you. But you know what the strangest thing was about meeting back up with Dave again, Ashley?"

"What's that?"

"Even though I'm now a grown man," he replied, "and I haven't seen Dave in two decades, I still feel like a little brother around him."

"Little brother?" she asked.

"Well let me back-story it a bit to when we were kids."

I thought, Where in hell is Mike going now?

"I never felt more alone in the world," he said, "than the day my parents dumped me off at Camp Marvins and sped on out—on their way to their own vacation."

"Yeah?" Ashley said, sipping her drink, clearly interested.

"Well, I showed up a few days late and all the kids seemed to know each other. I went into the cabin and lay down on my bed. The counselor ordered me outside to play with other kids, so I stood by a tree, wanting to be invisible. But I knew I wasn't invisible, I was conspicuous. You know the merry-go–round, the ones at the playground? I mean you've ridden them as a kid?"

"Yeah, sure," she replied.

"Well, I'm sure you guys were naturals, but I'd never been on one. But I tried to study the etiquette. If you want to get on, you have to spin the thing for the others before you jump on yourself."

"Yeah."

"Well, it took a while for me to get the courage to make my move. Only I was nervous and wasn't spinning it fast enough, so I picked up the pace and fell head-first—smack into the sand. Everyone laughed at me, and not just the kids on the merry-go-round."

"Wow," Ashley laughed, "for you to remember it so well now, it must have been traumatic."

"Oh, absolutely," Mike replied as he sipped his beer, "so I fell spinning a merry-go-round. As for how I felt at that moment, it ranks up there with the most traumatic moments of my life."

"Were you there?" Ashley asked me.

"I don't think so," I replied, "I don't remember."

"No he wasn't," Mike said. "I was sitting on a rock by myself a while later and you know what older boy comes up, sits down beside me, and asks my name?'"

Ashley smiled brightly. "Would that older boy be Dave, by any chance?"

"You are sharp, Ashley. Dave told me that about you. Yes, it was. I'm sure you don't remember this, Dave, but I remember you chatting me up about baseball."

"I don't remember," I said, feeling blind-sided by the story he was telling.

"Yeah," Mike said. "I loved baseball as a kid, and we were talking batting averages and pitchers, and that encounter changed everything. He introduced me to his friends, brought me in to his circle, and suddenly I was catapulted to being the cool kid in camp, being friends with the older kids."

Ashley put her arm around me and saddled up in couple-mode.

"What can I say?" I said. "I had been there myself."

"Yeah," Ashley said, "Dave's dad still talks about how bad he felt seeing Dave's forlorn expression the first time he left him there."

"Yeah, Dave told me about the 'Everything's dandy, dad' un-mailed letter the other night. I hadn't heard that one before."

"Oh yeah," Ashley replied, "that cracked me up when I first heard it. Like if they had read your mail, an eight-year-old boy using the word 'dandy' in the 1980s should have raised red flags."

"Well, what Dave did for me," Mike said, "especially at that age when kids can be mean, just speaks to his character."

"Aww," Ashley said, "that's all sweet," and gave me a kiss on the cheek.

"C'mon guys," I said, "you're embarrassing me. All I did was befriend a lonely kid."

"Well, it meant a lot to me," Mike said, patting my back.

Mike asked Ashley about her job. She said she liked it, but that it was not without its headaches. She talked about how clients could be difficult, then told of having to talk a client off a ledge that afternoon after first having him chew her out.

Mike added, "Well, sometimes it's less about getting your actual job done than managing others and securing the buy-in."

****

On our second drink, Mike gave me his wink.

Things were going smoothly, conversation was flowing, and I really didn't want to leave the scene. Then as Ashley turned for a moment, he nudged me, like, 'Now's the time.'

I nodded back OK.

I pulled out my phone and pretended to look at a message. "Oh Jeez," I said.

"What's wrong?" Ashley asked.

"The San Francisco office," I replied. "I'm terribly sorry. This will only take a few minutes, but I need to get back to them."

"That's the problem with time zones," Ashley said. "They wouldn't be hitting you up if it was 9 p.m. their time."

"Yeah, I know, I'm sorry. Would you excuse me for a moment?"

"Of course," Mike said, "totally understand. We'll be here. And maybe Ashley will tell me some good Dave stories."

"Uh-oh," I joked, "be right back."

On the street outside, I suddenly felt weak in the knees. *What the fuck am I doing?* I thought. I had just left Mike alone with my wife. Perhaps Mike could get a read on her and encourage her to talk more openly, but anything was possible. He had dressed up and was acting suave—quite different than before.

Suppose Ashley was attracted to him?

And how much did I really know about Mike? Sure, he had treated me like a friend, but he was a man as well. And here I was, giving him unfettered access—albeit brief—to my wife.

I tried to calm myself down. Ashley was out by herself all the time. She must always be getting hit on. As Mike had said, 'She has opportunities to stray every time she walks out the apartment door.'"

I found an angle from the window where I could see them talking by the bar. I wondered what Mike and Ashley were laughing about. Then I started thinking. A random guy hitting on her would see her wedding ring, assume his odds were low, and maybe not waste his time. But Mike knew what she had done, was capable of— he had insight and information. Sure, work people had those as well, but "the rumor" for Ashley was now a deterrent.

Was Mike using his time alone with her to really get a read on her, or might he be attempting to hit on her himself?

What the fuck am I doing out here?

This whole plan had been harried and last-minute. I hadn't any real time to think it through. On the other hand, Ashley wasn't going to flirt back with someone she thought was my old friend.

I looked again through the window. Mike was gesticulating as Ashley listened attentively. I felt helpless. I saw Mike put a hand on her shoulder, like he was saying, "I know, I know."

When eighteen minutes had passed, I couldn't wait any longer. Mike saw me walk in and shot me a look, holding up his hand to say, "Five more minutes." I turned around and went back outside. I thought of extended time in soccer games.

What the fuck was I doing? Was he really onto some great insight?

When I walked back in exactly five minutes later, I was prepared to shake my head no, that the alone-time with my wife was done. Instead he welcomed me back, saying, "Those damn west coast peeps."

"Pain in my ass," I replied, "So how are you guys doing?"

Ashley gave me an unusually bemused look and said, "We're doing great."

Mike asked the bartender to turn the TV to the U.S. Open. It was a replay from the afternoon. Nidal was playing some nobody in an early round. Mike started chatting her up about tennis and she yapped away right back at him. When Mike started in on players' individual strengths and weaknesses, Ashley replied, "I agree" or "Exactly."

Mike then added how he'd always wanted to go to Wimbledon and the French Open. Ashley gushed about both venues. Suddenly they were swapping stories of must-go vacation spots.

"Ashley and I honeymooned in Italy," I said.

"Have you ever been, Mike?" Ashley asked.

"Italy is my big European omission," Mike said. "It's next up on my list, though."

Ashley proceeded to name the various must-see places in Rome and Venice.

Mike mentioned that he liked a song that was playing.

"Oh yeah, I love this band," Ashley said, "I saw them in Boston last year."

"Yeah, I'm just not into that solo album he did."

"Me, either," Ashley replied. "Stick with the band stuff, Brandon."

I didn't know the lead singer had a solo anything. I excused myself to go to the men's room. I was feeling uneasy. Maybe tomorrow he'd say something like, "I observed her body language, and it's clear that she loves you, that you're the man in her world." But I needed to stop throwing up conversational air-balls and get my conversational mitt on.

As I walked back to the bar, Mike had moved into my chair, closer to Ashley, and had her laughing. "Hey buddy," he said, standing back up, "are we ready for another round?"

"Sure, I think I'll move on to a martini," I said, thinking a strong drink would help me get my game on.

"I like your style, buddy. Another drink, Ashley?"

"Absolutely," she said, "what kind of beer are you drinking?"

"Zlaty Bazant," Mike said. "It's from Slovakia. Have a taste, it's really good."

"Yeah, that is really good," Ashley replied.

"Care to join me? I'm getting another."

"Yeah, sure, why not? It's got an interesting taste, and why not mix-it up a bit."

"That a girl," Mike said, and ordered us the round.

I felt like a schmuck toasting them with my martini.

****

"How you doing, man?" Mike asked when Ashley went to the bathroom.

"I'm kind of wigging out about now," I replied.

"Chill out man, this is going well. I'm learning a lot. Trust me, I'll give you the whole download tomorrow. Why are you wigging?"

"I feel like I'm not even part of the conversation. Like it's just the two of you talking."

"Oh, I didn't realize. I thought we were just getting to know each other. I'll make a conscious effort to involve you."

"I wasn't saying that—"

"No, I will. I'm sorry about that. We can talk about camp days."

I gave Mike an "Are you fucking serious" look.

"What?" he asked.

"Jeez man, that's not what I meant. I don't want to make up shit about jamborees and freaking three legged races."

Mike laughed, and then apologized for laughing. "Relax bro, this has been enlightening," he said. "And everything with the two of you will be fine. Believe me. I'll share with you when we're alone and have more time."

Ashley was returning from the ladies room and I kind of backed away.

"Yeah, Giants tickets," Mike said to me. "PSL's are outrageously expensive, but I might be able to score a couple tickets for us. I have a friend with lower level twenty yard line."

"What's that?" Ashley asked.

"Giants tickets," Mike replied.

"Dave's uncle has season tickets. We went a few times, the last couple years."

"Oh yeah, you a Giants fan Ashley?"

"Not really. I don't really care for pro football. I like college though."

"Oh yeah, who's your team?"

"Virginia Tech."

And of course Mike engaged Ashley in a conversation about VT football. During a pause, Mike said, "I remember Dave as a mighty good second baseman. I played first base but dropped a lot of his throws. He was awfully patient."

I appreciated the gesture, but I didn't find it easy to respond to fake accolades directed at my pretend ten-year-old self.

I felt like a wet log.

****

Mike excused himself to go to the men's room, leaving me alone with Ashley.

"How are you doing?" I said.

"Great. I like Mike a lot. Thanks for arranging this."

"Yeah, I thought you'd like him," I said. "I mean it was cool to reconnect after all this time."

"Yeah, that's really cool," she said. "I guess FB can be good for something, right?"

"Yeah," I said. "I was surprised he found me, that he even remembered my last name."

I felt awkward and full of shit, like I was talking to just to talk.

"Are you OK?" I asked. "I mean, do you want to get going soon?"

"No, I'm good, this is fun. You?"

"I was just checking is all."

"Another round, guys?" Mike asked after he returned.

"Sure, why not?" Ashley said.

"Another martini, Dave?"

"No, I'll just have a beer—that Czech beer you guys are drinking."

Then Mike suggested tequila shots. "What do you say Ashley, you game? We'll do hornitos. It's far better than the gringo patron stuff."

"Why not?" she said.

When I hesitated Mike said with a laugh, "You're doing one, too, my man—you gotta love peer pressure."

"Ever do a vampire shot, Ashley?"

"No," she replied, "but I think I know what it is. I guess I'm doing one, right?"

"My kinda girl," he replied.

I wasn't sure what it was and listened as Mike explained it to my wife. I watched as he licked Ashley's neck and shook salt onto his wet saliva. He gave her the lime, telling her to keep it in her mouth; then he licked the salt off her neck, slammed the tequila and put his mouth to Ashley's as her tongue passed the lime to him.

She smiled when he told her it was her turn.

I watched as Ashley licked Mike's neck, poured the salt, licked it off, and did her shot. Only Mike was briefly playful with the lime, like she was going to have to go in and get it out of his mouth.

"C'mon," she said as he brought the lime to his lips before letting her snatch it.

"No cheating," she said afterwards, giving him a playful punch.

Mike laughed then turned to me, saying, "drink up buddy."

When he asked if I needed salt or lime, I replied, "I do mine straight."

I felt like a dumbass as soon as I said that.

"Excuse me, buddy," Mike said laughing.

So there I was, chugging my shot alone, as Mike went back to chatting with Ashley.

"How did that treat you, buddy?" Mike asked. "Hornitos is pretty smooth, right?"

"Yeah," I replied, "I just don't need the training wheels."

Another lame response, I thought.

"I like the process and tradition," Mike said, "the tequila, the lime, the salt—but I know what you mean about just doing it straight."

****

I thought about the vampire shot as I pissed. How was that getting a read on her?

Face it, I thought. Mike is hitting on Ashley. He has designs on my wife.

What other explanation was there?

But it was midnight. Ashley and I had to be up early. That was my exit strategy. I would be casual, give him a hug, and tell him to get back to me about those Giants tickets.

But then I walked back out to the bar. Even from forty feet away, I could see what was happening. Mike was kissing Ashley. She was kissing him back.

Jesus Christ, I thought. That motherfucker is making out with my wife. I went back to the bathroom, my heart racing. How stupid can I be?

And how could Ashley do that? She knew I'd only be gone for a minute. What would the freaking bartender, who knew us, be thinking? I waited another minute before going back out. From afar, I could see they were just talking now. I pretended like I hadn't seen anything when I walked back up.

"We were just talking about a nightcap back at the place," Ashley said.

"What do you say buddy?" Mike asked.

"It's past midnight. You sure, Ashley?"

"Yeah, why not? It's only a few blocks and it's not super-late, right?"

"Uh yeah, OK," I said.

****

When Mike went to the men's room I asked Ashley, "You sure about this?"

"Yeah, I mean you're OK with it, right?"

"Uh yeah, sure."

"We still have those Corona Lights, right?"

"Yeah, I think so."

"And we have vodka and cranberry juice?"

"Yeah."

"How are you doing?" she asked.

"I'm good, how are you?"

"Great, and I understand."

I thought, Understand what?

"I like Mike," she added. "I'm pretty sure we still have some Coronas."

She gave me a quick kiss and told me she loved me.

Mike came back out, signed the bill, and said, "Shall we?"

Ashley had just stuck her tongue in Mike's mouth, and now he was coming back with us to our apartment. My heart was freaking racing, and I thought, *I shouldn't have had that martini.*

Mike was essentially a stranger. And now, suddenly, we were saying hi to our doormen, and this guy was heading up the elevator with us to our apartment, our home.

****

Ashley turned on some music and offered Mike a seat on our sofa.

Jesus Christ, I thought, he was in our living room, looking around at our photos, sizing up our place, and Ashley was asking me to bring out some Coronas.

She had an alternative rock mix playing and was seated on the couch next to him when I came out with the beer. I sat on a chair to the side.

"I'm sure you hear this all the time, Dave," Mike said, "but you have a wife who is both super-gorgeous and super-cool."

"Oh please," Ashley said.

"You don't have to tell me that," I replied.

"Oh man," Mike said, when an Arctic Monkeys' song came on, "I love this song."

"It's a good song to dance to," Ashley said. "Do you dance, Mike?"

"Do I dance?" he repeated with an expression like *Dancing with the Stars* had nothing on him.

"We can move the coffee table," she suggested. "Can you help me with this, Dave?"

"What?" I said. "Yeah, OK."

Thirty seconds later, I was watching Mike dance with my wife in my living room. As Ashley shimmied away with Mike, I felt as inanimate as the chair I was sitting in.

When the song ended, Ashley lowered the music and said, "We have this video game. It's a little cheesy, but you have to check it out."

"Sure," Mike said.

I knew the game. I had watched Ashley dance to it for a whole afternoon with her eight-year old cousin. Some cartoon character comes out dancing to a song and points are awarded by how well you follow along, holding these sensor-batons.

"You're a champ at this, Ashley," Mike said, when the song ended. "You have two thousand points to my three hundred. Do you get your ass kicked at this like me, Dave?"

"I haven't played," I said, "but I'm sure I would."

"I think you had the batons on backwards," Ashley said.

"Now you're just being kind," Mike replied, "I'm no match for you."

The next song came on—a fast-paced country song.

"What, you're not joining me?" Ashley asked

"I'm still working on getting my two-step down," Mike replied, "but I'd love to watch you."

Ashley frowned, then smiled, before saying, "I'll be right back."

Mike leaned in to me and clicked bottles saying, "Cheers bro. This is a really nice place you have here. I'm impressed. How's the rent?"

"We own it," I replied.

"Wow, nice, it must have cost a pretty penny. I love the high ceilings and space—pretty atypical for Manhattan apartments."

Ashley darted back in, wearing a cowboy hat that I had bought her at a University of Texas football game, last year.

"You look cute as all get-out," Mike said as Ashley turned on the game and began her country music dance.

Ashley grew up in Virginia. I guess that's technically the South. She has a bit of a southern accent, much diminished from living here. She certainly can affect a strong southern accent when she's goofing around, but I've never known her to like country music. Maybe a couple very popular songs. But we don't ever have CMT playing on our TV.

She was doing the song as a goof mostly, and because she's good at it.

Mike clapped when it ended and Ashley said, "Oh stop."

"No that was a visual delight," Mike said. "I mean it. It had me thinking, why don't you put on some sultry music and show us more sultry moves?"

Ashley looked at me, then back at Mike, and said, "Yeah?"

"I would love it, Ashley," Mike said. "Right, Dave?"

"Uh, OK," I heard myself saying.

"Well, let me see what I got," she said, as she made a quick playlist on her iPod.

Suddenly, Ashley had Britney Spears' "Slave 4 U" playing.

I briefly wondered if I was hallucinating. Ashley was dancing in the middle of our living room, strutting around, flipping her dress up, performing for Mike.

I felt paralyzed.

"You OK, Dave?" Mike asked when the song ended.

"Yeah, I'm cruel—I mean—I'm cool."

Mike smiled and said, "Drink your beer, man, before it gets warm."

An old Madonna song came on next. Mike said, "Ashley?"

"Yeah, Mike."

"I loved how you danced in the last song, but 'Justify My Love' is a pretty sexy song. I would love it if you lost your dress in the middle of it."

"Excuse me?" Ashley replied.

"You have your bra and panties on underneath, right?" Mike said.

"Well, bra and thong," she replied.

"It's hardly more revealing than a bikini on the beach, right?"

Mike gave me a quick smile. I felt he was cribbing back the inverse of what I had told him about Ashley wearing bikinis.

"We still have some vodka left, right?" Ashley asked me.

"Do we?" I said.

"I'm pretty sure we do" Ashley replied, "and I'm going to need a shot for this, so long as you boys join me."

"Sounds good to me," Mike said.

And so there I was pouring the three of us shots, pouring Mike a shot, so that my wife would feel comfortable enough to take her dress off in front of him.

Mike toasted us, saying, "To a wonderful evening."

As soon as I drank it, I realized it wasn't a good idea—I felt drunk in a sedated way.

Ashley, on the other hand, was buzzing in an energetic "go off" way. And then she began dancing in her black dress as she restarted Madonna's "Justify my love."

"That's it," Mike said, "just go with it, girl."

I felt dazed, watching her.

"C'mon, Ashley," Mike said, "liberate yourself, even your dress wants you to free yourself from it."

Ashley smiled and gave me a look. I stared down at the floor.

"Just for a little bit," Mike said.

"OK," Ashley replied, "can you get the zipper?"

"Dave," Mike said to me, "would you like to do it?"

"Um, OK," I said, as Ashley walked toward me and turned around to give me access. I realized my hands were shaking as I unzipped the back of her dress.

"Thanks, honey," she said, giving me a quick kiss.

"OK," Ashley said, "I'm going to restart the song, K?"

"Absolutely, Ashley" Mike replied.

I watched as Ashley danced seductively around our living room, her eyes focused on Mike.

"So sexy," Mike said, "I love the way you dance."

And then I watched as Ashley pulled the strap down off her shoulders. It had a slow-motion quality to it, as the top of her dress came down to reveal her bra.

"Amazing," Mike said, "fan-fucking-tastic."

Ashley hesitated for a moment, but Mike said "Go with it, just a little more."

And I watched as Ashley shimmied out of her dress and it fell to our living room rug. She stepped out of it and hung it over the side of the sofa. Then she pranced back to the center of the living room in nothing but her bra and thong, and resumed dancing.

"Oh yeah, Ashley, shake them big titties of yours. Oh yes, I love it. Now how about turning around for me."

I watched in a surreal daze as my wife showed off her ass cheeks to Mike.

"What an amazing ass, Ashley," I heard Mike say.

The next was an old Joe Cocker song, "You Can Keep Your Hat On."

"Ever give a lap dance Ashley?" Mike asked.

Ashley smiled almost bashfully, "Um, no."

"Why don't you try it? I'm sure you'd be a natural. Just for a few seconds."

Ashley didn't even flash me a look. It was as if I wasn't there.

I watched my wife sit down on Mike's lap. I could see Mike straightening up, as if to get her to feel his hard-on under his jeans. Then he put his arms out and put his hands on her tits, over her bra, copping a feel.

My mouth was agape. He had his hands on my wife's fucking tits.

Mike whispered into her ear. Ashley whispered back into his. Then Mike again. Then Ashley. Then Ashley stood back up and asked if we were ready for another beer.

"Sounds great," Mike said.

It's already 1:30 a.m. on a Wednesday night, I thought.

"I really love your apartment," Mike said when she returned, "but I haven't seen beyond this room and the kitchen. What do you say, Ashley, can I get the grand tour?"

"Of course, where are my manners?" she said as she handed us both a beer.

When Mike stood up, I did, too. My heart was racing and I was trembling. Ashley was showing Mike the rest of our home, wearing nothing but her bra and thong.

"You've seen this bathroom," she said, her butt cheeks on total display as the two of us followed behind.

"This is our office, or our supposed office. Let's just say it's a work in progress."

"It's really spacious for Manhattan," Mike said.

"And here's our bedroom."

Ashley stepped in first, and then Mike, before he abruptly turned around. "Be a sport Dave," he said, "and give us a little alone time, bro."

"What?"

Mike looked back at Ashley before saying, "I think we're going to have a little private time now."

"What?"

I looked over at Ashley, who mouthed, "I love you," but made no forward movement toward me.

I mouthed back that I loved her too. Then I looked back at Mike.

"Just give us a few minutes, Dave."

"But Mike—" I said.

"It's OK, Dave, just relax, go back outside and enjoy your beer. It's all good, bro."

"But Mike, wait—" I said as he put his hand on the doorknob.

"It's cool buddy," he said.

I started to put my hand on the door. A few seconds later, he had pushed it closed and I heard the lock turn.

What the fuck?

A wave of panic overcame me. He'd just shut my bedroom door in my face and locked it. And now I was standing helplessly in the hallway. I stood in stunned, dazed disbelief.

Mike just locked me out of my own fucking bedroom. And Ashley's in there with him, in our bedroom, drunk and in her underwear.

I moved to knock on the door, but stopped myself. I had to think for a second about what I would say.

If I knocked, Mike would say, "What?"

And then I would say, "Can you open the door, please."

And he'd say something like he'd just said, "Dave, give us some time, enjoy your beer, hang out in the living room and watch TV."

Then what?

I could say, "Open this door right this fucking minute or I'm picking the lock."

That would probably prompt Ashley to come to the door.

I pictured her quietly saying, "It's OK, Dave, do you mind just giving us a little bit of privacy for a bit?"

I couldn't stand the thought of hearing something like that from her—being made to feel like an intruder.

Maybe she'd get a change of heart and come out on her own in a few minutes.

But she kissed him in the bar and gave him a fucking lap dance in our Goddamn living room.

And she seemed to have no problem with Mike shutting the door, basically in my face.

****

I heard Ashley's iDeck turn on. She was playing one of her "chill out" mixes I'd heard dozens of times. It seemed such an intimate thing to play.

I heard Mike say, "Turn it up."

I heard Ashley's playful, sweet laugh as the volume went up.

I walked back down the hallway and saw Ashley's dress draped over the living room sofa. I thought of a Radiohead song, the line, "this is really happening."

I knew I had to get a grip. Ashley had just told me she loved me. Perhaps they'd come back out in a few minutes and Mike would head back to Brooklyn.

Five minutes later, the music was still playing loudly and I was sitting on the living room couch with my head in my hands.

How could I have been so stupid? Good fucking God, what have I done? Mike is going to fuck Ashley tonight … in my own fucking bedroom … in my own fucking bed.

I felt sick to my stomach, and like I might cry.

I got up and sat down outside my bedroom door. But the music was so loud and there was no space between the songs.

I thought of Ashley saying, "I really like Mike" earlier at the bar.

Finally I got up and lay down on the living room sofa. It was after three, and I had to work tomorrow.

What have I done? I wondered. I just let another man lock me out of my own fucking bedroom and he probably just fucked my wife in our marital bed.

I hadn't been man enough to stop him. I should have broken things up and taken Ashley home as soon as I'd seen them kissing at the bar.

What would Ashley think of me now?

Will everything between us be different when I wake up tomorrow? Did I throw my marriage away tonight?

****

I woke up on the sofa in a hangover haze. I saw Ashley's dress over the foot of the sofa and realized there were sounds coming from the bedroom. It was 5:15.

I knew what was happening as I walked back up to the bedroom. I could hear the bed creaking. Ashley was moaning, "Oh God."

It was all too obvious. I was listening to my wife getting fucked. I heard Ashley's voice as I sat in the hallway by my bedroom door. "Oh God, Mike, oh yeah, Mike."

I wiped my eyes and listened to her moan—to the hard ball-slapping sounds of intense fucking.

What the fuck are you doing, dude? I said to myself, as I pulled my dick out through the fly of my boxers.

The ball slapping grew louder and the pace increased.

"Oh God, Mike, oh yeah, fuck me baby!"

"Yes, Mike, yes Mike, oh my God, Mike, I'm cumming, baby!"

Suddenly, I came. I didn't even have time to cup it. It landed on the carpet. I searched my pocket for a tissue.

But Mike was continuing to fuck my wife.

I put my forehead in my hand and felt a visceral knot in my stomach.

"Oh God, I love your cock, Mike, I'm about to cum again."

I wiped tears from my eyes.

"So am I, Ashley," I heard him say, "I'm so close, baby."

"I'm cumming, Mike, oh God, I'm cumming, Mike!"

"Oh fuck, yeah Ashley, so am I, baby, oh yeah, here it comes."

"Oh Mike, oooh Mike."

"Oh fuck, right inside you, baby."

The sounds from the bedroom quickly receded.

I didn't want to get caught listening by the bedroom door. So I stumbled my way back to the couch and lay there, my heart racing. Didn't Ashley know they'd wake me? Did she not even consider that? Or did she not care that I might hear her wake-up-fuck with Mike—in my fucking bedroom—in our fucking bed?

****

I heard the shower turn on.

Twenty minutes later, I heard footsteps and pretended to be asleep. I felt Mike looking down on me. Then I heard our apartment door shut.

I lay there in the quiet for a while, wondering what I could possibly say to Ashley. I tiptoed up the hallway and saw her sleeping. I showered in our other bathroom, so as not to wake her.

As I was about to leave, I stared at her sleeping—the woman I loved more than anything in the world.

"It's seven-thirty," I said. "You're going to be late for work."

"I'm calling in sick today," she said.

"Are you OK?"

"Yeah, but hung over and super-sleepy. And I haven't used one sick day this year. It's fine."

"OK," I said, "well I'm gonna head off now."

"How are you?" she asked.

"I'm OK."

"You sleep OK?"

"I'm hung over, too, but I slept OK."

"Where did you sleep?"

"The sofa in the living room."

"It's not bad, is it?"

"What?" I said.

"That sofa, I've napped there a lot. It's pretty comfy."

"It was fine," I said.

"David?" she said.

"Yeah?"

"Thank you. And I understand."

I looked at her puzzled, expressionless.

"Come here and give me a hug," she said. I leaned over and put my arms around her. The blanket fell slightly, exposing one of her breasts. Then she gave me a kiss and said, "I love you."

"I love you, too, Ashley."

"Have a great day at work," she said.

CHAPTER TWENTY-SIX

There was no way in hell I could even remotely have a great day at work.

I was a zombie and sick to my stomach.

After a meeting my boss asked, "Are you OK?"

"Yeah, I'm sorry, I'm just not feeling well."

"You sick? You want to go home?"

I ended up leaving a little early, but I didn't want to go home. I didn't know what to say to Ashley or what she would say to me. I went to Central Park and found a bench in a secluded area. Ashley was the most precious thing in the world to me, the one woman I couldn't see living without. What kind of meek little pussy would I seem to her now?

I thought about her comments in the morning. Telling me the sofa was comfy. Did she expect me to say, "Oh yeah, super comfy, I loved it, best sleep in years."

And what was she thanking me for? What did she mean, she understood? Understood fucking what?

Doesn't she know I'm aware she got fucked last night? Does she really think I went from having the door shut on me to peacefully drifting off on that couch? She doesn't think I was so drunk that I was unaware of what was happening in our bedroom, does she?

I thought of what she'd cried out—"I love your cock, Mike"—personalizing it, as he fucked her.

Fucking Mike, that asshole.

Thanks a lot, Mr. I'll help you with this bro.

What a stooge he'd made of me. He'd played me, pretending to be my friend and confidant. *Like yeah, Mike, thanks for the fucking insight.*

He probably had designs on Ashley the moment I stupidly sent him photos. Show me more photos Dave.

OK, Mike, here's some more. Oh and here's all Ashley's biographical info complete with interests, favorite books, you name it. Oh and you want time alone with her? OK, sure, I'll step outside for twenty minutes.

How easy I had made it for him. I'd fucking handed my wife to him on a silver fucking platter. God, the fucking power he must've felt. He probably knew he was closing the deal as soon as he was inside our apartment, the place where I lived—looking at photos on our walls, symbols of the life Ashley and I had built together.

And then he took the most sacred symbol—our marital bed—and fucked my wife in it. Mike had humiliated me in front of my own wife. He took the most precious thing in the world to me—my wife's pussy—and fucked it as his own.

What did the future portend for us now? How could I look Ashley in the eyes? How could she not view me differently? How could last night not have untold significance for us, our relationship, our marriage? She hadn't just let him fuck her last night, drunk. She'd let him give her a sober wake-up fuck as well.

I would be going home in a few hours. I kind of hoped she simply wouldn't bring it up. I could play dumb. I could pretend I was too drunk to be aware of what happened.

Ashley was showing Mike the bedroom and they both crashed, and then so did I. The living room sofa seemed as good a place as any. I hadn't been able to keep up with the party. Maybe they briefly cranked tunes, and then saw me on the sofa. And Mike was too drunk to go home, so he just crashed on the bed.

I could have slept through this morning. Ashley doesn't know I heard or was listening by the door. I could say something vague like "Did I help take your dress off?" and she could say, "Oh my God I barely even remember that."

Maybe we could write it off as just some weird, drunken night.

****

Tired and numb, sitting on the bench, I suddenly got a text

from Mike, saying, "Hey buddy, u around for mtg up after work & touching base?"

Fuck you, I thought,

I let his follow-up call go to voicemail.

"Hey buddy," he said, as I finally listened to his message, "I got a text from Ashley, but I don't want to respond without talking with you first. Let me know if you're around to meet up."

Good God, I thought, what did Ashley text him?

There was no choice. I had to know. I had to meet him.

"In a mtg," I texted back, "how's seven at the bar we hung out at?"

"See you then," he replied.

I texted Ashley that I had to meet a client after work.

She texted back, "K, I'll be here."

✱✱✱✱

I got to the bar a half hour early. I needed a drink and some time to think before Mike arrived.

Mike had pulled far more on me than Jim Murta ever had. Mike raised the stakes, upped the ante into the stratosphere.

It was still so hard to mentally process. It felt un-real. Mike had engineered a meeting, used my information to push her buttons, and used my bed, my bedroom to fuck my wife—relegating me to sleeping on the fucking couch.

I wondered if Ashley had called Tamara today with details. Would Tamara say, "I'm really impressed with the way Dave handled sleeping on the couch so maturely"?

I thought of punching Mike, but he'd probably end up kicking my ass.

Mike had a broad smile when he walked over and insisted on hugging me.

"So, how ya doing buddy?" he said as he sat beside me. "What you drinking?"

"Stella," I replied.

"Could we get two Stellas?" Mike said, and threw down his card.

"So how you doing bro?"

"OK."

"Were you as tired as I was today?"

I nodded.

"Yeah, bro, I hear you. I was dragging for sure."

"You OK?" he continued, "you seem a little shaken up."

"I'm a lot shaken up," I said, "can you freaking blame me?"

"I totally understand, man, it's a very normal reaction."

"Normal is nowhere near how I feel right now."

"It's gonna be OK, buddy. Relax, everything's gonna be fine."

"What are you saying? Everything is not fine."

"Chill bro, don't worry," he said, "cheers."

I clicked my glass mechanically with his.

"You said Ashley texted you?"

"Yeah, I want to get to that. But first, just talk to me Dave. I'm here for you. I really am. What's the matter? Were you surprised or blindsided by what happened last night?"

"Yes, you could say that. Blindsided, yeah, I was blindsided."

"Didn't expect it would happen so quickly?"

"I wasn't expecting this to happen at all, Mike. I thought this was about getting inside her head."

I looked around to make sure we weren't being overheard, before saying, "I didn't know it was about you trying to get inside my wife's pussy."

"It was about getting a read on her. And it turned out she was open to being with me. You said you wanted to know. Now you know. Now you have a baseline from which to go forward."

"What does that mean? Baseline? I know what the word means, but what do you mean?"

"Dave, if it hadn't been me, it would have been someone else. It was just a matter of time. Only you wouldn't have known about it. At least she wasn't running around behind your back. Or embarrassing you like that guy did. You don't want that, right?"

"No."

"Well, now you can begin to embrace that part of her sexuality and show that you support her, that you're there for her, that your love is unconditional. You do love her, right? You don't want to lose her?"

"Of course I love her. I told you the first time we talked that the thing that scared me the most was her leaving me. Do I love her? Are you kidding me? You know I do."

"Then you need to continue to show her that. And you did last night. By letting her follow her bliss. Letting her be who she is. Letting her explore her adventurous side. She's a very attractive young lady who is starting to bloom sexually. What's so wrong with that?"

"What's wrong with it?" I asked. "She's my wife, for one. Do you realize what my friends or family would think if they knew what happened last night?"

"Fuck 'em," Mike said. "I'm serious, fuck 'em. They will never know and who cares what they think anyway. I'm sure they have their own secrets. A lot happens behind closed doors."

"Not something like this. This is not normal."

"What the hell does 'normal' mean. Two kids and a white picket fence and vanilla sex once a week and church on Sundays. I mean who defines 'normal.' You want to follow every societal norm, being whoever society says you should be?"

"I don't know what the hell that's all supposed to mean," I said. "Mike, I'm just a little fucked in the head right now."

"It's OK, bro," he said, as he patted me on the back, "It may take a little while to accept. It was probably was a lot to take in. But I really am your friend, Dave. I mean that."

"Yeah, OK, Mike, whatever."

"Look, if you want to just sit here and watch some baseball and decompress, that's cool with me, too. We can just sit here and drink beer together."

"Mike," I said, "what I want to know, is what Ashley texted you."

"OK, but just calm down first, drink your beer, relax."

"I am calm, Mike. I just really want to know what she said."

"OK, OK, Ashley asked when she'd be seeing me again."

"Can I see the text, Mike, please?"

"Sure," he said grabbing his phone. "Here."

It was Ashley's cell number.

"Hey u, what did u do to me to last nite? omg I'm exhausted. took 2day off. when am i seeing u next?"

I stared at it, re-reading it, re-confirming her number, re-reading it again.

"You OK, bro?"

"Jesus," I muttered, as I handed his phone back.

"What are you thinking?"

"That I can't believe this is happening."

"I understand. It can be a lot to take in, but relax. I haven't responded back. I wanted to talk to you first. We don't have to figure out anything this minute. Let's watch a couple innings, chill out, and catch a buzz."

"You want a shot?" he asked.

"No."

"C'mon Dave, let's do a shot together. Pardon me, sir, we'll have two shots of Hornitos."

I sat there staring vacantly at the game until the shots arrived. "I take it we're not doing vampire shots?" I said.

Mike laughed. "That a boy" he said, "getting your humor back. We'll do them straight, my man, no training wheels tonight.

"It's all gonna be good bro," Mike said, as he clicked my glass.

"So you're gonna reply to her text?" I asked

"Yeah, how would you like me to handle it?"

"How do you mean?"

"I need to get back to Ashley, but I want your input."

I didn't know what to say.

"I was thinking the three of us meet again for dinner tomorrow night. What do you think?"

"What?" I said."

"Well, I can't do Saturday, I'm going to Atlantic City, so I was thinking, let's all meet for dinner tomorrow night."

Mike could see my distress.

"It's better that you're there supporting her, Dave. You don't want her carrying on any secret affairs. That's the kind of shit that damages marriages."

"And last night didn't damage it? Are you kidding?"

"I think you're going to find it strengthened it. In the long run, it will. The important thing is being there through the process. It's going to bring you closer."

"Mike, I heard you with Ashley this morning."

"What did you hear?"

"Mike, I heard you fucking my wife."

"Were you listening?"

"Yes."

"By the door?"

"At one point, yes."

"And it got you good and hard, didn't it?"

"Jeez, Mike."

"What? You talked to me about jerking off all summer thinking about that dude at that party fucking your wife. It's OK. You found it exciting. And nothing to be ashamed about."

"Jeez, Mike, please."

"What? It's a normal reaction. I bet you came real good, like you never had before. Hearing your wife all horned out like that."

"Mike, please, look, I'm just scared."

"Of what?"

"Oh gee, Mike, I don't know, like how about what Ashley will think of me, or how can she ever respect me now."

"She'll respect you a lot more now than that night she fucked the guy at the party right under your nose. She knows now that she's got a loving and supportive husband who will even make certain sacrifices to make sure her sexual needs are met."

"Oh man," I said.

"C'mon Dave, part of you wanted this."

"I didn't want this, Mike. I wasn't expecting this. I just wish I could go back to three months ago before everything happened."

"You need to focus on the future with her. I'm here to strengthen your relationship, not pull it apart."

"Strengthen my relationship by fucking my wife? Do you hear what you're saying?"

"It may sound unconventional or counterintuitive to you at first, but your acceptance of who she is, and being part of it all, is critical to rebuilding your relationship. I mean, Dave, you know that night at the party wasn't the first time."

"Did she say something to you to that effect?"

"I got strong indicators, yes. I mean, a wife doesn't typically spread her legs for a guy at a party her husband's at without some back context, you know?"

"What did she say?"

"When I get details, I'll let you know."

"Jesus," I muttered, "Mike, what are you going to text her?"

"Well, are you guys free tomorrow?"

"I have to check."

"Check with Ashley?"

"Yeah."

"OK," Mike replied, "so I'll text her that we talked on the phone and ask her if is she's up for dinner tomorrow—the three of us."

"Mike, why does it have to be tomorrow?"

"Because tomorrow is really the only night I'm free. After AC on Saturday, I'm going to the Open Sunday. Look, if Ashley can't do it tomorrow, we push it off to next week, but why not see if she can swing it? Rather than you and I figure this out, let's just see what she says, right?"

"Fine," I said in a what-recourse-do-I-have-if-she-wants-to-see-him kind of way.

"So, I'll text her now, we cool?" Mike asked.

"I guess so."

"You know, on second thought," Mike said, sipping his beer, "maybe you should text her."

"What?"

"Yeah, maybe it's better if the invite comes from you. It gives the control back to you. Like you're setting the agenda and taking charge."

"Please, are you freaking serious?"

"Dave I really am trying to help here. I'll text her if you prefer, but I just thought you'd show you were asserting control by giving the invite yourself."

I zoned out at the game on TV before saying, "Fine, I'll fucking text her."

"Hi Ash," I typed into my phone, "I'm still out w/a client, but I talked w/Mike & any interest in the 3 of us getting dinner tomorrow night?"

Five minutes later, she replied back, "Sure, count me in."

Mike smiled when he saw her reply and ordered us two more pints. "That wasn't so hard right?"

I was sinking into my chair.

Finally I said, "Mike, I'm not being accusatory, but last night was your goal all along, wasn't it, from the moment I sent you her photos? I mean this wasn't really about helping me gain insight now, was it?"

Mike patted my back. "It was about gaining insight, bro. You got insight, didn't you? You wondered if that guy at the party was a one-time thing. What did you call it—an aberrant event, right? Now you know it wasn't."

"But that was your goal? I mean, to fuck my wife."

"Hey, Dave, I'm always going to be honest with you. Yeah, I thought Ashley looked pretty damn hot and sexy in the pictures. And I got hard thinking about the possibilities. But if she had thrown the blockades down or acted like she wasn't up for anything, I would have respectfully backed off. And then I would have honestly told you, hey, I think it was a one-time thing. This was not about me. It was about her. As you said, seeing where her head was at."

"But that was why you asked me to tell you all her interests. I feel like I made it so easy for you. Like Virginia Tech football—"

"Bro, c'mon. So I follow college football. It was just the flow of the conversation. That was gonna happen anyway. It's not like I was talking about classical music. I don't know shit about that, and I wasn't going to pretend I did. We simply hit it off. There was chemistry between us. It just happened."

"It's just how easy she went along with it."

"Well, our talk when you stepped outside definitely greased the wheels."

"What do you mean?"

"I just got real with her. Talked about you."

"Talked about me? What about me?"

"That I was aware of what happened with that guy at the party. I told her we had talked a lot about it. And that opened things up. She started throwing questions my way."

"What did she ask? What did you say?"

"She asked what you had said about it and I talked in general terms."

"Meaning what?"

"I said you were hurt by it and scared of losing her. How much you love her. Then I said that you were also aroused by it. That you were turned on learning about a new side to her sexuality."

"Are you serious?"

"Yeah, she was curious. She wanted to know your take on all of that. She told me she loves you. That should make you feel good, right?"

"Yeah, but what did she think 'turned on' meant? That I've been masturbating? You didn't tell her about that, right Mike?"

"Relax Dave. No I didn't. Just that part of you was real turned on by it. Then I explained that it's not uncommon. That lots of guys react that way."

"Are you fucking kidding me?"

"I was just being honest. Telling her a few things you found too difficult to tell her yourself. I think she appreciated it."

I sat there stunned, incapable of responding, just listening.

"Dave," he continued, "I was just giving a bit of much-needed honesty to the situation. For the sake of your marriage, honesty is the key."

"Did you tell her we're not really camp friends?"

"No, honesty has its limits. That's a white lie that needs to stay a white lie. She needs to continue to think that and I certainly would never tell her otherwise. She would be very pissed at you, if she learned I was a guy you met in an online cuckold room, who you arranged to have meet her."

"She's never going to know that, right, Mike?"

"Of course not, never."

"I think I should probably get going, Mike," I said.

"It's going to be OK Dave, trust me. C'mon, give me a hug, c'mon, that a boy, all right, chill out, hang in there, and I'll see you tomorrow, bro."

****

I could feel myself shaking on my walk home. I felt more infinitely fucked than I had been just yesterday. Giving Mike alone time at the bar had sealed my fate. For all I knew he could have told her about how I constantly jerk off and cited Jim Murta's name. And he had all last night in my bed—when he wasn't fucking her— to expound on everything. He could have explained to her what the term 'cuckold' meant.

I'd revealed very intimate things to Mike. He could tell Ashley about knowing about my premature issues, and it would ring true. Now she'd believe anything he said about me.

And tomorrow I'd have to have dinner as if I had accepted or even initiated this whole fucking arrangement.

Good Lord, what the fuck have I gotten myself into?

****

I did five rotations around our block before walking into our apartment. Ashley was sprawled on the living room sofa, working on her laptop, when I arrived.

"How was your day?" I asked.

"Lazy. I slept in till eleven—didn't even make it to the gym."

"Wow, that is lazy for you."

"How was your day?" she asked.

"I'm exhausted, and the client tonight came up at the last minute. I'm probably just going to head to bed."

"OK. You don't mind if I catch up on emails and join you later?"

"Of course not."

"Do you know where we're going tomorrow night with Mike?"

"Not sure yet" I replied, "but I was also thinking I could rent a car when I get out of work and we could probably be down by the shore by four."

"What?"

"Isn't 'Hat Night' tomorrow night?"

"Yeah, I'm confused," she said, "I thought the plan was to meet Mike tomorrow—wasn't that what you texted me?"

"Yeah," I said, "but I just remembered 'Hat Night' was tomorrow. We could drive down if you wanted—I mean, you said you wanted to do that."

"I said Thursday night, if you could get tomorrow off, but you couldn't—it's too far to drive, just for one night—and we'd barely have any beach time."

"Well it was just one night last weekend."

"Dave, we got there at noon and had a day at the beach."

"OK," I said, "I was just throwing that out there, but forget it."

"Do you not want to meet up with Mike, tomorrow?"

"I do," I said, "I just remembered about 'Hat Night', but I hear you on arriving too late."

"Are you OK with that?"

"Yeah, Ash, of course, absolutely. Look I'm beat. I'm going to get some shuteye."

Ashley puckered her lips and said, "Mwah mwah," so I walked over to her, and she gave me a quick kiss goodnight.

****

I was under the covers in the Ottoman King that Ashley and I had bought last summer—the bed Mike had slept in last night. The marital bed he'd fucked my wife in.

Mike had made a royal sucker out of me.

What a conquest this must have been for him. He might have been playing it by ear, but his goal was fucking my wife in my bed, and he did it on the first night of meeting her. He'd locked me out of my own bedroom and gone in for the kill.

You got fucking played, boy, I said to myself. The motherfucker relegated you to the couch as he slept in your bed.

I thought of the way Ashley had personalized it, as he fucked her. "Oh God, I love your cock *Mike*, I'm about to cum." It echoed in my head with the sound of the bed squeaking.

I had popped a boner and whispered, "Oh God, Ashley."

I thought about what others might think if they knew.

He fucked your wife in your own marital bed—this bed you're lying in now—and you were too weak and meek to stop it. He made you look like a fucking pussy. He just strutted into your apartment and made your bedroom his home for the night. And he took the woman you love and cherish, in a candy from a baby way.

"I love your cock, Mike!"

Oh God, Ashley, I thought, you let him fuck you in our bed.

I came, super-hard under the covers.

And then I just felt scared and alone.

CHAPTER TWENTY-SEVEN

Friday was a half-day.

Crazy thoughts filled my head.

I found myself in an electronics store. Hiding a video camera in the room seemed too risky, but I wondered about getting a small audio recorder. If things happened again as they had two nights earlier, I felt compelled to try and capture it.

"Can I help you?" the salesman said.

"Um, yeah maybe, I'm looking for a recorder to do field recordings."

"Professional gear, semi-professional? What are you looking to record?"

"No, I'm just doing an amateur project," I said, "I need to get outdoor sounds, birds chirping, the sound of a freeway, thunder, that kind of thing."

Initially he showed me a crazy contraption.

"I'm just looking for something small."

"How about this? College students use it to record school lectures."

****

Ashley had to work the full day, so back in the apartment, I tested the audio on the recorder.

I turned on the kitchen faucet and recorded it from the living room. Then I turned on the shower and recorded it with the bathroom door shut. From the hallway I recorded our alarm clock.

I put on the headphones and listened to playback. The audio seemed pretty clear.

I put the recorder in the hallway where I'd sat two nights before, went into our bedroom and shut the door.

I knew what I was doing was crazy, fucked up.

I got on the bed and make it creak. I affected a girly falsetto: "Oh God, Mike, fuck me, fuck me, Mike, I love your cock, Mike." Then I bounced on the bed and cried out, "Oh God, I'm cumming!"

I went back outside and listened to the playback. I could hear the creaking. And I heard all my "oh God Mike's," though that was a bit creepy and I made sure to erase the recording immediately.

****

Ashley didn't get home until just before eight. "I've got to get my butt into the shower and pronto," she said.

I always loved showering with her. Just before the Jim Murta incident, we had a rain forest shower in Florida. The shower was the size of a bedroom with tiled marble floor and multiple jets. I loved lathering up her body, rubbing soap on her breasts, all sudsy and slippery.

I was lying on the bed pretending to read the *Journal* when she came out. I snuck peeks as she searched through her lingerie drawer. I watched her put on a white thong and bra.

She looked over at me and I felt like I should give her space, so I went into the kitchen and had a Corona.

Sitting at that kitchen counter, I didn't know what to think. I felt like I had no control over anything tonight.

When I went back in the bedroom, Ashley was wearing a sheer white mini tube dress. It wasn't Tamara slutwear, but it was pushing the envelope for Ashley, for sure. From behind, I could see her thong shadowing through.

"You look really good—beautiful," I said.

"Thanks, I still have to put makeup on. How much time do we have?'

"Well, it's 8:30, but we'll take a cab."

Ashley was making an effort to look extra good. She had done it for me—going out on the town or for work events—but mostly to present the two of us in the most favorable light. But now her motivation seemed simply to look as fuckable as possible for Mike.

When I complimented her dress, did she think I was a fool? Like, "Don't you know I'm wearing this for your friend?"

"We'll take a cab," I said when she came out. "Oh, I see you got a manicure."

"Yeah and a pedi, today at lunch, but you can't see that."

"Well, it looks good."

"Thanks, so ready to go?"

****

We arrived at the restaurant just before nine.

The place was dimly lit. Ashley spotted an empty booth by the bar, off from the main dining area. The hostess said they reserved those for parties of four or more, so Ashley explained that a third would be joining us shortly, and how, in addition to having food, we'd be ordering a few rounds of drinks. She followed that up with a few pleases.

"OK you sold me," the hostess said, and led us to the booth. It was a loungey, leather-type semi-circle table facing the bar and TVs.

That's when Mike arrived, again dressed in GQ-style.

Ashley and I both stood up to greet him. I watched the two of them hug.

"Damn, girl," Mike said, "you looking radiant in that dress—it's like it was made for you."

Then he turned to give me a hug, saying, "Great to see you again, buddy."

Ashley sat in the middle, with me to her left and Mike to her right.

"So," Mike said, "what are we all drinking? Personally, I hear a martini calling."

"I hear it calling as well," Ashley replied.

I nodded that I'd have one, too.

"A consensus," Mike said, "I like it. You guys ever have an Appletini? No? Trust me, you'll enjoy it."

After he ordered, Mike said, "This is a nice place, and these are great seats, perfect for watching games. What is that, the Mets-Giants? Are they playing in San Fran?"

"No, it's here at Citi," I said

"You guys ever been to San Francisco?" Mike asked, before adding, "What am I saying—Dave's like Mr. San Fran—I meant have you and Ashley been there?"

"Yeah, a few times," I said.

"We got engaged there," Ashley offered. "Well not San Francisco, but Napa Valley, on a trip there."

"Oh yeah?" Mike said. "I think Dave mentioned something like that. So how did my boy do it? Propose I mean."

"Well," Ashley started, "we went to a few vineyards. We were dragging though, 'cause it was like a hundred degrees. Or felt like it anyway. But we were staying in this boutique hotel up in the foothills, overlooking the Valley—"

"Yeah?" Mike said, paying close attention.

"It was a place called Presidio," I offered, just to contribute.

"Yeah," Ashley said, "and they had this outdoor area where you could bring out your own wine and watch the sunset. Dave had arranged for us to be in a more secluded area, an outdoor loveseat kind of thing with this ornate, floral top to it. Plush."

"Nice. So how did Dave actually propose?"

"Well," she continued, "after our first glass of wine, Dave said he was going to look over the ledge for a minute. Well, I knew something was up, 'cause he had been talking right before in a grandiose, sweet way about what I meant to him—and then he came back and got on one knee, and I was thinking 'Wow,' like, 'Take this moment in.' "

"Sounds really special," Mike said. "Were you nervous, Dave?"

"No," I said, "more like anxious."

"Oh c'mon," Ashley laughed, "you were nervous, I could tell."

"I was nervous about saying it right, the way I had it in my head, and not screwing things up. OK, fine, I was a little nervous."

"Who isn't?" Mike offered. "That's a monumental life moment."

Why, I thought, is Ashley talking to the guy who fucked my wife two nights before about how I proposed?

"Well, we had talked about marriage," Ashley continued. "I mean, you knew I was going to say yes, Dave?"

"Well, I guess, but you're never fully sure. I wasn't taking it for granted."

"So what did you say?" Mike asked, and then to Ashley, "What did he say?"

"It's kind of a blur," Ashley replied, "as much as, at the time, I was telling myself to 'remember this moment.' He was saying how much I meant to him, how much he loved me, how he wanted to spend his life with me. That kind of thing."

"He was getting deep there," Mike said, laughing casually. "That's the way to do it, my man. So then he showed you the ring?"

"Yeah," Ashley replied, "I had talked earlier about what I wanted, but I admit, it was prettier than I expected." She held her hand up to Mike, so he could examine it.

"Wow, that is beautiful indeed. And that's a great diamond. What is that, two-and-a-half carat?"

"Just over two, but it's a great cut."

"It sure is. My man knows how to treat the woman he loves right."

I was trying to keep from squirming.

"So, where was your wedding?" Mike asked.

"Castle on the Hudson," she replied, "in Tarrytown."

"Sure, I was at a wedding there myself—great views of the river up there."

✶✶✶✶

As dinner progressed, the same conversational pattern emerged—Mike and Ashley doing all the talking, with me having to fight to throw my two cents in.

There was also a physical dynamic going on. Ashley was at the center of this semicircle table, but she was tilted towards Mike. And he was now snug up against her. I hadn't changed my position, but now there was a good nine inches between our legs.

I Imagined Ashley's hand under the table—on his crotch.

After dinner Ashley asked, "So should we get another drink?"

"I don't know," I replied, "what are you thinking?"

"What do you think, Mike?" she said.

"Well," he replied, "do you guys have any drinks back at your place?"

"Yeah, definitely," Ashley replied.

"I don't know if we do," I said.

"I picked up more vodka tonight," she answered. "We can get beer on the way back."

I had anticipated this moment, but it still hit me hard.

"OK, yeah," I said.

The waitress dropped off the check and Ashley stopped Mike as he went to reach for it.

"You got it last time," Ashley said. "We'll get this, right?"

"Uh yeah, sure," I said, pulling out my wallet. I looked at the bill … $225 with tip.

What a schmuck I felt like, signing that tab. The guy fucks my wife and Ashley has me buy him dinner.

****

I felt like a spectator as we walked back to the apartment. Like Mike had the reins and I was just pulling the sleigh. I wanted to put my arm around Ashley. So finally I did, and she kind of leaned into me.

For the rest of that walk, it was Ashley and me as the couple. Mike was just with us, even if he was doing most of the talking.

We arrived at the deli and Ashley said, "So what do we think, Corona Lights?"

"Sure," I said.

"Do you need money?" Ashley replied.

"What?" I said. "Oh no, um, yeah, I'll go in and get them."

"Oh hey, let me get those," Mike said.

"No it's OK," Ashley said.

"I'll run in," I said.

"Oh and Dave?" Ashley said.

"Yeah?"

"We also need limes."

I didn't know what to think. I felt shell-shocked.

We walked back, the two of them talking as I lugged the twelve pack.

****

I could only imagine the sense of power Mike must have felt walking into our apartment. Unlike two nights ago, all three of us knew exactly where this was going, where the night was headed.

I was feeling second-class in my own home, as I put the beer away. Ashley cut a few limes and Mike was in our living room, looking at the photos on the mantle. "So, that's Ashley's mom and sister?" he said, as I handed him a Corona.

"Yeah," I said, "at Cape Cod last summer."

"Quite the attractive threesome," he said. "How old's Ashley's mom?"

"Fifty four," I replied.

"Damn, she's a good looking woman. She looks ten years younger."

"Yeah, I know."

"And these are your folks?" he continued, pointing to another photo. I nodded. "And that's your brother?"

"Yeah."

"Ashley, you were a beautiful bride," Mike said, pointing to our wedding day photo, as she walked in.

"Oh, thanks," she said.

"And an attractive groom," he said, turning back to me.

I smiled awkwardly.

He was inside my home, in my living room, inspecting personal photos of my wife and me. Ashley didn't seem to mind.

Maybe she naturally trusted him—being my "childhood friend" and all. She even pointed to the top of a bookshelf to show him more.

"That was in Napa," she said, "the night after Dave proposed."

"Yes, you're displaying your two-carat ring," he replied.

****

Mike was sitting on our sofa swigging his beer—the same sofa he would try to relegate me to again. I had to imagine he knew the irony or symbolism of sitting there, waiting for my wife to return from the bathroom. It was like he was doing a refined version of a victory lap.

"Should we put the Yankees game on?" he said. "We can mute the sound and get a score."

"Sure," I said.

"Looks like extra innings," he said.

"Oh yeah, top of the tenth."

Mike started talking about relief pitchers. So I mechanically rattled off a few.

"It can't be overstated," Mike said, "how critical it is to have a good reliever, y'know?"

Mike was probably just talking baseball, but I suspected that wasn't all he meant.

"A friend of mine gave me this," Ashley said, as she returned and sat beside Mike.

It was pot.

I was surprised, taken aback. Ashley and I had smoked pot with friends on occasion, but only when a friend offered.

Why now? I thought.

Had Mike suggested it to her in a communication I wasn't privy too? And who was this friend she got it from? If I had fifty guesses, I'd choose Tamara every time. She probably gave it to Ashley after work today. Had Ashley told Tamara about Mike?

"It smells good," he said. "Have you checked this out, Dave?"

"No, but yeah, it smells good," I said.

"So shall I roll up a few joints?" Mike said. "Or would you like to do the honors, Dave?"

I'd never rolled a joint in my life.

"It's been a long time," I said, "go for it, Mike."

And soon, there we were, sitting Indian style on the living room floor, the three of us getting high together.

I said, "I'm good," after the third toke.

I was already feeling it hard. It wasn't the laughing buzz I've sometimes experienced—maybe it was the alcohol. But I was nervous—on edge.

"Great timing, Mom," Ashley said as she looked at her cell phone.

"What?" I asked.

"She was just asking if I was around to talk. Um, Mom, it's eleven on a Friday night."

"Your mom's on Seattle time, right?" Mike asked.

I wondered how Mike knew that.

"Yeah," Ashley said, "time zones are pretty stupid."

"Stupid?" Mike said laughing. "Why, because they inconvenience you?"

"Look, no one even thought about time zones one thousand years ago."

"Well," Mike said laughing, "they didn't have squat one thousand years ago. They were lucky to have candlelight."

"That's my point," Ashley replied. "I don't know who invented time zones, but he was no Thomas Edison, I'll tell you that."

"Well," Mike said, "we need to get some scientists working on this. Anything else they should work at?"

"Well, while they're at it," Ashley replied, "they really need to make planes a lot faster, 'cause flights are way too long."

"What do you think a caveman would think if they heard this is how their descendants talked in the twenty-first century?" Mike asked.

"That I'm a spoiled little brat who doesn't even know how to make a simple fire with a pair of sticks."

Suddenly Mike and Ashley were both cracking up, touching each other, and I felt alone and isolated.

I was too stoned and paranoid to contribute.

These were the kind of silly conversations Ashley and I would have.

Mike looked over at me, as if realizing I was still there. "Say Dave," he said, "I scored some Giants tickets for October. They're lower level thirty yard line. You up for going, my man?"

"Yeah, sure," I replied.

Ashley gave a pouting expression.

"I'm sorry, Ashley," Mike said, "but I just have the two, and you said you don't like pro football."

"I don't," she said, "I was just kidding."

"But I just remembered," he said, "my buddy bailed on me for the U.S. Open. You up for going Sunday night?"

"Are you serious?"

"You bet, and they're pretty decent seats in Arthur Ashe. Are you game?"

"Absolutely," Ashley replied before suddenly catching herself and turning to me. "We don't have anything Sunday night, do we?"

"Um, no," I said, still in follow-along mode.

"Cool," Ashley said, "then I'm definitely in, Mike."

"Excellent."

Mike picked up the joint and passed it around again.

****

I came out of the bathroom and stopped suddenly.

Ashley and Mike were making out on the sofa.

I stood in the corner so as not to be noticed. I wanted to see how far it might go. Would she pull Mike's cock out of his pants and start sucking on it right then and there?

In my stoned state, part of me was saying, Just go for it Ashley, let me see it, pull it out and let's see you suck that big fat cock.

But then Ashley pulled away and whispered something in his ear. When she headed to the kitchen, I returned and sat down.

Mike motioned for me to come closer. "Hey bro, Ash and I were talking, and I think we're going to retreat to the other room for a bit, OK?"

I couldn't meet his eyes. Then Mike pointed to the game on TV. "Damn, it's going into the twelfth—you watching this?"

"Yeah, I see," I said.

But I was thinking about what Mike had just said. "We're going to retreat to the other room for a bit." The "other room" was my fucking bedroom. The "we" was him and Ashley without me, the "for a bit" could mean anything. And then he downplayed all that with the word "retreat."

When Ashley walked back in, she saw me on the chair and looked over at Mike. As though reading her mind, he replied, "Yeah, we talked, it's all good."

Ashley said, "Yeah?" and turned from Mike to me. "You good, Dave?"

"Yeah," I said, and then, "You?"

"Mmm hmm," she replied, "so do you mind if we take that joint? There's still most of the second one left if you want it—on top of the magazines."

"What?" I replied.

"The rest of that joint," she said, "if you wanted to smoke any more while watching your game."

"And there's a lighter's right there," she added.

"OK," I said, still stupefied.

Mike stood up and walked over to her.

I stood up as well.

Ashley saw me looking at the six-pack of Coronas in a bucket of ice. "Yeah," she said, "I left three Coronas for you in the fridge. Do you want me to get you one now, for the game?"

Before I answered she said, "Here, I'll get you one." After handing me the beer, she said, "So you'll be good?"

"Uh, yeah."

"The joint's on the coffee table."

"OK," I said.

Then she hugged me and whispered that she loved me. I told her I loved her as well, adding "so much." I wanted our embrace to continue. I wanted to feel her, savor her, hold her tight, kiss her, smother her and not let her go. I felt so deprived when she pulled away.

"See you in a bit, bro," Mike said. "I want to hear how this game turns out—promise?"

"Promise?" I said.

"How the Yankees game turns out."

"Oh OK," I said.

"Give me a hug, bro," he said.

"All right, we good?" he said, turning to Ashley and then back to me. "I want to hear about the game."

I stood there as they walked into the kitchen. I watched as Ashley picked up the bucket of iced Coronas and Mike grabbed the joint, a lighter and some cut-up limes, and the two of them headed off.

****

Mike was off to party with my wife in my bedroom. But the real party was going to be Mike having sex with Ashley. Had she blown him already, or was tonight the night for his first Ashley Martens blowjob?

I felt infinitely helpless.

There would be no banging on the door. If anything could have been accomplished from that, it would have been on the first night, in the first few minutes. I wondered if he even locked the door. Perhaps he knew he didn't have to bother, knowing I wouldn't be barging in.

And hey, we left Dave with a few Corona's, a joint, an exciting extra inning Yankees game to watch, and a comfy sofa to sleep on. As if I'd curl up all snug, enjoy my beer, and get into the Yankees game.

Ashley had another mix playing on her iPod. I heard the shower turn on. I thought of them showering naked together, Mike groping Ashley's soapy tits. I thought of Ashley sudsing up Mike's cock and stroking it. I thought of checking the door to see if it was locked.

But suppose it was just Mike in the shower? Suddenly I pictured Ashley saying, "Dave!" as she saw the doorknob start to turn.

****

I went back in the living room, waiting for the music to end.

I stared at the TV. The Yankees had just won in thirteen, but it meant nothing to me. I couldn't process it. Mike was spending his Friday night drinking beers, getting high, and fucking my wife in my bed.

Unable to hear over the music, I lay down on the sofa. The most precious thing in the world—Ashley—was now less mine than ever. I had foolishly given her away to Mike.

I imagined Mike saying, "Have you ever heard of the term 'cuckold'?" and then, when she seemed uninformed, explaining the whole lifestyle.

I imagined him saying, "He's sleeping on the couch for two of the last three nights. You just made Dave your cuckold, Ashley."

It's such a sickeningly humiliating and humbling label.

He could be telling her anything right now as the music blared on.

****

I woke up at 5 a.m. to noises coming from the bedroom. Only now, the music had stopped.

I heard the bed creaking and I grabbed the recorder. I wanted this. I wanted to be able to listen beyond the moment. I turned the recorder on and tiptoed down the hall.

They were into mid-fuck as I sat down and pointed the mic to the door. The "oh Gods" and "yeah Ashleys" from two nights earlier had become dirtier as the headboard banged against the wall.

"You're a little horndog, aren't you Ashley?" Mike said as he began grinding harder. "Say it to me, baby, tell me you're a horndog, Ashley."

"I'm a horndog Mike," she moaned.

"You're my little horndog, Ashley" he said.

"I'm your little horndog, Mike, your little fucking horndog, Mike."

"You love my cock, don't you, Ashley?"

"I love your cock, Mike."

"Oh yeah, that a girl, ride back on me, fuck back into it. Yeah, that's it, you've got my cock so hard, Ashley."

"You've got me so wet Mike."

"Mmm ... Your pussy loves my cock, don't it, Ashley?"

"It loves your cock, Mike."

"It's my pussy, ain't it, Ashley?"

"It's your pussy, Mike."

"Tell me that again as I fuck you."

"It's your pussy, Mike."

"Again?"

"It's your pussy, Mike," she half-screamed. "Oh my God, I'm about to cum again, oh fuck."

"Tell me 'you're my horndog,' as you cum, Ashley"

"I'm your horndog, Mike, I'm your little fucking horndog, Mike, oh my God, I'm cumming, oh fuck, oh my God, I'm fucking cumming ... oh God, yeah!"

"I'm about to cum, too, Ashley."

"Oh come inside me, Mike."

"I'm going to cum in your pussy."

"Cum in my pussy, Mike."

"Whose pussy is it, Ashley?"

"It's your pussy, Mike."

"Whose pussy?"

"It's your pussy, Mike."

"Oh yeah, Ashley, here it comes, oh fuck yeah, I'm cumming right inside you, baby."

I had a major boner, but I also felt like crying.

I tiptoed back to the sofa and slid the recorder under the couch. Mike had just fucked my wife and got her to say that her pussy was his, like it was his property. Maybe she was just saying that back to him because she was caught up in the sexual moment. But it seemed as if he'd gone bare and seeded my wife's pussy in my own fucking bed. What kind of positions he had her in, I could only imagine.

I felt meek, reduced, inadequate, helpless and emasculated. How could I possibly provide the sexual excitement he had just given her? How could I compete with Mike's cock? I had never heard her scream or dirty-talk with me like that. How was I going to go back to a normal sex life with Ashley after this? Wouldn't she always pine for what she had just had? I couldn't deliver the cloud nine-type of pleasure echoing from our bedroom, provided by a real man's cock, the kind of fucking Mike had just given her.

On an even baser level, how could she possibly respect me now? A real man and husband would have stopped the whole thing when he saw them making out in the bar that first night. Instead, I let Mike walk all over me, alpha-male me, in my own home, in front of my wife. And I'd just stood there frozen—a meek little coward—as he took my wife into my bedroom to fuck her.

What was he telling her about me? He could have told her anything. He could have disparaged me, reduced me in her eyes, told her I was a fucking cuckold, and elaborated in detail on what that is, or how he sees me.

What recourse did I have now? How could I come back down from Planet Pluto? There was no abort button or re-set control.

At this very moment, I thought, Mike's head is probably lying on my pillow, as he talks quietly with my wife in their post-fuck afterglow.

I thought of the satisfaction he must be feeling. How skillfully and easily he had played my ass. He wasn't just going to Jim Murta me. He had larger, bigger-picture aspirations. He had blocked me out, shut me out, locked me out, hard-cocked me out, and now he was trying to get my wife to cuck me out.

Lying there, I felt like the odd man out in my own fucking home, in my marriage to Ashley. I wondered if Mike would fuck her again in the morning. After all, none of us had to work today.

I felt very humiliated but also hard. I thought of listening to them fuck again and blowing my load on our bedroom door—my gesture—inexplicable, defiant, and utterly effete.

I began masturbating, on the sofa, under the blanket. I thought of Ashley exclaiming, "I'm your horndog, Mike," and suddenly came.

****

I heard the door open and could tell it was Mike walking down the hallway. When he entered the living room, he gave me a nudge.

"Oh hey," I said.

"Hey, bro," he said, "I gotta get going, but wanted to say goodbye. Sorry to wake you."

"It's OK," I replied.

"Hey," he whispered, "I got some more insight. She had seen a guy before that guy at the party. I gotta run—I'm meeting a buddy in an hour, going to A.C. for the night—but I'll give you the full download after this weekend. I think it'll explain things better."

"What do you mean?"

"Just chill, Dave. Let's meet up Monday. I'll probably get more of a picture tomorrow night."

"Tomorrow night?"

"Yeah, I'm taking Ashley to the Open, remember?"

"Oh," I said.

"Relax bro, this will be OK. I'm going to help you through this. I'm learning what makes Ashley tick. Believe me, I will share. You just sit tight and enjoy the weekend, OK?"

"OK," I said, but I didn't mean it.

CHAPTER TWENTY-EIGHT

In the quiet that followed, I thought of me lying on the couch and Ashley on our bed, and wondered what she must be thinking.

Was she thinking about us, our relationship, where things stood now, our future, how we'd be together moving forward?

Or was she thinking of what a good fuck Mike had been?

Was she feeling sexually satisfied, no longer frustrated, basking in the post-great-fuck moment?

Or was she thinking, "I never realized what a pussy my husband was. He didn't step in or fight for me, he just let his old friend come into our place and fuck me in our bed."

Maybe she even thought I had arranged this, that it had all been my idea, that I wanted it. Perhaps Mike had filled her head with those ideas. Maybe that's what her "I understand" comments were about.

Hell, Mike had made me text Ashley about Friday night. She had probably interpreted that as me being OK with—or even wanting—this.

And then the reality of Mike's U.S. Open invitation suddenly sank in. He had thrown it out so casually—as though it were an afterthought to inviting me to a Giants game.

Was it coincidence that his friend had bailed at the last minute?

Or had he secured the tickets after I'd told him what an avid tennis fan Ashley was?

Did it even matter?

He had invited her in front of me. Ashley had said yes, and now she wouldn't need to text, "When am I seeing you again?" She knew when she'd be seeing him again—tomorrow fucking night.

It would be just the two of them, going to the Open together like a couple.

I'd be the stooge husband left at home to sit and sulk.

Mike was taking my wife out tomorrow night on a fucking date.

Jesus Christ, I whispered.

In the last seventy-two hours, Mike had walked into my scene, my home, my life, my marriage, and turned it upside down.

How could I not have seen this coming? He saw a potentially horndog wife—as he had just called Ashley—and a husband who he thought he could get to acquiesce, or roll over, or de-man, or be a freaking doormat.

****

Suddenly Ashley came in and nudged me.

I opened my eyes and looked at her as she stood above me. She was in a bathrobe, looking groggy, her hair out of sorts. But my God, she looked beautiful, radiant, magnificent, blinding.

"Do you want to come into the bedroom?" she asked.

"Um yeah," I said, "sure, how are you? Tired?"

"Yeah, super-tired and I have to meet Tracy in three hours which is a big ugh."

She held out her hand and helped me up and continued holding it as we walked to our bedroom.

When we lay down together, she gave me a big hug, tightly and significantly—telling me she loved me without having to say it. It was a deep embrace in our own home, like she was happy to be my wife. She snuggled up on my shoulder as I ran my hand gently through her hair, and I listened as she drifted back to sleep.

Ashley looked so peaceful, like a small child or puppy dog, and I thought how much I loved this girl.

****

"Oh my God, it's one o'clock," Ashley awoke, startled. "I'm late! I'm gonna have to majorly scramble."

She gave me a quick kiss and hurled herself into the shower.

Ten minutes later, she was pulling on jeans and a top. As I lay on the bed I just watched, admiring her. The way she put on her earrings. Or stumbled around, looking for her purse. The way her cleavage became exposed as she gave me a kiss goodbye.

"I'm jealous," she said, "I wish I could crawl back into bed with you."

"Why not tell Tracy you're sick, that you have the flu?"

"I wish, but I'se gots to go."

"How about the mumps?" I said.

Ashley smiled.

"Or tell her you just got skunked," I said. "No, really, a skunk skunked you in Central Park this morning, and now I'm out getting tomato juice to give you a bath."

"That's cute," she said. "Enjoy the lazy Saturday. And be glad you're not trekking your out-of-towner friend all across town."

****

After she left, the apartment felt profoundly quiet. I waited until she was gone a half-hour, so there'd be no "I forgot something" possibility.

Then I chained the door and pulled out the recorder.

I knew I was mentally and emotionally playing with fire, but I wanted to hear how it had come out. I lay down our bed, right where it had all happened, and put my headphones on.

The audio was ultra clear. Apparently recorders have come a long way since I was a kid. The bed was squeaking loud and fast and I could hear Ashley crying out, "Oh God, oh God, Mike."

Then I heard Mike say it … "You're a little horndog, aren't you Ashley? Say it to me, tell me you're a horndog, Ashley."

I stopped it for a holy-shit moment.

I'm listening to my wife getting fucked in the bed that I'm lying on.

I resumed play and heard Ashley exclaim, "I'm a horndog, Mike."

"You're my little horndog, Ashley."

I stopped and thought about what he was doing—verbally taking her from her being A horndog, to HIS horndog.

Then I listened as Ashley exclaimed back, "I'm your little horndog, Mike, your little fucking horndog."

Adding the adjective "fucking" to horndog was Ashley's contribution. She had thrown it in all on her own as Mike pounded his big, hard, penis inside her.

Then I heard Ashley tell him, "I love your cock, Mike. You've got me so wet, Mike."

When Mike asked "Does your pussy love my cock, Ashley?" she replied, "It loves your cock, Mike."

And then the real verbal escalation began …

"Whose pussy is it Ashley?" … "It's your pussy, Mike."

I listened as Ashley exclaimed she was cumming again, and then the guttural way Mike said, "Fuck yeah—right inside you baby," as he came.

I rewound back to "It's your pussy, Mike," as the bed creaked loudly, and came myself.

****

I'm losing my mind, I thought, as I got off the bed.

I paced around my apartment, unsure of what to do with myself, when a text message arrived from Mike.

"Hey bro," he wrote, "just arrived in AC, we should come here sometime. Sending a few pics from the last few nites—just sent Ash as well—have a great wknd—be in touch."

I opened the photos.

The first one was from Wednesday night. Ashley had taken it when we were at the bar. Mike had his arm around me.

In the second photo Ashley and I posed by the bar; my arm was around her. Ashley was beaming, baring her ultra white teeth, and I looked more comfortable.

The third photo Mike had asked the bartender to take—one of all three of us. Ashley was in the center, looking straight ahead, and both of us had our arms around her.

The last two photos were from the night before, at the restaurant.

The first was of the three of us. Even though I had my arms around Ashley, I looked like the dejected outsider.

The next one—taken by the waitress—was of Mike and Ashley in her white dress. Mike had his arm around my smiling wife. The two of them looked like a New York City power couple.

I wondered why in hell he had sent them. What was the statement he was trying to make? Was this a victory lap or adding another cherry on top?

"In case you weren't already feeling low about what happened Dave, well here's a few photos to make you feel even lower."

Why else would he end the series with a photo of him with Ashley?

Jesus Christ, I thought, the whole thing was a storybook.

Dave meets Mike, photo one …

Dave with Ashley, photo two …

Dave introduces Mike to Ashley, photo three …

Dave looks like the third wheel, photo four …

Dave's no longer even there, as Mike has his arm around Ashley, photo five …

Yes it was chronological, but it seemed like Mike was sending me a message. The last photo felt like an exclamation point, as if to emphasize how Ashley's pussy was now his, how far he'd moved in on my girl.

He might as well have thrown in a photo of the U.S. Open tickets, to remind me he was taking my wife.

He had to be sending me a message with that text. Just in case my imagination and memory weren't enough, he was sending me the visual of how he's inserted himself into my marriage and relegated me to the fucking couch.

I wondered if he was showing those photos off to his friends in Atlantic City, explaining how he'd met me online, sensed I was a vulnerable stooge, and fucked my wife in my bed the very first night.

"She's super hot," I imagined his friend's saying, "and yeah, her husband looks like a pussy."

****

After pacing and thinking for a while, I sent the photos to my email and enlarged them on my computer.

I stared at the photo of Ashley and Mike from the night before. Mike's smile was completely confident. He had already fucked my wife two nights earlier, and he surely knew he'd be fucking her again in a few short hours.

Ashley also had to know that Mike would be coming back to our apartment, that my own bedroom would be off limits to me.

I looked at Ashley's smile and the way her tits, propped up in her white dress, pressed into Mike. She would be taking his big fat cock soon and would have known by then that I'd be no obstacle at all.

I enlarged the photo further and stared at Ashley's face and her mouth, the one that would be saying, "It's your pussy, Mike."

Oh God, Ashley.

I pulled up an image of a large cock and juxtaposed it next to the photo: Ashley and Mike on one side, the big cock photo on the other. Then I went under the sofa and grabbed the recorder.

I yanked my jeans and boxers down, hit play and began looking from one photo to the other.

It was stimuli overload—looking at Ashley posing with the guy she knew she'd be fucking in our bed a few hours later. And then looking at the type of big cock that Mike probably gave her last night—and then hearing the audio come on.

As soon as I heard Ashley repeat back to Mike, "It's your pussy, Mike," I knew I was about to lose it. But I knew she was about to orgasm and I wanted to wait for her.

As I heard her start to cum, I stared back and forth between Ashley and the cock and came hard.

I'm losing my freaking marbles, I thought, as I yanked off the headphones and went for a paper towel.

I felt alone. Like in some kind of mental Siberia, Mon-freaking-golia, Ant-fucking-Arctica.

Why would Mike send those photos to me?

Surely he didn't expect me to reply with, "That's a really nice photo of the three of us."

This was about Mike adding that additional cherry on top. It was a way to say, "I'm taking your wife out tomorrow and there's not a damn thing you're gonna do about it."

Jesus Christ, I thought, this guy is going caveman on my ass.

For all I knew he was going to frame the photo of Ashley and himself—the one I'd just masturbated to—and suggest she put it up on our bedroom nightstand.

I thought of having a talk with Ashley. Perhaps I'd suggest she skip tomorrow night. At the very least I could reassert my love for her.

****

I was on the sofa zoning out with the TV on, when Ashley unexpectedly arrived.

Then I saw Tracy walk in after her and stood up.

"It's good to see you Dave."

"You, too. Beautiful day," I said, "I just came back from the Park."

"I'm just dropping my bags off," Ashley said as she went into the bedroom.

"So, good day shopping, Tracy?"

"Yeah, we're only half done," she replied. "We're going to hit up stores in midtown now. I really miss the city, Dave."

"How are you?" Ashley asked as she came back and gave me a kiss.

"Good," I said. "So, going back out again?"

"Yeah," she said, hurriedly, "and then we're meeting up with Tamara and a friend of hers. I can call you if you want to meet us."

"I heard from Jack earlier," I lied, "and he wants me to check out his brother's band, but that may fall through, and if it does—"

"Sure," Ashley said, "just text me if you want to, and tell Jack I said 'hi'."

"Nice seeing you, Dave," Tracy said. "Sorry it was so brief, but if you don't do the band thing, swing by."

"Of course," I said, and gave her a hug.

So much for a talk tonight, I thought, so much for a Saturday night alone with Ashley.

****

I went into our bedroom after they left.

In Ashley's closet were new shopping bags from Nordstrom, Aldo, Zara, and Victoria fucking Secret.

I pulled out the pink box from Victoria Secret and noticed it was sealed with tape. I so wanted to look inside, but I didn't want to disturb anything. I didn't want Ashley coming back and asking, "Were you in my closet? Did you go through my bags?"

So I just sat on a chair with the door open, looking at her bags. What else could I conclude? These were her "fuck me" clothes for her big U.S. Open date tomorrow night. Why else would Ashley stash them in her closet? Inside those bags was some sexy outfit she'd wear out with Mike.

And whatever Victoria Secret lingerie she'd bought, well, Mike was going to see it before I would—Ashley's own freaking husband.

I thought of how Ashley said they'd be meeting up with Tamara later. With Tracy there, I was less concerned. Tracy's a conservative girl. There's no way Ashley would have told Tracy about Mike or Jim Murta. If Ashley had modeled her clothes for Tracy, she would have assumed Ashley was buying them to look sexy for me. Tracy would essentially be a conversational cock-block to Ashley discussing Mike with Tamara.

Mostly I felt deprived of a Saturday night with my wife. It would have been a chance to dial things down, take a time out from the mind-numbing stimuli, and reassert myself.

But Ashley loves the U.S. Open. It would be hard to last-minute "no" her on that.

I went onto Craigslist and looked at tickets. I could get a three-hundred-level nose-bleed for $150.

But what am I going to do, trail them in disguise with binoculars in tow?

I was just going to have to suck it up and take the emotional shellacking. Ashley had a sexy outfit in mind, and Mike was going to be her date for the evening.

****

I saw the joint in the living room and in a what-the-fuck kind of way, I took a few hits. "Thanks Tamara," I said aloud, "I'm smoking your weed, bitch."

I'm in a strange mental land, I thought.

Planes are flying backwards, and every car is blowing through the red light.

The life that I had assumed, expected, and taken for granted had become infinite question marks. Reliability and predictability had picked up their bags and scampered away.

Jim Murta had taken a swing at that piñata, but Mike was taking a caveman club to it. He was standing between me and my wife—that colonial house and family Ashley and I had imagined together.

I played a song on Ashley's iPod—some rap song from a British white guy, I believe. The verse/rap was about a pop star talking about losing it on drugs and booze. The chorus kept repeating as girls sang back to the singer, "You're pranging out."

To me the line meant, you've lost your shit, gone over the deep-end, have a first class ticket to coo-cooville.

And that's how I felt as I figured out how to loop the audio on the recorder. I could select a starting point and then loop the audio to keep repeating that section.

I looked at the photo Mike had sent and listened to Ashley say, "It's your pussy, Mike," and came three more times as the night progressed.

I fell asleep on our bed and only later woke up—with Ashley sleeping beside me.

CHAPTER TWENTY-NINE

Ashley was in her gym clothes when I awoke the following morning. I wasn't sure how I slept through her getting up.

"Hey there," I said, "why don't you lie back down with me for a minute."

I saw Ashley look over at our clock.

"It's not even nine," I said. "I know you want to bang the gym out, but c'mon."

"It's not like I want to go," she said, lying back down, "it's just that I have to. I've only gone once in the last three days."

I put my arm around her and she rolled over facing me. We began kissing, then making out. I felt goose pimples as she ran her hand over my back.

She pushed me away slightly, like she didn't have time for this, but then joined me in the embrace. I felt her hand go to my thigh and brush against my boner.

Oh yes, I thought as she pulled my dick from my boxers and began stroking it.

I tried to block out her words to Mike, but I couldn't. We were in the same bed Mike had fucked her in. "I'm your horndog, my pussy's yours, Mike …"

A half-minute later I came hard, splashing some onto Ashley.

She went into the bathroom to wash her hands.

"I'm sorry, Dave," she said, "but I really have to get going."

"Yeah, of course," I said. "Thank you for that—you're just so beautiful, I don't know, I kind of lost it there."

"I love you," she said as she kissed me goodbye.

I looked at her ass as she leaned over the dresser —the way her tight workout clothes showed off her ass cheeks.

"I have some errands to run," she said, "so I won't be back till the afternoon."

****

I had some errands to run myself.

It was opening day NFL Sunday and I turned on the pre-game show when I got home.

But in my head, the real countdown was Ashley leaving for the Open. Time was clicking down like the waiting for the ball to drop on New Year's Eve.

Ashley returned at three, saying, "I have to skedaddle big time," as I watched her strip naked and run for the shower.

When she came out, she was in her bathrobe. Her hair was wet, and she was holding her cell. "So," she said, "Mike's going to be in the area. He wants to know if he should meet me downstairs or if we're up for having a quick drink here?"

"Which would you prefer, Ash?"

"I'm cool with either," she replied, "but if he comes up here, I think we're out of beer."

"Yeah," I said.

"Well, I still have to get changed and put makeup on."

"OK."

"I mean I'm not going to be able to run out now."

"Oh yeah," I said. "Yeah, OK, I can run out."

"Thanks." She gave me a quick peck and went back into the bedroom.

****

What in hell am I doing? I thought, as I crossed the street to the bodega.

"That'll be thirteen-fifty," the guy at the counter said.

"For a six pack?"

"It's Corona Light."

"Whatever—here."

Within a few minutes of putting the beer away, the buzzer rang.

"Hi David," my doorman intercom'd, "Mike is here."

"Yeah, send him up."

Ashley came hustling in still in her robe and said, "He's friggin' early. You guys have a drink. Tell him I'll be out in ten."

"OK," I said as our doorbell rang.

He greeted me with a big smile and a "hey buddy" hug.

He was wearing shorts and a funky dark t-shirt.

I handed him a beer, opened one for myself, and explained that Ashley was still getting ready.

"How was A.C.?" I said.

"A blast. We have to go sometime. I lost a grand in blackjack in the first fifteen minutes."

"Wow, that sucks."

"Yeah, but I wound up winning it back and then some an hour later. You know how a split works?"

"Yeah, sure," I said, not following what he was saying.

He started asking me who was winning the one o'clock football games when Ashley emerged from the bedroom. She was wearing a white miniskirt and a pink, cleavage-revealing v-top with no bra. On her feet were these cute little pink sneakers that matched her top.

"Hi Mike," Ashley said, like I wasn't even in the room.

"Wow, Ashley," he said, "you look ravenous."

Ashley half-blushed and proceeded to hug him. As Ashley pulled back, Mike said, "How 'bout a kiss, gorgeous?"

She looked back at me for a moment, pausing, as if asking for a green light, and I kind of looked away, as though I wasn't fully aware of what was going on. With that, Ashley leaned in and kissed him. Soon they were making out, right there in front of me. I tilted my head down like it wasn't happening but then I saw Mike's hand on Ashley's ass.

I stood there frozen until they were done.

Mike pulled out the tickets and laid out a seating chart on our kitchen table, encouraging me to look as well.

"It's upper level," Mike said, "but center court and third row aisle. There are plenty of worse seats in the house."

"No, these look great," Ashley said, "I'm ultra-jazzed for checking out some tennis."

"Hey, Dave," Mike said, handing me his iPhone, "do you mind taking a quick photo?"

I was in stunned reactive mode and said, "OK."

Ashley, in her cute new outfit, put her arm around him, and I took the fucking picture. Mike reached for the phone and showed it to Ashley as she snuggled into him for a closer look.

"Aw, that's cute!" she said.

"Well, we should probably get going," Mike said.

"OK," Ashley replied, quickly finishing her beer.

"Wish I had an extra ticket," Mike said to me, "but it's tough to get three seats together without a fourth."

"I understand," I said.

"Dave's not much for tennis, anyway," Ashley offered.

"Yeah," I said, feeling like I had to say something, "besides I got the four o'clock games and the Giants play tonight at eight."

"That's right, Giants-Cowboys, right?"

"Yeah."

"Should be a good game, my man. Well, I guess we should get going."

Ashley gave me a quick kiss goodbye, and I watched as they left our apartment, Mike shutting the door behind me.

I imagined my doorman doing a slight double-take when Ashley said, "Bye Jimmy," with Mike by her side.

****

I felt horribly alone, helpless and jealous.

I imagined them walking to the subway holding hands, like a couple. Mike had done it. He'd succeeded. He was taking my wife out on a date to an event she loves and showing her a good time without me. And Ashley had bought a new outfit to look extra special for him—extra fuckable. She had leaned into Mike, tilted her head forward and made out with him in our kitchen, passionately, right in front of me.

What kind of message was Ashley sending, to tongue him back

as I just stood there? Talk about making me feel like a fucking third wheel. I was sure that had to have been Mike's idea. What's a date without a pre-date make-out moment in front of the sap husband who just stands there and awkwardly takes it?

What balls he had for pulling that stunt, and what lack of balls I had for sucking it up and taking it.

Then I thought of the handjob Ashley had given me earlier. She hadn't even contemplated putting her lips around it. *Is that only reserved for men with real cocks, Ashley? Like the guy you got all dolled up to see tonight? Or were you in a hurry to get to the gym and knew I would cum so very quickly anyway?*

Jesus fucking Christ.

Anyone could potentially run into Ashley and Mike at the Open and see them holding hands or making out.

Was someone from work going to tell me, "I could swear I saw Ashley with some other man?"

He had to know what he was putting me through. And the sinking torture as the clock slowly ticked away.

I thought again of the way they had made out earlier. Mike must have been delighted when she took his lead. Like he was saying, "C'mon, Ashley, just do it, make out with me in front of your husband, send him that message that you don't give a fuck, that you don't fucking care that he's standing there ... Fuck him, fuck Dave, let the pussy do some sulking tonight, fuck his feelings, let him cry later thinking about this. Send him a message like you did when you fucked Jim Murta. You don't give a shit. You'll make out right the fuck in front of him."

And she had done just that. She made out with him. She sucked face with him. She French-kissed Mike—with me barely five feet away.

And he had Ashley going to a public place, on a date, with the prospect of being seen on national TV within the realm of possibility.

I turned the TV to the pre-game, saw the match starting at Arthur Ashe, and set it on DVR.

****

I was fixing a drink to calm down, when my cell phone went off. It was a text message from Mike. I opened it up to find three photos attached.

The first was of Ashley and Mike sitting in their seats. Both of them were all smiles, like they were having a wonderful time—a wonderful time without me.

The second was of the court, with the caption "view from our seats."

Why didn't he just add, "Pretty sweet seats, eh, Dave? Too bad you're not here, but don't worry, I'm showing your wife a fantastic time."

The third and last photo was of the two of them in our kitchen. It was the one Mike had asked me to take before they left.

Sending that photo felt like the ultimate fuck-you.

I pictured Mike thinking, "Here's the photo I got YOU to take of the two of us before our big date. Look at that outfit she dressed up in for me, Dave. That's the outfit I'll be fucking her in. What do you think of that, Dave?"

I sent the photos to my email and enlarged them. This was the outfit Ashley picked out shopping. She probably had Mike, and Mike's cock and the way he had fucked her in her head as she bought it.

I looked at the photo I took of them. He was making a statement when he handed me the camera and he was making another one now.

You're such a pussy, I pictured him thinking, that I knew I'd get you to take it. Stare at the photo, Dave, look at the excitement in her eyes, look at the strength and confidence in mine … I'm with your wife tonight…feel like a cuckold now, buddy?

It felt like another, incredible, fucking cherry on top.

I thought of the immense power he must be feeling as he transmitted these trophy photos to me. The mental high-stepping he must be doing, sending them to the poor sap husband.

I looked back at Ashley, noting the twinkle in her eye as she sat next to Mike, and my heart ached like it never had before.

As I looked at the photo I imagined Ashley talking to me. "Look at my big titties, Dave, do you like how I'm displaying them out in public with Mike? I'm wearing the kind of top in public you'd have given me grief about three months ago. Do I look nice and sexy for Mike? You know how much I want to fuck him again. With his big fat juicy cock. These are his tits now, Dave. Just like it's his pussy. And it's all because you introduced us. Are you happy now? Are you happy knowing Mike's gonna give me another good hard fucking? The kind of fucking my pussy needs and you can't give me. Aren't man enough to give me. I made out with him in front of you and you did nothing."

Why did I take that photo of them in the kitchen? Why didn't I at least sabotage it by sticking my thumb in front or leaving out half their faces?

I could have said no, proving that I had some resolve and fiber of manhood. But instead, I took the picture.

I could picture Mike whispering in Ashley's ear, "We're gonna cuckold him; you're gonna cuckold him, Ashley. I'm gonna show you how. I'm gonna show you that the man you married is not much of a man at all. He's a pathetic little pussy. You can walk all over him. His cock can never satisfy you. You're getting what you need now—a real man's cock—a man who knows how to fuck you properly. Your pussy's mine now."

I thought of the power Mike must've felt, but also of the sense of power Ashley must be experiencing. Fucking Mike in our bed and making out in front of me. Showing me how she doesn't give a fuck. Leaving me to sleep on a couch, leaving me to wait for her date to end.

Oh God, Ashley, I so fucking love you.

I came hard looking at that photo.

I lay in bed, wondering what things would be like now. Would there be any way to find our way back from this?

And as one a.m. became two a.m., I started to cry.

****

Ashley woke me up when she lay down next to me.

"How was the Open?" I asked.

"Freaking awesome," she replied.

Then she planted a kiss on me, and I reciprocated until we were swapping tongue, making out for a good, long, minute. It gave me a hard-on, which felt reassuring. I was so grateful to have her home.

"Well, it's pretty late," she said. "I'm going to run into the bathroom and get ready for bed."

I was stroking my dick through my boxers under the covers. I had such a boner when she came back out. She lay down on her side and invited me to spoon with her.

But she quickly fell asleep, and I didn't want to move and wake her. So I just lay there, my boner up against her ass, until I fell back to sleep myself.

CHAPTER THIRTY

I had to work Labor Day Monday.

I didn't disturb Ashley, or tried not to, other than to give her a goodbye kiss as I was leaving.

The office was on skeleton crew, but I had a pitch to work on, for my boss' trip to San Francisco. An hour later, his boss called to tell me my boss was in the E.R. with kidney stones.

"We're going to put this one in your hands, Dave. Can you book yourself a 6 a.m. flight tomorrow?"

"Absolutely," I said, "consider it done."

I couldn't say no to the president.

As I scrambled to get ready by 4 p.m. I kept checking my phone—still nothing from Mike.

He'd said we'd meet Monday—how he'd be in touch. Was he sending me a message by not messaging me at all? When he didn't reply to my text, I finally called him.

"Hey buddy," he said, "I've been working the holiday myself. It's kind of hectic—how you doing, bro?"

In some weird way, his just picking up the phone was reassuring.

"Hey," he said, "do you think you could meet me over here on the east side?"

****

On the subway ride over, I wondered if he was illustrating a power shift—having me go to him now.

I was on my second beer when Mike arrived and gave me a hug. "So how you doing?" he asked.

"I'm OK," I replied, "actually, I'm not really OK, OK?"

"Talk to me man."

"I'm a bit fucked up with all that's taken place."

"Mmm hmm," he replied. "I understand that. It can be an adjustment at first, but it is all going to be OK."

"How's it going to be OK, Mike?" I asked, "how the fuck is this going to be OK?"

"Dave, chill out. I'm on your side, I'm your friend."

"I'm sorry, Mike," I said. Indeed, I needed this guy on my side.

"Here's how it's going to be, OK bro?" Mike replied, "Ashley loves you, she's told me that every night I've been with her."

"What did she say?"

"She said 'I love Dave' probably a half dozen times. She said you're a sweetheart. Does that make you feel better?"

"I guess," I said. "She didn't say anything about wanting to leave me?"

"Hell no, not at all! She said you're dependable, caring, trustworthy. You've been very good to her, and she loves you for that."

"You talk to her about me?"

"Sure, how else would I have heard how much she loves you?"

"What did you tell her Mike—c'mon you owe me that?"

"I simply told her the truth, Dave."

"The truth being what?"

"I said you confided in me about being hurt by what happened at the party, but that part of you was quite turned on by it."

"You told her I masturbated thinking about it?"

"I left it up to her to interpret," he said, "but I did say you got turned on imagining what happened."

"Jesus, Mike, if you're my friend as you say, why would you tell her that?"

"To help bring communication back into your marriage, Dave."

"Oh jeez, OK, thanks for consulting me there. Don't tell me Mike, you didn't tell her, you didn't tell Ashley what a cuckold is."

"Yeah, I did."

"Jesus, Mike, why?"

"It helped put a name and face to it," he said. "I explained you had read about it and were feeling those thoughts. I said how there are many husbands like that. I made it seem normal."

"Telling her what made things normal? Suggesting that I was some kind of fucking cuckold?"

"It began making sense to her. It helped her understand what's going on and why it's not really strange or unusual."

"Christ, fucking seriously, I trusted you, confided in you. Why did you have to go and say that shit to her?"

"It's not shit, Dave, it's real. And now she understands what an incredible and loving gift you are offering her."

"What?"

"I said you realized you weren't getting it done in the sex department, and that you love her so much, you will do anything to make her happy, even if it means recognizing certain limitations."

"Jesus, Mike, do you hear what you're saying? You're telling her I know I can't satisfy her."

"Well, have you been?"

"Before the Jim Murta incident we were good. Then afterwards ... well, I was working on that. I just needed to get my confidence back. And in the meantime, I was still getting her off by going down on her."

"And you still will. I'm sure you're a great pussy-licker."

I sat there stunned as Mike signaled for two more.

"Mike," I said, "why did you send me photos this weekend?"

"I wanted to keep you looped in. What did you think I meant by it?"

"You had her make out with you right in front of me. You weren't intending to rub my face in it?"

"Dave, I was exerting my power over Ashley. It's a process of taking control. And it turned her on, kissing me in front of you. That 'submissive' t-shirt you found was pretty revealing, you know?"

"How so?"

"There was someone before that Jim Murta guy. I mean, that thing at the party didn't just come out of nowhere."

"She told you that? There was another guy?"

"Let's just say some man a few months prior saw something in Ashley she didn't realize she had and helped her to learn about herself."

"That Ashley is submissive?"

"To a dominant man, yes. She's started showing that with me. And I have experience with subs and what makes them tick. I will be able to bring it out a whole lot more and help her explore that sexual side of herself."

"Mike, does Ashley have any respect for me now? Has she talked about that with you?"

"I think she has a new appreciation for you."

"Appreciation? How in hell so?"

"For letting her explore beyond your marriage. That's unconditional love in the truest sense. Sure, some people talk unconditional love, but you're actually proving it to her."

"Oh jeez, Mike, please."

"I'm serious," he replied, "look at it from Ashley's perspective."

"How?"

"She was going behind your back with the first guy. And that night of the party as well. Think of how liberating it is for her now. She can be open about her desires and longings. She has her husband's acceptance. She won't have to be afraid of losing you, because she knows you want her to be happy and satisfied. How can she not love you more for that?"

"I don't know, Mike. Do you know how fucked up all this sounds?"

"Dave, I know it's not without some emotional pain on your part—and I told Ashley that—but do you really believe she wouldn't stray if this hadn't happened between her and me? Only you wouldn't know about it, or be part of it. And that would be destructive. This is about building things up between the two of you. And it will take the pressure off you."

"Pressure? What pressure?"

"You're not going to have to beat yourself up about your performance issues or be scared you're not satisfying her. Once you accept this and see its benefits, you'll feel greatly relieved."

"Why, because you'll be fulfilling that role?"

"Dave, this isn't about me, it's about Ashley and her happiness. You will still be the central man in her life. But sexually, Ashley needs a strong man to take control, bring out the submissive side that she's anxious to explore."

"Jesus," I said in a daze.

"And it's good for you as well."

"How is this fucking good for me, Mike?"

"Well, beyond the pressure being off, you've told me how you've continually masturbated thinking of this Jim Murta guy. Well, now, you're getting to hear her get fucked. You've heard things that before you could only fantasize about. Don't tell me you haven't been jerking off, Dave."

"I don't want to talk about that, Mike."

"OK, how about you look me straight in the eye and tell me you haven't jerked off this past weekend."

"Jesus, Mike, that's private now, OK?"

"That's the problem, Dave, perhaps if you told Ashley about your fixation, she might let you watch us. Imagine the orgasm you'd have jerking off as you see me fuck your wife."

"You suggested that to her?"

"No, I'm going to wait and let you bring that up to her when you're ready, when you think you can handle that and you're both more comfortable and talking more openly."

"Good God," I mumbled.

"It's funny," he replied, "she said she's come to realize you're more submissive than she is—which is natural, by the way."

"What?"

"It's natural in this type of situation. She's submissive to a dominant man, and you're submissive to her."

"I meant what did she say about that?"

"That she saw a change in you after you learned she'd cheated."

"Change? How?"

"Well, she knew and knows you're scared of losing her. And you tried harder, took her out to dinner more, deferred to her, doted on her more.

"But it's more than that," he added, "I think she's starting to really like being the one in control in your relationship. I think there's an element of her that likes seeing you humbled."

"She said that?"

"In so many words," he replied. "I don't think she wanted to get caught, but you have to know it made it more exciting to her that night in the bathroom, fucking that guy as you knocked outside."

"What did she say about that night?"

"We didn't talk actual details."

"What did she say about this guy before Jim? Who was he, do I know him?"

"I don't think so."

"Who was he? Mike, you said you gained insight, learned about this other guy—so share it, like you said you would."

"I'm sure that in time she'll tell you. Be frank with her, Dave, and it will open doors to honest dialogue."

"What, so you're not going to tell me?"

"I don't want to act as the middleman. It needs to be between the two of you. And I understand if you need more time."

"Wow, OK, so I guess you didn't mean what you said on Saturday about giving me insight."

"Things changed, Dave. I'm trying to facilitate communication, which is not happening right now between the two of you."

"Yeah, but it hasn't stopped you from telling her it 'turned me on,' Mike? You planted that image in her head. You have her thinking I'm a fucking cuckold."

"Well, Dave, do you think you're not?"

"Fuck you, Mike."

"If you're going to be like that Dave, I can leave."

"I'm sorry," I said. "You just don't understand how life-altering crazy this is, if anyone I knew, knew ..."

"Fuck people you know. They won't find out, and your private life is private. You want Ashley to be happy, right?"

"Yeah, of course."

"I'm going to help you make her happy, Dave, and she will still always be yours, but—"

"But what?"

"If you want to see me fuck your wife with your own eyes, you are going to have to talk to her about it. I'm sure, if you're honest, she will more than agree."

"Jesus, Mike."

"Did Ashley kiss you when she got home last night?"

"Yeah," I said before adding, "why?"

Mike was clearly getting at something.

"Good girl," Mike said.

"Why?" I asked again.

"Because it shows she follows my instructions. I told her to. That's good. And she kissed you before brushing her teeth?"

"Yes, Mike, why?" I said, beginning to suspect the answer.

"We came back to your apartment at the end of night. We went up to the roof. Nice roof deck you have, by the way. Nothing like getting a BJ from a guy's wife, looking at that two-plus carat wedding ring on her hand, wrapped around your cock, knowing her husband is waiting up for her down below."

"You came in her mouth?" I said, my stomach in knots.

Mike looked me in the eye, patted me on my back and said, "Relax, Dave, I was just bringing out the sub in her. And she behaved like a good little sub for me."

I thought of guys I know. How any one of them would be clocking Mike in the face right about now. Then I thought how none of them would ever be remotely in this situation in the first place.

"Ashley tells me you're going to San Francisco tomorrow," he said.

"Yeah," I said.

"It will give me more alone time to work with her."

"Mike, please, why are you trying to make me a fucking cuckold?"

"Dave, I'm not trying to do anything, man. It was obvious from the first time we talked that you were mentally already going down this path, this slippery slope."

"Slippery slope?"

"To becoming a cuckold. I could sense those horns growing each time we talked."

"What are you talking about—horns?"

"You're growing a nice pair of cuckold horns, Dave—have you not heard the expression?"

"No."

"Google it when you get home tonight. Only Ashley can cuckold you, but I'd say she's doing a pretty good job of it already. I'm thinking you're gonna have a nice set of antlers before long, and I think, this is just the beginning, my friend."

I reached for my beer, and felt my hands start to tremble.

EPILOGUE

A few years ago, I started keeping a journal. My father encouraged the habit—he has over fifty, going back to the '80s. Mine mostly chronicled mundane work events and, occasionally, some longer-term career aspirations.

"You'll never read most or any of it again," he said, "but talking to yourself by writing it down has a funny way of giving you perspective."

My journal changed abruptly last summer. My last business entry ended the night Craig told me the rumor.

Soon, I had a new journal hidden in my closet. I tried to get as much as I could down while it was happening. This has been an attempt to give it some coherency.

I'm not exorcising demons, just trying to understand how all this happened.

And how I found myself in the world I am in now.